IVAN TUR

VIRGIN SOIL

Translated from the Russian
by

CONSTANCE GARNETT

Introduction by

V. S. PRITCHETT

GROVE PRESS, INC.
NEW YORK

Introduction by V. S. Pritchett from *The Gentle Barbarian:*
The Life and Work of Turgenev, by V. S. Pritchett, © 1977 by V. S. Pritchett.
Reprinted by permission of Random House, Inc.

ISBN: 0-394-17015-6
Grove Press ISBN: 0-8021-4101-3

Manufactured in the United States of America

Distributed by Random House, Inc., New York

GROVE PRESS, INC., 196 West Houston Street, New York, N.Y. 10014

Introduction

V. S. Pritchett

By the 1870s Turgenev's pre-eminence in Europe as the leading Russian novelist was unquestioned, but he was far from being known to the great public in Europe or America. In 1877 with the publication of *Virgin Soil*, his longest and most ambitious novel, he became world famous: a month after it was published fifty-two young men and women were arrested in Russia on charges of revolutionary conspiracy, and a shocked public in France, Britain, and America turned to the novel for enlightenment. Its effect on American readers was enormous: as powerful, in its way, as the effect of *Uncle Tom's Cabin* had been. For Turgenev the novel was one more attempt to present the Russian situation with detachment, and above all he sought to show to his critics that he had not lost touch with the younger generation.

Virgin Soil is his longest and most complex novel. One can't deny that it is very much a novel that has been willed—compare, for instance, the fatal example of "the great American novel" —nevertheless it does contain here and there some of Turgenev's finest things. He set out to portray the various types of educated young men and women who, under the influence of the Populist movement, had thrown up the life of their class "to go to the people," live among them, dress in the clothes of workers and peasants, and to work with them and even to conspire with them.

A quotation from the *Notebook of a Farmer* on the title page indicates that the novel will be a piece of practical social criticism: " 'Virgin Soil' should be turned up not by a harrow skimming over the surfaces, but by a plough biting deep into the earth." The Populists were skimmers, but there were many extremists among them. To Stasiulevich, his publisher, Turgenev wrote that he expected the novel would be as violently abused in Russia as *Fathers and Sons* had been.

> Hitherto the younger generation has been presented in our literature either as a crew of crooks and scoundrels...or as much as possible idealized.... I decided to choose the middle course and to get closer to the truth—to take the young people who are, for the most part, good and honest and show that despite their honesty their very course is so false and impractical that it cannot fail to lead them to complete fiasco.

Whether he succeeded or not, he said, the young would at any rate sense his sympathy if not for their aims, then for their personalities.

Turgenev feared the censor and indeed reluctantly suppressed things that might too obviously offend. The novel was published in two parts, and having passed the first, the censor's committee was in a difficulty about the more disturbing second part. One faction wanted to burn it and insist on the "correction" of the first part. The chairman gave an embarrassed casting vote in its favor, but said if he had known the whole book in the first place he would have banned it. In the end, as Turgenev expected, the novel was damned by the critics of both sides who were swayed by party feeling. The conservatives, the official classes, said Turgenev was a dangerous radical who himself was personally involved with conspiracy—and indeed he did give money to the paper of the Populist leader, Lavrov, but simply because he hoped it would take the place of Herzen's *The Bell* as a forum for political discussion. He knew enough about political opinion to know that its phases do not last long.

The Populists were a moral replacement of the Nihilists whose policy of rejection had soon spent itself. The conservatives, especially, derided the idea that one of his characters, the girl Marianna of the gentry class, would involve herself with the movement. The radical critics ranged from those who said he was an old man libeling the young to those who said he knew nothing about the genuine revolutionaries and that, in any case, his absence from Russia made him out of date. Turgenev proved to be more accurate than either party in his diagnosis, as he had been in the case of Bazarov in *Fathers and Sons*: almost immediately after the publication of his novel fifty-two young conspirators, including eighteen women, were arrested and put on trial.

Turgenev was easily affected by hostile criticism. Once more he said he was finished and, once more, that he would never write again. But presently he recovered and stood by what he had written and, like many gentle men who are bullied, he had his bitter malice and wit, and a sharp firm pride. Indeed, the novel itself has a satirical harshness which is exceptional in his works. He repeated one or two stinging epigrammatic judgments, one particularly on the notorious Oriental love of lying which so many Westerners have complained of in Russians:

A truthful man...that was the great thing! that was what touched her! It is a well known fact, though by no means easy to understand, that Russians are the greatest liars on the face of the earth and yet there is nothing they respect like the truth—nothing attracts them so much.

In the opening pages of *Virgin Soil*, we are pushed abruptly into a dirty attic and see a slovenly young man and a woman with coarse lips and teeth. Both are smoking and paying no attention to each other; nevertheless, we note their air of honesty, stoicism, and industry. From this moment we see how Turgenev's familiar world and manner have changed. The style is harder, more photographic; the grace has been replaced by the instant, the summary, and the laconic. He is now attempting a larger number of characters from a wider canvas of life and is about to involve them in an elaborate plot and to grip us with a long story of imposed suspense which he had said earlier was outside his instinct and competence. We remember that Tolstoy and Dostoevsky have overtaken him, in this sense, and have given the Russian novel a density where before it had only surface and extent. We remember that what he admired in Dickens was the variety of mood—indeed he wondered, after the book was done, if he had not taken too much of the caricaturist from him. We have certainly an impression of cartoon and in that the book has something in common with, say, Dostoevsky's *The Devils*.

Both Turgenev's conspirators and his innocents who "go to the people" strike one as living in a vacuum. Conspiracy is an urban matter and Turgenev is not by nature an urban novelist, although for once he does give us a picture of a Russian town, probably Orel, for its own sake. It is well photographed:

> It was Saturday night; there were no people on the street, but the taverns were still crowded. Hoarse voices broke from them, drunken songs and the nasal notes of the concertina; from doors suddenly opened streamed the filthy warmth, the acrid smell of alcohol, the red glare of lights. Before almost every tavern were standing little peasant carts, harnessed to shaggy, potbellied nags; they stood with their unkempt heads hanging down submissively, and seemed asleep.

Or:

> The coach crossed a wide market place, positively stinking of rush mats and cabbages, passed the governor's house with striped sentry boxes at the gates, a private house with a turret, a promenade set with trees recently planted and already dying, a bazaar filled with the barking of dogs and the clinking of chains and gradually reaching the boundaries of the town overtook a long long train of wagons, which had set off late for the sake of the cool of the night.

An un-Turgenevean scene, brutally observed, but it must be said well placed. For Nezhdanov, the young poet and idealist and, so to say, political guinea pig of the novel, is getting a first sight of the Russia he has vowed to live with and understand. But what one suspects already (as Richard Freeborn says in *Turgenev, A Study*) is that *Virgin Soil* is going to be a forerunner of the crude, black and white, schematic novels of the Socialist Realists of our time:

vi

The distinction Turgenev makes between the aims of the Populists and their persons was artificial, especially for a writer who had been used to accepting both the man and his ideas.

This change is certainly felt, and although one can say that Turgenev's effort of will in keeping in touch with Russian realities has some of the guilt of the absentee in it—a matter that was, as he put it, his fate—we know that he judged rightly when he said that the Populist movement was a pathos, that no root and branch change would take place for another twenty years at least. The central characters are nevertheless representative. The aristocratic young Nezhdanov has traits of Turgenev's character: like the young Turgenev, he is handsome and has chestnut hair; he has a double nature; he is secretly a poet but ashamed of his poetry; his real interest is political activity. He is an idealist, passionate, chaste, timid; ashamed of these qualities, he even tries to be coarse in his language: "Life did not come easily to him." His feelings push him forward, but beyond his power of performance. He is the Turgenevean mixture of Don Quixote and Hamlet, a throwback to "the superfluous man." When he "goes to the people" and solemnly dresses up in workman's clothes, the workmen see through him at once and make him drunk on raw vodka. Another time he is "beaten up" and makes a mess of everything.

Marianna, the brusque upper-class girl with whom he falls in love when he is tutoring in the grand house of the wordy liberal Sipyagin, is as innocent as he, but she is the new kind of young girl. She is a rebel who has cropped her hair, and (interesting when one remembers Turgenev's old-fashioned habits) she belongs to the generation who has also given up hand-kissing. When she boldly runs off with Nezhdanov to "go to the people" with him, she refuses to be married and they live together in chastity.

Marianna is a rebel, not a revolutionary—a rebel eager to leave her class, to be useful and to sacrifice herself. The real revolutionary is Mashurina, the unkempt, plain and awkward girl who silently loves Nezhdanov. She is quietly efficient in secret work, alert for traitors, spies, and mistrustful of some of the hangers-on of the movement, for example of Palkin, a cripple, a foolish yet far-seeing man, but a danger to the cause because he is an unstable and excitable chatterbox, easily flattered. It is Mashurina who will disappear deeper into conspiracy when Palkin's foolishness and swank give the group away.

The "hero" in Turgenev's eyes—although Palkin makes Turgenev's point in a prophetic speech about the dull, immovable men who will eventually rule Russia—is Solomin. Turgenev calls him an American type—he knew no Americans but America had provided a utopian dream for early revolutionaries (except Herzen, who called Americans "elderly children"). Turgenev rejected the traditional Russian respect for Germans as the practical race; he looked back on them as the dear deluded philosophers of his Romantic youth; so he turned to the English and made Solomin a Russian who had learned his trade in the cotton factories of Manchester and his politics from the English reformers of the industrial revolution. There may also be a hint of Engles in him.

Solomin is sympathetic to conspirators, protects them loyally but advises caution and gradualism to the headstrong. He is strong, healthy, hardworking, generous, sober, and resourceful, a man of sense. Inevitably he strikes one as being too good to be true; though as a still portrait he is well enough done. Turgenev is unable to make him move.

Markelov, a retired artillery officer and landowner, is the dour type of cantankerous conspirator, a lonely, unhappy man who can't farm his land effectively because he tries to run everything by giving orders in a military way. He is the same in conspiracy—too aggressive, given to acting independently and openly like a fanatical officer. He is certain to be arrested and to go grimly silent and still determined to Siberia.

These figures are well enough in the first volume of the novel which deceived the censors, for they are seen in the setting that Turgenev can always do well: the still, timeless scene of the great country house where the family and the guests dine and talk, where Sipyagin, the host, is mellifluous at the table, where his pretty wife flirts with the tutor in her boudoir, where the rebel girl gazes at Nezhdanov and sulks before her aunt, where people walk in the gardens and the carriages come and go. It is the same sort of paradise from the past as one finds in *A Nest of Gentlefolk*, in *Fathers and Sons*—but the characters are now hardened. Turgenev shows his contempt for the gentry openly, especially for the conceited and pompous young Kammer-junker, Kallomyetsov, who is an active "Red" hunter, vain of his certainty in spotting revolutionaries. He is far cruder than Pavel in *Fathers and Sons* or the other comical Frenchified asses of earlier novels. And Sipyagin, the bland, sporting, and mellifluous landowner with his skin-deep liberalism, is also ridiculed. The drawing room quarrels become edgy when the egregious Kallomyetsov says Sipyagin should be president of a commission that would decide everything.

Madame Sipyagin laughed more than ever.

"You must take care: Boris Andreivitch is sometimes such a Jacobin...."

"Jacko, Jacko, Jacko," called the parrot.

Valentine Mihalovna shook her handkerchief at him.

"Don't prevent sensible people from talking! Marianna, tell him to be quiet."

Marianna turned to the cage and began scratching the parrot's neck which he offered her at once.

"Yes," Madame Sipyagin said, "Boris Andreivich sometimes astonishes me. He has something...something of the tribune."

"*C'est parce qu'il est orateur*," Kallomyetsov interposed hotly. "Your husband has the gift of words, as no one else has; he's accustomed to success, too... *ses propres paroles le grisent*.... But he's a little off that, isn't he? *Il boude—*eh?"

"I haven't noticed it," she replied after a brief silence.

"Yes," Kallomyetsov pursued in a pensive tone, "he has been overlooked a little."

It is all drifting to a row about Marianna being a Nihilist because at this time she teaches in a village school.

The things we rely on Turgenev for are here: the naturalness of all kinds of talk and the silences in it—with him it is a pianist's gift—and his ear is just as fine when we get to the drunken and confused talk of the radicals in the second volume. His summary penetration into character does not fail. Madame Sipyagin, for example, is excellent.

> She was clever, not ill-natured—rather good-natured of the two, fundamentally cold and indifferent—and she could not tolerate the thought of anyone remaining indifferent to her.... Only, these charming egoists must not be thwarted: they are fond of power and will not tolerate independence in others. Women like Sipyagina excite and work upon inexperienced and passionate natures; for themselves they like regularity and a peaceful life.... Flirtation cost Sipyagina little; she was well aware that there was no danger for her and never could be.... With what a happy smile she retired into herself, into the consciousness of her inaccessibility, her impregnable virtue, and with what gracious condescension she submitted to the lawful embrace of her well-bred spouse.

But not until we get to the second volume does Turgenev break out of talk into dramatic scenes. Madame Sipyagin seems to be a development of Madame Odintsov of *Fathers and Sons* but done in acid. She spies on her niece, intercepts letters, and exposes the girl's love for Nezhdanov to her brother Markelov who had hoped to marry her. The point of this jealous intrigue is to show the extremes to which the apparently gracious Sipyagins will go to preserve the unity of their class. At the moment when the defiant Markelov dashes to support a local riot of the peasants and the conspiracy is betrayed, the hypocrisy of Sipyagin's liberalism comes out. Turgenev is a master of the exposure of relationships which have been undermined politically. There has been an excellent scene at the end of the first part of the novel in which Markelov begins to have the force of a tragic figure. As a man of honor, reckless and incapable of spite or jealousy, indifferent to enemies, and not deceived, Markelov does not spare his host:

> If we wait for the moment when everything, absolutely everything is ready, we shall never begin. If one weighs *all* the consequences beforehand, it is certain there will be some evil ones. For instance, when our predecessors organized the emancipation of the peasants, could they foresee that one result of this emancipation would be the rise of a whole class of money-lending landowners who would lend the peasant a quarter of mouldy rye for six roubles and extort then from him (here Markelov crooked one finger), first the full six roubles in labour and besides that (Markelov crooked another finger), a whole quarter of good rye and then (Markelov crooked a third), interest on top of that —in fact squeeze the peasant to the last drop. Our emancipators couldn't have foreseen that. And yet even if they had done, it was right to free the peasants and not to weigh all the consequences. And so I've made up my mind!

And when Markelov is arrested at the end of the book he is obdurate and does not repent. It is one of Turgenev's excellences that he is true to the basic character of people. Markelov is the incurable soldier when he reflects on his betrayal:

> It is I who am to blame, I didn't understand, I didn't say the right thing. I didn't go the right way to work. I ought simply to have given orders and if anyone had tried to hinder or resist, put a bullet through his head! What's the use of explanations here. Anyone not with us has no right to live... spies are killed like dogs, worse than dogs.

Turgenev is hard to follow in the facts of the conspiracy: there are too many hints and shadow figures, but one of them is well drawn. This is Palkin, the vain, chattering, and comic exhibitionist, the born mysterious contact-man longing to be trusted and knowing he cannot be; he is burdened by the knowledge of his own muddle-headedness. The scene in which Sipyagin flatters him, inflates his conceit, snubs him, and then slyly worms everything he wants out of him and dismisses him with contempt, is very subtle comedy. Into the mouth of this walking calamity Turgenev puts shrewd prophecy. Palkin defends Solomin to whom the intellectual revolutionaries are now cool: Russia needs sturdy, rough, dull men of the people.

> Just look at Solomin: his brain is clear as daylight, and he's as healthy as a fish.... Isn't that a wonder! Why hitherto with us in Russia has it always been the other way that to be a live man with feelings and a conscience, you had to be an invalid?

There are two more characters to whom a complete scene is given, who on the face of it have no relevance to the theme of the novel and who in fact seem to belong to a short story thrown in for a gentle relief. Turgenev was inclined to cut them out but was persuaded to let them stay. They are an elderly, childless pair of innocent doll-like, eccentric creatures, called Fomushka and Fimushka, the oldest inhabitants of the town, who have preserved themselves and their house as untouched models of the life of lesser gentry in the eighteenth century. They blissfully ignore everything that has happened since that time. They still drink chocolate because tea had not come in, they play duets, look at old albums, and sing sweet and old-fashioned songs about hopeless love in their cracked voices. They have one unbroken rule: they have never allowed their house serfs to be flogged, and if a servant turned out to be drunken and intolerable they bore with him, but after a while passed him on to a neighbor, saying "Let others take their turn with him."

> But such a disaster rarely befell them, so rarely that it made an epoch in their lives and they would say for instance "That was very long ago, it happened when we had that

rascal Aldoshka," or "When we had grandfather's fur cap with the fox tail stolen." They still had such caps.

The interesting thing is that this dream of an Arcadia in the past is often found in the Russian novel: in Oblomov's dream, for example, or even in the talk of the senile Iudushka in Shchedrin's *The Golovlyov Family*. In Turgenev, it is more than one of his "old portraits" or reminiscences. It is not antiquarian, it is really an incipient fairy tale or a fable without meaning which is budding in the depths of a people's mind. It is also a relief after the vulgar scene at the merchant's house that has preceded it, a holiday of the mind from the yearning for the future which rules the whole novel—the burden of Russia which the other characters bear. Fomushka and Fimushka bear no burden.

If *Virgin Soil* has not the sustained serenity of *Fathers and Sons* because the people in the right and the people in the wrong are too blatantly stated, it is an impressive attempt to have a final say. It can hardly be called an old man's book for Turgenev was in his late fifties when he wrote it. The strain we feel comes from his trying to pack too much into it, and not without artifice. To the critics who said that he was out of touch with the new Russia, Turgenev replied that he was closely in touch with the scores of young Russians who came to see him in Paris; but although they may have revealed themselves to him, they did not really bring their Russia with them and were more likely to present him with arguments than with intimacy.

If what we read in Anna Dostoevsky's diary of her life with her husband (and, of course, in Dostoevsky's novels) is true, the quality that was missing in Turgenev's young visitors was the fact that they lived in crowds, above all in one another's lives: their very homes, in whatever class, were normally wide open to their relations and their friends. They have the nature of people who live on the streets or in groups. It is in the nature of Dostoevsky's genius to show that when one of his characters appears a whole community or a confused common fate seems to be hanging out of his talking mouth. The soliloquists are never alone. Turgenev himself said that in Russia writing was easy for the novelist: the stories and people spring up around him and crowd in on him at once.

The political perspicacity of Turgenev is astonishing, and now that the state of our world has changed it seems closer to our political experience than it was to English or American admirers of Turgenev in 1900 who saw in him something close to the experience of a country gentleman of sensitive tastes. The only thing that really shocks in *Virgin Soil* is Nezhdanov's suicide: the "superfluous man," whom Turgenev invented, seems to die as a convenience in the interests of early Romanticism and Turgenev's preoccupation with death. One understands why Chekhov in the next generation was to get so sick of the superfluous man, as a political sob sister.

THE NAMES OF THE CHARACTERS IN THE BOOK

Alexéy (Al-yósha) Dmítritch Nezhdánov.
Síla Samsónitch Páklin.
Borís André-itch Sip-yágin. *+ Valentina*
Sem-yón Petróvitch Kallom-yétsev.
Valentína Mihálovna. *— Borís niece*
Mariánna Viként-yevna Sinétsky.
Ánna Zahárovna.
Sergéi Mihálitch Markélov. *Valentina brother*
Vassíly Fedótitch Solómin.
Mashúrina.
Ostrodúmov.
Golúshkin.
Vladímir Sílin.
Tat-yána Osipovna.
Pável Yegóritch.
Fímushka.
Fómushka.
Snandúliya (Snapótchka).

In transcribing the Russian names into English—
    a has the sound of *a* in *father*.
    e   ,,   ,,   *a* in *pane*.
    i   ,,   ,,   *ee*.
    u   ,,   ,,   *oo*.
    y is always consonantal except when it is
        the last letter of the word.
    g is always hard.

PART I

*' Virgin Soil should be turned up
not by a harrow skimming over
the surface, but by a plough biting
deep into the earth.'*—From the
Note-book of a Farmer.

1

AT one o'clock on a spring day of 1868, in Petersburg, a man of twenty-seven, carelessly and shabbily dressed, was mounting the back stairs of a five-storied house in Officers' Street. Tramping heavily with his over-shoes trodden down at heel, and slowly rolling his bulky, ungainly person as he moved, this man at last reached the very top of the stairs. He stopped before a half-open door, hanging off its hinges, and without ringing the bell, merely giving a noisy sigh, he swung into a small, dark ante-room.

'Is Nezhdanov at home?' he called in a deep and loud voice.

'He's not—I'm here, come in,' came from the next room another voice, a woman's, also rather gruff.

'Mashurina?' queried the new-comer.

'Yes, it's me. And you—Ostrodumov?'

'Pimen Ostrodumov,' he answered, and first carefully pulling off his rubber over-shoes, and then hanging his threadbare little old cloak on a nail, he went into the room from which the woman's voice had come.

This room, low-pitched and dirty, with its walls coloured a dingy green, was dimly lighted by two dusty windows. The only furniture in it was a small iron bedstead in the corner, a table in the middle, a few chairs, and a book-case crammed with books. Near the table was sitting a woman of thirty, bareheaded, in a black woollen gown, smoking a cigarette. When she saw Ostrodumov come in, she held out her broad red hand to him without speaking. He shook it, also without speaking, and, sinking into a chair, he pulled a half-smoked cigar out of his side pocket. Mashurina gave him a light, he began smoking, and without saying a word, or even exchanging glances, they both set to puffing rings of bluish

3

smoke into the close air, which was already saturated with tobacco fumes.

These two people had something in common, though in features they were not alike. About their slovenly figures, with coarse lips, and teeth, and noses (Ostrodumov was marked with smallpox too), there was an air of honesty and stoicism and industry.

'Have you seen Nezhdanov?' Ostrodumov inquired at last.

'Yes; he'll be here directly. He's gone to the library with the books.'

Ostrodumov turned aside and spat.

'How is it he's for ever gadding about now? There's no finding him.'

Mashurina took out another cigarette.

'He's bored,' she pronounced, carefully lighting it.

'Bored!' repeated Ostrodumov reproachfully. 'What self-indulgence! One would think we'd no work for him to do. Here are we praying we may get through all the work decently somehow, and he's bored!'

'Any letter come from Moscow?' inquired Mashurina, after a brief pause.

'Yes . . . the day before yesterday.'

'Have you read it?'

Ostrodumov merely nodded.

'Well . . . what's the news?'

'Oh—someone will have to go there soon.'

Mashurina took the cigarette out of her mouth.

'Why so? Everything's all right there, I'm told.'

'Yes, it's all right. Only one man's shown he's not to be depended on. So that . . . we must shift him, or else get rid of him altogether. Oh, and there are other things. They ask for you, too.'

'In the letter?'

'Yes.'

Mashurina shook back her heavy hair. Twisted up carelessly into a small knot behind, it fell in front over her forehead and eyebrows.

4

'Ah, well,' she declared; 'since the order's given, it's no use discussing it!'

'Of course not. Only it can't be done without money; and where are we to get the money?'

Mashurina pondered. 'Nezhdanov will have to produce it,' she said in an undertone, as though to herself.

'That's the very thing I've come about,' observed Ostrodumov.

'Have you got the letter with you?' Mashurina asked suddenly.

'Yes. Would you like to read it?'

'Yes, give it me . . . no, you needn't, though. We'll read it together . . . afterwards.'

'I tell the truth,' muttered Ostrodumov; 'you needn't doubt it.'

'Well, I don't doubt it.'

And both sank into silence again; and, as before, only the rings of smoke floated from their silent lips, and coiling feebly rose above their dishevelled heads.

The thud of over-shoes was heard in the ante-room.

'Here he is!' whispered Mashurina.

The door was opened slightly, and in the crack was thrust a head—but not the head of Nezhdanov.

It was a little round head with rough black hair, a broad, wrinkled forehead, very keen, little brown eyes under bushy eyebrows, a nose pointing in the air like a duck's, and a tiny, rosy, comical mouth. This head took a look round, nodded, smiled—showing a number of tiny white teeth—and came into the room, accompanied by its rickety little body, short arms, and somewhat bandy and lame little legs. Directly Mashurina and Ostrodumov caught sight of this head, the faces of both expressed a sort of condescending contempt, as though each of them were inwardly saying, 'Oh! it's only he!' and they did not utter a single word, did not stir a muscle. However, the reception accorded him not only failed to embarrass the visitor, but apparently afforded him positive gratification.

5

'What's the meaning of this?' he said in a squeaky voice.
'A duet? Why not a trio? And where's the first tenor?'

'Do you mean to inquire after Nezhdanov, Mr. Paklin?'
replied Ostrodumov with a serious face.

'Precisely so, Mr. Ostrodumov; I mean him.'

'He'll be here directly, most likely, Mr. Paklin.'

'It's very delightful to hear that, Mr. Ostrodumov.'

The little cripple turned to Mashurina. She sat scowling,
and went on deliberately puffing at her cigarette.

'How are you, dear . . . dear . . . There, how annoying!
I always forget your name and your father's.'

Mashurina shrugged her shoulders.

'And there's no need whatever to know them! You
know my surname. What more do you want? And what
a question: how are you! Can't you see I'm alive all
right?'

'True, most true!' cried Paklin, his nostrils dilating and
his eyebrows twitching; 'if you weren't alive, your humble
servant would not have the pleasure of seeing you here and
talking to you! Put my question down to a bad old-fashioned
habit. But as for your name and your father's . . . You
know it's rather awkward to say baldly, Mashurina! I'm
aware, it's true, that you even sign your letters so: Bona-
parte!—that's to say, Mashurina! But still, in conversation——'

'But who asks you to talk to me?'

Paklin laughed nervously, as though he were choking.

'There, that's enough, my dear creature—shake hands,
don't be cross; don't I know you've the best heart in the
world? and I've a good heart, too . . . Eh?'

Paklin held out his hand. . . . Mashurina looked at him
darkly. She shook hands with him, however.

'If you positively must know my name,' she said, with the
same gloomy face, 'by all means; my name's Fekla.'

'And mine, Pimen,' Ostrodumov added in his bass.

'Ah! that's very . . . very instructive! But that being so,
tell me, O Fekla! and you, O Pimen! tell me why you behave

6

with such unfriendliness, such persistent unfriendliness, to me, while I——'

'Mashurina thinks,' Ostrodumov interrupted, 'and she's not the only one who thinks it, that as you look at every subject from the ridiculous side, there's no relying upon you.'

Paklin turned sharply round on his heels.

'There she—that's the mistake people are continually making in criticising me, most honoured Pimen! In the first place, I'm not always laughing; and secondly, that would not in the least prevent your being able to rely upon me, which is proved, indeed, by the flattering confidence I've more than once enjoyed in your ranks! I'm an honest man, most reverend Pimen!'

Ostrodumov muttered something between his teeth, while Paklin shook his head and repeated, now without the faintest trace of a smile, 'No! I'm not always laughing! I'm anything but a light-hearted person! You need only look at me!'

Ostrodumov did look at him. And, in fact, when Paklin was not laughing, when he was silent, his face wore an expression almost of dejection, almost of terror; it became humorous and even malicious directly he opened his mouth. Ostrodumov said nothing, however.

Paklin again turned to Mashurina.

'Well, and how are your studies progressing? Are you successful in your truly philanthropic art? I should guess it's a difficult job helping the inexperienced citizen on his first entrance into the light of day?'

'No, not at all difficult, so long as he's not much bigger than you,' answered Mashurina, who had just taken her diploma as a midwife; and she smiled complacently. A year and a half before, she had left her own people, a family of poor nobles in South Russia, and had come to Petersburg with six roubles in her pocket; she had entered a lying-in institution, and by unceasing hard work had gained the coveted diploma. She was a single woman . . . and a very chaste single woman. Nothing wonderful in that, some sceptic will say, remembering what has been said of her exterior.

7

Something wonderful and rare, let us be permitted to say.

Paklin laughed again when he heard her retort.

'You're a smart person, my dear!' he cried. 'You had me there nicely! I deserve it. Why did I stay such a shrimp! But what can have become of our host?'

Paklin purposely changed the subject. He had never been able to resign himself to his diminutive stature and his unsightly little person altogether. He felt it the more keenly as he was a passionate admirer of women. What would he not have given to attract them! The consciousness of his pitiful exterior was a much sorer wound to him than his humble origin, or his unenviable position in society. Paklin's father had been simply a tradesman, who, through shifty dodges of one sort and another, had risen to the rank of titular councillor. He had been a successful go-between in legal business, and a speculator and agent for houses and property. He had made a respectable fortune; but drank heavily towards the end of his life, and left nothing at his death. Young Paklin (he had been named Sila Samsonitch, that is, Strength, son of Samson, which he also regarded as a jeer at his expense) had been educated at a commercial school, where he learned German thoroughly. After various rather disagreeable experiences, he got at last into a private business house for a salary of about a hundred and fifty pounds a year. On that sum he kept himself, a sick aunt, and a humpbacked sister. At the time of our story he was just twenty-eight. Paklin was acquainted with a number of students, young men who liked him for his cynical wit, the light-hearted venom of his audacious talk, and his one-sided but genuine and unpedantic learning. Only occasionally he suffered at their hands. One day he was somehow late at a political gathering. . . . As he came in, he began at once hurriedly making excuses. . . .

'Poor Paklin was afeared!' sang out someone in a corner, and they all roared with laughter. Paklin at last laughed himself, though his heart was sore. 'He spoke the truth, the ruffian!' he thought to himself. He made Nezhdanov's acquaintance at a Greek eating-house, where he used to go

8

and dine, and where he constantly expressed very free and
bold opinions. He used to declare that the chief cause of his
democratic frame of mind was the execrable Greek cookery,
which upset his liver.

'Yes . . . really . . . what has become of our host?'
repeated Paklin. 'I've noticed for some time past he's seemed
out of spirits. Can he be in love?—Heaven forfend!'

Mashurina scowled.

'He's gone to the library for some books; he's no time
to be in love and no one to be in love with.'

'How about you?' almost broke from Paklin's lips. 'I want
to see him,' he uttered aloud, 'because I have to talk to
him about an important affair.'

'What sort of affair?' put in Ostrodumov. 'Our affairs?'

'Perhaps yours . . . that is, our common affairs.'

Ostrodumov hummed. In his heart he was doubtful, but
then he reflected, 'Who can tell? He's such a slippery eel!'

'Here he comes at last,' said Mashurina suddenly, and in
her small unlovely eyes, that were fastened on the door of the
ante-room, there was a flash of something warm and tender,
a kind of deep inward spot of light. . . .

The door opened, and this time there entered a young
man of three-and-twenty, a cap on his head and a bundle of
books under his arm—Nezhdanov himself.

2

AT the sight of visitors in his room, he stopped short in the
doorway, took them all in in a glance, flung off his cap,
dropped the books straight on to the floor, and without a word
went up to the bed and sat down on the edge of it. His
handsome white face, which looked still whiter from the deep
red of his wavy chestnut hair, expressed dissatisfaction and
annoyance.

Mashurina turned slightly away, biting her lip; Ostrodumov growled: 'At last!'

Paklin was the first to approach Nezhdanov.

'What's wrong with you, Alexey Dmitrievitch, Hamlet of Russia? Has anyone offended you? or is it a causeless melancholy?'

'Stop that, please, Mephistopheles of Russia,' answered Nezhdanov irritably. 'I'm not equal to a contest with you in dull smartness.'

Paklin laughed.

'You don't express yourself very accurately; if it's smart, it's not dull; if it's dull, it's not smart.'

'Very well, very well. . . . You're a witty fellow, we all know.'

'And you're in a highly nervous condition,' Paklin drawled; 'or has something really happened?'

'Nothing has happened in special; but what's happened is that one can't set one's foot into the street in this filthy town, in Petersburg, without coming across some meanness, idiocy, hideous injustice, rottenness! Life here's impossible any longer.'

'So that's why you've advertised in the paper for a place as tutor and are ready to go away,' Ostrodumov growled again.

'I should think so; I shall get away from here with all the pleasure in life! If only some fool can be found to give me a situation!'

'You must first do your duty *here*,' said Mashurina significantly, still looking away.

'And that is?' queried Nezhdanov, turning sharply round to her.

Mashurina pressed her lips tightly together. 'Ostrodumov will tell you.'

Nezhdanov turned to Ostrodumov. But the latter only cleared his throat and grunted: 'Wait a bit.'

'No, joking apart now, really,' interposed Paklin; 'you have heard something's gone wrong?'

Nezhdanov bounded up on the bed, as though some force were tossing him upwards.

'What more would you have going wrong?' he shouted, his voice suddenly growing loud. 'Half Russia's dying of hunger. The *Moscow Gazette's* triumphant; they're going to introduce classicism; the students' benefit clubs are prohibited; everywhere there's spying, persecution, betrayal, lying, and treachery—we can't advance a step in any direction . . . and all that's not enough for him—he looks for something fresh to go wrong, he thinks I'm joking . . . Basanov's arrested,' he added, dropping his voice a little; 'they told me at the library.'

Ostrodumov and Mashurina both at once raised their heads.

'My dear fellow, Alexey Dmitrievitch,' began Paklin, 'you are excited—no wonder. . . . But had you forgotten what an age and what a country we live in? Why, among us a drowning man has to make for himself the very straw he's to clutch at! What's the good of being sentimental over it? One must face the worst, my dear fellow, and not fly into a rage, like a baby——'

'Ah, don't, please!' Nezhdanov interrupted fretfully, and his face worked as if he were in pain. 'You, we all know, are a man of energy, you're afraid of nothing and nobody——'

'Me afraid of nobody——!' Paklin was beginning.

'Who could have betrayed Basanov?' Nezhdanov went on. 'I don't understand it!'

'Why, to be sure, a friend. They're grand hands at that—friends are. You must be on the look-out with them! I, for instance, had a friend, and a capital fellow he seemed; thought such a lot of me, of my reputation! One day he came to me. . . . "Fancy!" he cried, "the ridiculous slanders they've been spreading about you; they declare you poisoned your own uncle; that you were introduced into some house, and at once took a seat with your back to the lady of the house, and persisted in sitting so the whole evening! And that she fairly cried, yes, cried at the insult! What absurdity!

11

what inanity! what fools can believe such a story?'' And what followed? Why, a year later I quarrelled with that very friend. . . . And he writes in a letter of farewell: "You who killed your own uncle! You who were not ashamed to insult a respectable lady by sitting with your back to her! . . ." and so on, and so on. That's what friends are!'

Ostrodumov exchanged glances with Mashurina. 'Alexey Dmitrievitch!' he blurted in his heavy bass—he obviously wanted to cut short the useless eruption of words that was beginning—'a letter has come from Vassily Nikolaevitch from Moscow.'

Nezhdanov gave a slight start and looked down.

'What does he write?' he asked at last.

'Well . . . they want me and her'—Ostrodumov indicated Mashurina—'to go.'

'What? they ask for her too?'

'Yes.'

'Well, where's the difficulty?'

'Why, of course the difficulty's—money.'

Nezhdanov got up from the bed and went up to the window.

'Is a great deal wanted?'

'Fifty roubles . . . can't do with less.'

Nezhdanov was silent for a space.

'I haven't got it now,' he muttered at last, drumming on the pane with his finger-tips; 'but . . . I could get it. I will get it. Have you the letter?'

'The letter? It . . . that's to say . . . of course.'

'But why do you always keep things back from me?' cried Paklin. 'Haven't I deserved your confidence? Even if I didn't fully sympathise . . . with what you are undertaking, could you suppose me capable of turning traitor or chattering?'

'Unintentionally . . . perhaps!' Ostrodumov said in his deep notes.

'Neither intentionally nor unintentionally. There's Madame Mashurina looking at me with a smile . . . but I say——'

'I'm not smiling,' snapped Mashurina.

'But I say,' pursued Paklin, 'that you, gentlemen, have no intuition; that you don't know how to distinguish who are your real friends! If a man laughs, you think he's not serious . . .'

'To be sure!' Mashurina snapped again.

'Here, for instance,' Paklin hurried on with renewed vigour, this time not even replying to Mashurina, 'you are in want of money . . . and Nezhdanov hasn't it at the moment . . . well, I can let you have it.'

Nezhdanov turned quickly round from the window.

'No . . . no, . . . what for? I will get it . . . I will draw part of my allowance in advance. . . . They do owe me something, if I remember. But, I say, Ostrodumov; show the letter.'

Ostrodumov first remained for some time motionless; then he looked round, then he stood up, bent right down, and, tucking up his trouser, pulled out of the leg of his high boot a carefully folded ball of blue paper; having pulled this ball out, he, for some unknown reason, blew on it and gave it to Nezhdanov.

The latter took the paper, unfolded it, read it attentively, and handed it to Mashurina. . . . She first got up from her chair, then she too read it, and returned it to Nezhdanov, though Paklin was holding out his hand for it. Nezhdanov shrugged his shoulders and passed the mysterious letter to Paklin. Paklin, in his turn, ran his eyes over it, and, compressing his lips with great significance, he laid it in solemn silence on the table. Then Ostrodumov took it, lighted a large match, which diffused a strong smell of brimstone, and first raising the paper high above his head, as though he would show it to all present, he burned it up completely in the match, not sparing his fingers, and flung the ashes into the stove. No one uttered a single word, no one even moved, during this operation. The eyes of all were cast down. Ostrodumov had a concentrated and business-like air. Nezhdanov's face looked wrathful; there were signs in Paklin of being ill at ease; Mashurina might have been at a solemn mass.

13

So passed two minutes. . . . Then a slight awkwardness came over all of them. Paklin first felt the necessity of breaking the silence.

'Well, then,' he began, 'is my sacrifice on the altar of the fatherland accepted, or not? Am I permitted to contribute, if not fifty roubles, at least twenty-five or thirty, to the common cause?'

Nezhdanov all at once flew into a perfect fury. His irritability had been growing, it seemed. . . . The solemn burning of the letter had by no means allayed it; it was only waiting for an excuse to break out.

'I have told you already that it's not wanted, not wanted . . . not wanted! I won't allow it and I won't accept it. I'll get the money, I'll get it directly. I don't need help from anyone!'

'All right, my dear fellow,' observed Paklin. 'I see, though you are a revolutionist, you're not a democrat!'

'Say at once that I'm an aristocrat!'

'Well, you are an aristocrat, really . . . to a certain degree.'

Nezhdanov gave a forced laugh.

'So you mean to hint at my being an illegitimate son. You needn't trouble, my kind friend. . . . Without your aid, I'm not likely to forget that.'

Paklin flung up his arms in despair.

'Alyosha, upon my word, what is the matter with you? How could you take my words like that! I don't know you to-day.' Nezhdanov made an impatient gesture of the head and shoulders. 'Basanov's arrest has upset you, but, you know, he used to behave so imprudently——'

'He used not to conceal his convictions,' Mashurina put in gloomily: 'it's not for us to find fault with him!'

'Of course; only he ought to have thought of others too, who may be compromised by him now.'

'Why do you suppose that of him?' . . . Ostrodumov boomed in his turn: 'Basanov's a man of strong will; he will never betray anyone. As for prudence . . . let me tell you,

14

we're not all equally able to be prudent, Mr. Paklin!'

Paklin was offended, and was about to retort, but Nezhdanov stopped him.

'Gentlemen,' he cried, 'be so good as to let politics alone for a time, please!'

A silence followed.

'I met Skoropihin to-day,' Paklin began at last, 'our great national critic and æsthetic enthusiast. What an intolerable creature! He's for ever boiling over and frothing, for all the world like a bottle of bad sour kvas. . . . The waiter, as he runs, holds it down with his finger instead of a cork, a fat raisin sticks in the neck—it goes on bubbling and hissing—and when once all the foam's flown out of it, all that's left at the bottom is a few drops of villainous sour stuff, which quenches no one's thirst, but only gives one a stomach-ache! . . . A most pernicious individual for young people to have to do with!'

The comparison Paklin had made, though true and apt, called up no smile on anyone's face. Only Ostrodumov observed that young people who were capable of taking an interest in æsthetic criticism deserved no pity, even if Skoropihin did lead them astray.

'But really, one moment,' Paklin exclaimed with warmth—the less sympathy he met with, the hotter he got,—'here we have a question, not political we admit, but important for all that. To listen to Skoropihin, every ancient work of art is no good, for the very reason that it is ancient. . . . If that's so, art is nothing but a fashion, and it's not worth while to talk seriously about it! If there is nothing stable, eternal, in it —then away with it! In science, in mathematics, for instance, you don't regard Euler, Laplace, Hauss as antiquated imbeciles, do you? Are you prepared to reckon them as authorities, while Raphael and Mozart are fools? Does your pride revolt against their authority? The canons of art are more difficult to arrive at than the laws of science . . . agreed; but they exist, and anyone who doesn't see them is blind; whether wilfully or not, makes no difference!'

15

Paklin ceased . . . and no one uttered a sound, as though all of them were holding water in their mouths, as though all were a little ashamed of him. Only Ostrodumov growled: 'And, all the same, I don't feel the least sorry for young men who are led astray by Skoropihin.'

'Oh, go to the devil with you!' thought Paklin. 'I'm off.'

He had come to see Nezhdanov with the object of communicating to him his views as to procuring the *Polar Star* from abroad (the *Bell* had already ceased to exist), but the conversation had taken such a turn that it seemed better not even to raise the question. Paklin was already reaching after his cap, when suddenly, without any premonitory noise or knocking, there was heard in the ante-room a marvellously pleasant, manly, and mellow baritone, the very sound of which had somehow a suggestion of exceptional good breeding, good education, and even good perfume.

'Is Mr. Nezhdanov at home?'

They all looked at one another in amazement.

'Mr. Nezhdanov at home?' repeated the baritone.

'Yes,' answered Nezhdanov at last.

The door was opened discreetly and smoothly, and slowly removing his glossy hat from his comely short-cropped head, a man of about forty, tall, well-made, and dignified, came into the room. He was dressed in a very handsome cloth coat, with a superb beaver collar, though the month of April was drawing to its close. He struck all, Nezhdanov, Paklin, even Mashurina . . . even Ostrodumov! by the elegant self-possession of his carriage and the cordial ease of his address. They all instinctively rose on his entrance.

3

THE elegantly dressed man advanced to Nezhdanov, and, smiling benevolently, began: 'I have already had the pleasure of meeting you and even having some conversation with you, Mr. Nezhdanov, the day before yesterday, if you remember, at the theatre.' The visitor paused, as though waiting for something. Nezhdanov bent his head slightly, and flushed. 'Yes. . . . I have come to see you to-day in consequence of the advertisement you have put in the papers. I should be glad to have a few words with you, if only I'm not disturbing the lady and gentlemen present'—(the visitor bowed to Mashurina, and waved a hand wearing a grey Swedish glove in the direction of Paklin and Ostrodumov)—'if I'm not interrupting them. . . .'

'No . . . why, . . .' Nezhdanov replied with some difficulty. 'My friends will excuse . . . Won't you sit down?'

The visitor gave his figure an affable bend, and politely taking hold of the back of a chair, drew it towards himself, but did not sit down—seeing that everyone in the room was standing. He merely looked about him with his clear though half-closed eyes.

'Good-bye, Alexey Dmitritch,' Mashurina brought out abruptly; 'I'll come in later.'

'And I,' added Ostrodumov, 'I too 'll come . . . later on.'

Passing by the visitor as though intentionally slighting him, Mashurina took Nezhdanov's hand, shook it vigorously and walked out, without saluting anyone. Ostrodumov followed her, making a quite unnecessary amount of noise with his boots, and even snorting more than once, as though to say: 'So much for you with your beaver collar!'

The visitor followed them both with a civil but rather inquisitive glance; then he bent it upon Paklin, as though

17

expecting that he too would follow the example of the two retreating guests. But Paklin, whose face had worn a peculiar forced smile from the moment of the stranger's appearance, edged away, and shrank into a corner. Then the visitor sank into the chair. Nezhdanov also took a seat.

'My surname's Sipyagin—you have heard it, perhaps,' the stranger began with proud modesty.

But first we must relate how Nezhdanov had met him at the theatre.

There had been a performance of Ostrovsky's drama, *Don't Sit in Another Man's Sledge,* on the occasion of a visit of Sadovsky from Moscow. The part of Rusakov was, as is well-known, one of the famous actor's favourite parts. In the morning, Nezhdanov had gone to the box-office, where he found a good many people. He had intended to take a ticket for the pit, but at the very instant he went up to the desk, an officer, standing behind him, held out a three-rouble bill right across Nezhdanov, and shouted to the clerk: 'He'— (*i.e.* Nezhdanov)—'is sure to want change, and I don't, so give me, please, a ticket for the front row, at once. . . . I'm in a hurry!'

'I beg your pardon,' Nezhdanov rejoined sharply, 'I, too, want a ticket for the front row,' and thereupon he flung into the little window three roubles—all the ready money he had. The clerk gave him a ticket, and in the evening Nezhdanov made his appearance in the aristocratic division of the Alexandrinsky Theatre.

He was shabbily dressed, had muddy boots and no gloves; he felt ill at ease and exasperated at himself for feeling so. Next him on the right was sitting a general, studded with stars; on the left the same elegantly dressed man, the privy councillor Sipyagin, whose visit two days later had so disturbed Mashurina and Ostrodumov. Every now and then the general took a passing look at Nezhdanov as though at something improper, unexpected, and even offensive; Sipyagin, on the other hand, cast upon him furtive but by no means hostile glances. All the persons surrounding

18

Nezhdanov struck one, to begin with, rather as personages than persons; and then they were all intimately acquainted with one another, and exchanged brief remarks, or even simple exclamations and words of welcome—some of them speaking across Nezhdanov; while he sat motionless and awkward in his wide, comfortable arm-chair, like a kind of pariah. There were bitterness and shame and disgust in his soul; he did not gain much pleasure from Ostrovsky's comedy and Sadovsky's acting. And suddenly, marvellous to relate, during an *entr'acte,* his neighbour on the left, not the starred general, but the other, who wore no sign of distinction of any kind, addressed him softly and courteously, with a kind of ingratiating gentleness. He began speaking of Ostrovsky's play, wished to learn from Nezhdanov, as 'a representative of the younger generation', what was his opinion of it? Astonished, almost scared, Nezhdanov at first answered abruptly and in monosyllables . . . his heart was positively throbbing; but then he got angry with himself; what was he agitated for? wasn't he a man like all the rest? And he proceeded to lay down his opinions unconstrainedly, without reserve, and spoke in the end so loudly, with such enthusiasm, that he obviously annoyed his starred neighbour. Nezhdanov was a fervent admirer of Ostrovsky; but for all his appreciation of the talent shown by the author in the comedy, *Don't Sit in Another Man's Sledge,* he could not approve of the unmistakable intention to depreciate civilisation in the burlesqued character of Vihorev. His courteous neighbour listened to him with great attention and with sympathy, and in the next *entr'acte* began talking to him again, not this time of Ostrovsky's play, but of various general topics, of life, of science, and even of politics. He was obviously interested in the eloquent young man. Nezhdanov, far from being constrained, even, as the phrase goes, let off steam a little, as much as to say, 'All right, if you want to know—here you are, then!' In his neighbour, the general, he roused more than simple discomfort—positive indignation and suspicion. At the close of the performance, Sipyagin took leave in a very cordial way of Nezhdanov, but did not seek to learn his surname, nor did he mention his own. While he was waiting on the stairs for his carriage, he jostled against a friend of his, an *aide-de-camp* to the Tsar, Prince G.

'I was looking at you from my box,' the prince said to him, grinning over his perfumed moustaches. 'Do you know whom you were talking to?'

'No, do you?'

'The lad's no fool, eh?'

'Far from it; who is he?'

Then the prince bent over to his ear and whispered in French, 'My brother—yes; he's my brother, a natural son of my father's . . . his name's Nezhdanov. I will tell you about it some day. . . . My father hadn't expected him; that's why he called him Nezhdanov—that is, unexpected. However, he provided for him . . . *il lui a fait un sort.* . . . We let him have an allowance. He's a fellow with brains . . . he's had, thanks to my father again, a good education. But, he's gone utterly crazy, a sort of republican. . . . We don't receive him. . . *Il est impossible!*. But good-bye, they're calling my carriage!' The prince departed, and the next day Sipyagin read in the paper the advertisement Nezhdanov had inserted, and he went to see him. . . .

'My surname's Sipyagin,' he told Nezhdanov, as he sat on a basket-chair facing him, and looked at him with his ingratiating eyes. 'I learned from the papers that you want a position as tutor, and I have come to you with this proposal. I am married; I have one son—nine years old, a boy—to speak frankly—of excellent abilities. We spend the greater part of the summer and autumn in the country, in the province of S——, four miles from the chief town of the province. Well, would you care to go there with us for the vacation, to teach my son the Russian language and history—the subjects you mentioned in your advertisement? I venture to think you will like me, my family, and the very situation of our place. There's a first-rate garden, streams, splendid

20

air, a roomy house. . . . Will you consent? If so, I have only to inquire your terms, though I do not imagine,' added Sipyagin with a faint grimace, 'that any difficulties could arise between us on that score.'

All the while Sipyagin was speaking, Nezhdanov stared fixedly at him, at his small head, thrown a little back, at his low and narrow but clever forehead, his delicate Roman nose, his pleasant eyes, his well-cut lips, from which the amiable words seemed to flow in an easy stream, at his long whiskers drooping after the English fashion—he stared and was puzzled. 'What does it mean?' he thought. 'Why does this man seem to be making up to me? He's an aristocrat—and I! How have we come together? And what brought him to me?'

He was so absorbed in his reflections that he did not open his mouth even when Sipyagin paused at the end of his speech, awaiting a reply. Sipyagin stole a glance at the corner where Paklin was ensconced, his eyes fixed as intently upon him as Nezhdanov's—was it the presence of this third person which prevented Nezhdanov from speaking out? Sipyagin raised his eyebrows high, as though submitting to the strangeness of the surroundings into which he had dropped, by his own act, however, and raising his voice also, he repeated his question.

Nezhdanov started.

'Of course,' he said rather hurriedly, 'I consent . . . gladly. . . . Though I must own . . . that I can't help feeling some astonishment . . . seeing that I have no recommendation . . . and indeed the opinions I expressed the day before yesterday at the theatre were rather calculated to dissuade you. . . .'

'There you are utterly mistaken, dear Alexey . . . Alexey Dmitritch! isn't that it?' declared Sipyagin smiling; 'I am, I venture to say, well known as a man of liberal, progressive ideas; on the contrary, your opinions, with the exception of all that is peculiar to youth, ever prone—don't be angry with me—to some exaggeration—those opinions of yours are in no way opposed to my own, and, indeed, I am delighted with their youthful enthusiasm!'

Sipyagin talked without the faintest hesitation; his even, rounded speech dropped 'smooth as honey upon oil'.

'My wife shares my way of thinking,' he went on; 'her views, very likely, approach yours even more closely; that's natural enough; she is younger! When, the day after our meeting, I read your name in the papers—you had published your name with your address, contrary, I may mention in passing, to the ordinary practice, though I had found out your name already at the theatre—well—that—that fact struck me. I saw in it—in this coincidence—the . . . excuse the superstitious phrase . . . so to say, the finger of fate! You referred to recommendations; but I need no recommendation. Your appearance, your personality attract me. That is enough for me. I am accustomed to believe my eyes. And so—may I reckon on it? You agree?'

'Yes . . . of course . . .' answered Nezhdanov, 'and I will try to justify your confidence; only let me mention one thing now: I am ready to teach your son, but not to look after him. I am not fit for that—and in fact I don't want to tie myself down, I don't want to lose my freedom.'

Sipyagin waved his hand lightly in the air as though driving away a fly.

'Don't be uneasy. . . . You're not made of that clay; and I don't want anyone to look after him either—I am trying to find a teacher, and I have found him. Well, now, how about terms? financial considerations, filthy lucre?'

Nezhdanov was at a loss what to say. . . .

'Come,' said Sipyagin, bending his whole person forward and affectionately touching Nezhdanov's knee with his fingertips, 'between gentlemen such questions are settled in a couple of words. I offer you a hundred roubles a month; travelling expenses there and back are my affair, of course. You agree?'

Nezhdanov blushed again.

'That is far more than I meant to ask . . . I——'

'Very good, very good . . .' interposed Sipyagin . . . 'I look on the matter as settled, then . . . and on you as one of my household.' He got up from his chair and suddenly grew bright and expansive as though he had received a present. In all his gestures there appeared a certain affable familiarity, even playfulness. 'We will set off in a day or two,' he said in an easy tone; 'I like to meet the spring in the country, though by the nature of my occupations I'm a prosaic creature and chained to town. And so let us reckon your first month as beginning from to-day. My wife and son are already at Moscow. She started before me. We shall find them in the country, in the bosom of nature. We will travel together . . . as bachelors. . . . He, he!' Sipyagin gave a little affected nasal laugh, 'And now——'

He drew out of the pocket of his overcoat a black and silver pocket-book and took out of it a card.

'This is my address here. Come round . . . to-morrow. Yes . . . at twelve o'clock. We will have some more talk. I will develop some of my ideas on education . . . Oh—and we'll fix the day of our departure.' Sipyagin took Nezhdanov's hand. 'And do you know?' he added, his voice lowered and his head held aslant, 'if you need any advance . . . Please don't stand on ceremony! Just a month in advance!'

Nezhdanov simply did not know what to reply, and with the same perplexity he gazed at the face so bright and cordial, and at the same time so alien to him, which was bent so close to him and smiling so kindly at him.

'You don't want it? eh?' whispered Sipyagin.

'If you'll allow me, I'll tell you that to-morrow,' Nezhdanov articulated at last.

'Excellent! And so—till we meet! Till to-morrow!'

Sipyagin dropped Nezhdanov's hand, and was about to go away. . . .

'Allow me to ask,' said Nezhdanov suddenly, 'you told me just now that you found out my name at the theatre? From whom did you learn it?'

'From whom? Oh, from a friend of yours, and I think a relation, Prince . . . Prince G.'

'The *aide-de-camp* of the Tsar?'

'Yes.'

Nezhdanov flushed more hotly than before, and opened his mouth . . . but he said nothing. Sipyagin again pressed his hand, but this time in silence, and bowing first to him, then to Paklin, he put on his hat just in the doorway and went out, still wearing his complacent smile on his face; in it could be discerned the consciousness of the profound impression which his visit must have produced.

4

SIPYAGIN had scarcely crossed the threshold when Paklin leaped up from his chair, and, rushing up to Nezhdanov, began to congratulate him.

'Well, you have made a fine catch!' he declared, giggling and tapping his feet. 'Why, do you know who that is? Sipyagin, everyone knows him, a *kammerherr*, a pillar of society of a sort, a future minister!'

'I know absolutely nothing of him,' Nezhdanov declared sullenly.

Paklin threw up his arms in despair.

'That's just our misfortune, Alexey Dmitritch, that we know no one! We want to produce an effect, we want to turn the whole world upside down, but we live outside that world, we only have to do with two or three friends, and go revolving in a narrow little circle——'

'I beg your pardon,' interposed Nezhdanov: 'that's not true. We only don't care to consort with our enemies; but as for men of our own stamp, as for the people, we are continually entering into relations with them.'

'Stay, stay, stay, stay!' Paklin in his turn interposed. 'In the first place: as for enemies, let me remind you of Gœthe's lines:

"*Wer den Dichter will versteh'n*
Muss im Dichter's Lande gehn . . ."

but I say:

"*Wer die Feinde will versteh'n*
Muss im Feinde's Lande gehn . . ."

To avoid one's enemies, not to know their manners and habits, is ridiculous! Ri . . . di . . . cu . . . lous! . . . Yes! yes! If I want to shoot a wolf in the forest I have to know all his holes! . . . Secondly, you talked just now of entering into relations with the people. . . . My dear soul! In 1862 the Poles went "into the forest"; and we are going now into the same forest; that's to say, to the people, who are just as dark and obscure to us as any forest!'

'Then what's to be done, according to you?'

'The Hindoos fling themselves under the wheels of Juggernaut,' Paklin went on gloomily; 'it crushes them, and they die—in bliss. We too have our Juggernaut. . . . It crushes us indeed, but gives us no bliss.'

'Then what do you say's to be done?' Nezhdanov repeated almost with a shriek. 'Write novels with a "tendency", or what?'

Paklin flung wide his arms and bent his head towards his left shoulder.

'Novels, in any case, you could write, since you have a literary turn. . . . There, don't be angry, I won't. I know you don't like one to refer to it; besides, I agree with you: spinning out that sort of work with "padding" and all the new-fangled phrases too:—"'Ah! I love you!' she bounded. . . . 'It's nothing to me,' he grated." It is anything but a lively job. That's why I repeat, form ties with all classes, from the highest downwards! We mustn't rest all our hopes on fellows like Ostrodumov! They're honest, excellent fellows, but then they're dense! dense! Just look at our worthy friend.

25

Why, the very soles of his boots aren't what clever people wear! Why, what made him go away from here just now? He didn't like to remain in the same room, to breathe the same air, as an aristocrat!'

'I must ask you not to speak slightingly of Ostrodumov before me,' Nezhdanov interposed emphatically. 'He wears thick boots because they're cheaper.'

'I did not mean——' Paklin was beginning.

'If he doesn't care to remain in the same room with an aristocrat,' Nezhdanov continued, raising his voice, 'I applaud him for it; but the great thing is he knows how to sacrifice himself; he will face death, if need be, which you and I will never do!'

Paklin made a piteous little grimace, and pointed to his wasted, crippled little legs.

'Is fighting in my line, my friend Alexey Dmitritch? Good heavens! But never mind all that . . . I repeat, I'm heartily glad of your connection with Mr. Sipyagin, and I even foresee great advantages from that connection, for our cause. You will get into a higher circle! You will see those lionesses, those women of "velvet body worked by springs of steel", as it says in the *Letters from Spain*; study them, my dear boy, study them! If you were an epicurean, I should be positively afraid for you . . . upon my word, I should! But that's not your object in taking such an engagement, of course?'

'I am taking an engagement,' Nezhdanov caught him up, 'for the sake of bread and butter . . . And to get away from all of you for a time!' he added to himself.

'To be sure! to be sure! And so I say to you: study them! What a perfume that gentleman has left behind him!' Paklin sniffed with his nose in the air. 'It's the veritable *ambre* that the mayoress dreamed of in the *Revisor*!

'He questioned Prince G. about me,' Nezhdanov muttered thickly, taking up his position again at the window: 'he probably knows my whole story now.'

'Not probably, but certainly! What of it? I'll bet you it was just that that gave him the idea of taking you as a tutor!

Say what you like, you're an aristocrat yourself by blood, you know. And, of course, that means you're one of themselves! But I've stayed too long with you; it's time I was at the office, at the exploiter's! Good-bye for the present, my dear boy!'

Paklin was going towards the door, but he stopped and turned round.

'Listen, Alyosha,' he said in an ingratiating tone: 'you refused me just now; you will have money now, I know, but still allow me to make some sacrifice, however trifling, for the common cause! There's no other way I can help, so let me at least with my purse! Look; I put a ten-rouble bill on the table! Is it accepted?'

Nezhdanov made no answer, and did not stir.

'Silence gives consent! Thanks!' cried Paklin joyfully, and he disappeared.

Nezhdanov was left alone. . . . He went on staring through the window-pane into the dark, narrow court, into which no ray of sunshine fell even in summer, and dark too was his face.

Nezhdanov was the son, as we are already aware, of Prince G., a rich adjutant-general, and of his daughter's governess, a pretty 'institute-girl,' who had died on the day of his birth. Nezhdanov had received his early education at a boarding-school from an able and strict Swiss schoolmaster, and afterwards had gone to the university. He had himself wished to study law; but the general, his father, who detested the Nihilists, had made him enter 'in æsthetics', as with a bitter smile Nezhdanov used to put it, that is, in the faculty of history and philology. Nezhdanov's father had been in the habit of seeing him only three or four times a year, but he took an interest in his welfare, and when he died bequeathed him, in memory of 'Nastenka' (his mother), a sum of 6000 roubles, the interest of which was paid him by way of a 'pension', by his brothers, the Princes G. Paklin had not been wrong in describing him as an aristocrat; everything in him betrayed good birth: his little ears, hands and feet, the delicate but rather small features of his face, his soft skin, his fluffy hair, even his rather mincing but musical voice. He was terribly nervous, terribly self-conscious, impressionable, and even capricious; the false position in which he had been put from his very childhood had made him irritable and quick to take offence; but his inborn magnanimity had saved him from becoming suspicious and distrustful. This same false position of Nezhdanov's was the explanation of the contradictions to be met in his character. Daintily clean and fastidious to squeamishness, he forced himself to be cynical and coarse in his language; an idealist by nature, passionate and chaste, bold and timid at the same time, he was as ashamed of his timidity and of his purity as of some disgraceful vice, and made a point of jeering at ideals. His heart was soft and he shunned his fellows; he was easily enraged, and never harboured ill-feeling. He was indignant with his father for having made him study 'æsthetics'; ostensibly, as far as anyone could see, he took interest only in political and social questions, and professed the most extreme views (in him they were more than a form of words!); secretly, he revelled in art, poetry, beauty in all its manifestations . . . he even wrote verses. He scrupulously concealed the book in which he scribbled them, and of all his friends in Petersburg, only Paklin—and that solely through the intuition peculiar to him—suspected its existence. Nothing so deeply offended, so outraged Nezhdanov as the faintest allusion to his poetical compositions—to that, as he considered, unpardonable weakness. Thanks to his Swiss schoolmaster, he knew a good many facts, and was not afraid of hard work; he even worked with positive fervour, though rather spasmodically and irregularly. His comrades loved him . . . they were attracted by his uprightness of character, his goodness and purity; but Nezhdanov had been born under no lucky star; life did not come easily to him. He was deeply conscious of this himself, and knew he was lonely in spite of the devotion of his friends.

He still stood at the window, thinking, thinking mournfully and drearily of the journey before him, of the new, unexpected turn in his life. He did not regret leaving Petersburg—he was leaving nothing in it specially precious to him; besides, he knew he would return in the autumn. And still a mood of dread and doubt came over him; he felt an involuntary dejection.

'A nice teacher I shall make!' crossed his mind, 'a fine sort of schoolmaster!' He was ready to reproach himself for having undertaken the task of education, and yet such a reproach would have been unjust. Nezhdanov possessed a fair amount of knowledge, and, in spite of his uneven temper, children were at ease with him, and he, too, readily grew fond of them. The depression which came upon Nezhdanov was that feeling preceding every change of place—that feeling known to all melancholy, all brooding natures. To people of a bold, sanguine character it is unknown: they are rather disposed to rejoice when the daily routine of life is broken up, when their habitual surroundings are changed. Nezhdanov became so deeply absorbed in his meditations that by degrees, almost unconsciously, he began translating them into words; the emotions passing over him were already ranging themselves into rhythmic cadences.

'Oof, the devil!' he cried aloud, 'I do believe I'm on the high road to a poem!'

He shook himself, turned away from the window. Catching sight of Paklin's ten-rouble note lying on the table, he thrust it in his pocket and set to walking up and down the room.

'I must take an advance,' he mused to himself; 'a good thing this gentleman offers it. A hundred roubles . . . and from my brothers—from their excellencies—a hundred roubles . . . fifty for debts, fifty or seventy for the journey . . . and the rest for Ostrodumov. And what Paklin gives—he can have too. And we shall have to get something from Merkulov too.'

Even while he was making these calculations in his head, the same cadences were again astir within him. He stopped, fell to dreaming . . . and, his eyes fixed on the distance, he stood rooted to the spot. Then his hands, gropingly, as it were, felt for and opened a drawer in the table and drew out from the very bottom of it a manuscript-book.

He sank on to a chair, his eyes still turned away, took up a pen, and humming to himself, at times shaking back his hair, with much blotting and scratching out, he set to tracing line after line.

The door into the ante-room was half opened, and Mashurina's head appeared. Nezhdanov did not notice her and went on with his work. Long and intently Mashurina gazed upon him, and, with a shake of her head to right and left, drew back. . . . But Nezhdanov all at once drew himself up, looked round, and exclaiming with vexation, 'Oh you!' he flung the book into the table drawer.

Then Mashurina advanced with a firm step into the room.

'Ostrodumov sent me to you,' she observed jerkily, 'to find out when you can get the money. If you can let us have it to-day we will start this evening.'

'To-day I can't,' rejoined Nezhdanov, and he frowned; 'come to-morrow.'

'At what o'clock?'

'Two o'clock.'

'Very well.'

Mashurina was silent for a little. All at once she held out her hand to Nezhdanov.

'I think I interrupted you—forgive me; and besides . . . I'm just going away. Who knows whether we shall meet again? I wanted to say good-bye to you.'

Nezhdanov pressed her chilly red fingers.

'You saw that gentleman here?' he began; 'we came to terms. I am going to him as a tutor. His estate is in S—— province, near S—— itself.'

A rapturous smile flashed across Mashurina's face.

'Near S——! Then perhaps we shall see each other again. They may possibly send us there.' Mashurina sighed. 'Ah, Alexey Dmitritch. . . .'

'What?' inquired Nezhdanov.

Mashurina assumed a concentrated look.

'Never mind. Good-bye. Never mind.'

Once more she pressed Nezhdanov's hand and retreated.

'And in all Petersburg there is no one cares for me like that . . . queer creature!' was Nezhdanov's thought. 'But why need she have interrupted me? . . . It's all for the best, though!'

The following morning Nezhdanov betook himself to Sipyagin's town residence, and there, in a magnificent study, filled with furniture of a severe style, in full harmony with the dignity of a liberal politician and modern gentleman, he sat before a huge bureau, on which lay, in orderly arrangement, papers of no use to anyone, beside gigantic ivory knives which never cut anything. For a whole hour he listened to the liberal-minded master of the house, and was immersed in the smooth flood of his clever, affable, condescending words. At last he received a hundred roubles in advance, and ten days later the same Nezhdanov, half-reclining on a velvet sofa in a reserved first-class compartment, beside this same clever liberal politician and modern gentleman, was being carried to Moscow on the jolting lines of the Nikolavsky railway.

5

In the drawing-room of a large stone house, with columns and a Greek façade, built in the twenties of the present century by a landowner noted for devotion to agriculture and for the free use of his fists, the father of Sipyagin, his wife, Valentina Mihalovna, a very handsome woman, was from hour to hour expecting her husband's arrival, for which she had been prepared by a telegram. The decoration of the drawing-room bore the stamp of a modern, refined taste; everything in it was charming and attractive—everything, from the agreeably varied tints of the cretonne upholstery and draperies to the different lines of the china, bronze, and glass knick-knacks, scattered about on the tables and *étagères*—all fell into subdued harmony and blended together in the bright May sunshine which streamed freely in at the high, wide-open windows. The air of the room, heavy with the scent of lilies-of-the-valley (great nosegays of these exquisite spring flowers made patches of white here and there), was stirred from time to time by an inrush of the light breeze which was softly fluttering over the luxuriant leafage of the garden.

A charming picture! And the lady of the house, Valentina Mihalovna, completed the picture—lent it life and meaning. She was a tall woman of thirty, with dark brown hair, a dark but fresh face of one uniform tint, recalling the features of the Sistine Madonna, with marvellous deep, velvety eyes. Her lips were rather wide and colourless, her shoulders rather high, her hands rather large. . . . But, for all that, anyone who had seen how freely and gracefully she moved about the drawing-room, at one time bending her slender, somewhat constricted figure over her flowers and sniffing them with a smile; at another moving some Chinese vase, then rapidly readjusting her glossy hair and half-closing her divine eyes before the glass—anyone, we say, would certainly have exclaimed, to himself or aloud, that he had never met a more fascinating creature!

A pretty, curly-headed boy of nine, in a Scotch kilt, with bare legs, much pomaded and befrizzed, ran impetuously into the drawing-room, and stopped suddenly on seeing Valentina Mihalovna.

'What is it, Kolya?' she asked. Her voice was as soft and velvety as her eyes.

'Well, mamma,' the boy began in confusion, 'auntie sent me here. . . . She told me to bring her some lilies-of-the-valley . . . for her room. . . . She has none.'

Valentina Mihalovna took her little son by the chin and lifted his little pomaded head.

'Tell your auntie to send to the gardener for lilies; those lilies are mine. . . . I don't want them touched. Tell her I don't like my arrangements disarranged. Can you repeat my words?'

'Yes, I can . . .' muttered the boy.

'Well, then, . . . say them.'

'I will say . . . I will say . . . you won't let her have them.'

Valentina Mihalovna laughed. Her laugh, too, was soft.

'I see it's no use giving you messages. Well, never mind; tell her anything you think of.'

The boy hurriedly kissed his mother's hand, which was completely covered with rings, and rushed headlong away.

Valentina Mihalovna followed him with her eyes, sighed, and went up to a cage of gold wire, on the walls of which a green parrot was clambering, warily hooking on by his beak and his claws; she teased him with her finger-tip; then sank into a low lounge, and, taking from a carved round table the last number of the *Revue des Deux Mondes,* she began to skim its pages.

A respectful cough made her look round. In the doorway stood a handsome footman in livery and a white cravat.

'What is it, Agafon?' inquired Valentina Mihalovna, still in the same soft voice.

'Semyon Petrovitch Kallomyetsev is here. Shall I show him up?'

'Ask him up, of course. And send word to Marianna Vikent-yevna to come down to the drawing-room.'

Valentina Mihalovna flung the *Revue des Deux Mondes* on a little table, and, leaning back on the lounge, she turned her eyes upwards and looked thoughtful, which suited her extremely.

From the very way Semyon Petrovitch Kallomyetsev, a young man of two-and-thirty, entered the room, easily, carelessly, and languidly, from the way he suddenly beamed politely, bowed a little on one side, and drew himself up like elastic afterwards, from the way he spoke, half-condescendingly, half-affectedly, respectfully took Valentina Mihalovna's hand, and effusively kissed it—from all this one might judge that the visitor was not an inhabitant of the province, a mere casual country neighbour, even one of the richest, but a real Petersburg swell of the highest fashion. He was dressed, too, in the best English style: the coloured border of his white cambric handkerchief peeped in a tiny triangle out of the flat side-pocket of his tweed jacket; a single eyeglass dangled on a rather wide black ribbon; the pale dull tint of his Suède gloves corresponded with the pale grey of his check trousers. Close shorn was Mr. Kallomyetsev, and smoothly shaven; his rather feminine face, with its small eyes set close together, its thin depressed nose, and its full red lips, was expressive of the agreeable ease of a well-bred nobleman. It was all affability . . . and it very easily turned vindictive, even coarse; someone or something had but to vex Semyon Petrovitch, to jar on his conservative, patriotic, and religious principles—oh! then he became pitiless! All his elegance evaporated instantly; his soft eyes glowed with an evil light; his little pretty mouth gave forth ugly words—and appealed, with piteous whines appealed, to the strong arm of the government!

Semyon Petrovitch's family had sprung from simple market-gardeners. His great-grandfather had been known in the parts from which he came as Kolomentsov. . . . But his grandfather even had changed his name to Kollometsov; his father wrote it Kallometsev, finally Semyon Petrovitch had inserted the *y*, and quite seriously regarded himself as an aristocrat of the purest blood; he even hinted at his family's being descended from the Barons von Gallenmeier, one of whom had been the Austrian field-marshal in the Thirty Years' War. Semyon Petrovitch was in the ministry of the Court, he had the title of a *kammeryunker*. He was prevented by his patriotism from joining the diplomatic service, for which he seemed destined by everything, his education, his knowledge of the world, his popularity with women, and his very appearance . . . *mais quitter la Russie! jamais!* Kallomyetsev had a fine property, and had connections; he had the reputation of a trustworthy and devoted man—*un peu trop féodal dans ses opinions*—as the distinguished Prince B——, one of the leading lights of the Petersburg official world, had said of him. Kallomyetsev had come to S—— province on a two months' leave to look after his property, that is to say, 'to scare some and squeeze others'.

34

Of course, there's no doing anything without that.

'I expected to find Boris Andreitch here by now,' he began, politely swaying from one foot to the other, and with a sudden sidelong look in imitation of a very important personage.

Valentina Mihalovna made a faint grimace.

'Or you would not have come?'

Kallomyetsev all but fell backwards, so unjust, so inconsistent with the facts did Valentina Mihalovna's question seem to him.

'Valentina Mihalovna!' he cried, 'heavens! could you suppose . . .'

'Well, well, sit down. Boris Andreitch will be here directly. I have sent the carriage to the station for him. Wait a little . . . You will see him. What time is it now?'

'Half-past two,' replied Kallomyetsev, pulling out of his waistcoat pocket a big gold watch decorated with enamel. He showed it to Madame Sipyagin. 'Have you seen my watch? It was a present from Mihail, you know, the Servian prince . . . Obrenovitch. Here's his crest, look. We are great friends. We used to go hunting together. A capital fellow! And a hand of iron, as a ruler should have! Oh, he won't stand any nonsense! No-o-o!'

Kallomyetsev sank into an easy chair, crossed his legs, and began in a leisurely way to draw off his left glove.

'If only we had someone like Mihail here in our province!'

'Why? Are you discontented with anything?'

Kallomyetsev puckered up his nose.

'Yes, always that provincial council! That provincial council! What good is it? It simply weakens the administration and arouses . . . superfluous ideas. . . .' (Kallomyetsev waved his bare left hand, freed from the compression of the glove) '. . . and impossible expectations.' (Kallomyetsev breathed on his hand.) 'I have talked of this at Petersburg . . . *mais bah!* The wind's not in that quarter now. Even your husband . . . imagine! But of course he's a well-known liberal!'

Madame Sipyagin drew herself up on the little lounge.

'What? You, M'sieu Kallomyetsev, you in opposition to the government!'

'I? In opposition? Never! On no account! *Mais j'ai mon franc parler*, I sometimes criticise, but I always submit!'

'And I do just the opposite; I don't criticise and I don't submit.'

'*Ah! mais c'est un mot!* I will, if you will allow me, repeat your remark to my friend, *Ladislas—vous savez—*he is writing a society novel, and has already read me some chapters. It will be magnificent! *Nous aurons enfin le grand monde russe peint par lui-même.*'

'Where is it to appear?'

'In the *Russian Messenger,* of course. It is our *Revue des Deux Mondes.* I see you are reading that.'

'Yes, but do you know it is getting very dull?'

'Perhaps . . . perhaps. . . . And the *Russian Messenger,* perhaps, for some time past—to speak in the language of the day—has been just a wee bit groggy.'

Kallomyetsev laughed heartily; he thought it very amusing to say 'groggy', and even 'a wee bit'.

'*Mais c'est un journal qui se respecte,*' he went on. 'And that's the chief thing. I, I must admit, take very little interest in Russian literature; such plebeians are always figuring in it nowadays. It's positively come to the heroine of a novel being a cook, a plain cook, *parole d'honneur!* But Ladislas's novel I shall certainly read. *Il y aura le petit mot pour rire . . .* and the tendency! the tendency! the Nihilists will be exposed. I can answer for Ladislas's way of thinking on that subject, *que est très correct.*'

'More than one can say for his past,' remarked Madame Sipyagin.

'*Ah! jetons un voile sur les erreurs de sa jeunesse!*' cried Kallomyetsev, and he pulled off his right glove.

Again Valentina Mihalovna faintly fluttered her eyelids. She was in the habit of making rather free use of her marvellous eyes.

'Semyon Petrovitch,' she observed, 'may I ask you why it is

36

that in speaking Russian you use so many French words? I
fancy . . . excuse my saying so . . . that's gone out of fashion.'

'Why? why? Everyone has not such a perfect mastery of
our mother-tongue as you, for instance. As for me, I recognise
the Russian language as the language of imperial decrees, of
government regulations; I prize its purity. I do homage to
Karamzin! . . . But the Russian, so to say, everyday language
. . . does it really exist? How, for instance, could you trans-
late my exclamation *de tout à l'heure*? *C'est un mot!* It's
a word! . . . Fancy!'

'I should say: that's a clever saying.'

Kallomyetsev laughed.

'A clever saying! Valentina Mihalovna! But don't you
feel there's . . . something scholastic directly. . . . All the
raciness has gone. . . .'

'Well, you won't convince me. But what is Marianna
doing?' She rang the bell; a page appeared.

'I gave orders to ask Marianna Vikentyevna to come down
to the drawing-room. Hasn't my message been taken to her?'

Before the page had time to answer, there was seen in the
doorway behind him a young girl in a loose dark blouse,
with her hair cropped short, Marianna Vikentyevna, Sipyagin's niece.

6

'I BEG your pardon, Valentina Mihalovna,' she said, going
towards Madame Sipyagin; 'I was busy and I lingered.'

Then she bowed to Kallomyetsev, and, moving a little aside,
seated herself on a small ottoman near the parrot, who had
begun flapping his wings and craning towards her directly
he caught sight of her.

'Why are you sitting so far away, Marianna?' observed

37

Madame Sipyagin, following her with her eyes to the ottoman. 'Do you want to be close to your little friend? Only fancy, Semyon Petrovitch,' she turned to Kallomyetsev, 'that parrot's simply in love with dear Marianna.'

'That does not astonish me!'

'And me he can't endure.'

'Well, that is astonishing! You tease him, I suppose?'

'Never; quite the contrary. I give him sugar. But he will take nothing from me. No . . . it's a case of sympathy . . . and antipathy.'

Marianna glanced up from under her eyelids at Madame Sipyagin . . . and Madame Sipyagin glanced at her.

These two women did not like each other. In comparison with her aunt, Marianna might almost have been called 'a plain little thing'. She had a round face, a large hawk nose, grey eyes, also large and very clear, thin eyebrows, thin lips. She had cropped her thick dark-brown hair, and she looked unsociable. But about her whole personality there was something vigorous and bold, something stirring and passionate. Her feet and hands were tiny; her strongly knit, supple little body recalled the Florentine statuettes of the sixteenth century; she moved lightly and gracefully.

Marianna's position in the Sipyagins' household was a rather difficult one. Her father, a very clever and energetic man of half-Polish extraction, gained the rank of a general, but was suddenly ruined by being detected in a gigantic fraud on the government; he was brought to trial . . . condemned, deprived of his rank and his nobility, and sent to Siberia. Afterwards he was pardoned . . . and brought back; but he did not succeed in climbing up again, and died in extreme poverty. His wife, Sipyagin's sister, the mother of Marianna (she had no other children), could not endure the blow which had demolished all her prosperity, and died soon after her husband. Sipyagin gave his niece a home in his own house; but she was sick of a life of dependence; she strove towards freedom with all the force of her uncompromising nature, and between her and her aunt there raged a constant though hidden warfare. Madame Sipyagin considered her a Nihilist and an atheist; Marianna, for her part, hated Madame Sipyagin, as her unconscious oppressor. Her uncle she held aloof from, as she did, indeed, from everyone else. She simply held aloof from them; she was not afraid of them; she had not a timid temper.

'Antipathy,' repeated Kallomyetsev; 'yes, that's a strange thing. Everyone is aware, for instance, that I'm a deeply religious man, orthodox in the fullest sense of the word; but a priest's flowing locks—his mane—I can't look at with equanimity; I have a sensation of positive nausea.'

And Kallomyetsev, with a reiterated wave of his clenched fist, tried to express his sensations of nausea.

'Hair in general terms seems rather to worry you, Semyon Petrovitch,' observed Marianna; 'I am sure you can't look at anyone with equanimity whose hair is cropped like mine.'

Madame Sipyagin slowly raised her eyebrows and bent her head, as though amazed at the free and easy way in which young girls nowadays enter into conversation; while Kallomyetsev gave a condescending simper.

'Of course,' he replied, 'I cannot but feel regret for lovely curls like yours, Marianna Vikentyevna, which have fallen beneath the remorseless scissors; but I have no feeling of antipathy; and, in any case, . . . your example would have . . . would have . . . *proselytised* me!'

Kallomyetsev could not find the Russian word, and did not want to speak French after his hostess's observations.

'Thank goodness, dear Marianna does not wear spectacles yet,' put in Madame Sipyagin, 'and has not parted with cuffs and collars, though she does study natural science, to my sincere regret; and is interested in the woman question too . . . Aren't you, Marianna?'

This was all said with the object of embarrassing Marianna; but she was not embarrassed.

'Yes, auntie,' she answered, 'I read everything that's written about it; I try to understand exactly what the question is.'

'That's what it is to be young!'—Madame Sipyagin turned

to Kallomyetsev; 'you and I don't care about these things now—eh?'

Kallomyetsev smiled sympathetically; he was bound to bear with the lady's jesting humour.

'Marianna Vikentyevna,' he began, 'is filled with the idealism . . . the romanticism of youth . . . which in time . . .'

'But I am slandering myself,' Madame Sipyagin interrupted: 'I take an interest in such questions too. I'm not quite elderly yet, you know.'

'And I take an interest in all such subjects,' Kallomyetsev exclaimed hurriedly; 'only I would forbid talking about it.'

'You would forbid talking about it?' Marianna repeated inquiringly.

'Yes! I would say to the public: I don't hinder your taking an interest . . . but as for talking . . . hush!'—he put his finger to his lips—'anyway, talking *in print*—I would prohibit—unconditionally!'

Madame Sipyagin laughed.

'What? You would have a commission appointed in some department to decide the question, wouldn't you?'

'And why not a commission? Do you think we should decide the question worse than all the hungry penny-a-liners, who can never see beyond their noses, and fancy they are . . . geniuses of the first rank? We would appoint Boris Andreevitch president.'

Madame Sipyagin laughed more than ever.

'You must take care; Boris Andreevitch is sometimes such a Jacobin——'

'Jackó, jackó, jackó,' called the parrot.

Valentina Mihalovna shook her handkerchief at him.

'Don't prevent sensible people from talking! . . . Marianna, quiet him.'

Marianna turned to the cage and began scratching the parrot's neck, which he offered her at once.

'Yes,' Madame Sipyagin continued, 'Boris Andreevitch sometimes astonishes me. He has something . . . something of the tribune in him.'

'*C'est parce qu'il est orateur!*' Kallomyetsev interposed hotly in French. 'Your husband has the gift of words, as no else has; he's accustomed to success, too . . . *ses propres paroles le grisent* . . . add to that a liking for popularity . . . But he's a little off all that, isn't he? *Il boude?*— eh?'

Madame Sipyagin glanced towards Marianna.

'I have not noticed it,' she replied after a brief silence.

'Yes,' Kallomyetsev pursued in a pensive tone; 'he has been overlooked a little.'

Madame Sipyagin again indicated Marianna with a significant glance.

Kallomyetsev smiled and grimaced, as much as to say, 'I understand.'

'Marianna Vikentyevna!' he exclaimed suddenly, in a voice unnecessarily loud, 'are you intending to give lessons in the school again this year?'

Marianna turned round from the cage.

'And does that, too, interest you, Semyon Petrovitch?'

'To be sure; indeed it interests me very much.'

'You would not prohibit that?'

'I would prohibit Nihilists from even thinking about schools; but, under clerical guidance, and with supervision of the clergy, I would found schools myself!'

'Really, now? Well, I don't know what I am going to do this year. Everything turned out so badly last year. Besides, there's no school in summer-time.'

When Marianna talked, her colour gradually deepened as though her words cost her an effort, as though she were forcing herself to go on. There was still a great deal of self-consciousness about her.

'You are not sufficiently prepared?' inquired Madame Sipyagin with a quiver of irony in her voice.

'Perhaps not.'

'What?' Kallomyetsev exclaimed again. 'What do I hear? Merciful heavens! is preparation needed to teach the little peasant wenches their A B C?'

But at that instant Kolya ran into the drawing-room shouting: 'Mamma! mamma! papa is coming!' and after him there
came rolling in on her fat little feet a grey-haired lady in a cap
and yellow shawl, and she too announced that dear Boris
would be here directly! This lady was Sipyagin's aunt, Anna
Zaharovna by name. All the persons who were in the drawing-room jumped up from their places and rushed into the
ante-room, and from there down the stairs out to the principal
entrance. A long avenue of lopped fir-trees led from the highroad straight to this entrance; already a carriage was dashing
along it, drawn by four horses. Valentina Mihalovna, standing in front of all, waved her handkerchief, Kolya uttered a
piercing shout; the coachman deftly drew up the heated horses,
the groom flew headlong from the box and almost tore the
carriage door off, lock, hinges, and all; and, with an amiable
smile on his lips, in his eyes, over his whole face, Boris Andreevitch alighted, flinging his cloak off with a single easy gesture.
Quickly and gracefully Valentina Mihalovna flung both arms
about his neck, and kissed him three times. Kolya was stamping and tugging at his father's coat-tails behind . . . but he
first kissed Anna Zaharovna, taking off his very uncomfortable
and hideous Scotch travelling cap as a preliminary; then he
exchanged greetings with Marianna and Kallomyetsev, who
had also come out on the doorstep—(he gave Kallomyetsev
a vigorous English 'shake-hands', working his arm up and
down, as though he were tugging at a bell-rope)—and only then
turned to his son; he took him under his arms, lifted him up,
and drew him close to his face.

While all this was taking place, Nezhdanov crept stealthily
with a guilty air out of the carriage and stood near the front
wheel, keeping his cap on and looking up from under his
brows. . . . Valentina Mihalovna, as she embraced her husband, glanced sharply over his shoulder at this new figure;
Sipyagin had told her beforehand that he was bringing a tutor
along with him.

The whole party, still exchanging welcomes and shaking
hands with the newly arrived master, moved up the steps,

along both sides of which were ranged the principal men- and maid-servants. They did not kiss his hand—that 'Asiaticism' had long been abandoned—but merely bowed respectfully; and Sipyagin responded to their salutations with a motion more of the nose and brows than of the head.

Nezhdanov too moved slowly up the broad steps. Directly he entered the ante-room, Sipyagin, who had been already on the look-out for him, presented him to his wife, Anna Zaharovna and Marianna; while to Kolya he said, 'This is your tutor, mind you obey him! give him your hand!' Kolya timidly stretched out his hand to Nezhdanov, then stared at him; but apparently finding nothing in him striking or attractive, clung again to his 'papa'. Nezhdanov felt ill at ease just as he had that time at the theatre. He had on an old, rather ugly great-coat; his face and hands were covered with the dust of the road. Valentina Mihalovna said something affable to him; but he did not quite catch her words and made no response; he only noticed that she gazed with peculiar brightness and affection at her husband and kept close to his side. He did not like Kolya's befrizzed, pomaded head of hair; at the sight of Kallomyetsev he thought, 'What a smug little phiz!' and to the others he paid no attention whatever. Sipyagin twice turned his head with dignity as though looking round at his household gods, a position which threw his long hanging whiskers and rather round little head into striking relief. Then he called to one of the footmen in his powerful resonant voice, which showed no trace of the fatigues of the journey: 'Ivan! take this gentleman to the green room and carry his trunk up there,' and informed Nezhdanov that he could rest now, unpack, and set himself to rights, and dinner would be ready at five o'clock precisely. Nezhdanov bowed, and followed Ivan into the 'green room', which was on the second storey.

The whole party passed into the drawing-room. There words of welcome were repeated once more; a half-blind old nurse came in with a curtsy. From regard for her years, she was allowed by Sipyagin to kiss his hand, and then, with apologies

43

to Kallomyetsev, he retired to his own room, escorted by his
wife.

7

THE spacious and comfortable room to which the servant conducted Nezhdanov looked out on the garden. Its windows
were open and a light breeze was faintly fluttering the white
blinds; they swelled out like sails, rose and fell again. Gleams
of golden light glided slowly over the ceiling; the whole room
was full of a fresh, rather moist fragrance of spring.
Nezhdanov began by dismissing the servant, unpacking his
trunk, washing and changing his clothes. The journey had
utterly exhausted him; the constant presence for two whole
days of a stranger, with whom he had had much varied and
aimless talk, had worked upon his nerves; something bitter, not
quite weariness nor quite anger, was secretly astir in the very
bottom of his soul; he raged against his faint-heartedness,
and still his heart sank.

He went up to the window and began looking at the garden.
It was an old-world garden, of rich black soil, such a garden
as one does not see this side of Moscow. It was laid out on
a long, sloping hill-side, and consisted of four clearly marked
divisions. In front of the house for two hundred paces stretched
the flower-garden, with straight little sandy paths, groups of
acacias and lilacs, and round flower-beds; on the left, past the
stable-yard, right down to the threshing-floor, lay the fruit-
garden closely planted with apple, pear, and plum trees,
currants and raspberries; just opposite the house rose inter-
secting avenues of limes forming a great close quadrangle.
The view on the right was bounded by the road, shut in by a
double row of silver poplars; behind a clump of weeping
birches could be seen the round roof of a green-house. The

whole garden was in the tender green of its first spring foliage; there was no sound yet of the loud summer buzz of insects; the young leaves twittered, and chaffinches were singing somewhere, and two doves cooed continually in the same tree, and a solitary cuckoo called, shifting her place at each note; and from the distance beyond the mill-pond came the caw in chorus of the rooks, like the creaking of innumerable cart-wheels. And over all this fresh, secluded, peaceful life the white clouds floated softly, with swelling bosoms like great, lazy birds. Nezhdanov gazed, listened, drank in the air through parted chilling lips.

And his heart grew lighter; a sense of peace came upon him too.

Meanwhile, in the bedroom downstairs, there was talk about him. Sipyagin was telling his wife how he had made his acquaintance, and what Prince G. had told him, and what discussions they had had on the journey.

'A good brain!' he repeated, 'and plenty of information; it's true, he's a red republican, but, as you know, that's nothing to me; these fellows have ambition, anyway. And besides, Kolya's too young to pick up any nonsense from him.'

Valentina Mihalovna listened to her husband with an affectionate though ironical smile, as though he had been confessing a rather strange, but amusing prank; it was positively agreeable to her that her *seigneur et maître,* so solid a man, so important an official, was still as capable of perpetrating some sudden mischievous freak as a boy of twenty. Standing before the looking-glass in a snow-white shirt and blue silk braces, Sipyagin set to brushing his hair in the English fashion with two brushes, while Valentina Mihalovna, tucking up her little shoes under her on a low Turkish lounge, began to tell him various pieces of news about the estate, about the paper factory, which—sad to say—was not doing as well as it should, about the cook, whom they would have to get rid of, about the church, off which the stucco was peeling, about Marianna, about Kallomyetsev. . . .

45

Between the husband and wife there existed a genuine harmony and confidence; they did really live 'in love and good counsel', as they used to say in old times; and when Sipyagin, on completing his toilet, asked Valentina Mihalovna in chivalrous fashion for 'her little hand', when she gave him both, and with tender pride watched him kissing them alternately, the feeling expressed in both faces was a fine and genuine feeling, though in her it was reflected in eyes worthy of a Raphael, in him in the commonplace 'peepers' of a civilian general.

Precisely at five o'clock Nezhdanov went down to dinner, which was announced not even by a bell, but the prolonged boom of a Chinese *gong*. The whole party were already assembled in the dining--room. Sipyagin, above his high cravat, greeted him cordially once more, and assigned him a place at the table between Anna Zaharovna and Kolya. Anna Zaharovna was an old maid, the sister of Sipyagin's deceased father; she smelt of camphor, like stored-up clothes, and had an anxious and dejected air. Her position in the household was that of Kolya's nurse or governess; her wrinkled face expressed her displeasure when Nezhdanov was seated between her and her little charge. Kolya stole sidelong glances at his new neighbour; the sharp child soon guessed that his tutor was ill at ease, that he was embarrassed; he did not raise his eyes, and scarcely ate anything. Kolya was pleased at this; till then he had been afraid his tutor might turn out to be cross and severe. Valentina Mihalovna too glanced at Nezhdanov.

'He looks like a student,' was her thought, 'and he's not seen much of the world; but his face is interesting and the colour of his hair's original, like that apostle whom the old Italian masters always depict as red-haired; and his hands are clean.' Everyone at the table indeed glanced at Nezhdanov and, as it were, had pity on him, leaving him in peace for the present; he was conscious of this and was glad of it, and at the same time, for some reason or other, irritated. The conversation at table was kept up by Kallomyetsev and

46

Sipyagin. They talked about the provincial council, the governor, the highway-rates, the terms of redemption, their common acquaintances in Petersburg and Moscow, of Mr. Katkov's school then just beginning to become influential, the difficulty of getting workmen, fines and damage caused by cattle, but also of Bismarck, of the war of 1866 and of Napoleon III, whom Kallomyetsev dubbed a capital fellow. The young *kammerjunker* gave expression to the most retrograde opinions; he went so far at last as to propose—ostensibly as a joke, it's true—the toast given by a gentleman, a friend of his, at a certain birthday banquet: 'I drink to the only principles I acknowledge,' the ardent landowner had exclaimed, 'to the knout and to Roederer '

Valentina Mihalovna frowned, and observed that this quotation was *de très mauvais goût*. Sipyagin, on the contrary, expressed the most liberal opinions; amicably, and rather carelessly, he opposed Kallomyetsev; he even jeered at him a little.

'Your apprehensions in regard to the emancipation, my dear Semyon Petrovitch,' he said to him, among other things, 'remind me of a memorial drawn up by our respected and excellent friend Alexey Ivanitch Tveritinov in 1860, and read by him everywhere in the Petersburg drawing-rooms. There was one particularly nice sentence describing how the liberated peasant would infallibly go, torch in hand, over the face of the whole country. You should have seen dear good Alexey Ivanitch, with distended cheeks and round eyes, bringing out of his infantine mouth, "T-t-torch! t-t-torch! he will go about t-torch in hand!" Well, the emancipation is an accomplished fact. . . . Where is the peasant with the torch?'

'Tveritinov,' Kallomyetsev answered in a gloomy tone, 'was only so far wrong that it's not peasants but other people who are going about with torches.'

At those words Nezhdanov, who till that instant had hardly noticed Marianna—she was sitting at the farther diagonal corner—suddenly exchanged glances with her and at once

felt that they—that sullen girl and he—were of the same
faith, of the same camp. She had made no impression of
any kind on him when Sipyagin had introduced him to her;
why was it her eye that he caught at this moment? He put the
question to himself at that point: Wasn't it shameful, wasn't
it disgraceful to sit and listen to such opinions without protest-
ing, giving grounds by his silence for believing that he shared
them? A second time Nezhdanov glanced at Marianna, and he
fancied that he read the answer to his question in her eyes:
'Wait a little,' they seemed to say, 'it's not time now . . .
it's not worth while . . . later on; there's always time. . . .'

It was pleasant to him to think that she understood him.
He listened again to the conversation. . . . Valentina
Mihalovna had taken her husband's place and was speaking
out even more freely, even more radically than he. She could
not comprehend, 'positively could not com-pre-hend', how a
man of education, still young, could adhere to old-fashioned
conventionalism like that!

'I am sure, though,' she added, 'that you only say so for
the sake of a paradox! As for you, Alexey Dmitritch,' she
turned with a cordial smile to Nezhdanov (he was inwardly
amazed that she knew his name and his father's), 'I know you
don't share Semyon Petrovitch's apprehensions; Boris
described to me your talks with him on the journey.'

Nezhdanov flushed, bent over his plate, and muttered something unintelligible; he was not so much shy as unaccustomed
to exchange remarks with such distinguished personages.
Madame Sipyagin still smiled upon him; her husband supported her patronisingly. . . . But Kallomyetsev deliberately
stuck his round eyeglass between his nose and his eyebrow,
and stared at the student who dared not share his 'apprehensions'. But to confuse Nezhdanov in *that* way was a
difficult task; on the contrary, he drew himself up at once,
and stared in his turn at the fashionable official; and just as
suddenly as he had felt a comrade in Marianna, he felt a foe
in Kallomyetsev! And Kallomyetsev was conscious of it;
he dropped his eyeglass, turned away, and tried to laugh . . .

but unsuccessfully; only Anna Zaharovna, who secretly adored him, inwardly took his part, and was still more indignant at the uninvited neighbour who was separating her from Kolya.

Shortly afterwards the dinner came to an end. The party moved on to the terrace to drink coffee; Sipyagin and Kallomyetsev lighted cigars. Sipyagin offered Nezhdanov a genuine regalia, but he refused it.

'Ah! to be sure!' cried Sipyagin; 'I'd forgotten; you only smoke your cigarettes!'

'Curious taste,' Kallomyetsev observed, between his teeth.

Nezhdanov almost exploded. 'I know the difference between a regalia and a cigarette well enough, but I don't care to be under obligations,' almost broke from his lips. . . . He restrained himself; but at once scored this second piece of insolence as a 'debt' to pay back against his enemy.

'Marianna!' Madame Sipyagin observed all at once, in a loud voice, 'you need not stand on ceremony before a stranger . . . you may smoke your cigarette, and welcome. Besides,' she added, turning towards Nezhdanov, 'I have heard that in your set all the young ladies smoke?'

'Quite so,' Nezhdanov answered dryly. It was the first word he had spoken to Madame Sipyagin.

'Well, I don't smoke,' she went on, with an ingratiating light in her velvety eyes. . . . 'I am behind the age.'

In a leisurely, circumspect fashion, as though in defiance of her aunt, Marianna drew out a cigarette and a box of matches, and began smoking. Nezhdanov, too, smoked a cigarette, lighting it from Marianna's.

It was an exquisite evening. Kolya and Anna Zaharovna went off into the garden; the rest of the party remained about an hour longer on the terrace, enjoying the air. The conversation became rather lively. . . . Kallomyetsev attacked literature; Sipyagin on that point, too, showed himself a liberal, championed the independence of literature, pointed out its utility, and even referred to Chateaubriand and the fact that the Emperor Alexander Pavlovitch had bestowed on him the order of St. Andrei the First-Called! Nezhdanov

49

did not take part in the discussion; Madame Sipyagin looked at him with an expression which seemed on one hand to approve of his discreet reserve, and on the other to be a little surprised at it.

Everyone went back to the drawing-room for tea.

'We have a very bad habit, Alexey Dmitritch,' said Sipyagin to Nezhdanov; 'we play cards every evening, and what's more, a prohibited game . . . think of that! I won't invite you to join us . . . but Marianna will be so good as to play us something on the piano. You're fond of music, I hope, eh?' And without waiting for an answer, Sipyagin picked up a pack of cards. Marianna sat down to the piano, and played neither well nor ill a few of Mendelssohn's 'Songs without Words'. *'Charmant! charmant! quel toucher!'* Kallomyetsev, from a distance, shrieked as though he had been scalded; but this ejaculation was vociferated rather from politeness; and Nezhdanov too, in spite of the hope expressed by Sipyagin, had no passion for music.

Meanwhile Sipyagin and his wife, Kallomyetsev and Anna Zaharovna had sat down to cards. . . . Kolya came to say good-night, and after receiving a blessing from his parents and a large glass of milk instead of tea, he went off to bed; his father shouted after him that to-morrow he would begin his lessons with Alexey Dmitritch. Soon afterwards, seeing that Nezhdanov was hanging aimlessly about in the middle of the room, turning over the leaves of a photograph album with an embarrassed air, Sipyagin told him not to stand on ceremony, but to go and rest, as he must certainly be tired after the journey; that the great principle of his house was freedom.

Nezhdanov availed himself of this permission, and, saying good-night to everyone, went away; in the doorway he stumbled against Marianna, and, again looking into her eyes, was again convinced that he should find a comrade in her, though she did not smile, but positively frowned upon him.

He found his room all filled with fragrant freshness; the windows had stood open the whole day. In the garden just opposite his windows the nightingale was trilling its soft, melodious lay; there was a warm, dull glow in the night sky above the rounded tree-tops; it was the moon making ready to float upwards. Nezhdanov lighted a candle; the grey night-moths flew in from the garden in showers, and went towards the light, while the wind blew them back and set the candle's bluish-yellow light flickering.

'Strange!' thought Nezhdanov, as he lay in his bed. . . . 'They seem good people, liberal, positively human . . . but I feel so sick at heart. The *kammerherr* . . . *kammerjunker*. . . . Well, morning brings good counsel. . . . It's no good sentimentalising.'

But, at that instant, in the garden a watchman knocked loudly and persistently on his board, and a long drawn-out shout was heard:

'Li-isten there-re!'

'Ri-i-ight!' answered another lugubrious voice.

'Ugh! mercy on us!—it's like being in prison!'

8

Nezhdanov woke up early, and without waiting for a servant to make his appearance he dressed and went out into the garden. It was very large and beautiful, this garden, and was kept in splendid order; hired labourers were scraping the paths with spades; among the intense green of the bushes peeped the red kerchiefs of peasant-girls armed with rakes. Nezhdanov made his way to the lake: the fog of early morning had already disappeared from it, but the mist still clung about in parts, in shady nooks in the banks. The sun, not yet high in the sky, beat with rosy light over the broad, silky, leaden-hued surface. Some carpenters were busily at work near the washing-platform; a new, freshly painted boat lay there, feebly rocking from side to side, stirring a faint eddy in the water about it. The men's voices were heard seldom, and in reserved fashion: about everything there was a feeling of morning, of the peace and rapid progress of morning work, a feeling of order and regularity of life. And behold, at a bend of the avenue Nezhdanov saw before him the very personification of order and regularity—Sipyagin.

He wore an overcoat of a pea-green colour, made like a dressing-gown, and a striped cap; he leaned on an English bamboo cane, and his freshly shaven face was beaming with satisfaction; he had come out to look round his estate. Sipyagin greeted Nezhdanov cordially.

'Aha!' he cried, 'I see you're one of the young and early!' (He probably meant by this not very appropriate saying to express his approval of the fact that Nezhdanov had, like himself, not stayed late in bed). 'We drink tea all together in the dining-room at eight, and lunch at twelve; at ten you will give Kolya your first lesson in Russian, and at two the history lesson. To-morrow, the 9th of May, is his name-day, and there will be no lessons; but I should like you to begin to-day.'

Nezhdanov bowed, while Sipyagin parted from him in the French fashion, raising his hand several times in rapid succession to his lips and nose, and walked on, smartly swinging his cane and whistling, not at all like an important official or dignitary, but like a good-natured Russian *country gentleman*.

Till eight o'clock Nezhdanov stayed in the garden enjoying the shade of old trees, the freshness of the air, the song of the birds; the booming of the gong summoned him to the house, and he found the whole party in the dining-room. Valentina Mihalovna behaved very affably to him; in her morning dress she struck him as perfectly beautiful. Marianna's face wore its usual absorbed and sullen expression. At ten o'clock exactly the first lesson took place in the presence of Valentina Mihalovna; she had first inquired of Nezhdanov whether she would be in his way, and she behaved the whole time very discreetly. Kolya turned out to be an intelligent boy; after the first inevitable awkwardness and hesitation, the lesson went off satisfactorily. Valentina Mihalovna was left apparently well content with Nezhdanov, and several times she addressed him in an ingratiating manner. He held off . . . but not too much so. Valentina Mihalovna was present also at the second lesson, on Russian history. She declared with a smile that on that subject she needed a teacher no less than Kolya himself, and behaved as quietly and sedately as during the first lesson. From three till five o'clock Nezhdanov sat in his own room, wrote letters to Petersburg, and felt neither well nor ill: he was free from boredom and from depression; his overwrought nerves were gradually being soothed. They were unhinged again at dinner-time, though Kallomyetsev was absent, and the ingratiating friendliness of his hostess was unchanged; but that very friendliness rather irritated Nezhdanov. Moreover, his neighbour, the old maiden lady Anna Zaharovna, was obviously sulky and antagonistic, while Marianna was still serious, and Kolya even kicked him rather too unceremoniously. Sipyagin, too, seemed out of spirits. He was very much dissatisfied with the overseer of his paper-mill, a German whom he had engaged at a high salary. Sipyagin began abusing Germans in general, declaring that he was, to a certain extent, a Slavophil, though not a fanatic, and mentioned a young Russian, a certain Solomin, who, it was rumoured, had brought a neighbouring merchant's factory into excellent working order; he had a great desire to make the acquaintance of this Solomin. Towards evening Kallomyetsev, whose property was only eight miles from Arzhano, Sipyagin's village, arrived. There arrived, too, a Mediator, one of those landowners so aptly described by Lermontov in two famous lines:

'A cravat to the ears, and a coat to the heels,
A moustache and a squeak, and eyes muddy and thick.

There came, too, another neighbour with a dejected, tooth-less countenance, but exceedingly sprucely dressed; and the district practitioner, a very ignorant doctor, who liked to show off with learned terms; he asserted, for instance, that he preferred Kukolnik to Pushkin because there was so much 'protoplasm' in Kukolnik. They sat down to play cards. Nezhdanov withdrew to his own room and read and wrote till after midnight.

The following day the 9th of May, was Kolya's patron saint's day. The whole family in three open carriages, with grooms on footboards up behind, drove to church, though it was not a quarter of a mile off. Everything was done in grand and pompous style. Sipyagin had put on the ribbon of his order; Valentina Mihalovna was dressed in a charming Parisian gown of a pale lilac colour, and in church, during the service, she said her prayers over a tiny prayer-book bound in crimson velvet; this little book completely dumbfoundered several old men, one of whom could not resist asking his neighbour: 'Is it a witch's charm, God forgive her, she's using, or what, eh?' The scent of the flowers that filled the church was blended with the powerful odour of new peasants' coats smelling of sulphur, tarred boots, and bast shoes, and above these and other smells rose the overwhelming sweetness of the incense. The deacons and choristers sang with astounding conscientiousness with the aid of some factory hands who had joined them; they even made an effort at part-singing! There was a moment when everyone present felt . . . something like dismay. The tenor voice (it belonged to a factory hand, Klima, a man in a galloping consumption), all alone and unsupported, broke into a chromatic series of flat minor notes; they were terrible, those notes, but if they had been cut out the whole concert would promptly have gone to pieces. . . . However, the thing was got through somehow. Father Ciprian, a priest of the most respectable appearance, in full vestments, delivered a very edifying discourse from a manuscript book; unfortunately, the conscientious father had thought it necessary to introduce the names of some wise Assyrian kings, the pronunciation of which cost him great pains, and though he succeeded in proving some degree of erudition, he was

54

hot and perspiring from the exertion. Nezhdanov, who had not been at church for a long while, hid himself in a corner among the peasant women; they scarcely glanced at him, crossing themselves persistently, bowing low, and discreetly wiping their babies' noses; but the little peasant girls in new coats, and strings of glass drops on their foreheads, and the boys in belted smocks, with embroidered shoulder-straps and red gussets, stared intently at the new worshipper, turning right round facing him. . . . And Nezhdanov looked at them, and various were his thoughts.

After the service, which lasted a very long while—for the thanksgiving of St. Nikolai the Wonder-worker, as is well-known, is almost the most lengthy of all the services of the Orthodox Church—all the clergy, at Sipyagin's invitation, moved across to the manor-house. After performing a few more rites proper to the occasion—even sprinkling the rooms with holy water—they were regaled with a copious lunch, during which the edifying but rather exhausting conversation usual at such times was maintained. Both the master and the mistress of the house, though they never lunched at that time of the day, ate and drank a little. Sipyagin went so far as to tell an anecdote, thoroughly proper, but mirth-moving, and this, in face of his red ribbon and his dignity, produced an impression which might be described as comforting, and moved Father Ciprian to a sense of gratitude and amazement. In return, and also to show that he too on occasion could impart some piece of information, Father Ciprian described a conversation he had had with the bishop, when the latter made a tour of his diocese, and summoned all the priests of the district to see him at the monastery in the town. 'He was severe, very severe with us,' Father Ciprian declared; 'first he cross-questioned us about our parish, our arrangements, and then he began an examination. . . . He turned to me: "What's your church's dedication-day?" "The Transfiguration of our Saviour," said I. "And do you know the anthem for that day?" "I should hope so, indeed!" "Sing it!" Well, I began at once: "Thou wert transfigured on the

55

mountain, O Christ our Lord. . . ." "Stop! what is the Transfiguration, and how must we understand it?" "In one word," said I, "Christ wished to show Himself to His disciples in His glory!" "Good," said he, "here's a little image for you to wear in memory of me." I fell at his feet. "I thank your Reverence!" . . . So he did not send me empty away.'

'I have the honour of his Reverence's personal acquaintance,' Sipyagin observed majestically. 'A most worthy pastor!'

'Most worthy indeed!' Father Ciprian re-echoed. 'Though he makes a mistake in putting too much trust in the diocesan superintendents. . . .'

Valentina Mihalovna mentioned the peasant school, referring to Marianna as the future schoolmistress; the deacon (the supervision of the school was intrusted to his charge), a man of Titanic build, with long waving hair vaguely recalling the combed tail of an Orlov horse, tried to express his approval; but not reckoning on the strength of his lungs, brought out such a deep note that he intimidated himself and alarmed the others. Soon after this the clergy retired.

Kolya in his new short jacket with gold buttons was the hero of the day; he received presents and congratulations; his hands were kissed on the front stairs and the back stairs, by factory-hands, house-servants, old women and young women, and peasants—the latter, just as in the old serf days, were buzzing round tables laid out before the house with pies and pots of vodka. Kolya was abashed, and delighted, and proud, and shy, all at once; he caressed his parents and ran out of the room; but at dinner Sipyagin ordered up champagne, and before drinking to his son's health he made a speech. He spoke of the significance of 'serving one's country', and the way he would wish his Nikolai (so he dubbed him) to go . . . and what was due from him: first, to his family; secondly, to his class, to society; thirdly, to the people,—yes, gentlemen, to the people; and fourthly, to the government! Gradually warming up, Sipyagin rose at last to genuine eloquence, while, like Robert Peel, he thrust one hand into a fold of his dress-coat; he became impressive at the word 'science', and ended his speech by the Latin exclamation *laboremus*, which he at once translated into Russian. Kolya, with a glass in his hand, had to go the length of the table to thank his father, and be kissed by everyone. Again it happened to Nezhdanov to exchange a look with Marianna. . . . They were both, probably, feeling the same thing. . . . But they did not speak to one another.

Everything he saw struck Nezhdanov, however, more as amusing and even interesting than as vexatious and distasteful, while the courteous lady of the house, Valentina Mihalovna, impressed him as a clever woman who knew she was playing a part and was at the same time secretly glad that there was another person clever and penetrating enough to comprehend her. . . . Nezhdanov probably did not suspect how greatly his vanity was flattered by her attitude to him.

The next day lessons began again, and daily life moved on its accustomed way.

A week passed by imperceptibly. . . . What were Nezhdanov's experiences and reflections can best be understood by an extract from a letter to Silin, his best friend, who had been a schoolfellow of his at the gymnasium. Silin did not live in Petersburg, but in a remote provincial town, with a well-to-do relative, on whom he was utterly dependent. His position was such that it was no use for him even to dream of getting away from there; he was a weakly, timid, and limited man, but of a singularly pure nature. He took no interest in politics, had read some few middling books, played on the flute to while away the time, and was afraid of young ladies. Silin loved Nezhdanov passionately—he was in general fervent in his attachments. To no one did Nezhdanov reveal himself so unreservedly as to Vladimir Silin; when he wrote to him he always felt as if he were in communion with some dear and intimate being inhabiting another world, or with his own conscience. Nezhdanov could not even imagine the possibility of living with Silin again as a comrade in the same town. . . . He would most likely have grown colder to him at once, they had so little in common; but he wrote a great deal to him with eagerness and complete openness. With others—on paper at least—he was always, as it were, showing off or artificial; with Silin—never! Silin, who was a poor hand with his pen, answered very little, in short awkward sentences; nor did Nezhdanov need voluminous replies; he knew without that that his friend drank in every word of his, as the dust in the road drinks in a drop of rain, kept his secrets as a holy thing, and, buried in a dreary solitude from which he would never emerge, simply lived in his friend's life. To no one in the world had Nezhdanov spoken of his relations with him; they were very precious to him.

'Well, dear friend—my pure Vladimir,' so he wrote to him— he always called him pure, and with good reason—'congratulate me: I have fallen into a snug berth, and can now rest and rally my forces. I am living as a tutor in the house of a rich swell, Sipyagin. I'm teaching his little son, feeding sumptuously (I have never been so well fed in my life!), sleeping soundly, walking to my heart's content in lovely country, and, what is the chief thing, I have escaped for a time from the care of my Petersburg friends; and though at first I was devoured by the most savage *ennui*, now I feel somehow better. Soon I must set to the work you know of (as the proverb has it: If you call yourself a mushroom you must go into the basket), and that's just what they let me come here for; but meanwhile I can lead a delicious animal existence, grow fat, and perhaps write verses, if the fit takes me. Impressions of the country, as they call it, I put off for another time. The estate seems well managed, though the factory, perhaps, is in rather a bad way. As for the peasants, some seem rather unapproachable; and the hired servants have all such decorous faces. But we will go into all that later on. The people of the house are cultivated, liberal; Sipyagin is always so condescending—oh! so condescending; and then all of a sudden he flies off into eloquence—a most highly cultivated person! The lady of the house is a perfect beauty—

a sly puss, I should fancy; she fairly watches over one; and oh, isn't she soft!—not a bone in her body! I am afraid of her; you know what my manners are like with ladies! There are neighbours—wretched creatures—and one old lady, who worries me. . . . But I am most interested in a girl—whether she is a relation or a companion, goodness knows; I have hardly spoken two words to her, but I feel she's made of the same clay as myself. . . .'

Here followed a description of Marianna's appearance and all her ways; then he went on:

'That she's unhappy, proud, self-conscious, reserved, and, most of all, unhappy, I feel no doubt about. Why she's unhappy, so far I don't know. That she's honest is clear to me: whether she is good-natured is still a question. Are there any entirely good-natured women who are not stupid? And is it necessary there should be? However, I know little enough of women in general. The lady of the house does not like her . . . and she reciprocates. . . . But which of them is in the right I don't know. I should suppose that it's rather the lady who is in the wrong . . . seeing that she's so very polite to her, while the girl's very eyebrows twitch with nervousness when she speaks to her patroness. Yes, she's a very nervous creature; in that, too, she's like me. And she's *out of joint* like me, though probably not in just the same way.

'When all this is a little clearer I will write to you. . . .

'She scarcely ever speaks to me, as I said just now; but in the few words she has addressed to me (always suddenly and unexpectedly) there is a sort of rough frankness. . . . I like it.

'By the way, is your relation still keeping you on short commons? Isn't he beginning to think of his end?

'Have you read the article in the *Messenger of Europe* on the last pretenders in the province of Orenburg? That happened in 1834, my dear boy! I don't care for that journal, and the author's a Conservative; but it's an interesting thing, and sets one thinking. . . .'

9

MAY had already passed into its second half. The first hot days of summer had come.

At the end of his history lesson one day Nezhdanov went out into the garden, and from the garden into a birchwood which adjoined it on one side. Part of this wood had been cut down by timber merchants fifteen years before, but all the clearings were overgrown with thick young birch trees. The trunks of the trees stood close like columns of soft dull silver, striped with greyish rings; the tiny leaves were of a uniform shining green, as though someone had washed them and put varnish on them; the spring grass pushed up in little sharp tongues through the dark even layer of last year's fallen leaves. Little narrow paths ran up and down all over the wood; yellow-beaked blackbirds with a sudden cry, as though in alarm, fluttered across the paths, low down, close to the earth, and dashed like mad into the bushes. After walking for half an hour, Nezhdanov sat down at last on a felled stump, surrounded by grey, ancient chips; they lay in little heaps as they had fallen, struck off by the axe. Many times had the winter snow covered them and melted from off them in the spring, and no one had touched them. Nezhdanov sat with his back to a thick hedge of young birches, in the dense, soft shade. He thought of nothing; he gave himself up utterly to the peculiar sensation of the spring in which, for young and old alike, there is always an element of pain . . . the restless pain of expectation in the young . . . the settled pain of regret in the old. . . .

Suddenly Nezhdanov heard the sound of approaching footsteps.

It was not one person coming, and not a peasant in shoes or heavy boots, nor a bare-foot peasant woman. It seemed as though two persons were walking at a slow, even pace. . . .

There was the light rustle of a woman's dress. . . .

Suddenly there came the sound of a hollow voice—the voice of a man: 'And so that is your last word?—never?'

'Never!' repeated another voice—a woman's—which seemed to Nezhdanov familiar, and an instant later, at a turn in the path, which at that point skirted the young birches, Marianna stepped out, escorted by a dark, black-eyed man, whom Nezhdanov had never seen till that instant.

Both stopped, as if they had been shot, at the sight of Nezhdanov, while he was so astounded that he did not even get up from the stump on which he was sitting. . . . Marianna blushed up to the roots of her hair, but at once smiled contemptuously. For whom was the smile meant—for herself for having blushed, or for Nezhdanov? . . . Her companion knitted his bushy brows, and there was a gleam in the yellowish whites of his uneasy eyes. Then he looked at Marianna, and both of them, turning their backs on Nezhdanov, walked away in silence, at the same slow pace, while he followed them with a stare of amazement.

Half an hour later he went home and to his room, and when, summoned by the booming of the gong, he went into the drawing-room, he saw in it the same swarthy stranger who had come upon him in the copse. Sipyagin led Nezhdanov up to him and introduced him as his *beau-frère*, the brother of Valentina Mihalovna—Sergei Mihalovitch Markelov.

'I hope you will be good friends, gentlemen!' cried Sipyagin, with the majestically affable though absent-minded smile characteristic of him.

Markelov performed a silent bow; Nezhdanov responded in a similar manner . . . while Sipyagin, with a slight toss of his little head and a shrug of his shoulders, moved away, as much as to say, 'I have done my duty by you . . . and whether you really do become friends is a matter of no importance to me!'

Then Valentina Mihalovna approached the couple, who stood immovable, and again presented them to one another, and with the peculiar caressing brightness which she seemed

able at will to shed over her marvellous eyes, she addressed
her brother:

'How is it, *cher Serge*, you've quite forgotten us? you did
not even come for Kolya's name-day. Or have you had such
piles of work? He's introducing new arrangements with his
peasants,' she turned to Nezhdanov—'very original ones too;
three-quarters of everything for them, and one quarter for
himself; and even then he thinks he gets too much.'

'My sister's fond of joking,' Markelov in his turn addressed
himself to Nezhdanov; 'but I'm prepared to agree with her
that for *one* man to take a quarter of what belongs to a
hundred at least, is certainly too much.'

'And have you, Alexey Dmitrievitch, noticed that I'm fond
of joking?' inquired Madame Sipyagin, still with the same
caressing softness both of eyes and voice.

Nezhdanov found no reply; and at that moment Kallomyetsev was announced. The lady of the house went to meet
him, and a few moments later the butler appeared and in a
sing-song voice announced that dinner was on the table.

At dinner Nezhdanov could not help watching Marianna
and Markelov. They sat side by side, both with eyes downcast, and lips compressed, with a severe, gloomy, almost
exasperated expression. Nezhdanov kept wondering too how
Markelov could be Madame Sipyagin's brother. There was so
little resemblance to be discerned between them. One thing,
perhaps—both were of dark complexion; but in Valentina
Mihalovna the uniform tint of her face, arms, and shoulders
constituted one of her charms . . . while in her brother it
attained that degree of swarthiness which polite people
describe as 'bronzed', but which, to the Russian eye, inevitably
suggests a leather gaiter. Markelov had curly hair, a rather
hooked nose, full lips, sunken cheeks, a contracted chest, and
sinewy hands. He was sinewy and dry all over; and he spoke
in a harsh, abrupt, metallic voice. His eyes were sleepy,
his face surly, a regular dyspeptic! He ate little, and busied
himself in rolling up little pellets of bread, only occasionally
casting a glance at Kallomyetsev, who had just returned from

62

the town, where he had seen the governor, upon a matter rather unpleasant for him, Kallomyetsev. Upon this point he was studiously silent, though on other subjects he launched out freely.

Sipyagin, as before, pulled him up when he went too far. He laughed a great deal at his anecdotes, his *bons mots,* though he opined, *'qu'il est un affreux réactionnaire.'* Kallomyetsev declared among the rest that he had been thrown into perfect raptures over the name the peasants—*oui, oui! les simples moujiks!*—give to the lawyers—*'Loiars! loiars!'* he repeated in ecstasy: *'ce peuple russe est délicieux.'* Then he related how once when visiting a peasant-school he had put to the pupils the question: 'What is an ornithorhincus?' And as no one was able to answer, not even the teacher, then he, Kallomyetsev, put them another question: 'What is a wendaru?' quoting the line of Hemnitser: The senseless wendaru that apes the other beasts.' And no one had answered that either. So much for your peasant schools!

'But excuse me,' remarked Valentina Mihalovna, 'I don't know myself what those animals are.'

'Madam!' cried Kallomyetsev, 'there's not the slightest necessity for you to know.'

'And what need is there for the peasants to know?'

'Why, because it is better for them to know of an ornithorhincus or a wendaru than of Proudhon—or even Adam Smith!'

But at this point Sipyagin again pulled him up, maintaining that Adam Smith was one of the leading lights of human thought, and that it would be a good thing if all were to imbibe his principles . . . (he poured himself out a glass of Château Yquem . . .) with their mothers' (he held it to his nose and sniffed at the wine) milk! . . . He emptied the glass; Kallomyetsev drank too, and praised the wine.

Markelov paid no special attention to the flights of the Petersburg *kammerjunker,* but twice he looked inquiringly at Nezhdanov, and, tossing up a pellet of bread, all but flung it straight at the loquacious visitor's nose. . . .

Sipyagin let his brother-in-law alone; Valentina Mihalovna, too, did not address him; it was clear that both husband and wife were in the habit of regarding Markelov as an unaccountable creature, whom it was better not to provoke.

After dinner, Markelov went off to the billiard-room to smoke a pipe, and Nezhdanov went to his own room. In the corridor he came upon Marianna. He was about to pass her . . . she stopped him with an abrupt gesture.

'Mr. Nezhdanov,' she began in a not quite steady voice, 'it ought really to be just the same to me what you think about me; but all the same I consider . . . I consider . . . (she was at a loss for a word . . .) I consider it fitting to tell you, that when you met me to-day in the copse with Mr. Markelov . . . Tell me, no doubt you wondered why it was we were both confused, and why we had come there, as though by appointment?'

'It certainly did strike me as a little strange,' Nezhdanov began.

'Mr. Markelov,' Marianna broke in, 'made me an offer, and I refused him. That's all I had to say to you; so—good-night. You can think of me what you choose.'

She turned swiftly away and walked with rapid steps along the corridor.

Nezhdanov went to his room, sat down at his window and pondered. 'What a strange girl! and why this wild freak, this uninvited confidence? What is it—a desire to be original, or simply affectation, or pride? Most likely pride. She can't put up with the smallest suspicion. . . . She can't endure the idea that anyone should judge her falsely. A strange girl!'

So mused Nezhdanov; and on the terrace below there was a conversation about him; and he heard it all very clearly.

'I know by instinct,' Kallomyetsev was asserting, 'that that's a red republican. While I was serving on special commission under the governor-general of Moscow, *avec Ladislas,* I got a quick scent for these gentlemen—the reds—and for dissenters too. I've a wonderfully keen nose, at times.' At this point Kallomyetsev described incidentally how he had once, in the environs of Moscow, caught by the heel an old dissenter, whom he had dropped in upon with the police, and who had all but jumped out of his cottage window. . . . 'And there he had been sitting as quiet as could be, till that minute, the rascal!'

Kallomyetsev forgot to add that the same old man, when shut up in prison, had refused all food, and starved himself to death.

'And your new tutor,' continued the zealous *kammerjunker*, 'is a red, not a doubt of it! Have you noticed that he never bows first?'

'And why should he bow first?' observed Madame Sipyagin; 'quite the contrary—I like that in him.'

'I am a guest in the house in which he is employed,' cried Kallomyetsev—'yes, yes employed for money, *comme un salarié*. . . . Consequently I am his superior, and he *ought* to bow first.'

'You are very exacting, Kallomyetsev,' interposed Sipyagin, with especial stress on the *y* in his name; 'all that, if you'll excuse my saying so, strikes one as rather out of date. I have purchased his services, his work, but he remains a free man.'

'He does not feel the curb,' continued Kallomyetsev, 'the curb, *le frein!* All these reds are like that. I tell you I've a wonderfully sharp nose for them! Ladislas might perhaps compare with me in that respect. If he fell into my hands, that tutor, I'd straighten him up a bit! Wouldn't I make him sit up! He'd sing a very different tune; and shouldn't he touch his hat to me! . . . it would be sweet to see him!'

'Rotten drivel, little blustering idiot!' Nezhdanov was almost shouting from above. . . . But at that instant the door of his room opened, and into it, to the considerable astonishment of Nezhdanov, walked Markelov.

10

NEZHDANOV rose from his place to meet him, while Markelov
went straight up to him, and, without a bow or a smile, asked
him, was he Alexey Dmitriev Nezhdanov, student of the
Petersburg University?

'Yes . . . certainly,' answered Nezhdanov.

Markelov pulled an open letter out of his side pocket. 'In
that case, read this. From Vassily Nikolaevitch,' he added,
dropping his voice significantly.

Nezhdanov unfolded and read the letter. It was something
of the nature of a half-official circular, in which the bearer,
Sergei Markelov, was recommended as one of 'us', fully
deserving of confidence; there followed, further, an exhortation concerning the urgent necessity of concerted action, and
the propaganda of certain principles. The circular was
addressed to Nezhdanov among others, also as being a trustworthy person.

Nezhdanov held out his hand to Markelov, asked him to
sit down, and himself dropped into a chair. Markelov began,
without a word, by lighting a cigarette. Nezhdanov followed
his example.

'Have you had time yet to make friends with the peasants
here?' Markelov asked at last.

'No; I've not had time yet.'

'You've not been here long, then?'

'I shall soon have been here a fortnight.'

'Been very busy?'

'Not very.'

Markelov coughed grimly.

'H'm! The peasants here are rather a wretched lot,' he
resumed; 'an ignorant lot. They want teaching. There's
great poverty, but no one to explain to them what their
poverty comes from.'

'Those who were your brother-in-law's serfs, as far as I can judge, aren't poor,' remarked Nezhdanov.

'My brother-in-law's a humbug; he knows how to hoodwink people. The peasants about here are no good, certainly; but he has a factory. That's where one must make an effort. One need only stick the spade in there and the whole ant-heap will be on the move directly. Have you any books with you?'

'Yes . . . but not many.'

'I'll let you have some. But how is it you haven't?'

Nezhdanov made no answer. Markelov, too, was silent, and only blew the smoke out of his nostrils.

'What a beast that Kallomyetsev is, though!' he observed suddenly. 'At dinner I was thinking of getting up, going up to that worthy, and pounding that impudent face of his to atoms, for an example to others. But no! There's business of more importance just now than slaying *kammerjunkers*. Now's not the time to lose one's temper with fools for saying stupid things; it's time to prevent them doing stupid things.'

Nezhdanov nodded his head in confirmation, while Markelov again puffed away at his cigarette.

'Here, among all the servants, there's one sensible fellow,' he began again; 'not your servant Ivan . . . he's a dull fish, but another one . . . his name's Kirill, he waits at the sideboard'—(this Kirill had the character of being a sad drunkard) —'you notice him. A drunken brute . . . but we can't afford to be squeamish, you know. And what have you to say of my sister?' he added suddenly, raising his head and fixing his yellow eyes on Nezhdanov. 'She's even more of a humbug than my brother-in-law. What do you think of her?'

'I think she's a very agreeable and amiable lady . . . and, moreover, she's very beautiful.'

'H'm! With what delicate precision you gentlemen from Petersburg express yourselves! . . . I can only admire it! Well . . . and as regards . . .' he began, but suddenly he scowled, his face darkened, and he did not complete his sentence. 'I see we must talk things over thoroughly,' he began again. 'We can't do it here. Who the devil can tell? They're listening at the door, I dare say. Do you know what I would suggest? To-day's Saturday; to-morrow, I suppose, you won't give my nephew any lessons? Will you?'

'I have a rehearsal of the week's work with him at three to-morrow.'

'A rehearsal! As if you were on the stage! It must be my sister who invents those expressions. Well, it's all the same. Would you care to come to me at once? My place is only eight miles from here. I have good horses: they fly like the wind—you shall stay the night, and spend the morning—and I'll bring you back to-morrow by three o'clock. Do you agree?'

'By all means,' said Nezhdanov. Ever since Markelov's entrance he had been in a state of excitement and embarrassment. His sudden intimacy with him confused him; at the same time he felt drawn to him. He felt, he realised, that there was before him a person, dull, very likely, but unmistakably honest and strong. And then that strange meeting in the copse, Marianna's unexpected explanation. . . .

'Well, that's capital!' cried Markelov. 'You get ready meanwhile, and I'll go and order the coach to be put to. You needn't ask any questions of the heads of the house here, I hope?'

'I will mention it to them. I imagine I couldn't absent myself without.'

'I'll tell them,' said Markelov. 'Don't you be uneasy. They'll be frowning over their cards now; they won't notice your absence. My brother-in-law aims at becoming a political personage, but all he has to back him is that he plays cards splendidly. After all, though, men have made their fortunes that way! . . . So you get ready. I will make arrangements at once.'

Markelov went away; and an hour later Nezhdanov was sitting beside him on a broad leather cushion, in a wide,

68

roomy, very old, and very comfortable coach; the squat little coachman on the box-seat whistled incessantly a wonderfully sweet bird's note; the three piebald horses, with black plaited manes and tails, galloped swiftly along the even road; and, already swathed in the first shadows of night (it struck ten just as they started), trees, bushes, fields, plains, and ravines, advancing and retreating again, glided smoothly by.

Markelov's small property (it consisted of not more than six hundred acres, and yielded about seven hundred roubles of revenue—it was called Borzyonkovo) was two miles from the provincial town, while Sipyagin's property was six miles from it. To reach Borzyonkovo they had to drive through the town. The new friends had not had time to exchange half a hundred words before they caught glimpses of the wretched little artisans' huts in the outskirts, with tumble-down, wooden roofs, with dim patches of light in the warped windows, and then under their wheels they heard the rumble of the stone pavements of the town; the coach rocked, swaying from side to side, and, shaken at every jolt, they were carried past the dull stone houses of merchants, with two storeys and façades, churches with columns, taverns. . . . It was Saturday night; there were no people in the streets, but the taverns were still crowded. Hoarse voices broke from them, drunken songs, and the nasal notes of the concertina; from doors suddenly opened streamed the filthy warmth, the acrid smell of alcohol, the red glare of lights. Before almost every tavern were standing little peasant carts, harnessed to shaggy, pot-bellied nags; they stood with their unkempt heads hanging down submissively, and seemed asleep; a ragged, unbelted peasant in a big winter cap, which hung in a bag over his neck, would come out of a tavern, and, his breast propped against the shafts, stay motionless, feebly fumbling and moving his hands as though looking for something; or a wasted factory-hand, his cap awry, and his cotton shirt flying open, would take a few irresolute steps, barefoot—his boots having remained in the tavern—stop short, scratch his spine, and, with a sudden groan, go back again.

'The Russian's a slave to drink!' observed Markelov gloomily.

'It's sorrow drives him to it, Sergei Mihalovitch!' pronounced the coachman without turning round. Before each tavern he ceased whistling, and seemed to sink into deep thought.

'Get on! get on!' responded Markelov, with a savage tug at his own coat collar. The coach crossed a wide market-place, positively stinking of rush-mats and cabbage, passed the governor's house with striped sentry-boxes at the gates, a private house with a turret, a promenade set with trees, recently planted and already dying, a bazaar, filled with the barking of dogs and the clanking of chains, and, gradually reaching the boundaries of the town, and overtaking a long, long train of wagons, which had set off so late for the sake of the cool of the night, again emerged into the fresh air of the open country, on to the highroad planted with willows, and again moved on more smoothly and swiftly.

Markelov—a few words must be said about him—was six years older than his sister, Madame Sipyagin. He had been educated in an artillery school, which he left as an ensign; but just after attaining the rank of a lieutenant he had to retire, through a misunderstanding with the commander—a German. From that time forth he hated Germans, particularly Russian Germans. His resignation embroiled him with his father, whom he scarcely saw again till the day of his death; he inherited the little property from him, and settled in it. In Petersburg he had associated frequently with various intellectual and advanced people, whom he had positively adored; they completely formed his way of thinking. Markelov had read little— and chiefly books relating to the cause—Herzen in especial. He had retained his military habits; he lived like a Spartan and a monk. A few years before he had fallen passionately in love with a girl; but she had jilted him in the most unceremonious fashion, and had married an adjutant—also a German. Markelov began hating adjutants too. He used to try to write articles on the defects of our artillery, but he had not the slightest faculty of exposition; not a single article could he ever work out to the end, and yet he continued to cover large sheets of grey paper with his sprawling, illegible, childish handwriting. Markelov was a man obstinate and dauntless to desperation, who could neither forgive nor forget, for ever resenting his own wrongs and the wrongs of all the oppressed, and ready for anything. His limited intellect went for one point only; what he did not understand, for him did not exist; but he scorned and hated treachery and falseness. With people of the higher class, with the 'reacs', as he expressed it, he was short, and even rude; with the poor he was simple; with a peasant as friendly as with a brother. He managed his estate fairly well; his head was in a whirl of socialistic plans, which he could no more carry out than he could finish his articles on the defects of the artillery. As a rule, he did not succeed—at any time, or in anything; in the regiment he had been nick-named 'the unsuccessful'. Sincere, upright, a passionate and unhappy nature, he was capable at any moment of appearing merciless, bloodthirsty, of deserving to be called a monster, and was equally capable of sacrificing himself, without hesitation and without return.

The coach, at the second mile from the town, suddenly plunged into the soft gloom of an aspen wood, with the whisper and rustle of unseen leaves, with the fresh, keen forest fragrance, with vague patches of light overhead and tangled shadows below. The moon had already risen on the horizon, red and broad, like a copper shield. Darting out from under the trees, the coach faced a small manor-house. Three lighted-up windows stood out like shining squares on the face of the low-pitched house, which hid the moon's disc. The gates stood wide open and seemed as though they were never shut. In the courtyard in the half-dark could be seen a high trap with two white, hired horses fastened on behind. Two puppies, also white, ran out from somewhere and gave vent to piercing but not savage barks. People were moving about in the house. The coach rolled up to the steps, and with some difficulty getting out, and feeling with his foot for the iron carriage-step, put, as is usually the case, by the local blacksmith in the most inconvenient position, Markelov said to Nezhdanov: 'Here we are at home; and you will find guests here whom you know very well but don't at all expect to meet. Please come in.'

11

THESE guests turned out to be our old friends, Ostrodumov and Mashurina. They were both sitting in the small and very poorly furnished drawing-room of Markelov's house, drinking beer and smoking by the light of a kerosene lamp. They were not surprised at Nezhdanov's arrival; they knew Markelov intended to bring him with him; but Nezhdanov was much surprised at seeing them. When he came in, Ostrodumov observed, 'How are you, brother?' and that was all. Mashurina first turned crimson all over, then held out her hand. Markelov explained to Nezhdanov that Ostrodumov and Mashurina had been sent down 'on the cause', which was bound shortly now to take practical shape; that they had come from Petersburg a week ago; that Ostrodumov was remaining in S—— province for propaganda purposes, while Mashurina was going to K—— to see a certain person there.

Markelov suddenly grew hot, though no one had contradicted him. He gnawed his moustache, and with flashing eyes began to speak in a hoarse, agitated, but distinct voice of hideous acts of injustice that had been committed, of the necessity for immediate action, maintaining that practically everything was ready, and none but cowards could procrastinate; that some violence was as essential as the lancet's prick to the abscess, however ready to break the abscess might be! He repeated this simile of the lancet several times; it obviously pleased him; he had not invented it, but had read it in some book. It seemed that, having lost all hope of Marianna's reciprocating his feelings, he felt he had nothing now to lose, and only thought how to set to work as soon as might be 'for the cause'. His words came like the blows of an axe, with absolute directness, sharply, simply, and vindictively; monotonous and weighty, they fell one after another from his blanched lips, recalling the sharp, abrupt bark of a grim old watchdog. He said he knew the peasants of the neighbourhood and the factory hands well, and that there were capable people among them—Eremey of Goloplyok, for instance—who would be ready for anything you like any minute. The name of Eremey from the village of Goloplyok was constantly on his tongue. At every tenth word he struck the table with his right hand, not with the palm, but with the edge of his hand, while he thrust his left hand into the air, with the first finger held apart from the rest; and those hairy, sinewy hands, that finger, the droning voice, and the blazing eyes produced a powerful impression. On the road Markelov had said little to Nezhdanov; his anger had been rising . . . but now it broke out. Mashurina and Ostrodumov applauded him with a smile, a glance, sometimes a brief exclamation, but in Nezhdanov something strange was taking place. First he tried to reply; he referred to the harm done by haste, by premature, ill-considered action; above all, he was surprised to find it all so decided, that no doubt was felt, and no consciousness of the necessity of examining into the circumstances of the place, nor even of trying to find out precisely what the people wanted. . . . But afterwards his nerves were wrought upon and quivering like harpstrings, and in a sort of desperation, almost with tears of rage in his eyes, his voice breaking into a scream, he began speaking in the same spirit as Markelov, going further even than he had done. What impulse was working in him it would be hard to say. Was it remorse for having been, as it were, lukewarm of late? was it vexation with himself or with others, or the longing to stifle some worm gnawing within? or indeed was it a desire to show off before the comrades he was meeting again? . . . or had Markelov's words really influenced him—fired his blood? Till the very dawn the conversation continued; Ostrodumov and Mashurina did not stir from their seats, while Markelov and Nezhdanov did not sit down. Markelov stood on the same spot, for all the world like a sentinel, while Nezhdanov kept walking up and down the room with unequal steps, now slowly, now hurriedly. They talked of the measures and means to be employed, of the part each ought to take on himself; they examined and tied up in parcels various tracts and leaflets; they referred to a merchant, a dissenter, one Golushkin, a very trustworthy though uneducated man; to the young propagandist, Kislyakov, who was, they said, very able, though over-hasty, and had too high an opinion of his own talents; the name of Solomin, too, was mentioned. . . .

'Is that the man who manages a cotton factory?' inquired Nezhdanov, remembering what had been said of him at the Sipyagin's table.

'Yes, that is he,' answered Markelov; 'you must get to know him. We have not tested him thoroughly yet, but he's a capable, very capable, fellow.'

Eremey of Goloplyok again figured in the conversation; to him were added the Sipyagins' Kirill and a certain Mendeley, also nicknamed the Sulker; only it was difficult to reckon on the Sulker—he was bold as a lion when sober, but a coward when he was drunk, and he almost always was drunk.

'And your own people, now,' Nezhdanov inquired of Markelov, 'are there any you can rely on?'

Markelov replied that there were some. He did not mention one of them by name, however, but went off into a discourse upon the artisans of the towns and the seminarists, who would be the more useful from their great bodily strength, and, if only it came to fighting with fists, would do great things! Nezhdanov made inquiries about the nobility. Markelov answered that there were five or six young noblemen; one of them, to be sure, was a German, and he the most radical of the lot, but, of course, there was no reckoning on a German . . . he might turn sulky or betray them any moment. But there, they must wait to see what news Kislyakov would send them. Nezhdanov inquired too about the army. At that

Markelov hesitated, tugged at his long whiskers, and explained at last that there was nothing, so far, decisive. . . . Perhaps Kislyakov would have something to disclose.

'And who is this Kislyakov?' cried Nezhdanov impatiently.

Markelov smiled significantly, and said that he was a man . . . such a man. . . .

'I know him very little, though,' he added; 'I have only seen him twice altogether. But the letters that man writes!— such letters!! I will show you them. . . . You will be astonished. Such fire! And his activity! Five or six times he has raced right across Russia and back . . . and from every station a letter of ten—twelve pages!'

Nezhdanov looked inquiringly at Ostrodumov, but he sat like a statue, not an eyebrow twitching, while Mashurina's lips were compressed in a bitter smile, but she, too, was dumb as a fish. Nezhdanov tried to question Markelov about his reforms in a socialistic direction on his estate . . . but at this Ostrodumov interposed.

'What's the good of discussing that now?' he observed. 'It makes no difference; everything must be transformed afterwards.'

The conversation turned again into a political channel. Nezhdanov was still devoured by a secret worm gnawing within; but the keener the inward torture, the more loudly and positively he spoke. He had drunk only one glass of beer, but from time to time it struck him that he was completely drunk; his head was in a whirl, and his heart throbbed painfully. When at last, at four o'clock in the morning, the discussion ceased, and, stepping over a little page asleep in the ante-room, they separated and went to their respective rooms, Nezhdanov, before he lay down, stood a long time motionless, his eyes fixed on the floor before him. He mused upon the continual, heart-rending note of bitterness in all Markelov had uttered. The man's pride could not but be wounded; he was bound to be suffering, his hopes of personal happiness were shattered, and yet how he forgot himself—how utterly he gave himself up to what he held for the truth! 'A limited nature,' was Nezhdanov's thought. . . . 'But isn't it a hundred times better to be such a limited nature than such . . . such as I, for instance, feel myself to be?'

But at once he struggled against his own self-depreciation. 'Why so? Am not I, too, capable of sacrificing myself? Wait a bit, my friends. . . . And you, Paklin, shall be convinced in time that though I am an æsthetic, though I do write verses . . .'

He pushed his hair back angrily, ground his teeth, and, hurriedly pulling off his clothes, flung himself into the damp, chill bed.

'Sleep well!' Mashurina's voice called through the door. 'I am next door to you.'

'Good-night,' answered Nezhdanov, and then it came into his mind that she had not taken her eyes off him all the evening.

'What does she want?' he muttered, and at once felt ashamed of himself. 'Ah, to sleep as soon as may be!'

But it was hard to master his overwrought nerves . . . and the sun stood high in the sky when at last he fell into a heavy, comfortless sleep.

The next morning he got up late with a headache. He dressed, went to the window of his attic room, and saw that Markelov had practically no farm at all. His little box of a house stood on a ravine not far from a wood. A little granary, a stable, a cellar, a little hut with a half tumble-down thatch-roof, on one side; on the other, a diminutive lake, a patch of kitchen garden, a hemp-field, another little hut with a similar roof; in the distance an outhouse, a barn, and an empty threshing-floor—this was all the wealth that could be seen. It all seemed poor, decaying, and not exactly neglected or run wild, but as though it had never thrived, like a tree that has not taken root well. Nezhdanov went downstairs. Mashurina was sitting behind the tea-urn in the dining-room, evidently waiting for him. He learned from her that Ostrodumov had gone off, on the cause, and would not be back for a fortnight; and Markelov had gone to see after his labourers. As

May was drawing to a close and there was no pressing work to be done, Markelov had a plan for felling a small birch copse without outside help, and had set off there early in the morning.

Nezhdanov felt a strange weariness at heart. So much had been said overnight of the impossibility of delaying longer, it had so often been repeated that the only thing left to do was 'to act'. But how act? in what direction, and how without delay? It was useless to question Mashurina; she knew no hesitation, she had no doubts as to what she had to do; it was to go to K——. Beyond that she did not look. Nezhdanov did not know what to say to her; and after drinking some tea, he put on his cap and went off in the direction of the birch copse. On the way he fell in with some peasants carting manure, formerly serfs of Markelov's. He began to talk to them . . . but did not get much out of them. They too seemed weary, but with an ordinary physical weariness, not at all like the feeling he was experiencing. Their former master, according to them, was a good-natured, simple gentleman, but queerish; they predicted his ruin, because 'he didn't understand how things should be done, and wanted to do things his own way, not as his fathers did before. And he's too wise, too—you can't make him out, do what you will; but a good-hearted gentleman, if ever there was one.' Nezhdanov went on farther and came upon Markelov himself.

He was walking surrounded by a whole crowd of workmen; from a distance it could be seen that he was talking and explaining something to them; then he gave a despairing wave of the hand, as though he gave it up! Beside him was his bailiff, a dull-eyed young man, with no trace of authority in his bearing. This bailiff continually repeated, 'That shall be as you please, sir,' to the intense annoyance of his master, who looked for more independence from him. Nezhdanov went up to Markelov, and on his face he saw traces of the same spiritual weariness he was feeling himself. They exchanged greetings; Markelov began speaking at once, briefly though, of the questions discussed overnight, of the impending revolution;

77

but the expression of weariness did not leave his face. He was all over dust and perspiration; shavings of wood, green strands of moss were clinging to his clothes; his voice was hoarse. . . . The men standing round him were silent; they were half scared, half amused. . . . Nezhdanov looked at Markelov, and Ostrodumov's words re-echoed again in his head: 'What's the good? It makes no difference, it will all have to be transformed afterwards!' One labourer who had been in fault somehow began entreating Markelov to let him off the fine for his mistake. . . . Markelov at first flew into a rage, and shouted furiously at him, but afterwards he forgave him. . . . 'It makes no difference . . . it will all have to be changed later on. . . .' Nezhdanov asked him for horses and a conveyance to return home; Markelov seemed surprised at his wish, but answered that everything should be ready directly.

He went back to the house with Nezhdanov. . . . He was staggering as he walked, from exhaustion.

'What's the matter with you?' asked Nezhdanov.

'I am worn out!' said Markelov savagely. 'However you talk to these people, they can't understand anything, and they won't carry out instructions. . . . They positively don't understand Russian. The word "part" they know well enough . . . but "participation". . . . What is participation? They can't understand. And yet it's a Russian word, too, damn it! They imagine I want to make them a present of part of the land!' Markelov had conceived the idea of explaining to the peasants the principles of co-operation, and introducing it on his estate, but they resisted. One of them had gone so far as to say in this connection, 'There was a pit deep enough before, but now there's no seeing the bottom of it' . . . while the other peasants had with one accord given vent to a profound sigh which had crushed Markelov utterly.

On reaching the house he dismissed his attendant retinue, and began to see about the carriage and horses, and about lunch. His household consisted only of a little page, a cook, a coachman, and a very aged man with hairy ears, in a long-skirted cotton coat, who had been his grandfather's valet. This old man was for ever gazing with profound dejection at his master; he did nothing, however, and was scarcely perhaps fit to do anything; but he was always there, crouched up on the doorsill.

After a lunch of hard-boiled eggs, anchovies, and cold hash —the page handed the mustard in an old pomatum pot and vinegar in an eau-de-cologne bottle—Nezhdanov took his seat in the same coach in which he had come overnight; but instead of three horses they only harnessed two; the third had been shod and lamed. During lunch Markelov had said little, eaten nothing, and had drawn his breath painfully. . . . He had uttered two or three bitter words about his property, and again waved his hand as though to say . . . 'It makes no difference, it will all have to be changed afterwards.' Mashurina asked Nezhdanov to take her as far as the town; she wanted to go there to do some shopping. 'I can walk back, or else get a lift in some peasant's cart.' Markelov escorted them both to the steps, and said vaguely that he should shortly come for Nezhdanov again; and then . . . then—(he shook himself and plucked up his spirits again)—they must come to a definite arrangement; that Solomin should come too; that he, Markelov, was only waiting for news from Vassily Nikolaevitch, and then it only remained to 'act' promptly—since the peasants (the same peasants who did not understand the word 'participation') would not consent to wait longer!

'Oh, you were going to show me the letters of that—what's his name—Kislyakov?' said Nezhdanov.

'Later . . .' Markelov replied hurriedly. . . . 'Then we will do everything—altogether.'

The carriage started.

'Be in readiness!' Markelov's voice was heard for the last time. He was standing on the steps, and beside him, with the same unchanged dejection on his face, straightening his bent back, clasping his hands behind him, diffusing an odour of rye bread and cotton fustian, and hearing nothing, stood the model servant, the decrepit old valet.

All the way to the town Mashurina was silent; she only

79

smoked a cigarette. As they drew near the barrier she suddenly gave a loud sigh.

'I'm sorry for Sergei Mihalovitch,' she observed, and her face darkened.

'He's quite knocked up with worry,' remarked Nezhdanov; 'I think his land's in a poor way.'

'That's not why I'm sorry for him.

'Why, then?'

'He's an unhappy man, unlucky! Where could one find a better fellow? But no—no one wants him anywhere.'

Nezhdanov looked at his companion.

'Do you know something about him, then?'

'I know nothing . . . but one sees it for oneself. Good-bye, Alexey Dmitritch.'

Mashurina got out of the coach, and an hour later Nezhdanov was driving into the courtyard of the Sipyagins' house. He did not feel very well. . . . He had spent a night without sleep . . . and then all the discussions . . . the talk. . . .

A beautiful face peeped out of a window and smiled graciously to him. . . . It was Madame Sipyagin welcoming him on his return.

'What eyes she has!' was his thought.

12

A GREAT many people had come to dinner, and after dinner Nezhdanov profited by the general bustle to slip away to his own room. He wanted to be by himself if only to review the impressions he carried away from his expedition. At table Valentina Mihalovna had looked at him several times attentively, but apparently had not got a chance of speaking to him; Marianna, since that unexpected avowal which had so astounded him, seemed ashamed of herself and avoided him.

Nezhdanov took up a pen; he felt a desire to converse on paper with his friend Silin; but he could not think what to say even to his friend; or perhaps, so many contradictory thoughts and sensations were clashing together in his head that he did not attempt to disentangle them, and put it all off to another day. Among the party at dinner had been Mr. Kallomyetsev too; never had he shown more arrogance and gentlemanly superciliousness; but his free and easy remarks had had no effect on Nezhdanov: he did not notice them. He seemed shut in by a sort of cloud; it stood like a veil of half-darkness between him and the rest of the world—and, strange to say, across this veil he could discern only three faces, and all three women's faces, and all three had their eyes persistently fastened upon him. They were: Madame Sipyagin, Mashurina, and Marianna. What did it mean? And why precisely these three? What had they in common? And what did they want with him?

He went early to bed, but could not get to sleep. He was haunted by thoughts, gloomy, though not exactly painful . . . thoughts of the inevitable end, of death. They were familiar thoughts. For long he was turning them this way and that, at one time shuddering at the probability of annihilation, then welcoming it, almost rejoicing in it. He felt at last the peculiar excitement he knew so well. . . . He got up, sat down to his writing-table, and, after thinking a little, almost without correction, wrote the following verses in his secret book:

'My dear one, when I come
To die—this is my will:
Heap up and burn my writings all,
That they may die in the same hour!
With flowers then deck me all about
And let the sun shine in my room;
Musicians place about my doors,
And let them play no mournful dirge!
But as in hours of revelry,
Let the gay fiddles shrilly twang
A rollicking, seductive waltz!
Then, as upon my dying ear

That reckless music dies away,
I too would die, dropping asleep,
And mar not with a useless moan
The peace that comes with coming death.
I'd pass away to other worlds,
Rocked to my sleep by the light strains
Of the light pleasures of our earth!'

When he wrote the words 'my dear one', he was thinking of
Silin. He declaimed his verses in an undertone to himself, and
was surprised at what had come from his pen. This scepticism,
this indifference, this light-minded lack of faith, how did it all
agree with his principles? with what he had said at Markelov's? He flung the book in the table-drawer, and went back
to his bed. But he only fell asleep at dawn when the first larks
were trilling in the paling sky.

The next day he had just finished his lesson, and was sitting
in the billiard-room. Madame Sipyagin came in, looked
round, and, going up to him with a smile, asked him to come
to her room. She was wearing a light barège dress, very
simple and very charming; the sleeves ended in a frill at the
elbow; a wide ribbon clasped her waist, her hair fell in thick
curls on her neck. Everything about her seemed overflowing
with kindness and sympathetic tenderness, a restrained,
emboldening tenderness—everything: the subdued brilliance
of her half-closed eyes, the soft languor of her voice, her
gestures, her very gait. Madame Sipyagin conducted Nezhdanov to her boudoir, a bright, charming room, filled with the
scent of flowers and perfumes, the pure freshness of a woman's
garments, a woman's constant presence; she made him sit
down in an easy-chair, seated herself near him, and began to
question him about his journey, about Markelov's doings, with
such tact, such gentleness, such sweetness! She showed sincere
interest in her brother, whom, till then, she had not once mentioned in Nezhdanov's hearing; from some of' her words it
could be gathered that the feeling Marianna had inspired in
him had not escaped her; her tone was slightly mournful . . .
whether because his feeling was not reciprocated by Marianna,

or because her brother's choice had fallen on a girl he really knew nothing of, was left undefined. But what was principally clear: she was obviously trying to win Nezhdanov, to arouse his confidence in her, to make him cease to be shy. Valentina Mihalovna went so far as to reproach him a little for having a false idea of her.

Nezhdanov listened to her, looked at her arms and her shoulders, at times glanced at her rosy lips, the faintly waving coils of her hair. At first his answers were very short; he felt a slight tightening in his throat and his chest . . . but gradually this sensation was replaced by another, disturbing enough too, but not devoid of a certain sweetness: he had never expected such a distinguished and beautiful lady, such an aristocrat, would be capable of taking an interest in him, a mere student; and she was not simply taking an interest in him, she seemed to be flirting a little with him. Nezhdanov asked himself why she was doing all this, and he found no answer; nor, indeed, was he very anxious to find one. Madame Sipyagin talked of Kolya; she even began by assuring Nezhdanov that it was simply with the object of talking seriously about her son, to learn his views on the education of Russian children in general, that she wished to get to know him better. The suddenness with which this wish had sprung up might have struck anyone as curious. But the root of the matter did not lie in what Valentina Mihalovna had just said, but in the fact that she had been overtaken by something like a wave of sensuality; a craving to conquer, to bring to her feet this stubborn creature, had asserted itself. . . .

But at this point we must go back a little. Valentina Mihalovna was the daughter of a very stupid and unenergetic general, with only one star and a buckle to show for fifty years' service, and a very sly and intriguing Little Russian, endowed, like many of her countrywomen, with an exceedingly simple, and even foolish, exterior, from which she knew how to extract the maximum of advantage. Valentina Mihalovna's parents were not well-to-do people; she got into the Smolny

Convent, however, and there, though she was regarded as a republican, she stood high in favour because she studied industriously and behaved sedately. On leaving the Smolny Convent, she lived with her mother (her brother had gone into the country, her father, the general with the star and the buckle, was dead) in a clean but very chilly flat; when people talked in their rooms, the breath could be seen coming in steam from their mouths; Valentina Mihalovna used to laugh and declare it was 'like being in church'. She was plucky in bearing all the discomforts of a poor, cramped style of living: she had a wonderfully good temper. With her mother's aid, she succeeded in keeping up and forming acquaintances and connections: everyone talked about her, even in the highest circles, as a very charming, very cultivated girl, of the very best breeding. Valentina Mihalovna had several suitors; she had picked out Sipyagin from all the rest, and had very simply, rapidly, and adroitly made him in love with her. . . . Though, indeed, he soon recognised himself that a better wife for him could not have been found. She was clever, not ill-natured . . . rather good-natured of the two, fundamentally cold and indifferent . . . and she could not tolerate the thought of anyone remaining indifferent to her. Valentina Mihalovna was full of that special charm which is peculiar to attractive egoists; in that charm there is no poetry nor true sensibility, but there is softness, there is sympathy, there is even tenderness. Only, these charming egoists must not be thwarted: they are fond of power, and will not tolerate independence in others. Women like Sipyagina excite and work upon inexperienced and passionate natures; for themselves they like regularity and a peaceful life. Virtue comes easy to them, they are inwardly unmoved, but the constant desire to sway, to attract, and to please lends them mobility and brilliance: their will is strong, and their very fascination partly depends on this strength of will. Hard it is for a man to hold his ground when for an instant gleams of secret softness pass unconsciously, as it seems, over a bright, pure creature like this; he waits, expecting that the time is coming, and now the ice will melt; but the clear ice only

84

reflects the play of the light, it does not melt, and never will he see its brightness troubled!

Flirtation cost Sipyagina little; she was well aware that there was no danger for her, and never could be. And meantime, to make another's eyes grow dim and then sparkle again, to set another's cheeks flushing with desire and dread, another's voice quivering and breaking, to trouble another soul—oh, how sweet that was to her soul! How pleasant it was late at night, as she lay down to untroubled slumbers in her pure, fresh nest, to recall those restless words and looks and sighs! With what a happy smile she retired into herself, into the consciousness of her inaccessibility, her impregnable virtue, and with what gracious condescension she submitted to the lawful embraces of her well-bred spouse! Such reflections were so soothing that she was often positively touched and ready to do some deed of mercy, to succour a fellow-creature. . . . Once she had founded a tiny almshouse after a secretary of legation, madly in love with her, had tried to cut his throat! She had prayed most sincerely for him, though the sentiment of religion had been feeble in her from her earliest years.

And so she talked to Nezhdanov, and tried in every way to bring him to her feet. She admitted him to her confidence, she, as it were, revealed herself to him, and with sweet curiosity, with half-maternal tenderness, watched this very nice-looking, interesting, and severe young radical slowly and awkwardly beginning to respond to her. In a day, an hour, a minute—all this would disappear, leaving no trace; but meanwhile she found it pleasant, rather amusing, rather pathetic, and even rather touching. Forgetting his origin, and knowing how such interest is appreciated by people who are lonely and among strangers, Valentina Mihalovna began questioning Nezhdanov about his youth, his family. . . . But guessing instantly by his confused and short replies that she had made a blunder, Valentina Mihalovna tried to smooth over her mistake, and opened her heart even more ingenuously to him. . . . As in the languid heat of noonday a full-blown rose opens its fragrant petals, which are soon folded up close again by the bracing coolness of night.

She did not succeed, however, in fully effacing her mistake. Nezhdanov, touched on a sore spot, could not feel confiding as before. The bitter feeling he had always with him, always rankling at the bottom of his heart, was astir again; his democratic suspicion and self-reproach were awakened. 'This wasn't what I came here for,' he thought; Paklin's sarcastic advice recurred to him . . . and he took advantage of the first instant of silence to get up, make a curt bow, and go out 'looking very foolish', as he could not help whispering to himself.

His embarrassment did not escape Valentina Mihalovna . . . but to judge from the little smile with which she watched him go out, she interpreted this embarrassment in a manner flattering to herself.

In the billiard-room Nezhdanov came upon Marianna. She was standing with her back to the window, not far from the door of the boudoir, her arms folded tightly. Her face happened to be in almost black shadow; but her fearless eyes were looking so inquiringly, so fixedly at Nezhdanov, such scorn, such insulting pity were visible on her tightly closed lips, that he stood still in perplexity. . . .

'You have something to say to me?' he said involuntarily.

Marianna did not at once answer. 'No . . . or rather yes; I have. But not now.'

'When, then?'

'Wait a little. Perhaps—to-morrow; perhaps—never. You see, I know very little—of what you are really like.'

'Still,' began Nezhdanov, 'it has sometimes struck me . . . that we have——'

'And you don't know me at all,' Marianna interrupted. 'But there, wait a little. To-morrow, perhaps. Now I have to go to my . . . mistress. Good-bye till to-morrow.'

Nezhdanov took two steps forward, but suddenly turned back. 'Oh, by the way, Marianna Vikentyevna . . . I have been continually meaning to ask you: won't you let me go to the school with you—to see what you do there—before it's shut?'

'Certainly. . . . But it's not of the school that I wanted to talk to you.'

'What, then?'

'To-morrow,' repeated Marianna.

But she did not put it off till the next day; a conversation between her and Nezhdanov took place the same evening in one of the avenues of limes, not far from the terrace.

13

SHE went up to him first.

'Mr. Nezhdanov,' she began in a hurried voice, 'you are, I fancy, completely fascinated by Valentina Mihalovna?'

She turned without waiting for an answer, and walked along the avenue; and he walked beside her.

'What makes you think that?' he asked after a brief pause.

'Isn't it so? If not, she has played her cards badly to-day. I can fancy how carefully she has been at work, how she has laid her little nets.'

Nezhdanov uttered not a word; he only stared from one side at his strange companion.

'Listen,' she continued; 'I'm not going to pretend; I don't like Valentina Mihalovna—and you know that well enough. I may strike you as unjust . . . but you should first consider . . .'

Marianna's voice broke. She was flushed and moved. . . . Emotion with her almost always took the form of seeming angry. 'You are probably asking yourself,' she began again, 'why is this young lady telling me all this? You must have thought the same, I suppose, when I told you something . . . about Mr. Markelov?'

She suddenly stooped down, picked a small mushroom, broke it in half and flung it away.

'You are wrong, Marianna Vikentyevna,' observed Nezhdanov; 'on the contrary, I thought I had inspired you with confidence—and that idea was a very pleasant one.'

Nezhdanov was not telling quite the truth; this idea had only just entered his head.

Marianna glanced at him instantly. Up till then she had looked away persistently.

'It's not so much that you inspire confidence,' she said as though reflecting; 'you are completely a stranger, you see. But your position—and mine—are very much alike. We are both alike unhappy; that's a bond between us.'

'Are you unhappy?' inquired Nezhdanov.

'And you—aren't you?' answered Marianna.

He said nothing.

'Do you know my story?' she began quickly; 'the story of my father? his exile?—no? well, then, let me tell you that he was brought up, tried, found guilty, deprived of his rank . . . and everything—and sent to Siberia. Then he died . . . my mother died too. My uncle, Mr. Sipyagin, my mother's brother, took care of me; I live at his expense; he's my bene-factor and Valentina Mihalovna's my benefactress—and I repay them with the blackest ingratitude, because, I suppose, I have a hard heart—and the bread of charity is bitter—and I'm not good at bearing insulting condescension—and I can't put up with patronage . . . and I'm not good at hiding things; and when I'm for ever being hurt with little pin-pricks, I only keep from crying out because I'm too proud.'

As she uttered these disconnected sentences, Marianna walked more and more rapidly. All at once she stood still.

'Do you know that my aunt—simply to get me off her hands—means to marry me . . . to that loathsome Kallom-yetsev? Of course she knows my ideas—why, in her eyes, I'm a Nihilist!—while he, I'm not attractive to him, of course —I'm not pretty, you see; but I might be sold. That would be another act of charity, you know.'

'Why then didn't you . . .' Nezhdanov began, and he hesitated.

Marianna glanced at him for a moment. 'Why didn't I accept Mr. Markelov's offer, do you mean? Isn't that it? Well, but what could I do? He's a good man. But it's not my fault; I don't love him.'

Marianna again walked on in front as though she wished to save her companion from any obligation to reply to this unexpected confession.

They both reached the end of the avenue. Marianna turned quickly into a narrow path that ran through the densely planted firs, and walked along it. Nezhdanov followed Marianna. He was conscious of a twofold perplexity; it was amazing that this shy girl could suddenly be so open with him, and he wondered still more that her openness did not strike him as strange, that he felt it natural.

Marianna turned round suddenly and stood still in the middle of the path, so that it came to pass that her face was about a yard from Nezhdanov's and her eyes were fixed straight upon his.

'Alexey Dmitritch,' she said, 'don't suppose my aunt is ill-natured. . . . No! she is all deceit, she's an actress, she poses, she wants everyone to adore her as a beauty, and to worship her as a saint! She makes a sympathetic phrase, says it to one person, and then repeats the phrase to a second and a third, and always with the same air of only just having thought of it, and that's just when she uses her wonderful eyes! She understands herself very well; she knows she's like a Madonna, and she cares for no one! She pretends she's always worrying over Kolya, but all she does is to talk about him with intellectual people. She wishes no harm to anyone. . . . She's all benevolence! But they may break every bone in your body in her presence . . . it's nothing to her! She wouldn't stir a finger to save you; while if it were necessary or useful to her . . . then . . . oh, then!'

Marianna ceased; her wrath was choking her. She resolved to give it vent—she could not restrain herself; but speech failed her in spite of herself. Marianna belonged to a special class of unhappy persons (in Russia one may come across them pretty often). . . . Justice satisfies but does not requite them, while injustice, which they are terribly keen in detecting, revolts them to the very depths of their being. While she was talking, Nezhdanov was looking at her intently; her flushed face, with her short hair slightly dishevelled, and the tremulous twitching of her thin lips, impressed him as menacing, and significant, and beautiful. The sunlight, broken up by the thick network of twigs, fell on her brow in a slanting patch of gold, and this tongue of fire seemed in keeping with the excited expression of her whole face, her wide-open, fixed, and flashing eyes, the thrilling sound of her voice.

'Tell me,' Nezhdanov asked her at last, 'why did you call me unhappy? Is it possible you know about my past?'

Marianna nodded her head.

'Yes.'

'That is . . . how did you know of it? Someone has talked to you about me?'

'I know . . . your origin.'

'You know. . . . Who told you?'

'Why, the very Valentina Mihalovna whom you're so fascinated by! She didn't fail to mention in my presence, passing over it lightly, as her way is, but plainly—not with sympathy, but as a liberal who is superior to all prejudices—that there was, to be sure, a fact of interest in the life of our new tutor! Don't be surprised, please: Valentina Mihalovna, in the same incidental way, and with commiseration, informs almost every visitor that there is, to be sure, in her niece's life a . . . fact of interest: her father was sent to Siberia for taking bribes! She may fancy herself an aristocrat—she's simply backbiting and posing, your Sistine Madonna!'

'Excuse me,' remarked Nezhdanov, 'why is she "mine"—'

Marianna turned away, and again walked along the path.

'You had such a long conversation with her,' she uttered thickly.

'I hardly said a single word,' answered Nezhdanov; 'she was talking all the while alone.'

Marianna walked on in silence; but at this point the path turned aside, the pines, as it were, made way, and a small lawn stretched before them, with a hollow weeping birch in the middle and a round seat encircling the trunk of the old tree. Marianna sat down on this seat; Nezhdanov placed himself beside her; the long hanging branches, covered with tiny green leaves, swayed above both their heads. Around them lilies-of-the-valley peeped out white in the fine grass, and from the whole clearing rose the fresh scent of the young herbage, sweetly refreshing after the oppressive resinous odour of the pines.

'You want to come with me to look at the school here,' began Marianna. 'Well, then, let us go. . . . Only . . . I don't know. It will not be much pleasure to you. You've heard—our principal teacher is the deacon. He's a good-natured man, but you can't imagine what he talks about to his pupils! There is one boy among them. . . . His name is Garasei. He's an orphan, ten years old, and fancy, he learns faster than any of them!'

In suddenly changing the subject of conversation, Marianna herself seemed transformed. She grew rather pale and quiet . . . and her face expressed confusion, as though she began to be ashamed of all she had been saying. She apparently wanted to get Nezhdanov upon a question of some sort—the schools or the peasantry—anything, if only they might not continue in the same tone as before. But at that minute he was in no humour for 'questions'.

'Marianna Vikentyevna,' he began, 'I will speak to you openly. I did not at all anticipate all that . . . has just passed between us.' (At the word 'passed' she started a little.) 'I think we have suddenly become very . . . very intimate. And it was bound to be so. We have long been getting closer to one another, but we did not put it into words. And so I, too, will speak to you without reserve. You are wretched and miserable in this house, but your uncle, though he's limited, still, so far as I can judge, he's a humane man, isn't he? Won't he understand your position and stand by you?'

'My uncle? To begin with, he's not a man at all: he's an official—a senator or a minister . . . I don't know. And secondly . . . I don't want to complain and slander people for nothing. I'm not wretched at all here; that's to say, I'm not oppressed in any way; my aunt's tiny pin-pricks are really nothing to me. . . . I'm absolutely free.'

Nezhdanov looked in bewilderment at Marianna.

'In that case . . . all you told me just now . . .'

'You are at liberty to laugh at me,' she said quickly; 'but if I am unhappy—it's not for my own unhappiness. It sometimes seems to me that I suffer for all the oppressed, the poor, the wretched in Russia. . . . No, I don't suffer, but I am indignant—I am in revolt for them . . . that I'm ready for them . . . to lay down my life. I am unhappy because I'm a young lady—a hanger-on, because I can do nothing—am fit for nothing! When my father was in Siberia, while I was left with mother in Moscow—ah! how I longed to go to him! not that I had any great love or respect for him—but I so much wanted to know for myself, to see with my own eyes, how convicts and how prisoners live. . . . And what disgust I felt for myself and all those easy-going, prosperous, well-fed people! . . . And afterwards, when he came back, broken down, crushed, and began humiliating himself, fretting and trying to get on . . . ah . . . that was hard! How well he did to die . . . and mother, too! But, you see, I was left behind. . . . For what? To feel that I've a bad nature, that I'm ungrateful, that nothing is right with me, and that I can do nothing—nothing for anything or anybody!'

Marianna turned away. Her hand had slid on to the garden seat. Nezhdanov felt very sorry for her; he stroked the hand . . . but Marianna at once pulled it away, not because Nezhdanov's action struck her as unsuitable, but that he might not—God forbid!—imagine that she was asking for his sympathy.

Through the branches of the pines there was a glimpse of a woman's dress.

Marianna drew herself up. 'Look, your Madonna has sent

92

her spy out. That maid has to keep watch on me and report to her mistress where I am and with whom. My aunt most likely supposed that I was with you, and thinks it improper, especially after the sentimental scene she has been rehearsing with you. And, indeed, it's time to go back. Come along.'

Marianna got up; Nezhdanov, too, rose from his seat. She glanced at him over her shoulder, and suddenly there passed over her face an expression almost childish, charming, a little embarrassed.

'You're not angry with me? You don't think I, too, have been showing off to you? No, you don't think that,' she went on, before Nezhdanov could answer her in any way. 'You see, you are, like me, unhappy, and your nature, too, is . . . bad, like mine. To-morrow we will go to the school together, for we are friends now, you know.'

As Marianna and Nezhdanov approached the house, Valentina Mihalovna watched them with a spy-glass from the balcony, and with her usual sweet smile she slowly shook her head; then returning through the open glass door into the drawing-room, where Sipyagin was already seated at preference with the toothless neighbour, who had dropped in for tea, she observed in a loud, drawling tone, each syllable distinct: 'How damp the night air is! It's dangerous!'

Marianna glanced at Nezhdanov, while Sipyagin, who had just taken a point from his partner, cast a truly ministerial glance, sidelong and upwards, upon his wife, and then trans-ferred this same cool, sleepy, but penetrating look to the young couple coming in from the dark garden.

14

A FORTNIGHT more passed. Everything went its accustomed way. Sipyagin arranged the duties of the day, if not like a minister, at least like the director of a department, and maintained the same lofty, humane, and somewhat fastidious deportment; Kolya had his lessons; Anna Zaharovna fretted in continual, suppressed anger; visitors came, talked, skirmished at cards, and apparently were not bored; Valentina Mihalovna continued to amuse herself with Nezhdanov, though a' shade of something like good-natured irony was blended with her amenities. With Marianna Nezhdanov grew unmistakably intimate, and to his surprise found that her temper was even enough, and that he could talk to her about anything without coming into violent opposition. In her company he twice visited the school, though at his first visit he was convinced that he could do nothing there. The reverend deacon was in full possession of it with Sipyagin's consent, and, indeed, by his wish. The worthy father taught reading and writing fairly, though on an old-fashioned method; but at examinations he propounded questions decidedly ridiculous; for instance, he one day asked Garasei how he would explain the expression, "the waters in the firmament", to which Garasei, by the instruction of the same worthy father, was to reply, 'That is inexplicable.'

Moreover, the school, such as it was, was closed soon after—for the summer months—till autumn. Remembering the exhortation of Paklin and of others, Nezhdanov tried, too, to make friends with the peasants; but soon he realised that he was simply, so far as his powers of observation enabled him, studying them, not doing propaganda work at all. He had spent almost the whole of his life in town, and between him and the country people there was a gulf over which he could not cross. Nezhdanov succeeded in exchanging a few words with the drunkard Kirill, and even with Mendeley; but, strange to say, he was, as it were, afraid of them, and, except some very brief abuse of things in general, he got nothing out of them. Another peasant, called Fityuev, nonplussed him utterly. This peasant had a face of exceptional energy, almost that of some brigand chief. . . . 'Come, he's sure to be some use,' Nezhdanov thought. . . . But Fityuev turned out to be a wretched outcast; the mir had taken his land away from him, because he—a healthy and positively powerful man —*could not* work.

'I can't!' Fityuev would sob, with deep inward groans and with a long-drawn sigh; 'I can't work! kill me! or I shall lay hands on myself!' And he would end by begging alms—a halfpenny for a crust of bread. . . . And a face out of a canvas of Rinaldo Rinaldini!

The factory folk, too, were no good to Nezhdanov; all these fellows were either terribly lively or terribly gloomy . . . and Nezhdanov could not get on at all with them. He wrote a long letter on this subject to his friend Silin, complaining bitterly of his own incapacity, and ascribing it to his wretched education and disgusting artistic temperament! He suddenly came to the conclusion that his vocation, in propaganda work, was with the written, not the spoken, living word; but the pamphlets he planned did not work out. Everything he tried to put on paper made on him the same impression of something false, far-fetched, artificial in tone and language, and twice—oh horror!—he caught himself unconsciously wandering off into verse or into a sceptical, personal effusion. He positively brought himself—an extraordinary sign of confidence and intimacy!—to speak of this to Marianna . . . and was again surprised by finding a fellow-feeling in her, of course not with his literary bent, but with the moral malady which he was suffering from, and with which she, too, was familiar. Marianna was quite as much up in arms against all things artistic as he was; yet the reason she had not loved and married Markelov was in reality just that there was not a trace of the artistic nature in him! Marianna, of course, had not the courage to recognise this even to herself; but we know that it is what remains a half-suspected secret for ourselves that is strongest in us.

So the days went by slowly, unequally, but not drearily.

Something curious was taking place in Nezhdanov. He was discontented with himself, with his activity, or rather his inactivity; his words almost constantly had a ring of bitter and biting self-reproach; but in his soul—somewhere very deep within it—there was a kind of happiness, a sense of a certain peace. Whether it was the result of the country quiet, the fresh air, the summer, the good food, and the easy life, or whether it came from the fact that he was now, for the first time in his life, tasting the sweetness of close contact with a woman's soul—it would be hard to say; but, in fact, his heart was light, even though he complained—and sincerely —to his friend Silin.

This frame of mind was, however, suddenly and violently destroyed in a single day.

On the morning of that day he received a note from Vassily Nikolaevitch, in which he was directed in conjunction with Markelov, while awaiting further instructions, at once to make friends with and come to an understanding with the aforementioned Solomin, and a certain merchant, Golushkin, an Old Believer, living in S——. This note threw Nezhdanov into violent agitation; he could read reproach for his inactivity in it. The bitterness that had all this time only raged in words was stirred up again from the bottom of his heart.

Kallomyetsev came to dinner greatly perturbed and exasperated. 'Imagine,' he cried in a voice almost lachrymose, 'what a horrible thing I have just read in the paper: my friend, my dear Mihail, the Servian prince, has been murdered by some miscreants in Belgrade! This is what these Jacobins and revolutionists come to, if we don't put a firm stop to them!' Sipyagin 'begged leave to remark' that this revolting murder was probably not the work of Jacobins, 'whose existence can hardly be supposed in Servia,' but of men of the party of Karageorgievitch, the enemies of

Obrenovitch. . . . But Kallomyetsev would hear nothing, and, in the same lachrymose voice, began again describing how the murdered prince had loved him, what a splendid gun he had given him! . . . Gradually branching off and getting more and more indignant, Kallomyetsev turned from foreign Jacobins to home-bred Nihilists and Socialists, and at last broke into a perfect philippic. Clutching a large, white roll with both hands, and breaking it in half over his soup-plate, quite in the style of real Parisians at the 'Café Riche', he expressed his longing to crush, to grind to powder, all who were in opposition to anyone or anything whatever! That was precisely his expression. 'It is high time,' he declared, lifting his spoon to his mouth, 'it's high time!' he repeated, as he gave his glass to the servant for sherry. He referred reverentially to the great Moscow journalists, and *Ladislas, notre bon et cher Ladislas,* was continually on his lips. And all through this he kept his eyes on Nezhdanov as though to transfix him with them. 'There, that's for you!' he seemed to say. 'Take that! I meant it for you! And there's more like it!' At last Nezhdanov could endure it no longer, and he began to retort. His voice, it is true, was a little uncertain and hoarse—not from fear, of course; he began to champion the hopes, the principles, the ideals of the younger generation. Kallomyetsev at once answered in a high pipe—indignation in him was always expressed by falsetto—and began to be abusive.

Sipyagin majestically took Nezhdanov's part; Valentina Mihalovna, too, agreed with her husband; Anna Zaharovna tried to distract Kolya's attention, and cast looks of fury in all directions from under her cap; Marianna sat as though turned to stone.

But suddenly, on hearing the name of *Ladislas* uttered for the twentieth time, Nezhdanov fired up, and with a blow on the table he cried: 'A fine authority! As though we didn't know what kind of a creature this *Ladislas* is! He, a hired puppet from his birth up, and nothing more!'

'Ah—a—a—so that—that's,' whined Kallomyetsev, stuttering with fury. . . . 'Is that how you allow yourself to refer to a man who enjoys the respect of persons of position like Count Blazenkrampf and Prince Kovrizhkin!'

Nezhdanov shrugged his shoulders. 'A great recommendation truly; Prince Kovrizhkin, the flunkey enthusiast——'

'*Ladislas* is my friend,' shrieked Kallomyetsev; 'he's my comrade . . . and I——'

'So much the worse for you,' interrupted Nezhdanov; 'it implies that you share his way of thinking, and my remarks apply to you as well.'

Kallomyetsev was livid with wrath.

'Wh-what You l-laugh! You—you ought—instantly—be——'

'What are you pleased to do with me *instantly?*' Nezhdanov interrupted a second time with ironical politeness.

There is no knowing how this scuffle between the two enemies would have ended, if Sipyagin had not cut it short at the very commencement. Raising his voice and assuming an air in which it was hard to say which was the predominant element—the solemn authority of the statesman, or the dignity of the master of the house—he declared with calm insistence that he did not wish to hear any such intemperate expressions at his table; that he had long ago made it his rule (he corrected himself—his sacred rule) to respect every sort of conviction, but only on the understanding (here he raised his forefinger, adorned with a signet ring) that they were maintained within the limits of decorum and good breeding; that though on the one hand he could not but censure a certain intemperance in the language of Mr. Nezhdanov, pardonable, however, at his years, on the other hand he could not approve of the severity of Mr. Kallomyetsev's attacks on persons of the opposite camp, a severity to be attributed, however, to his zeal for the public welfare.

'Under my roof,' so he concluded, 'under the roof of the Sipyagins, there are neither Jacobins nor puppets, there are only well-meaning people, who, when once they understand one another, are bound to end by shaking hands!'

Nezhdanov and Kallomyetsev both held their peace, but they did not shake hands; apparently the hour of mutual comprehension had not come for them. Quite the contrary; they had never felt such intense mutual hatred. The dinner was concluded in unpleasant and awkward silence; Sipyagin tried to relate a diplomatic anecdote, but fairly gave it up in despair half-way through. Marianna stared doggedly at her plate. She did not care to show the sympathy aroused in her by Nezhdanov's remarks—not from cowardice, oh no! but she felt bound before everything not to betray herself to Madame Sipyagin. She felt her penetrating, persistent eyes fixed on her. And Madame Sipyagin did actually keep her eyes fixed on her, on her and Nezhdanov. His unexpected outburst at first astounded the sharp-witted lady; then all of a sudden she saw, as it were, a light upon it, so much so that involuntarily she murmured. Ah! . . . she suddenly divined that Nezhdanov was drifting away from her—Nezhdanov, who had so lately been in her grasp. Then something must have happened. . . . Could it be Marianna? Yes, of course it was Marianna . . . He attracted her . . . yes, and he . . .

'Steps must be taken,' was how she concluded her reflections, and meanwhile Kallomyetsev was choking with indignation. Even when playing preference, two hours later, he uttered the words 'Pass!' or 'I buy!' with an aching heart, and in his voice could be heard a hoarse tremolo of wounded feeling, though he put on an appearance of 'being above it'! Sipyagin alone was in reality positively pleased with the whole scene. He had had a chance to show the power of his eloquence, to still the rising storm. . . . He knew Latin, and Virgil's *Quos ego!* was familiar to him. He did not consciously compare himself to Neptune quelling the tempest; but he thought of him with a sort of sympathy.

15

As soon as it seemed possible, Nezhdanov went away to his
room and locked himself in. He did not want to see anyone,
anyone except Marianna. Her room was at the very end of
the long corridor which intersected the whole top storey.
Nezhdanov had only once, and then only for a few instants,
been to her room; but it struck him that she would not be
angry if he knocked at her door, that she even wished to have
a talk with him. It was rather late, about ten o'clock; the
Sipyagins, after the scene at dinner, had not thought it necessary to disturb him, and were still playing cards with Kallomyetsev. Valentina Mihalovna had twice inquired after
Marianna, as she too had vanished soon after dinner.

'Where is Marianna Vikentyevna?' she asked first in
Russian, then in French, not addressing herself to anyone
in particular, but rather to the walls, as people are wont to do
when they are greatly astonished; but soon she too was
absorbed in the game.

Nezhdanov walked once or twice up and down his room,
then he went along the corridor to Marianna's door and softly
knocked. There was no answer. He knocked once more, tried
the door. . . . It appeared to be locked. But he had hardly
got back to his own room, and sat down to the table, when
his own door gave a faint creak, and he heard Marianna's
voice:

'Alexey Dmitritch, was that *you* came to me?'

He jumped up at once and ran into the corridor; Marianna
was standing at his door, a candle in her hand, pale and
motionless.

'Yes . . . I . . .' he whispered.

'Come along,' she answered, and walked along the corridor,
but before she got to the end she stopped and pushed open a
low door with her hand. Nezhdanov saw a small, almost

empty room. 'We had better go in here, Alexey Dmitritch, here no one will disturb us.' Nezhdanov obeyed. Marianna set the candle down on the window-sill and turned round to Nezhdanov.

'I understand why it was that you wanted to see me,' she began; 'it is very wretched for you living in this house, and so it is for me too.'

'Yes; I wanted to see you, Marianna Vikentyevna,' answered Nezhdanov, 'but it isn't wretched for me here since I have come to know you.'

Marianna smiled thoughtfully.

'Thanks, Alexey Dmitritch; but tell me, can you intend to stay here after all this hideous business?'

'I don't suppose they'll let me stay here, they'll dismiss me!'

'Wouldn't you dismiss yourself?'

'Of my own accord? . . . No.'

'Why?'

'You want to know the truth? because *you* are here.'

Marianna bent her head and moved a little farther away into the room.

'And besides,' Nezhdanov went on. 'I am *bound* to stay here. You know nothing—but I want, I feel I ought, to tell you everything.'

He stepped up to Marianna and seized her by the hand. She did not take it away, but only looked into his face. 'Listen!' he cried on a sudden powerful impulse, 'listen to me!' And at once, without sitting down, though there were two or three chairs in the room, still standing in front of Marianna and keeping hold of her hand, with impulsive heat, with an eloquence unexpected by himself, Nezhdanov told her of his plans, his intentions, the reasons that had made him accept Sipyagin's offer, of all his ties, his acquaintances, his past, all that he had always concealed, that he had never spoken openly of to anyone! He told her of the letters he received, of Vassily Nikolaevitch, of everything—even of Silin! He spoke hurriedly, without reluctance, or the faintest hesitation, as though he were reproaching himself for not having initiated Marianna into all his secrets before, as though he were seeking her pardon. She heard him attentively, greedily; for the first minute she was bewildered. . . . But that feeling vanished at once. Gratitude, pride, devotion, resolution, that was what her soul was overflowing with. Her face, her eyes were bright; she laid her other hand on Nezhdanov's hand, her lips were parted in rapture. . . . She had suddenly grown marvellously beautiful!

He stopped at last, looked at her, and as it were for the first time saw *that* face, which seemed at the same time so dear and so familiar to him.

He gave a deep, long sigh. . . .

'Ah! I have done well to tell you everything!'—his lips were hardly able to utter the words.

'Yes, oh, so well, so well!' she repeated, also in a whisper. She unconsciously imitated him, and, indeed, her voice failed her too. 'And it means, you know,' she went on, 'that I am at your disposal, that I want too to be of use to your cause, that I am ready to do anything that is wanted, to go where I am ordered, that I have always, with my whole soul, yearned for the thing that you . . .'

She too was silent. Another word, and tears of emotion would have fallen in floods. All her strong nature was suddenly soft as wax. The thirst for activity, for sacrifice, immediate sacrifice—that was what mastered her.

The steps of someone in the corridor could be heard—cautious, rapid, light steps.

Marianna suddenly drew herself up, freed her hands; she was at once transformed and alert. Something scornful, something audacious came over her face.

'I know who is spying on us at this minute,' she said, so loudly that each of her words resounded distinctly in the corridor. 'Madame Sipyagin is spying on us . . . but I don't care a bit for that.'

The sound of steps ceased.

'What then?' Marianna said, turning to Nezhdanov, 'what

am I to do? how am I to help you? Tell me . . . tell me soon! What's to be done?'

'What?' said Nezhdanov; 'I don't know yet . . . I got a letter from Markelov.'

'When? when?'

'This evening. I must go with him to-morrow to the factory to see Solomin.'

'Yes . . . yes. . . . That's a splendid man, now, Markelov. He's a real friend.'

'Like me?'

Marianna looked Nezhdanov straight in the face.

'No . . . not like you.'

'How? . . .'

She turned suddenly away.

'Ah! don't you understand what you have become to me, and what I am feeling at this moment? . . .'

Nezhdanov's heart beat violently; involuntarily he looked down. This girl, who loved him—him, a poor homeless devil—who believed in him, who was ready to follow him, to go with him towards the same aim—this exquisite girl—Marianna, at that instant, was to Nezhdanov the incarnation of everything good and true on earth—the incarnation of all the love of mother, sister, wife, that he had known nothing of—the incarnation of fatherland, happiness, struggle, freedom!

He raised his head, and saw her eyes again bent upon him. . . .

Oh, how that clear, noble glance sank into his soul!

'And so,' he began in an unsteady voice, 'I am going to-morrow. . . . And when I come back, Marianna Vikentyevna'—(he suddenly found it awkward to use this formal address)—'I will tell you what I find out, what is decided. Henceforth everything I do, everything I think, everything, you shall be the first to know . . . Marianna.'

'Oh, my friend!' cried Marianna, and again she clasped his hand, 'and I make the same promise to you, dear.'

This last word came as easily and simply from her as though

it could not be otherwise, as though it were the 'dear' of long, intimate companionship.

'Can I see the letter?'

'Here it is, here.'

Marianna skimmed through the letter, and almost with reverence she raised her eyes upon him.

'Do they intrust such important commissions to you, Alexey?'

He smiled at her in answer, and put the letter in his pocket.

'Strange,' he said, 'why, we have made known our love to each other—we love one another—and there has not been a word said about it between us!'

'What need?' whispered Marianna, and suddenly she flung herself on his neck, pressed her head to his shoulder. . . . But they did not even kiss—they would have felt it ordinary and somehow dreadful—and at once they separated, after tightly clasping each other's hands again.

Marianna turned away to get the candle, which she had put on the window-sill of the empty room, and only then something like embarrassment came over her. She extinguished it, and, gliding quickly along the corridor in the darkness, she returned to her own room, undressed and went to bed, still in the darkness—she felt it somehow comforting.

16

THE next morning when Nezhdanov woke up he felt no embarrassment at the recollection of what had happened overnight; on the contrary, he was filled with a kind of serene and sober happiness, as though he had done something which ought really to have been done long before. Asking for two days' leave from Sipyagin, who consented at once, though stiffly, to his absence, Nezhdanov went to Markelov's. Before starting he succeeded in getting an interview with Marianna. She, too, was not at all ashamed or embarrassed; she looked calmly and resolutely at him, and calmly addressed him by his Christian name. She was only excited about what he would learn at Markelov's, and begged him to tell her everything.

'That's a matter of course,' answered Nezhdanov.

'And after all,' he reflected, 'why should we be disturbed? In our friendship, personal feeling has played . . . a secondary part—though we are united for ever. In the name of the cause? Yes, in the name of the cause!'

So fancied Nezhdanov, and he did not suspect how much of truth, and how much of falsehood, there was in his fancies.

He found Markelov in the same weary and morose frame of mind. They dined after a fashion, and then set off in the same old coach (they hired from a peasant a second trace-horse, a colt, who had never been in harness before—Markelov's horse was still lame) to the merchant Faleyev's big cotton factory, where Solomin lived. Nezhdanov's curiosity was aroused; he felt eager to make a closer acquaintance with a man of whom he had heard so much of late. Solomin was prepared for their visit; when the two travellers stopped at the gates of the factory and gave their names, they were promptly conducted into the unsightly little lodge occupied by the 'superintendent of the machinery'. He was himself in the chief wing of the building; while one of the workmen ran to fetch him, Nezhdanov and Markelov had time to go to the window and look about them. The factory was apparently in a flourishing condition and overburdened with work; from every side came the brisk, noisy hum of unceasing activity, the snorting and rattling of machines, the creaking of looms, the hum of wheels, the flapping of straps, while trollies, barrels, and loaded carts moved in and out; there was the sound of loudly shouted instructions, bells and whistles; workmen in smocks with belts round the waist, their hair bound round with a strap, work-girls in print dresses hurried by; horses were led by in harness. . . . There was the busy hum of the labour of thousands of human beings strained to their utmost. Everything moved in regular, rational fashion, at full speed; but not only was there no attempt at style or neatness, there was not even any trace of cleanliness to be observed in anything anywhere; on the contrary, on all sides one was impressed by neglect, filth, grime. Here a window was broken and there the plaster was peeling off, the boards were loose, a door yawned wide open; a great, black puddle, covered with an iridescent film of slime, stood in the middle of the principal courtyard; farther on lay some discarded bricks; bits of matting and sail-cloth, boxes, scraps of rope lay wallowing in the mud; shaggy and lean dogs crept about, not even barking; in a corner under a fence sat a pot-bellied, dishevelled little boy of four, covered from head to foot with soot, crying hopelessly as though he had been deserted by the whole world; beside him, besmeared with the same soot, a sow, surrounded by a litter of spotted sucking pigs, was inspecting some cabbage stalks; ragged linen was fluttering on a line; and what an odour, what a stench everywhere! A Russian mill, in fact; not a German or a French factory.

Nezhdanov glanced at Markelov.

'I have heard so much talked about Solomin's great abilities,' he began, 'that, I confess, all this disorder rather surprises me; I didn't expect it.'

'It isn't disorder,' answered Markelov grimly, 'it's the Russian sluttishness. For all that, it's turning over millions! And he has to adapt himself to the old ways, and to practical needs, and to the owner himself. Have you any notion what Faleyev's like?'

'Not the slightest.'

'The greatest skinflint in Moscow. A bourgeois—that's the word for him!'

At that instant Solomin came into the room. Again Nezhdanov was fated to be disappointed in him, as in the factory. At first sight Solomin gave one the impression of being a Finn or, still more, a Swede. He was tall, lean, broad-shouldered, with light eyebrows and eyelashes; he had a long yellow

106

face, a short broad nose, very small greenish eyes, a placid expression, large prominent lips, white teeth, also large, and a cleft chin covered with a faint down. He was dressed as a mechanic or stoker; an old pea-jacket with baggy pockets on his body, a crumpled oilskin cap on his head, a woollen comforter round his neck, and tarred boots on his feet. He was accompanied by a man about forty, in a rough peasant coat, with an exceedingly mobile gipsy face and keen jet-black eyes, with which he at once scanned Nezhdanov, as soon as he came into the room. . . . Markelov he knew already. His name was Pavel; he was said to be Solomin's right hand.

Solomin approached his two visitors without haste, pressed the hand of each of them in his horny, bony hand, without a word, took a sealed packet out of the table-drawer and handed it, also without a word, to Pavel, who at once went out of the room. Then he stretched, and cleared his throat; flinging his cap off his head with one wave of his hand, he sat down on a wooden, painted stool, and, motioning Markelov and Nezhdanov to a similar sofa, he said, 'Please sit down'.

Markelov first introduced Solomin to Nezhdanov; he again shook hands with him. Then Markelov began talking of the 'cause', and mentioned Vassily Nikolaevitch's letter. Nezhdanov handed the letter to Solomin. While he read it, attentively and deliberately, his eyes moving on from line to line, Nezhdanov watched him. Solomin was sitting near the window; the sun, now low in the sky, threw a glaring light on his tanned, slightly perspiring face and his light, dusty hair, showing up a number of golden threads among them. His nostrils quivered as his breath came and went while he read, and his lips moved as though he were forming each word; he held the letter with a strong grip, rather high up with both hands. All this, for some unknown reason, pleased Nezhdanov. Solomin gave the letter back to Nezhdanov, smiled at him, and again began listening to Markelov. The latter talked and talked, but at last he ceased.

'Do you know what,' began Solomin, and his voice, rather hoarse, but young and powerful, pleased Nezhdanov too, 'it's not quite convenient here at my place; let us go to your house, it's not more than five miles to you. I suppose you came in the coach?'

'Yes.'

'Well . . . then there will be room for me. In an hour my work is over and I am at liberty. We will have a talk. Are you at liberty?'—he addressed Nezhdanov.

'Till the day after to-morrow.'

'That's capital. We will stay the night with Mr. Markelov. Can we do that, Sergei Mihalitch?'

'What a question! Of course you can.'

'Well, I'll be ready directly. Only let me clean myself up a bit.'

'And how are things going with you at the factory?' Markelov inquired significantly.

Solomin looked away.

'We will have a talk,' he said a second time. 'Wait a little. . . . I'll be back directly. . . . I've forgotten something.'

He went out. If it had not been for the good impression he had made on Nezhdanov, the latter would probably have thought, and perhaps even have said to Markelov, 'Isn't he shuffling out of it?' But no question of the sort even entered his head.

An hour later, at the time when from every floor of the vast building, on every staircase, and at every door the noisy crowd of factory hands were streaming out, the coach, in which were seated Markelov, Nezhdanov, and Solomin, drove out of the gates on to the road.

'Vassily Fedotitch! is it to be done?' Pavel, who had escorted Solomin to the gate, shouted after him.

'No; wait a little' . . . answered Solomin. 'That refers to a night operation,' he explained to his companion.

They reached Borzyonkovo; and had supper, rather for the sake of manners. Then cigars were lighted and the talk began, one of those interminable, midnight, Russian talks, which of the same form and on the same scale are hardly to be found in any other people. Here too, though, Solomin did not fulfil Nezhdanov's expectations. He spoke noticeably little . . . so little that one might say he was almost continually silent; but he listened intently, and if he uttered any criticism or remark, then it was sensible, weighty, and very brief. It turned out that Solomin did not believe that a revolution was at hand in Russia; but not wishing to force his opinions on others, he did not try to prevent them from making an attempt, and looked on at them, not from a distance, but as a comrade by their side. He was very intimate with the Petersburg revolutionists, and was to a certain extent in sympathy with them, since he was himself one of the people; but he realised the instinctive aloofness from the movement of the people, without whom 'you can do nothing,' and who need a long preparation, and that not in the manner nor by the means of these men. And so he stood aside, not in a hypocritical or shifty way, but like a man of sense who doesn't care to ruin himself or others for nothing. But as for listening . . . why not listen, and learn too, if one can? Solomin was the only son of a deacon; he had five sisters, all married to village priests or deacons; but with the consent of his father, a steady, sober man, he had given up the seminary, had begun to study mathematics, and had devoted himself with special ardour to mechanics; he had entered the business of an Englishman, who had come to love him like a father, and had given him the means of going to Manchester, where he spent two years and learned English. He had lately come into the Moscow merchant's factory, and though he was exacting with subordinates, because that was the way of doing things he had learned in England, he was in high favour with them; 'he's one of ourselves,' they used to say. His father was much pleased with him; he used to call him 'a very steady-going chap,' and his only complaint was that his son didn't want to get married.

During the midnight conversation at Markelov's, Solomin was, as we have said already, almost completely silent; but when Markelov began discussing the expectations he had formed of the factory hands, Solomin, with his habitual brevity, observed that with us in Russia, factory workers are not what they are abroad—they're the meekest set of people.

'And the peasants?' inquired Markelov.

'The peasants? There are pretty many of the close-fisted, money-lending sort among them now, and every year there'll be more; but they only know their own interest; the rest are sheep, blind and ignorant.'

'Then where are we to look?'

Solomin smiled.

'Seek and ye shall find.'

He was almost constantly smiling, and the smile, like the man himself, was peculiarly guileless, but not meaningless. To Nezhdanov he behaved in quite a special way; the young student had awakened a feeling of interest, almost of tenderness, in him.

During this same midnight discussion, Nezhdanov suddenly got flushed and hot, and broke into an outburst; Solomin softly got up, and, moving across the room with his large tread, he closed a window that stood open behind Nezhdanov's head. . . .

'You mustn't get cold,' he remarked naïvely in reply to the orator's puzzled look.

Nezhdanov began questioning him as to what socialistic ideas he was trying to introduce into the factory in his charge, and whether he intended to arrange for the work-people to have a share of the profits.

'My dear soul!' answered Solomin, 'we have set up a school and a tiny hospital, and, to be sure, our master struggled against that like a bear!'

Once only Solomin lost his temper in earnest, and struck the table such a blow with his powerful fist that everything shook upon it, not excepting a forty-pound weight that lay near the inkstand. He had been told of some legal injustice, the oppressive treatment of a workmen's guild. . . .

When Nezhdanov and Markelov started discussing how 'to act', how to put their plans into execution, Solomin still listened with curiosity, even with respect; but he did not himself utter a single word. This conversation lasted till four o'clock. And what, what did they not discuss? Markelov, among other things, alluded mysteriously to the indefatigable traveller Kislyakov, to his letters, which were becoming more and more interesting; he promised to show Nezhdanov some of them, and even to let him take them home, since they were very lengthy, and not written in a very legible hand; and over and above this there was a great deal of erudition in them, and there were verses too, only not frivolous ones, but of a socialistic tendency! From Kislyakov, Markelov passed to soldiers, adjutants, Germans; he got at last to his articles on the artillery; Nezhdanov talked of the antagonism between Heine and Börne, of Proudhon, of realism in art; while Solomin listened, listened and pondered and smoked, and, still smiling and not saying a single smart thing, he seemed to understand better than anyone what lay at the root of the matter.

It struck four. . . . Nezhdanov and Markelov were almost dropping with fatigue, while Solomin had not turned a hair. The friends separated, but first it was mutually agreed to go the next day to the town to see the merchant Golushkin on propaganda business. Golushkin himself was very zealous, and moreover he promised proselytes! Solomin expressed a doubt whether it was worth while to visit Golushkin. However, he agreed later that it was worth while.

17

MARKELOV'S guests were still asleep when a messenger came to him with a letter from his sister, Madame Sipyagin. In the letter Valentina Mihalovna wrote to him of various trifling domestic details, asked him to send her back a book he had borrowed—and incidentally, in the postscript, told him of an 'amusing' piece of news: that his former flame, Marianna, was in love with the tutor, Nezhdanov—and the tutor with her; that she, Valentina Mihalovna, was not repeating gossip—she had seen it all with her own eyes, and heard it with her own ears. Markelov's face grew dark as night . . . but he did not utter one word; he gave orders to give the book to the messenger, and when he saw Nezhdanov coming downstairs he said, 'Good morning' to him, just as usual—even gave him the promised packet of Kislyakov's epistles; he did not stop with him, though, but went out 'to see after things'. Nezhdanov went back to his room, and looked through the letters. The young propagandist talked incessantly of himself, of his feverish activity; according to his own statement, he had during the last month journeyed through eleven districts, been in nine towns, twenty-nine villages, fifty-three hamlets, one farm, and eight factories; sixteen nights he had passed in hay-lofts, one in a stable, one even in a cow-shed (he mentioned, in a parenthetical note, that fleas did not affect him); he had got into mud huts, into workmen's barracks; everywhere he had taught, preached, distributed pamphlets, and collected information by the way; some facts he had noted on the spot, others he carried in his memory on the latest system of mnemonics; he had written fourteen long letters, twenty-seven short ones, and eighteen notes, four of which were written in pencil, one in blood, one in soot and water; and all this he had managed to do because he had mastered the systematic disposition of his time, taking as his models Quintin Johnson, Karrelius, Sverlitsky, and other writers and statisticians. Then he talked again of himself, his lucky star; and how and with what additions he had completed Fourier's theory of the passions; declared that he was the first to reach the 'bed-rock', that he should 'not pass from the world without leaving a trace behind,' that he himself wondered that he, a boy of two-and-twenty, should already have solved all the problems of life and of science, and that he should turn Russia upside down,

that he would 'give her a shaking'! *Dixi!!* he added at the
end of the line. This word, *Dixi*, occurred frequently in
Kislyakov's effusions, and always with two exclamation
marks. In one of the letters there was a socialistic poem,
addressed to a girl, and beginning with the words:

'Love not me, but the idea!'

Nezhdanov marvelled inwardly, not so much at Mr.
Kislyakov's self-conceit as at Markelov's honest simplicity
. . . but then came the thought, 'Good taste be hanged!
Mr. Kislyakov even may be of use.'

The three friends all met in the dining-room for morning
tea, but the previous night's discussion was not renewed
between them. Not one of them was disposed to talk, but
only Solomin was placidly silent; both Nezdanov and
Markelov were inwardly perturbed.

After tea they set off to the town; Markelov's old servant,
sitting on his locker, followed his former owner with his
habitual dejected glance.

The merchant, Golushkin, with whom Nezhdanov was to
make acquaintance, was the son of a wealthy merchant in
the wholesale drug business—an Old Believer of the Fedosian
sect. He had not increased his father's fortune by his own
efforts, as he was, as it is called by the Russians, a *joueur*,
an epicurean of the Russian stamp, and had no sort of
aptitude for business. He was a man of forty, rather stout,
and ugly, pock-marked, with small pig's eyes; he talked in
a great hurry, stumbling, as it were, over his words,
gesticulating with his hands, swinging his legs, and going off
into giggles . . . and in general making the impression of a
blockhead and a coxcomb of extraordinary vanity. He considered himself a man of culture, because he wore German
clothes, and was hospitable, though he lived in filth and disorder, had rich acquaintances, and used to go to the theatre
and 'protect' low music-hall actresses, with whom he communicated in an extraordinary would-be French jargon. The
thirst for popularity was his ruling passion; for the name of

Golushkin to be thundering through the world! As once Suvarov or Potemkin, why not now Kapiton Golushkin? It was just this passion, overcoming even his innate meanness, which had flung him, as he with some self-complacency expressed it, into the *opposition* (he had at first pronounced this foreign word simply *position,* but afterwards he had learned better), and brought him into connection with the Nihilists; he uttered freely the most extreme views, laughed at his own Old Believers' faith, ate meat in Lent, played cards, and drank champagne like water. And he never got into trouble, because, he used to say, 'I have every authority bribed just where it's needed, every hole is sewn up, all mouths are shut, all ears are deaf.' He was a widower and childless; his sister's sons hung about him with timorous servility . . . but he used to call them unenlightened clowns and barbarians, and would hardly look at them. He lived in a large stone house, rather sluttishly kept; in some rooms the furniture was all of foreign make—in others there was nothing but painted chairs and an American-leather sofa. Pictures were hung everywhere, and all of them were wretched daubs—red landscapes, pink marine views, Moller's 'Kiss', and fat, naked women, with red knees and elbows. Though Golushkin had no family, there were a great many servants and dependents of different kinds under his roof; it was not from generosity that he kept them, but, again, from a desire for power, so as to have a public of some sort at his command to show off before. 'My clients,' he used to call them when he was in a bragging mood; he never read a book, but he had a capital memory for learned expressions.

The young men found Golushkin in his study. Dressed in a long coat, with a cigar in his mouth, he was pretending to read the newspaper. On seeing them, he at once jumped up, and fussed about, turning red, shouting for some refreshment to be brought immediately, asking questions, laughing—all at the same time. Markelov and Solomin he knew; Nezhdanov was a stranger to him. Hearing that he was a student, Golushkin laughed again, shook his hand a second

time, and said: 'Capital! capital! our forces are growing.
. . . Learning is light, ignorance is darkness. I've not a
ha'porth of learning myself, but I've insight—that's how I've
got on!'

It struck Nezhdanov that Mr. Golushkin was nervous and
ill at ease . . . and that was actually the fact. 'Look out,
brother Kapiton! mind you don't come a cropper in the
mud!' was his first thought at the sight of any new person.
Soon, however, he recovered himself, and in the same
hurried, lisping, muddled language began talking of Vassily
Nikolaevitch, of his character, of the necessity of pro-pa-gan-
da (he had that word very pat, but he articulated it slowly);
of how he, Golushkin, had discovered a capital new recruit,
most trustworthy; of how it seemed now that the time was at
hand, was ready for . . . for the lancet (at this he glanced
at Markelov, who did not, however, stir a muscle); then, turning to Nezhdanov, he started singing his own praises, with
as much zest as the great correspondent, Kislyakov, himself.
He said that he had long left the ranks of the benighted,
that he knew well the rights of the proletariat (that word, too,
he had a firm hold of), that though he had actually given
up commerce and taken to banking operations—to increase his
capital—that was only that the aforesaid capital might be
ready at any moment to serve . . . the good of the common
movement, the good, so to speak, of the people; and that he,
Golushkin, had in reality the greatest contempt for money!
At this point a servant came in with refreshments, and
Golushkin cleared his throat expressively, and asked wouldn't
he begin with a little glass of something? and set the example
by gulping down a wineglass of pepper-brandy.

The visitors partook of the refreshments. Golushkin thrust
some huge morsels of caviar in his mouth, and drank with
unflagging punctuality, saying, 'Come, gentlemen, a glass of
good Macon now.'

Addressing himself again to Nezhdanov, he asked where
he had come from, and how long and where he was staying;
and learning that he was living at Sipyagin's, he cried: 'I

know that gentleman. No good!' and then proceeded to abuse all the landowners of the province of S——, on the grounds, not only of their having no public spirit, but of their not even understanding their own interests. . . . Only, strange to say, though his language was strong, his eyes strayed restlessly about, and a look of uneasiness could be detected in them. Nezhdanov could not quite make out what sort of a person he was, and in what way he was of use to them. Solomin was silent, as usual; and Markelov had such a gloomy face that Nezhdanov asked him at last what was wrong with him. To which Markelov replied and there was nothing wrong with him, in the tone in which people commonly answer when they mean to give you to understand that there is something, but not for you to know. Golushkin again started abusing someone or other, then he passed to praise of the younger generation: 'such talented fellows,' he declared, 'are appearing among us nowadays! such talent! Ah! . . .'

Solomin cut him short with the question, who was the trustworthy young man he had spoken of, and where had he picked him up? Golushkin giggled, repeated twice, 'Ah, you shall see, you shall see,' and began cross-questioning him about his factory, and its 'shark' of an owner, to which Solomin replied in monosyllables. Then Golushkin poured out champagne for all; and, bending down to Nezhdanov's ear, he whispered, 'To the republic!' and drank off his glass at a gulp. Nezhdanov sipped his; Solomin remarked that he didn't drink wine in the morning; Markelov angrily and resolutely drained his glass to the last drop. He seemed devoured by impatience; 'here we are wasting our time,' he seemed to say, 'and not coming to the real matter to be discussed.' . . . He struck a blow on the table, exclaimed sternly, 'Gentlemen!' and was about to speak. . . .

But at that instant there came into the room a sleek man with a foxy face and a consumptive appearance, in a merchant's dress of nankeen, with both hands outstretched like wings. Bowing to the party collectively, the man communicated something to Golushkin in a whisper: 'I'll come directly,' the latter replied hurriedly. 'Gentlemen,' he added, 'I must beg you to excuse me . . . Vasya here, my clerk, has told me of a *leetle* affair' (Golushkin pronounced it thus purposely, by way of being jocose) 'which absolutely necessitates my absenting myself for a while; but I hope, gentlemen, that you will consent to take a meal with me to-day at three o'clock; and then we shall be much more at liberty!'

Neither Solomin nor Nezhdanov knew what answer to make; but Markelov answered at once with the same sternness in his face and voice: 'Of course we will; it would be rather too much of a farce if we didn't.'

'I am greatly obliged,' said Golushkin hastily and, bending to Markelov, he added: 'A thousand roubles I devote to the cause in any case . . . have no doubt about that!'

And so saying he waved his right hand three times, with the thumb and little finger sticking out, as a sign of his good faith.

He escorted his guests to the door, and standing in the doorway, shouted, 'I shall expect you at three!'

'You may expect us!' Markelov alone responded.

'Well, my friends,' observed Solomin, when they were all three in the street, 'I'm going to take a cab and go back to the factory. What are we to do till dinner-time? Waste our time idling about? And, indeed, our worthy merchant . . . it strikes me . . . is like the goat in the fable, neither good for wool nor for milk.'

'Oh, there shall be some wool,' observed Markelov grimly. 'He was just promising some money. Or isn't he nice enough for you? We can't be particular. We're not so much courted that we can afford to be squeamish.'

'I'm not squeamish!' said Solomin calmly; 'I'm only asking myself what good my presence can do. However,' he added with a glance at Nezhdanov, and a smile, 'I will stay, by all means. Even death, as they say, is sweet in good company.'

Markelov raised his head.

117

'Let's go, meanwhile, to the public gardens; it's a lovely day. We can look at the people.'

'Very well.'

They went, Markelov and Solomin in front, Nezhdanov behind them.

18

STRANGE was the state of his mind. In the last two days so many new sensations, new faces. . . . For the first time in his life he had come close to a girl, whom, in all probability, he loved; he was present at the beginning of the thing to which, in all probability, all his energies were consecrated. . . . Well? was he rejoicing? No. Was he wavering, afraid, confused? Oh, certainly not. Was he, at least, feeling that tension of his whole being, that impulse forward into the front ranks of the battle, to be expected as the struggle grew near? No again. Did he believe, then, in this cause? Did he believe in his own love? 'Oh, damned artistic temperament! sceptic!' his lips murmured inaudibly. Why this weariness, this disinclination to speak even, without shrieking and raving? What inner voice did he want to stifle with those ravings? But Marianna, that noble, faithful comrade, that pure, passionate nature, that exquisite girl, did not she love him? Was not that an immense happiness, to have met her, to have gained her friendship, her love? And these two walking in front of him at this moment, this Markelov, this Solomin, whom he knew so little as yet, but to whom he felt so drawn, were they not fine types of the Russian nature, of Russian life, and was not it a happiness, too, to know them, to be friends with them? Then why this undefined, vague, gnawing sensation? How and why this dejection? 'If you're a brooding pessimist,' his lips murmured again, 'a damned fine revolutionist you'll make! You ought to be writing rhymes, and sulking and nursing your own petty thoughts and sensations, and busying yourself with psychological fancies and subtleties of all sorts, but at least don't mistake your sickly, nervous whims and irritability for manly indignation, for the honest anger of a man of convictions! O Hamlet, Hamlet, how to escape from the shadow of your spirit! How cease to follow you in everything, even in the loathsome enjoyment of one's own self-depreciation!'

'Alexey! Friend! Hamlet of Russia!' he heard suddenly, like the echo of these reflections, in a familiar squeaky voice. 'Is it you I see before me?'

Nezhdanov raised his eyes, and with amazement beheld Paklin!—Paklin, in quite an Arcadian get-up, a summer suit of flesh-colour, with no cravat round his neck, a large straw hat with a blue ribbon pushed on to the back of his head, and in varnished shoes!

He at once limped up to Nezhdanov and grasped his hands.

'First of all,' he began, 'though we are in a public garden, I must, for old custom's sake, embrace . . . and kiss you . . . Once, twice, thrice! Secondly, you must know that if I had not met you to-day, you would certainly have seen me to-morrow, as I knew your abode, and am, indeed, in this town with that object . . . how I got here, we will talk of hereafter; and thirdly, introduce me to your companions. Tell me briefly who they are, and them who I am, and then let's proceed to enjoy ourselves!'

Nezhdanov acted on his friend's request, named him, Markelov and Solomin, and told what each of them was, where he lived, what he did, and so on.

'Capital!' cried Paklin; 'and now let me lead you all far from the madding crowd, though there's not much of it here, certainly, to a secluded seat, where I sit, at moments of contemplation, to enjoy the beauties of nature. There's a wonderful view: the governor's house, two striped sentry-boxes, three policemen, and not one dog! Don't be too much surprised at the remarks with which I'm so perseveringly trying to amuse you! I'm the representative, in my friends' opinion, of Russian wit . . . no doubt that's why I'm lame.'

Paklin led his friends to the 'secluded seat', and made them sit down on it, after dislodging two beggar women as a preliminary. The young men proceeded to 'exchange ideas', generally a rather tedious process, especially at a first meeting, and a particularly unprofitable occupation at all times.

'Stay!' Paklin cried suddenly, turning to Nezhdanov. 'I must explain to you how it is I'm here. You know I always take my sister away somewhere every summer; when I found out that you had gone off into the neighbourhood of this town, I remembered that there were two wonderful creatures living in this very town, a husband and wife, who are connections of ours . . . on my mother's side. My father was a tradesman'—(Nezhdanov was aware of the fact, but Paklin mentioned it for the benefit of the other two)—'but my mother was of noble family. And for ages they've been inviting us to come and see them! There! thought I . . . the very thing. They're the kindest people, it'll do my sister any amount of good—what could be better? Well, and so here we are. And it was just as I thought! I can't tell you how nice it is for us here! But what types! what types! you really must make their acquaintance! What are you doing here? Where are you going to dine? And why is it you were here, of all places?'

'We are going to dinner with a man called Golushkin . . . a merchant here,' answered Nezhdanov.

'At what o'clock?'

'Three.'

'And you are seeing him upon . . . upon . . .' Paklin took a comprehensive look at Solomin, who was smiling, and Markelov, whose face grew darker and darker. . . .

'Come, Alyosha, tell them . . . make some sort of Masonic sign, do . . . tell them they needn't be on their guard with me . . . I'm one of you . . . of your party. . . .'

'Golushkin, too, is one of us,' observed Nezhdanov.

'Now, I've a brilliant idea! There's a long while yet to

three o'clock. Listen, let's go and see my relations!'

'Why, you're crazy! How could we? . . .'

'Don't worry yourself about that! I'll take all that on myself. Imagine: it's an oasis! Not a glimpse of politics, nor literature, nor anything modern has penetrated into it. A queer podgy sort of little house, such as you never see anywhere now; the very smell in it's antique; the people antique, the atmosphere antique . . . take it how you will, it's all antique, Catherine the Second, powder, hoops, eighteenth century! Just fancy a husband and wife, both very old, the same age, and without a wrinkle; round, chubby, spruce little things, a perfect pair of little poll-parrots; and good-natured to stupidity, to saintliness, no bounds to it! They tell me "boundless" good-nature often goes with an absence of moral feeling. . . . But I can't enter into such subtleties; I only know that my little old dears are the very soul of good-nature! Never had any children. The blessed innocents! That's what they call them in the town: blessed innocents. Both dressed alike in sort of striped gowns, and such good stuff: you can never see anything like that either nowadays. They're awfully like each other, only one has a mob-cap on her head, and the other a skull-cap, though that has the same sort of frilling as the mob-cap, only no strings. If it weren't for that difference, you wouldn't know which was which; especially as the husband has no beard. Their names are Fomushka and Fimushka. I tell you people ought to pay at the door to look at them, as curiosities. They love one another in the most impossible way; but if anyone comes to visit them, it's "Delighted, so good of you!" And such hospitable creatures! they show off all their little tricks at once to amuse you. There's only one thing: one mustn't smoke; not that they're dissenters, but tobacco upsets them. . . . You see, no one smoked in their day. However, they can't stand canaries either, because that bird was very rarely seen in their day too. . . . And that's a great blessing, you'll admit! Well? will you come?'

'Really, I don't know,' began Nezhdanov.

'Stay; I haven't told you everything yet; their voices are just alike; with your eyes shut you wouldn't know which was speaking. Only Fomushka speaks just a little more expressively. Come, my friends, you are now on the brink of a great undertaking—perhaps, a terrible conflict. . . . Why shouldn't you, before flinging yourselves into those stormy deeps, try a dip . . .'

'In stagnant water?' Markelov put in.

'And what if so? Stagnant it is, certainly; but fresh and pure. There are ponds in the steppes which never get putrid, though there's no stream through them, because they are fed by springs from the bottom. And my old dears have such springs too in the bottom of their hearts, and pure as can be. It all comes to this, would you like to know how people lived a century, a century and a half ago, make haste then and follow me. Or soon a day and hour will come—it's bound to be the same hour for both—and my poll-parrots will be knocked off their perches, and all that's antique will end with them, and the podgy little house will fall down, and the place of it will be overgrown with what, my grandmother used to tell me, always grows over the place where man's handiwork has been—that's to say, nettles, burdock, thistles, wormwood, dock leaves; the very street will cease to be, and men will come and go and never see anything like this again in all the ages!'

'Well!' cried Nezhdanov, 'let's be off directly!'

'I'm ready, with the greatest pleasure, indeed,' observed Solomin. 'It's not in my line, but it's interesting; and if Mr. Paklin can really guarantee that we should not be putting anyone out by our visit, then . . . why . . .'

'Don't worry yourself!' Paklin cried in his turn; 'they'll be simply transported—that's all. No need of ceremony in this case! I tell you, they're blessed innocents; we'll make them sing to us. And you, too, Mr. Markelov, do you agree?'

Markelov shrugged his shoulders angrily.

'I'm not going to stay here alone! lead the way, if you please.'

The young men got up from the seat.

'You've a formidable gentleman there,' Paklin whispered to Nezhdanov, indicating Markelov, 'the very image of John the Baptist eating locusts . . . the locusts without the honey! But he,' he added with a nod in Solomin's direction, 'is delightful! What a jolly smile! I've noticed the only people who smile like that are those who're superior to other people— without being aware of it.'

'Are there ever people like that?' asked Nezhdanov.

'Not often; but there are some,' answered Paklin.

19

FOMUSHKA and Fimushka, otherwise Foma Lavrentyevitch and Evfimiya Pavlovna Subotchev, both belonged to the same family of pure Russian descent, and were considered to be almost the oldest inhabitants of the town of S——. They had been married very early, and a very long time ago had installed themselves in the wooden house of their ancestors on the outskirts of the town, had never moved from there, and had never changed their mode of life or their habits in any respect. Time seemed to have stood still for them; no 'novelty' had crossed the boundary of their 'oasis'. Their fortune was not large; but their peasants sent them up poultry and provisions several times a year, just as in the old days before the emancipation. At a fixed date the village elder appeared with the rents and a brace of woodcocks, supposed to be shot on the manorial forest domains, though the latter had in reality long ceased to exist. They used to regale him with tea at the drawing-room door, present him with a sheep-skin cap and a pair of green wash-leather mittens, and bid him God-speed. The Subotchevs' house was filled with house-serfs, as in the old serf days. The old manservant Kalliopitch, clothed in a jerkin of extraordinarily stout cloth with a stand-up collar and tiny steel buttons, announced in a sing-song chant that 'dinner is on the table,' and dozed standing behind his mistress's chair, all quite in the old style. The sideboard was in his charge; he had the care of 'the various spices, cardamums and lemons', and to the question, 'Hadn't he heard that all serfs had received their freedom?' he always responded, 'To be sure, folks would for ever be talking some such idle nonsense; that like enough there was freedom among the Turks, but he, thank God, had escaped all that.' A girl, Pufka, a dwarf, was kept for entertainment, and an old nurse, Vassilyevna, used to come in during dinner with a large dark kerchief on her head, and talk in a thick voice of all the news—of Napoleon, of the year 1812, of Antichrist, and white niggers; or else, her chin propped in her hand, in an attitude of woe, she would tell what she had dreamed and what it portended, and what fortune she had got from the cards. The Subotchevs' house itself was quite different from all the other houses in the town; it was entirely built of oak and had windows exactly square. The double windows for winter were never taken out all the year round! And there were in it all kinds of little ante-rooms and passages, lumber-rooms and store-closets, and raised landings with balustrades and alcoves raised on rounded posts, and all sorts of little back premises and cellars. In front was a little palisade, and behind a garden, and in the garden outbuildings of every sort, granaries, cellars, ice-houses . . . a perfect nest of them! And it was not that there were many goods stored in all these outhouses; some, indeed, were tumbling down; but it had all been so arranged in old days, and so it had remained. The Subotchevs had only two horses, ancient, grey, and shaggy; one was covered with white patches from age; they called it the Immovable. They were—at most once a month—harnessed to an extraordinary equipage, known to the whole town, and presenting a resemblance to a terrestrial globe with one quarter cut out in front, lined within with foreign yellow material, closely dotted with big spots like warts. The last yard of that stuff had been woven in Utrecht or Lyons in the time of the Empress Elizabeth! The Subotchevs' coachman, too, was an exceedingly aged man, redolent of train-oil and pitch; his beard began just under his eyes, while his eyebrows fell in little cascades to meet his beard. He was so deliberate in all his movements that it took him five minutes to take a pinch of snuff, two minutes to stick his whip in his belt, and more than two hours to harness the Immovable alone. His name was Perfishka. If, when the Subotchevs were driving, their carriage had to go ever so little uphill, they were invariably alarmed (they were as frightened, however, going downhill), hung on to the straps of the carriage, and both repeated aloud: 'God grant the horses—the horses . . . the strength of Samuel, and make us . . . us light as a feather, light as a feather! . . .'

The Subotchevs were regarded by everyone in the town as eccentric, almost as mad; and indeed they were conscious themselves that they were not in touch with the life of the day . . . but they did not trouble themselves very much about that: the manner of life to which they had been born and bred and married they adhered to. Only one peculiarity of that manner of life had not clung to them: from their birth up they had never punished anyone, never had anyone flogged. If any servant of theirs proved to be an irreclaimable thief or drunkard, first they were patient and bore with him a long while, just as they would have put up with bad weather; and at last tried to get rid of him, to pass him on to other masters: let others, they would say, take their turn of them for a little. But such a disaster rarely befell them, so rarely that it made an epoch in their lives, and they would say, for instance, 'That was very long ago, it happened when we had that rascal Aldoshka,' or, 'when we had grandfather's fur cap with the fox's tail stolen.' The Subotchevs still had such caps. Another distinguishing trait of the old world was, however, not noticeable in them: neither Fimushka nor Fomushka was very religious. Fomushka went so far as to profess some of Voltaire's views; while Fimushka had a mortal dread of ecclesiastical personages; they had, according to her experience, the evil eye. 'The priest comes in to call on me,' she used to say, 'and then I look round and the cream's turned sour!' They rarely went to church, and fasted in the Catholic fashion, that's to say, ate eggs, butter, and milk. This was known in the town, and of course did not improve their reputation. But their goodness carried everything before it; and though the queer Subotchevs were laughed at and regarded as lunatics and innocents, they were all the same, in fact, respected. Yes; they were respected . . . but no one visited them. This, however, was no great affliction to them. They were never bored when they were together, and therefore they were never apart and desired no other company. Neither Fomushka nor Fimushka had once been ill; and if either of them ever contracted some slight ailment, then they both drank lime-flower water, rubbed warm oil on their stomachs, or dropped hot tallow on the soles of their feet, and it was very soon over. They always spent the day in the same way. They got up late, drank chocolate in the morning in tiny cups of the shape of a cone; 'tea,' they used to declare, 'came into fashion after our time.' They sat down opposite to one another, and either talked (and they always found something to talk about!) or read something out of *Agreeable Recreations, The Mirror of the World,* or *Aonides,* or looked at a little old album bound in red morocco with gold edges, which once belonged, as an inscription recorded, to one Mme. Barbe de Kabyline. How and when this album had come into their hands they did not know themselves. In it were several French and many Russian poems and prose extracts, after the fashion, for example, of the following short meditations on Cicero: 'In what disposition Cicero entered upon the office of quæstor, he explains as follows: Invoking the gods to testify to the purity of his sentiments in every position with which he had hitherto been honoured, he deemed himself by the most sacred bonds bound to the worthy fulfilment thereof, and to that intent he, Cicero, not only suffered himself not the indulgence of the pleasures forbidden by law, but refrained even from those lighter distractions which are held to be indispensable by all.' Below stood the inscription: 'Composed in Siberia in hunger and cold.' A good specimen, too, was a poem entitled 'Tirsis', where these lines were to be met:

> 'A settled peace is over all,
> The dew's asparkle in the sun,
> Nature it soothes, with freshness cool,
> Giving new life to the day begun!
> Tirsis alone, with soul dismayed,
> Sorrows, pines, so lone and so sad.
> His darling Aneta is far away,
> And what can then make Tirsis glad?'

and the impromptu composition of a captain who had come on a visit in 1790, dated 'May 6th':

> 'Never shall I forget
> Thee, lovely hamlet!
> For ever shall I recall
> How sweetly the time passed!
> What kindness I received
> In thy noble owner's hall!
> Five memorable happy days,
> In a circle worthy of all praise!
> With old and young ladies, not a few,
> And other int'resting people too.'

On the last page of the album instead of verses there were recipes for remedies against stomach-ache, spasms, and worms. The Subotchevs dined at twelve o'clock punctually, and always upon old-fashioned dishes: curd fritters, sour cucumber soups, salt cabbage, pickles, hasty pudding, jelly puddings, syrups, jugged poultry with saffron, and custards, made with honey. After dinner they took a nap for just one hour and no longer, waked up, again sat opposite one another, and drank cranberry syrup and sometimes an effervescent drink called 'forty winks', which, however, almost all popped out of the bottle, and afforded the old people great amusement and Kalliopitch great annoyance; he had to wipe up 'all over the place,' and he kept up a long grumble at the butler and the cook, whom he regarded as responsible for the invention of this beverage . . . 'What sort of good is there in it? it only spoils the furniture' Then the Subotchevs again read something, or laughed at the pranks of the dwarf Pufka, or sang duets of old-fashioned songs (their voices were exactly alike, high, feeble, rather quavering, and hoarse—especially just after their nap—but not without charm), or they played cards, always the same old games, cribbage, piquet, or even boston with double dummy! Then the samovar made its appearance; they drank tea in the evening. . . . This concession they did make to the spirit of the age, though they always thought it a weakness, and that the people were growing noticeably feebler through this 'Chinese herb'. As a rule, however, they refrained from criticising modern times or exalting the old days; they had never lived in any other way from their birth up; but that other people might live differently, better even, they readily admitted so long as they were not required to change their ways. At seven o'clock Kalliopitch served the supper, with the inevitable cold, sour hash; and at nine o'clock the high striped feather-beds had already taken into their soft embraces the plump little persons of Fomushka and Fimushka, and untroubled sleep was not slow in descending upon their eyelids; and everything was hushed in the old house; the lamp glowed, amid the fragrance of musk; the cricket chirped; and the kind-hearted, absurd, innocent old couple slept sound.

To these eccentrics, or, as Paklin expressed it, 'poll-parrots', who were taking care of his sister, he now conducted his friends.

His sister was a clever girl, and not bad-looking. Her eyes were magnificent, but her unfortunate deformity had crushed her, deprived her of all self-confidence and joyousness, made her distrustful and even ill-tempered. And her name was very unfortunate, Snanduliya! Paklin had tried to make her change it to Sofya, but she clung obstinately to her queer name, saying that that was just what a hunchback ought to be called—Snanduliya. She was a good musician, and played the piano well: 'Thanks to my long fingers,' she observed with some bitterness; 'hunchbacks always have fingers like that.'

The visitors came upon Fomushka and Fimushka at the very minute when they had waked up from their after-dinner nap and were drinking cranberry water.

'We are stepping into the eighteenth century,' cried Paklin, directly they crossed the threshold of the Subotchevs' house.

And they were, in fact, confronted by the eighteenth century in the very hall, in the shape of low bluish screens covered with black cut-out silhouettes of powdered cavaliers and ladies. Silhouettes, introduced by Lavater, were much in vogue in Russia in the eighties of last century. The sudden appearance of so large a number of visitors—no less than four —produced quite a sensation in the secluded house. They heard a stampede of feet, both shod and naked; more than one woman's face was thrust out for an instant and then vanished again; someone was shut out, someone groaned, someone giggled, someone whispered convulsively, 'Get along with you, do!'

At last Kalliopitch made his appearance in his shabby jerkin, and, opening the door into the 'salon', he cried in a loud voice:

'Your honour, Sila Samsonitch with some other gentlemen!'

The old people were far less flustered than their servants. The irruption of four full-sized men in their drawing-room, comfortably large as it was, did indeed bewilder them a little, but Paklin promptly reassured them by presenting, with various odd phrases, Nezhdanov, Solomin, and Markelov to them in turn as good quiet fellows and not 'crown people'. Fomushka and Fimishka had a special dislike for 'crown'— that is, official—people.

Snanduliya, who appeared at her brother's summons, was far more agitated and ceremonious than the old Subotchevs. They asked their visitors, both together, and in exactly the same phrases, to sit down, and begged to know what they would take—tea, chocolate, or an effervescent beverage with jam? When they heard that their guests wanted nothing, since they had not long before lunched at the merchant Golushkin's and would shortly dine there, then they did not press them, and, folding their little hands across their persons in precisely the same manner, they entered upon conversation.

At first the conversation flagged rather, but soon it grew livelier. Paklin diverted the old people hugely with Gogol's well-known story of the mayor who succeeded in getting into a church when it was full, and of the pie that was equally successful in getting into the mayor; they laughed till the tears ran down their cheeks. They laughed, too, in exactly the same way, with sudden shrieks, ending in a cough, with their whole faces flushed and heated. Paklin had noticed that, as a rule, quotations from Gogol have a very powerful and, as it were, convulsive effect upon people like the Subotchevs, but, as he was not so much anxious to amuse them as to show them off to his friends, he changed his tactics, and managed so that the old people were soon quite at ease and animated. Fomushka brought out and showed the visitors his favourite carved wood snuff-box, on which it had once been possible to distinguish thirty-six figures in various attitudes; they had long ago been effaced, but Fomushka saw them, saw them still, and could distinguish them and point them out. 'See,' he said, 'there's one looking out of window; do you see, he's put his head out . . .' and the spot to which he pointed with his chubby finger with its raised nail was just as smooth as all the rest of the snuff-box lid. Then he drew the attention of his guests to a picture hanging above his head, painted in oils; it represented a hunter in profile galloping full-speed on a pale bay-coloured steed, also in profile, over a plain of snow. The hunter wore a tall white sheepskin cap with a blue streamer, a tunic of camel's hair, with a velvet border and a belt of wrought gold; a glove embroidered in silk was tucked into the belt, and a dagger, mounted in silver and black, hung from it. In one hand the hunter, who was very youthful and plump in appearance, held a huge horn, decked with red tassels, and in the other the reins and whip. All the four legs of the horse were suspended in the air, and on each of them the artist had conscientiously portrayed a horse-shoe, and even put in the nails. 'And observe,' said Fomushka, pointing with the same chubby finger to four semi-circular marks in the white ground behind the horse's legs, 'the prints in the snow—even these he has put in!' Why it was that there were only four of these prints—not one was to be seen farther back—on that point Fomushka was silent.

'And you know that it is I,' he added after a brief pause, with a modest smile.

'What!' exclaimed Nezhdanov, 'did you hunt?'

'I did . . . but not for long. Once the horse threw me at full gallop, and I injured my "kurpy", so Fimushka was frightened . . . and so she wouldn't let me. I have given it up ever since.'

'What did you injure?' inquired Nezhdanov.

'The *kurpy*,' repeated Fomushka, dropping his voice.

His guests looked at one another. No one knew what sort of thing a *kurpy* might be; at least, Markelov knew that the shaggy tuft on a Cossack or Circassian cap is called a *kurpy*, but surely Fomushka could not have injured that! But to ask him exactly what he understood by the word was more than anyone could make up his mind to do.

'Well, now, since you've shown off,' Fimushka observed suddenly, 'I will show off, too.'

Out of a diminutive 'bonheur du jour', as they used to call the old-fashioned bureau on tiny crooked legs, with a convex lid which folded up into the back of the bureau, she took a water-colour miniature in an oval bronze frame, representing a perfectly naked child of four years old, with a quiver on her shoulder and a blue ribbon round her breast, trying the points of the arrows with the end of her little finger. The child was very curly and smiling, and had a slight squint. Fimushka showed the miniature to her visitors.

'That was I!' she observed.

'You?'

'Yes, I. In my childhood. There was an artist, a French-

131

man, who used to come and see my father—a splendid artist!
And so he painted a picture of me for my father's birthday. And what a nice Frenchman he was! He came to see
us afterwards, too. He would come in, scraping his foot as he
bowed, and then giving it a little shake in the air, and would
kiss your hand, and when he went away he would kiss his
own fingers and bow to right and to left, and before and
behind! He was a delightful Frenchman!'

They praised his work; Paklin even professed to discern
a certain likeness.

Then Fomushka began talking of the French of to-day,
and expressed the opinion that they must all be very wicked!

'Why so, Foma Lavrentyevitch?'

'Why, only see what names they have now!'

'What, for instance?'

'Why, such as Nozhan-Tsent-Lorran (Nogent Saint
Lorraine), a regular bandit's name!'

Fomushka inquired incidentally, 'Who is the sovereign now
in Paris?'

They told him 'Napoleon,' and that seemed to surprise and
pain him.

'Why so?'

'Why, he must be such an old man,' he began, and stopped,
looking round him in confusion.

Fomushka knew very little French, and read Voltaire in a
translation (in a secret box under the head of his bed he kept
a manuscript translation of *Candide*), but he occasionally
dropped expressions like 'That, my dear sir, is *fausse parquet*'
(in the sense of 'suspicious', 'untrue'), at which many people
laughed till a learned Frenchman explained that it was an old
parliamentary expression used in his country until the year
1789.

Seeing that the conversation had turned on France and the
French, Fimushka screwed up her courage to inquire about
one thing which was very much on her mind. She first
thought of applying to Markelov, but he looked very ill-
tempered; she might have asked Solomin . . . but no! she

thought, 'he's a plain sort of person; he's sure not to know French.' So she addressed herself to Nezhdanov.

'There's something, my dear sir, I should like to learn from you,' she began, 'excuse me! My cousin, Sila Samsonitch, you must know, makes fun of an old woman like me, and my old-fashioned ignorance.'

'How so?'

'Why, if anyone wants to put the question, "What is it?" in the French dialect, ought he to say, "Ke-se-ke-se-ke-se-là?" '

'Yes.'

'And can he also say, "Ke-se-ke-se-là?" '

'Yes, he can.'

'And simply, "Ke-se-là?" '

'Yes, he could say that too.'

'And all that would be the same?'

'Yes.'

Fimushka pondered deeply, and threw up her hands.

'Well, Silushka,' she said at last, 'I was wrong and you were right. But these Frenchmen! Poor things!'

Paklin began begging the old people to sing them some little ballad. . . . They both laughed and wondered how such an idea could occur to him; they soon consented, however, but only on the condition that Snanduliya sat down to the harpsichord and accompanied them—she would know what. In one corner of the drawing-room there turned out to be a diminutive piano, which not one of them had noticed at the beginning. Snanduliya sat down to this 'harpsichord', struck a few chords. . . . Such toothless, acid, wizened, crazy notes Nezhdanov had never heard before in his life; but the old people began singing promptly:

> 'Is it to feel the smart,'

began Fomushka,

> 'That's hid in love,
> The gods gave us a heart
> Attuned to love?'

133

'Was there a love-sick heart,'

responded Fimushka,

> 'In the world ever,
> Quite free from woe and smart?'

> 'Never! never!'

put in Fomushka.

> 'Never! never!'

repeated Fimushka.

> 'Pain is of love a part
> Ever! ever!'

they both sang together.

> 'Ever! ever!'

Fomushka warbled alone.

'Bravo!' cried Paklin; 'that's the first verse, now the second.'

'Certainly,' answered Fomushka; 'only, Snanduliya Samsonovna, how about the shake? There ought to be a shake after my verse.'

'To be sure,' replied Snanduliya, 'you shall have your shake.'

Fomushka began again:

> 'Has ever lover loved
> And known not grief and pain?
> What lover has not sighed
> And wept and sighed again?'

And then Fimushka:

> 'The heart is rocked in grief
> As a ship floats on the main,
> Why was it given, then?'

> 'For pain! for pain! for pain!'

cried Fomushka, and he waited to give Snanduliya time for the shake.

Snanduliya performed the shake.

'For pain! for pain! for pain!'

repeated Fimushka.

And then both together:

'Take, gods, my heart away,
Again! again! again!
Again! again! again!'

And the song wound up with another shake.

'Bravo! bravo!' they all shouted, with the exception of Markelov, and they even clapped their hands.

'And do they feel,' thought Nezhdanov directly the applause ceased, 'they are performing like some sort of buffoons? Perhaps they don't, and perhaps they do feel it and think "Where's the harm? no one's the worse for it; we amuse others, in fact!" And if you look at it properly, they're right, a thousand times right!'

Under the influence of these reflections, he began suddenly paying them compliments, in acknowledgment of which they merely made a sort of slight curtsey, without leaving their chairs. . . . But at that instant, out of the adjoining room, probably a bedroom or maids'-room, where a great whispering and bustle had been audible a long while, appeared the dwarf, Pufka, escorted by the old nurse, Vassilyevna. Pufka proceeded to squeal and play antics, while the nurse one minute quieted her, and the next egged her on.

Markelov, who had long shown signs of impatience (as for Solomin, he simply wore a broader smile than usual) turned sharply upon Fomushka.

'I shouldn't have thought you,' he began in his abrupt fashion, 'with your enlightened intellect (you're a follower of Voltaire, aren't you?) could be amused by what ought to be a subject for compassion—I mean deformity.' Then he remembered Paklin's sister, and could have bitten his tongue off; while Fomushka turned red, murmuring, 'Why—why, I didn't . . . she herself——'

And then Pufka fairly flew at Markelov.

'What put that idea into your head,' she squeaked in her lisping voice, 'to insult our masters? They protect a poor wretch like me, take me in, give me meat and drink, and you must grudge it me. You envy another's luck, I suppose. Where do you spring from, you black-faced, worthless wretch, with moustaches like a beetle's?' Here Pufka showed with her thick, short finger what his moustaches were like. Vassilyevna's toothless gums were shaking with laughter, and her mirth was echoed in the next room.

'Of course I can't presume to judge you,' Markelov addressed Fomushka; 'to protect the poor and the crippled is a good action. But allow me to observe, to live in luxury, wallowing in ease and plenty, even without injuring others, but not to lift a finger to aid your fellow-creatures, doesn't imply much virtue; I, for one, to tell the truth, attach no value to that sort of goodness!'

Here Pufka gave a deafening howl, she had not understood a word of all Markelov said; but the 'black-browed fellow' was scolding . . . how dared he. Vassilyevna, too, muttered something indistinct, while Fomushka folded his little hands across his breast, and turning towards his wife, 'Fimushka, my darling', he said, all but sobbing, 'do you hear what the gentleman says? You and I are sinners, miscreants, Pharisees . . . we're wallowing in luxury, oh! oh! . . . we ought to be turned into the streets . . . and have a broom put in our hands to work for our living. Oh, ho! ho!' Hearing these mournful words, Pufka howled louder than ever. Fimushka's eyes puckered up, the corners of her mouth dropped, she was just drawing in a deep breath so as to give full vent to her emotions.

There's no knowing how it would have ended if Paklin had not intervened.

'What's the meaning of this? upon my word,' he began with a wave of the hand and a loud laugh, 'I wonder you're not ashamed of yourselves. Mr. Markelov meant to make a little joke, but as he has such a very solemn face, it sounded rather alarming, and you were taken in by it! That's enough! Evfimiya Pavlovna, there's a dear, we've got to go in a minute, so, do you know what? you must tell all our fortunes before parting . . . you're a great hand at that. Sister! get cards!'

Fimushka glanced at her husband, and he was sitting now completely reassured; she, too, was reassured.

'The cards,' she said; 'but I've quite forgotten, my dear sir, it's long since I had them in my hand.'

But of her own accord she took out of Snanduliya's hands a pack of aged, queer ombre cards.

'Whose fortune shall I tell?'

'Oh, everyone's,' said Paklin; while to himself he said, 'What a mobile old thing! you can turn her any way you like . . . she's a perfect darling! Everyone's, granny, everyone's,' he went on aloud; 'tell us our fate, our character, our future . . . tell us everything!'

Fimushka began shuffling the cards, but suddenly she threw down the whole pack.

'I don't need to use the cards!' she cried; 'I know the character of each of you without that. And as the character is, so is the fate. He, now' (she pointed to Solomin) 'is a cool man, constant; he, now' (she shook her finger at Markelov) 'is a hot, dangerous man . . .' (Pufka put out her tongue at him); 'as for you' (she looked at Paklin), 'there's no need to tell you; you know yourself—a weathercock! As for this gentleman' (she indicated Nezhdanov, and hesitated).

'What is it?' he said; 'tell me, please; what sort of man am I?'

'What sort of man are you? . . . ' said Fimushka slowly, 'you're to be pitied—that's all.'

Nezhdanov shuddered.

'To be pitied? why so?'

'Oh! I pity you—that's all.'

'But why?'

'Oh, for reasons! My eye tells me so. Do you think I'm a fool? Oh, I'm cleverer than you, for all your red hair. . . . I pity you . . . that's your fortune!'

All were silent . . . they looked at one another, and were still silent.

'Well, good-bye, dear friends,' Paklin cried, 'we've stayed too long and tired you, I'm afraid. It's time these gentlemen were off . . . and I'll see them on their way. Good-bye; thanks for your kind reception.'

'Good-bye, good-bye, come again, don't stand on ceremony,' Fomushka and Fimushka cried with one voice. . . . Then Fomushka struck up suddenly like a refrain:

'Many, many years of life.'

'Many, many years,' Kalliopitch chimed in quite unexpectedly in the bass, as he opened the door to the young men.

And all four of them suddenly emerged into the street before the podgy little house; while at the window they heard Pufka's squeaky voice: 'Fools . . . ' she shouted, 'fools! . . .'

Paklin laughed aloud; but no one responded. Markelov scanned each in turn as though he expected to hear some word of indignation. . . .'

Solomin alone smiled his ordinary smile.

20

'WELL, now,' Paklin was the first to begin, 'we have been in the eighteenth century; now lead the way full trot to the twentieth. . . . Golushkin's such an advanced man that it wouldn't do to reckon him in the nineteenth.'

'Why, do you know him?' inquired Nezhdanov.

'The earth is full of his glory; and I said, "lead the way", because I meant to come with you.'

'How's that? why, you don't know him, do you?'

'Get along! Did you know my poll-parrots?'

'But you introduced us!'

'Well, and do you introduce me. You can have no secrets from me, and Golushkin's an open heart. You'll see he'll be delighted to see someone new. And we don't stand on ceremony here in S——!'

'Yes,' muttered Markelov, 'people seem unceremonious here certainly.'

Paklin shook his head.

'That's, perhaps, meant for me. . . . So be it! I've deserved the reproach. But I say, my new acquaintance, defer for a time the gloomy reflections your bilious temperament inspires in you! And most of all——'

'And you, sir, my new acquaintance,' Markelov interrupted emphatically, 'let me tell you . . . by way of a word of warning, I never have the faintest taste for joking at any time, and especially not to-day! And what do you know about my temperament? It strikes me that we've not long—that it's the first time we've set eyes on each other.'

'There, there, don't be cross, and don't swear. I'll believe you without that,' said Paklin, and turning to Solomin: 'Oh, you,' he exclaimed, 'you whom the keen-sighted Fimushka herself called a cool man—and there certainly is something refreshing about you—say, had I the slightest intention of doing anything unpleasant to anyone, or of joking unseasonably? I only suggested going with you to Golushkin; and besides, I'm an inoffensive creature. It's not my fault that Mr. Markelov has a bilious complexion.'

Solomin shrugged up first one shoulder, then the other; it was a habit of his when he could not make up his mind at once what to answer.

'There's no mistake,' he said at last, 'you couldn't give offence to anyone, Mr. Paklin, and you don't want to; and why shouldn't you go to Mr. Golushkin's? We shall, I should fancy, spend our time just as pleasantly there as at your cousin's, and just as profitably.'

Paklin shook his finger at him.

'Oh! I see there's malice in you too! But you're going to Golushkin's yourself, aren't you?'

'To be sure, I'm going. To-day's a day lost, anyway.'

'Well, then, *en avant, marchons,* to the twentieth century! to the twentieth century! Nezhdanov, you're an advanced man, lead the way!'

'All right, come along; only, don't repeat the same jokes too often, for fear of our thinking you're running out of your stock.'

'There'll always be plenty at your service,' retorted Paklin gaily, and he hurried, advancing as he said, not by leaps and bounds, but by limps and bounds.

'An amusing chap, very,' Solomin remarked as he walked behind him arm-in-arm with Nezhdanov; 'if—which God forbid—they send us all to Siberia, there'll be someone to amuse us!'

Markelov walked in silence behind the rest.

Meanwhile in the house of the merchant Golushkin every measure was being taken to provide a 'chic' dinner. A fish-soup, very greasy and very disagreeable, was concocted, various *pâtés chauds* and *fricassées* were prepared (Golushkin, as a man on the pinnacle of European culture, though an Old Believer, went in for French cookery, and had taken a cook from a club, where he had been discharged for dirtiness); and, what was most important, several bottles of champagne had been got out and put in ice.

The host himself met the young men with the awkward tricks peculiar to him, a hurried manner and much giggling. He was, as Paklin had predicted, overjoyed to see him; he inquired about him: 'I suppose he's one of us?' and without waiting for an answer, cried, 'There, of course he's bound to be!' Then he told them that he had just come from that 'queer fish' of a governor, who was always worrying him on behalf of some—deuce knows what!—benevolent institution.
. . . And it was absolutely impossible to say whether Golushkin was more pleased at having been received at the governor's, or at having succeeded in abusing him in the

presence of advanced young men. Then he introduced them to the proselyte he had promised. And this proselyte turned out to be none other than the sleek, sickly little man with the foxy face who had come in with a message in the morning, and whom Golushkin addressed as Vasya, his clerk. 'He's not much of a talker,' Golushkin declared, pointing to him with all five fingers at once, 'but devoted heart and soul to our cause.' Vasya confined himself to bowing, blushing, blinking, and smirking so effectually that again it was impossible to say whether he was a vulgar blockhead or a consummate knave and scoundrel.

'But to dinner, gentleman, to dinner.'

After partaking freely of the preliminary appetisers on the sideboard, they sat down to the table. Immediately after the soup, Golushkin ordered up the champagne. In frozen flakes and lumps it dropped from the neck of the bottle into the glasses. 'To our . . . our enterprise!' cried Golushkin, with a wink and a nod in the direction of the servants, as though to give them to understand that in the presence of outsiders they must be on their guard! The proselyte Vasya still continued silent, and though he sat on the extreme edge of his chair and conducted himself in general with a servility utterly out of keeping with the convictions to which, in the words of his patron, he was devoted heart and soul, he drank away at the wine with desperate eagerness! . . . The others, however, talked; that is to say, their host talked—and Paklin; Paklin especially. Nezhdanov was inwardly fretting; Markelov was angry and indignant, just as indignant, though in a different way, as at the Subotchevs'; Solomin was looking on, observant.

Paklin was enjoying himself! With his smart speeches he greatly delighted Golushkin, who had not the faintest suspicion that the 'little lame chap' kept whispering to Nezhdanov, who was sitting beside him, the cruellest remarks at his, Golushkin's, expense He positively imagined that he was something of a simpleton, who might be patronised . . . and that was partly why he liked him. Had Paklin been sitting next him, he would have poked him in the ribs with his finger or slapped him on the shoulder; as it was, he winked at him across the table and nodded his head in his direction . . . but between him and Nezhdanov was seated first Markelov, like a storm-cloud, and then Solomin. However, Golushkin laughed convulsively at every word Paklin uttered, and even laughed on trust in advance, slapping himself on the stomach, and showing his bluish gums. Paklin soon saw what was required of him, and began abusing everything (it was a congenial task for him)—everything and everybody; conservatives, liberals, officials, barristers, judges, landowners, district councils, local assemblies, Moscow and Petersburg!

'Yes, yes, yes, yes,' put in Golushkin; 'to be sure, to be sure! Our mayor here, for instance, is a perfect ass! A hopeless noodle! I tell him one thing and another . . . but he doesn't understand a word; he's just such another as our governor!'

'Is your governor a fool?' inquired Paklin.

'I tell you he's an ass!'

'Have you ever noticed, does he grunt or snuffle?'

'What?' asked Golushkin in some bewilderment.

'Why, don't you know? In Russia our great civilians grunt; and our great army men talk through their noses; and it's only the very highest dignitaries who both grunt and snuffle at once.'

Golushkin roared with laughter till the tears ran down.

'Yes, yes,' he stuttered, 'he snuffles. . . . He's an army man!'

'Ugh, you booby!' Paklin was thinking to himself.

'Everything's rotten with us, go where you will,' bawled Golushkin, a little later. 'Everything's rotten, everything!'

'Most honoured Kapiton Andreitch,' Paklin observed sympathetically—(he had just been whispering to Nezhdanov, 'What makes him keep moving his arms about, as if his coat were too tight in the armholes?')—'Most honoured Kapiton Andreitch, trust me, half-measures are no use now.'

142

'Half-measures!' screamed Golushkin, suddenly ceasing to laugh, and assuming a ferocious expression, 'there's only one thing now: to tear it all up from the roots! Vasya, drink, you dirty dog you, drink!'

'And so I am drinking, Kapiton Andreitch,' responded the clerk, emptying his glass down his throat.

Golushkin, too, tossed off a glassful.

'How is it he doesn't burst?' Paklin whispered to Nezhdanov.

'It's practice does it!' rejoined Nezhdanov.

But the clerk was not the only one who drank. By degrees the wine affected them all. Nezhdanov, Markelov, even Solomin, gradually took part in the conversation.

At first in a sort of disdain, in a sort of vexation with himself for not keeping up his character, for doing nothing, Nezhdanov began to maintain that the time had come to cease to play with mere words, the time had come to 'act'— he even alluded to the 'bed-rock having been reached!' And then, without noticing that he was contradicting himself, he began to ask them to point out what real existing elements they could rely on—to declare that he couldn't see any. No sympathy in society, no understanding in the people.

He got no answer, of course; not because there was no answer to be given, but that everyone was by now talking on his own account. Markelov kept up a monotonous, insistent drone with his dull, angry voice ('for all the world as if he were chopping cabbage,' remarked Paklin). Precisely what he was talking of was not quite clear; the word 'artillery' could be distinguished in a momentary lull . . . he was probably referring to the defects he had discovered in its organisation. Germans and adjutants seemed also to be coming in for their share. Even Solomin observed that there were two ways of waiting: waiting and doing nothing, and waiting while pushing things forward.

'Progressives are no use to us,' said Markelov gloomily.

'Progressives have hitherto worked from above,' observed Solomin; 'we are going to try working from below.'

'No use, go to the devil, no use in it!' Golushkin cut in furiously; 'we must act at once, at once!'

'In fact, you want to jump out of the window?'

'I'll jump out!' clamoured Golushkin. 'I will! and so'll Vasya! If I tell him, he'll jump out! Eh, Vasya? You'd jump, wouldn't you?'

The clerk drank off a glass of champagne.

'Where you lead, Kapiton Andreitch, there I follow. I shouldn't dare think twice about it.'

'You'd better not! I'd twist you into a ram's horn.'

Before long there followed what in the language of drunkards is known as a 'regular Babel'. A mighty clamour and uproar arose.

Like the first flakes of snow, swiftly whirling, crossing and recrossing in the still mild air of autumn, words began flying, tumbling, jostling against one another in the heated atmosphere of Golushkin's dining-room—words of all sorts —progress, government, literature; the taxation question, the church question, the woman question, the law-court question; classicism, realism, nihilism, communism; international, clerical, liberal, capital; administration, organisation, association, and even crystallisation! It was just this uproar which seemed to rouse Golushkin to enthusiasm; the real gist of the matter seemed to consist in this, for him. . . . He was triumphant! 'Here we are! Out of the way or I'll kill you! . . . Kapiton Golushkin's coming!' The clerk Vasya at last reached such a point of tipsiness that he began snorting and talking to his plate, and suddenly shouted like one possessed: 'What the devil's the meaning of a *pro*gymnasium?'

Golushkin all at once got up, and throwing back his crimson face, in which an expression of coarse brutality and swagger was curiously mingled with the expression of another feeling, like a secret misgiving, even trepidation, he bawled, 'I will sacrifice another thousand! Vasya, out with it!' to which Vasya responded in an undertone, 'He's going it!'

Paklin, pale and perspiring (for the last quarter of an hour he had vied with the clerk in drinking), Paklin, jumping up from his place, and lifting both hands high above his head, cried brokenly, 'Sacrifice! he said, sacrifice! Oh, degradation of that sacred word! Sacrifice! No one dares to rise to thee, no one has the strength to fulfil the duties thou enjoinest, at least no one of us here present—and this lout, this vile money-bag, gloats over his swollen gains, scatters a handful of roubles, and shouts of sacrifice! And asks for gratitude; expects a wreath of laurel—the mean scoundrel!' Golushkin either did not hear or did not understand what Paklin said, or possibly took his words for a joke, for he vociferated once more, 'Yes! a thousand roubles! Kapiton Andreitch's word is sacred!' He suddenly thrust his hand into his side-pocket. 'Here it is, here's the cash! There, pocket it, and remember Kapiton!' As soon as he reached a certain pitch of excitement, he used to talk of himself in the third person, like a little child. Nezhdanov picked up the notes flung on the wine-stained cloth. Since there was nothing to stay for after this, and it was now late, they all got up, took their caps, and went away.

In the open air they all felt giddy, especially Paklin.

'Well? where are we going now?' he managed to articulate with some difficulty.

'I don't know where you're going,' answered Solomin; 'I'm going home.'

'To your factory?'

'Yes.'

'Now, in the middle of the night, on foot?'

'What of it? there are neither wolves nor brigands here, and I'm quite well and able to walk. It's cooler walking at night.'

'But, I say, it's three miles!'

'Well, what if it were four? Good-bye, my friends!'

Solomin buttoned up his coat, pulled his cap over his forehead, lighted a cigar, and set off with long strides up the street.

'And where are you going?' said Paklin, turning to Nezhdanov.

'I'm going to his place.' He indicated Markelov, who was standing stock-still, his arms folded across his breast. 'We have horses here and a carriage.'

'Oh, that's capital . . . and I, my dear boy, am going to the oasis, to Fomushka and Fimushka. And do you know what I would say to you, my dear boy? There's madness there and madness here . . . only that madness, the eighteenth-century madness, is closer to the heart of Russia than the twentieth century. Good-bye, gentlemen; I'm drunk, don't be angry with me. Just let me say one thing! There's not a kinder and a better woman on earth than my sister, Snanduliya; and you see what she is—a hunchback, and her name's Snanduliya! That's how it always is in this world! Though it's quite right that should be her name. Do you know who Saint Snanduliya was? A virtuous woman, who visited the prisons and healed the wounds of the prisoners and the sick. Well, good-bye! good-bye, Alexey—man to be pitied! And you call yourself an officer . . . ugh! misanthrope! good-bye!'

He trailed away, limping and swaying from side to side, towards the oasis, while Markelov and Nezhdanov sought out the post station where they had left their coach, ordered the horses to be put to, and half an hour later they were driving along the highroad.

21

THE sky was overcast with low clouds, and although it was not perfectly dark, and in front the cart-ruts could be distinguished standing out on the road, to right and left everything was in shadow, and the outlines of separate objects fell together into big confused patches of darkness. It was a dim, treacherous night; the wind blew in gusty, damp squalls, bringing with it the scent of rain and of broad fields of corn. When they had passed the oak bush which served as a landmark, and had to turn off into the by-road, driving was still more difficult; the narrow track was quite lost at times. . . . The coachman drove more slowly.

'I hope we're not going to lose our way,' observed Nezhdanov, who had been silent till then.

'No; we shan't lose our way!' answered Markelov. 'Two misfortunes don't come in one day.'

'Why, what was the first misfortune?'

'What? Why, we've wasted our day for nothing—don't you reckon that as anything?'

'Yes . . . of course. . . . That awful Golushkin! We oughtn't to have drunk so much wine. My head aches now . . . fearfully.'

'I wasn't speaking of Golushkin; he at any rate gave us some money, so that was at least something gained by our visit!'

'Surely you don't regret Paklin's having taken us to his . . . what was it he called them—poll-parrots?'

'There's nothing to regret in it . . . and there's nothing to rejoice at either. I'm not one of those who take interest in such trifles. . . . I was not referring to that misfortune.'

'What, then?'

Markelov made no reply, he simply turned a little in his corner, as though he were wrapping himself up. Nezhdanov could not quite make out his face; only his moustaches stood out in a black transverse line; but ever since the morning he had been conscious of something in Markelov it was better not to touch upon—some obscure, secret irritation.

'Tell me, Sergei Mihalovitch,' he began after a long pause, 'are you in earnest in admiring Mr. Kislyakov's letters, that you gave me to read this morning? You know—excuse the crudity of the expression—it's all perfect rubbish!'

Markelov drew himself up.

'In the first place,' he began in a wrathful voice, 'I don't at all share your opinion about those letters. I think them very remarkable . . . and conscientious! And secondly, Kislyakov toils and slaves, and, what's more, he *believes*; he believes in our cause, he believes in revolution! I must tell you one thing, Alexey Dmitrievitch, I notice that *you*— you are very luke-warm in our cause; you don't believe in it!'

'What makes you think that?' Nezhdanov articulated slowly.

'What? Why, every word you say, your whole behaviour! To-day at Golushkin's, who was it said he didn't see what elements we could depend on? You! Who asked us to point to any? You! And when that friend of yours, that grinning ape and buffoon, Mr. Paklin, began declaring, with eyes upturned to heaven, that not one of us was capable of sacrifice, who was it backed him up, who was it nodded his head in approval? Wasn't that you? Say what you please of yourself, and think of yourself what you like . . . that's your affair . . . but I know of people who are capable of renouncing everything that makes life sweet, even the bliss of love, to be true to their convictions, not to betray them! Oh, to-day, *you* are not capable of that, of course!'

'To-day? And why to-day?'

'Come, no humbug, for God's sake, you happy Don Juan, you myrtle-crowned lover!' shouted Markelov, totally oblivious of the coachman, who, though he did not turn round on the box, could hear everything perfectly distinctly. It is true the coachman was at that instant far more interested in the road than in any wrangling on the part of the gentlemen sitting behind him, and he cautiously and rather timorously urged on the centre horse, who shook his head and backed, letting the coach slide down a sort of rocky prominence, which certainly ought not to have been there at all.

'Excuse me, I don't quite understand you,' said Nezhdanov.

Markelov gave a forced, vindictive chuckle.

'You don't understand me! Ha! ha! ha! I know all about it, my fine gentleman! I know whom you had a love-scene with yesterday; I know who it is you've fascinated with your good looks and your fine talk; I know who lets you into her room . . . after ten o'clock at night!'

'Master!' the coachman suddenly addressed Markelov, 'take the reins . . . I'll get down and have a look . . . I think we've got off the road. . . . There seems a sort of ravine here, or something. . . .'

The coach was, in fact, all on one side. Markelov clutched the reins handed him by the coachman, and went on as loudly as ever: 'I don't blame you, Alexey Dmitritch! You profited . . . of course. You were right. I only say that I don't wonder at your luke-warmness over our cause; you'd something else, I say again, in your heart. And I say, too, for my own part, what man can guess beforehand what will take girls' hearts, or understand what it is they want! . . .'

'I understand you now,' Nezhdanov began, 'I understand your mortification, guess who has spied on us and lost no time in telling you. . . .'

'It's not merit in this case,' Markelov went on, affecting not to hear Nezhdanov, and intentionally dwelling on and prolonging each word, 'not any extraordinary qualities of mind or body. . . . No! It's simply . . . the cursed luck of all illegitimate children . . . of all . . . bastards!'

The last phrase Markelov uttered abruptly and rapidly, and at once was still as death.

Nezhdanov felt himself grow pale all over in the darkness, and spasms passed over his face. He could scarcely restrain himself from flying at Markelov, seizing him by the throat. . . . 'This insult must be washed out in blood, in blood. . . .'

'I've found the road!' cried the coachman, making his appearance at the right front wheel. 'I made a little mistake, kept too much to the left . . . it's no matter now! We'll be there in no time; there's not a mile before us. Be pleased to sit still!'

He clambered on to the box, took the reins from Markelov, turned the shaft horse's head. . . . The coach, after two violent jolts, rolled along more easily and evenly, the darkness seemed to part and to lift, there was a smell of smoke, in front rose a sort of hillock. Then a light twinkled . . . and vanished. . . . Another glimmered. . . . A dog barked. . . .

'Our huts,' said the coachman; 'ah, get along, my pretty pussies!'

The lights came more and more often to meet them.

'After that insult,' Nezhdanov began at last, 'you will readily understand, Sergei Mihalovitch, that I cannot spend a night under your roof; I am therefore, unpleasant as it is to me, forced to ask you to lend me your coach, when you reach home, so that I may return to the town; to-morrow I will find means of getting home; and then you shall receive from me the communication you doubtless expect.'

Markelov did not at once reply.

'Nezhdanov,' he said all at once in a low, but despairing voice, 'Nezhdanov! For God's sake come into my house, if only to let me beg on my knees for your forgiveness! Nezhdanov! Forget . . . Alexey! forget, forget my senseless words! Oh, if anyone could feel how miserable I am!' Markelov struck himself on the breast with his fist, and it seemed to give forth a hollow groan. 'Alexey! be magnanimous! Give me your hand! . . . Don't refuse to forgive me!'

Nezhdanov held out his hand—irresolutely—still he held it out. Markelov squeezed it so that he almost cried out.

The coachman stopped at the steps of Markelov's house.

'Listen, Alexey,' Markelov was saying to him a quarter of an hour after in his room. . . . 'dear brother,' he kept addressing him by this familiar, endearing term; and in this affectionate familiarity to the man in whom he had discovered a successful rival, to whom he had only just offered a deadly insult, whom he had been ready to kill, to tear to pieces, there was the expression of irrevocable renunciation, and humble, bitter supplication, and a sort of claim too. . . . Nezhdanov recognised this claim by beginning to address Markelov in the same familiar way.

'Listen, Alexey! I said just now I had refused the happiness of love, renounced it so as to be wholly at the service of my convictions. . . . That was nonsense, bragging! I have never been offered anything of that sort, I have had nothing to renounce! I was born without gifts, and so I have remained. . . . And perhaps it was right it should be so. Since I can't attain to that, I have to do something else! Since you can combine both . . . can love and be loved . . . and at the same time serve the cause . . . well, you're a fine fellow! I envy you . . . but it's not so with me. I can't. You are happy! You are happy! I can't.'

Markelov said all this in a subdued voice, sitting on a low chair, his head bent and his arms hanging loose at his sides. Nezhdanov stood before him, plunged in a sort of dreamy attention, and though Markelov called him happy, he neither looked nor felt happy.

'I was deceived in my youth,' . . . Markelov went on; 'she was an exquisite girl, and yet she jilted me . . . and for whom? For a German! for an adjutant! while Marianna——'

He stopped. . . . For the first time he had uttered her name, and it seemed to burn his lips.

151

'Marianna did not deceive me; she told me plainly that she didn't care for me. . . . And how should she care for me? Well, she has given herself to you . . . Well, what of that? was she not free?'

'Oh, stay, stay!' cried Nezhdanov, 'what is it you are saying? Given herself? I don't know what your sister has written to you; but I swear to you——'

'I don't say physically; but morally she has given herself, in heart, in soul,' interposed Markelov, who was obviously comforted for some reason or other by Nezhdanov's exclamation. 'And she has done well. As for my sister . . . Of course she had no intention of wounding. . . . At least, she didn't care about it one way or another; but she must hate you, and Marianna too. She was not lying . . . but there, enough of her!'

'Yes,' thought Nezhdanov to himself: 'she hates us.'

'Everything is for the best,' Markelov continued without changing his position. 'Now the last ways of retreat are cut off for me, now there is nothing to hinder me! Never mind Golushkin's being a blockhead; that's of no consequence. And Kislyakov's letters . . . they're absurd, perhaps . . . but we must look to the principal thing. According to him, everything's ready everywhere. You don't believe that, perhaps?'

Nezhdanov made no answer.

'You are right, perhaps; but you know if we wait for the moment when everything, absolutely everything, is ready, we shall never begin. If one weighs *all* the consequences beforehand, it's certain there will be some evil ones. For instance: when our predecessors organised the emancipation of the peasants, could they foresee that one result of this emancipation would be the rise of a whole class of money-lending landowners, who would lend the peasant a quarter of mouldy rye for six roubles, and extort from him' (here Markelov crooked one finger) 'first the full six roubles in labour, and besides that' (Markelov crooked another finger) 'a whole quarter of good rye, and then' (Markelov crooked a third) 'interest on the top of that?—in fact, they squeeze the peasant to the last drop! Our emancipators couldn't have foreseen that, you must admit! And yet, even if they had foreseen it, they'd have done right to free the peasants, and not to weigh all the consequences! And so, I have made up my mind!'

Nezhdanov looked questioningly, in perplexity, at Markelov; but the latter looked away into the corner. His brows were contracted and hid his eyes; he bit his lips and gnawed his moustache.

'Yes, I have made up my mind!' he repeated, bringing his dark hairy fist down on his knee. 'I'm an obstinate man, you know . . . I'm not half a Little-Russian for nothing.'

Then he got up, and, staggering as though his legs were failing him, he went into his bedroom, and brought out from there a small portrait of Marianna framed under glass.

'Take it,' he said in a mournful but steady voice; 'I did it once. I draw very badly; but look, I think it's like.' (The sketch, a pencil drawing taken in profile, was really like.) 'Take it, brother; it's my last bequest. Together with this portrait I give up to you all my rights . . . I never had any . . . but you know, Alexey, everything! I give you everything, Alexey . . . and her, dear brother; she's a good . . .'

Markelov paused; the heaving of his breast was visible.

'Take it. You're not angry with me, Alexey? Then take it. I have nothing now. . . . I don't want that.' Nezhdanov took the portrait; but a strange sensation oppressed his heart. It seemed to him that he had no right to accept this gift; that if Markelov had known what was in his, Nezhdanov's, heart, he would not, perhaps, have given him the portrait. He held in his hand the little round piece of paper carefully set in its black frame with a mount of gold paper, and he did not know what to do with it. 'Here is a man's whole life in my hand,' was the thought that occurred to him. He realised what a sacrifice Markelov was making, but why, why was it to him? Should he give back the portrait? No!

that would be a still crueller affront. . . . And after all, wasn't that face dear to him? didn't he love her?

Nezhdanov with some inward misgiving turned his eyes upon Markelov . . . wasn't he looking at him, trying to read his thoughts? But Markelov was again staring into the corner and gnawing his moustache.

The old servant came into the room with a candle in his hand.

Markelov started.

'It's time for bed, dear Alexey!' he cried. 'Morning brings better counsel. I will give you horses, you will drive home, and good-bye, brother.

'And good-bye to you, too, old fellow!' he added suddenly, turning to the servant and slapping him on the shoulder. 'Think of me kindly!'

The old man was so astounded that he all but dropped the candle, and his eyes, bent on his master, expressed something other—and more—than his habitual dejection.

Nezhdanov went to his room. He was miserable. His head was still aching from the wine he had drunk, there were noises in his ears, and lights dazzling before his eyes, even though he shut them. Goulshkin, the clerk Vasya, Fomushka, Fimushka, kept revolving before him; in the distance, Marianna's image seemed distrustful, would not come near. Everything he had said or done himself struck him as such lying and affectation, such superfluous and humbugging nonsense . . . and the thing that ought to be done, the aim that ought to be striven for, was not to be found anywhere, unattainable under lock and bar, buried in the bottomless pit. . . .

And he was beset with the unceasing desire to get up, go to Markelov, and say to him, 'Take back your present, take it back!'

'Ugh! what a loathsome thing life is!' he cried at last.

The next morning he went off early. Markelov was already on the steps, surrounded by peasants. Whether he had called them together, or they had come of themselves, Nezhdanov could not make out; Markelov said good-bye to him, very briefly and dryly . . . but he seemed to be about to make some important communication to the peasants. The old servant was hanging about the steps with his unvarying expression.

The coach quickly passed through the town, and moved at a furious pace directly the open country was reached. The horses were the same, but the coachman, either because Nezhdanov was living in a grand house, or for some other reason, was reckoning on something handsome 'for vodka' . . . and we all know that when a coachman has had vodka, or is confidently expecting it, the horses trot their best. It was June weather, though fresh; lofty clouds were gambolling over the sky, there was a strong, steady breeze; the road, after the previous day's rain, was not dusty; the willows rustled, gleamed, and rippled, everything was moving, fluttering; the peewit's cry came whistling from the distant slopes, across the green ravines, just as though the cry had wings and was flying on them; the crows were glossing themselves in the sun; something like black fleas was moving across the straight line of the bare horizon—it was the peasants ploughing their fallow land a second time.

But Nezhdanov let it all pass by unseen; he did not even notice that he was driving into Sipyagin's property; he was overcome by his brooding thoughts.

He started, though, when he saw the roof of the house, the upper storey, Marianna's window. 'Yes,' he said to himself, and there was a glow of warmth in his heart; '*he* was right, she's a good girl, and I love her.'

22

HE hurriedly changed his clothes and went to give Kolya his lesson. Sipyagin, whom he met in the dining-room, bowed to him with chilly politeness, and muttering through his teeth, 'Had a pleasant visit?' went on to his study. The statesman had already decided in his diplomatic mind that directly the vacation was over he would promptly pack this tutor off to Petersburg, as he was 'positively too red', and meanwhile he would keep an eye on him . . . '*Je n'ai pas eu la main heureuse cette fois-ci,*' he thought to himself; however, '*j'aurais pu tomber pire.*' Valentina Mihalovna's sentiments towards Nezhdanov were far more energetic and defined. She could not endure him now. . . . He—this little scrub of a boy!—had affronted her. Marianna had not been mistaken; it was she, Valentina Mihalovna, who had been spying on her and Nezhdanov in the corridor. . . . The distinguished lady was not above such a proceeding. In the course of the two days his absence had lasted, though she had said nothing to her 'thoughtless' niece, she had repeatedly given her to understand that she was aware of everything; that she would have been indignant, had she not been half-contemptuous, half-compassionate. . . . Her face was filled with restrained, inward contempt, her eyebrows were raised with something of irony and, at the same time, of pity whenever she looked at or spoke to Marianna; her superb eyes rested with tender perplexity, with mournful disgust, on the self-willed girl who, after all her 'fancies and eccentricities,' had come to . . . to . . . to kissing . . . in dark rooms . . . with a paltry little undergraduate!

Poor Marianna! Her stern, proud lips knew nothing as yet of any man's kisses.

Valentina Mihalovna had, however, given her husband no hint of the discovery she had made; she contented herself by accompanying a few words addressed to Marianna in his presence by a significant smile, in no way relevant to their apparent meaning. Valentina Mihalovna felt positively rather remorseful for having written the letter to her brother . . . but, all things considered, she preferred to repent and have done it, than be spared her penitence at the price of the letter not having been written.

Of Marianna, Nezhdanov had a glimpse in the dining-room at lunch. He thought her looking thin and yellow; she was not at all pretty that day; but the rapid glance she flung at him the instant he came into the room went straight to his heart. On the other hand, Valentina Mihalovna looked at him as though she were continually repeating inwardly, 'I congratulate you! Well done! Very smart!' and at the same time she wanted to discover from his face whether Markelov had shown him the letter or not. She decided at last that he had shown it.

Sipyagin, hearing that Nezhdanov had been to the factory of which Solomin was the manager, began cross-questioning him about 'that manufacturing enterprise which presents so many striking points of interest'; but being shortly convinced from the young man's answers that he had really seen nothing there, he relapsed into majestic silence, with the air of reproaching himself for having expected any valuable information from such an undeveloped person! As they left the dining-room, Marianna managed to whisper to Nezhdanov, 'Wait for me in the old birch copse, Alexey; I will come directly I can get away.' Nezhdanov thought, 'She, too, calls me Alexey, just as he did.' And how sweet that familiarity was to him, though rather terrible too! and how strange, and how incredible, if she had suddenly begun addressing him as Mr. Nezhdanov again, if she had been more distant to him! He felt that that would be misery to him. Whether he was in love with her he could not be sure yet; but that she was precious to him, and near, and necessary— yes, above all, necessary—that he felt to the very depths of his being.

The copse to which Marianna had sent him consisted of some hundreds of old birch-trees, mostly of the weeping variety. The wind had not dropped; the long bundles of twigs nodded and tossed like loosened tresses in the breeze; the clouds, as before, flew fast and high up in the sky, and when one of them floated across the sun, everything grew—not dark—but of one uniform tint. Then it floated past, and suddenly glaring patches of light were waving everywhere again, in tangled, medley riot, mingled with patches of shade . . . the rustle and movement were the same; but a kind of festive delight was added. With just such joyous violence, passion makes its way into a heart distraught and darkened by trouble. . . . And just such was the heart Nezhdanov carried within his breast.

He leaned against the trunk of a birch-tree, and began waiting. He did not really know what he was feeling, and indeed he did not want to know; he felt at once more disturbed and more light of heart than at Markelov's. He longed before all things to see her, to speak to her; the chain which so suddenly binds two living creatures together had him fast just then. Nezhdanov bethought himself of the rope flung to the quay when the ship is ready to be made fast. . . . Now it is twisted tight about a post, and the ship is at rest.

In harbour! God be thanked!

Suddenly he trembled. There was a glimpse of a woman's dress on the path in the distance. It was she. But whether she was coming towards him, or going away from him, he could not be sure, until he saw that the patches of light and shadow glided *from below upwards* over her figure . . . so she was approaching. They would have moved *from above downwards* if she had been walking away. A few instants more and she was standing near him, before him, with a bright face of greeting, a tender light in her eyes, a faint but gay smile on her lips. He snatched her outstretched hands, but at first could not utter a word; she, too, said nothing. She had walked very quickly and was a little out of breath; but it could be seen she was immensely overjoyed that he was overjoyed to see her.

She was the first to speak.

'Well,' she began, 'tell me quickly what you've decided on!'

Nezhdanov was surprised.

'Decided! . . . why, were we to have decided on anything just now?'

'Oh, you know what I mean! Tell me what you talked about. Whom did you see? Have you made friends with Solomin? Tell me everything, everything! Stay a minute—let's go over there, further. I know a place . . . that's not so visible.'

She drew him after her. He followed her obediently right through the tall, scanty, dry grass.

She led him to the place she meant. There lay a great birch-tree that had fallen in a storm. They sat down on the trunk.

'Come, tell me!' she repeated, but she went on herself at once: 'Ah, how glad I am to see you, dear! I thought these two days would never pass. You know, Alexey, I'm certain now that Valentina Mihalovna overheard us.'

'She wrote to Markelov about it,' said Nezhdanov.

'To Markelov!'

Marianna did not speak for a minute, and gradually crimsoned all over, not from shame, but from another stronger passion.

'Wicked, malicious woman!' she murmured slowly; 'she had no right to do that. . . . Well, never mind! Tell me, tell me everything.'

Nezhdanov began talking. . . . Marianna listened to him with a sort of stony attention, and only interrupted him when she noticed that he was hurrying things over, slurring over incidents. All the details of his visits were not, however, of equal interest to her; she laughed over Fomushka and Fimushka, but they did not interest her. Their life was too remote from her.

'It's just as if you were telling me about Nebuchadnezzar,' was her comment.

But what Markelov said, what Golushkin even thought (though she soon realised what sort of a creature he was), and, above all, what were Solomin's ideas, and what he was like—these were the points she wanted to hear about, and took to heart. 'When? when?'—that was the question that was continually in her head and on her lips when Nezhdanov was talking, while he seemed to avoid everything which could give a positive answer to that question. He began to notice himself that he laid stress precisely on those incidents which were of least interest to Marianna . . . and was constantly returning to them. Humorous descriptions made her impatient; a sceptical or dejected tone wounded her. . . . He had constantly to come to the 'cause', the 'question'. Then on that subject no amount of talk wearied her. Nezhdanov was reminded of a summer he had spent with some old friends in the country before he was a student, when he used to tell stories to the children, and they, too, did not appreciate descriptions nor expressions of personal, individual sensation . . . they, too, had demanded action, facts! Marianna was not a child, but in the directness and simplicity of her feelings she was like one.

Nezhdanov praised Markelov with warmth and sincerity, and spoke with special appreciation of Solomin. Speaking almost in enthusiastic terms about him, he asked himself, what precisely was it gave him such a high opinion of that man? He had uttered nothing specially brilliant; some of his sayings seemed indeed directly opposed to his, Nezhdanov's, convictions. . . . 'He's a well-balanced character,' was his conclusion; 'that's it, businesslike, cool, as Fimushka said, a solid fellow; calm, strong force; he knows what he wants, and has confidence in himself, and arouses confidence in others; there's no excitement . . . and balance! balance! . . . That's the great thing; just what I haven't got.' Nezhdanov was silent, absorbed in reflection. . . . Suddenly he felt a caressing hand on his shoulder.

He raised his head; Marianna was looking at him with anxious, tender eyes.

'My dear! What is it?' she asked.

He took her hand from his shoulder, and for the first time kissed that strong little hand. Marianna gave a slight smile as though wondering how such a polite attention could occur to him. Then she in her turn grew thoughtful.

'Did Markelov show you Valentina Mihalovna's letter?' she asked at last.

'Yes.'

'Well . . . how was he?'

'He? He's the noblest, most unselfish fellow! He . . .' Nezhdanov was on the point of telling Marianna about the portrait—but he checked himself, and only repeated, 'the noblest fellow.'

'Oh, yes, yes!'

Marianna again fell to musing, and suddenly turning round towards Nezhdanov on the trunk which served them both for a seat, she said with vivid interest:

'Well, then, what did you decide?'

Nezhdanov shrugged his shoulders.

'Why, I've told you . . . nothing . . . as yet; we shall have to wait a little longer.'

'Wait longer? . . . What for?'

'Final instructions.' ('Of course that's a fib,' Nezhdanov thought.)

'From whom?'

'From . . . you know . . . Vassily Nikolaevitch. And, oh yes, we must wait too till Ostrodumov comes back.'

Marianna looked inquiringly at Nezhdanov.

'Tell me, did you ever see Vassily Nikolaevitch?'

'I have seen him twice . . . just a glimpse, that was all.'

'What is he? . . . a remarkable man?'

'How shall I tell you? He's the head now, and controls everything. We couldn't do without discipline in our work; obedience is essential.' ('And that's all rot,' was his inward comment.)

'What's he like to look at?'

'Oh, stumpy, heavy, dark. . . . High cheek-bones, like a

Kalmik . . . a coarse face. Only he has very keen, bright eyes.'

'And how does he talk?'

'He does not talk, so much as command.'

'Why was he made head?'

'Oh, he's a man of character. He wouldn't stick at anything. If necessary he'll kill anyone. And so he's feared.'

'And what's Solomin like?' inquired Marianna, after a short pause.

'Solomin's not handsome either; only he has a nice, simple, honest face. You see faces like that among divinity students—the good ones.'

Nezhdanov described Solomin in detail. Marianna gazed a long, long time at Nezhdanov; then she said as though to herself: 'You have a good face too; I think life would be sweet with you, Alexey.'

That saying touched Nezhdanov; he took her hand again, and was lifting it to his lips . . .

'Defer your civilities,' said Marianna smiling—she always smiled when her hand was kissed; 'you don't know; I've a sin to confess to you.'

'What have you done?'

'Why, in your absence I went into your room, and there on your table I saw a manuscript book of verses . . .'—(Nezhdanov started; he remembered that he had forgotten the book and left it on the table in his room)—'and I must confess, I couldn't overcome my curiosity, and I read it. They are your verses, aren't they?'

'Yes; and do you know, Marianna, the best possible proof of how devoted I am to you and how I trust you is that I'm hardly angry with you.'

'Hardly? Then, however little, you are angry? By the way, you call me Marianna—that's right; I can't call you Nezhdanov, I must call you Alexey. And the poem beginning: "My dear one, when I come to die," is that yours too?'

'Yes . . . yes. But please leave off. . . . Don't torment me.'

Marianna shook her head.

'It's very melancholy—that poem. . . . I hope you wrote it before you knew me. But it's real poetry so far as I can judge. It seems to me you might have been an author, only I know *for certain* that you have a better, higher vocation than literature. It was all very well to be busy with that—before, when nothing else was possible.'

Nezhdanov bent a rapid glance upon her.

'You think so? Yes, I agree with you. Better failure in this than success in the other.'

Marianna rose impulsively.

'Yes, my dearest, you are right!' she cried, and her whole face was radiant, glowing with the fire and light of rapture, with the softening of generous emotion: 'you are right, Alexey! But perhaps we shall not fail at once; we shall succeed, you will see—we shall be useful, our life shall not be spent in vain, we will go and live among the people. . . . Do you know any trade? No? well, never mind, we will work, we will devote to them, our brothers, all we know. I will cook, and sew, and wash, if need be. . . . You shall see, you shall see. . . . And there'll be no merit in it—but happiness, happiness. . . .' Marianna broke off; but her eyes—fixed eagerly on the distant horizon, not that which spread out before her, but another unseen, unknown horizon perceived by her—her eyes glowed. . . .

Nezhdanov bent down before her.

'O Marianna!' he whispered, 'I'm not worthy of you!'

She suddenly shook herself.

'It's time to go home, high time!' she said, 'or they'll be looking for us again directly. Though Valentina Mihalovna, I think, has given me up. In her eyes I'm ruined!'

Marianna uttered this word with such a bright and happy face that Nezhdanov could not help smiling too as he looked at her, and repeated, 'Ruined!'

'But she's terribly offended,' Marianna went on, 'that you're not at her feet. But that's all of no consequence, there's something I must talk of. . . . You see, it will be impossible for me to stay here. . . . I shall have to run away.'

163

'Run away?' repeated Nezhdanov.

'Yes, run away. . . . You're not going to stay, are you? We will go together—we must work together. . . . You'll come with me, won't you?'

'To the ends of the earth!' cried Nezhdanov, and there was a sudden ring of emotion and a kind of impetuous gratitude in his voice. 'To the ends of the earth!' At that instant he would certainly have gone with her wherever she wished, without looking back.

Marianna understood him, and gave a short blissful sigh.

'Then take my hand, Alexey, only don't kiss it; and hold it tight, like a comrade, like a friend—there, so!'

They walked together to the house, pensive, blissful; the young grass caressed their feet, the young leaves stirred about them; patches of light and shade flittered swiftly over their garments; and they both smiled at the restless frolic of the light, and the merry bluster of the wind, and the fresh glitter of the leaves, and at their own youth and one another.

PART II

23

DAWN was already beginning in the sky on the night after Golushkin's dinner, when Solomin, after about four miles of brisk walking, knocked at the gate in the high fence surrounding the factory. The watchman let him in at once, and, followed by three sheep-dogs, vigorously wagging their shaggy tails, he led him with respectful solicitude to his little lodge. He was obviously delighted at his chief's successful return home.

'How is it you're here to-night, Vassily Fedotitch? we didn't expect you till to-morrow.'

'Oh, it's all right, Gavrila; it's nice walking at night.' Excellent, though rather exceptional, relations existed between Solomin and his workpeople; they respected him as a superior and behaved with him as an equal, as one of themselves; only in their eyes he was a wonderful scholar! 'What Vassily Fedotitch says,' they used to repeat, 'is always right! for there's no sort of study he hasn't been through, and there isn't an Anglisher he's not a match for!' Some distinguished English manufacturer had once, as a fact, visited the factory; and either because Solomin spoke English to him, or that he really was impressed by his knowledge of his business, he kept clapping him on the shoulder, and laughing, and inviting him to come to Liverpool to see him; and he declared to the workpeople in his broken Russian, 'Oh, she's very good man, yours here! Oh! very good!' at which the workpeople in their turn laughed heartily, but with some pride; feeling, 'So our man's all that! One of us!'

And he really was one of them, and theirs.

Early the next morning Solomin's favourite, Pavel, came into his room; waked him, poured him water to wash with, told him some piece of news, and asked him some question. Then they had some tea together hurriedly, and Solomin, pulling on his greasy, grey working pea-jacket, went into the factory, and his life began to turn round again, like a huge flywheel.

But a fresh break was in store for it.

Five days after Solomin's return to his work, a handsome little phæton, with four splendid horses harnessed abreast, drove into the factory yard, and a groom in pale pea-green livery was conducted by Pavel to the lodge, and solemnly handed Solomin a letter, sealed with an armorial crest, from 'His Excellency Boris Andreevitch Sipyagin'. In this letter, which was redolent, not of scent, oh, no! but of a sort of peculiarly distinguished and disgusting English odour, and was written in the third person, not by a secretary but by his Excellency himself, the enlightened owner of the Arzhano estate first apologised for addressing a person with whom he was not personally acquainted, but of whom he, Sipyagin, had heard such flattering accounts. Then he 'ventured' to invite Mr. Solomin to his country seat, as his advice might be of the utmost service to him, Sipyagin, in an industrial undertaking of some magnitude; and in the hope of Mr. Solomin's kindly consenting to do so, he, Sipyagin, was sending his carriage for him. In case it should be impossible for Mr. Solomin to get away that day, he, Sipyagin, most earnestly begged Mr. Solomin to appoint him any other day convenient to him, and he, Sipyagin, would gladly place the same carriage at his, Mr. Solomin's, disposal. There followed the usual civilities, and at the end of the letter was a postscript in the first person, 'I hope you will not refuse to dine with me *quite simply*—not evening dress'. (The words 'quite simply' were underlined.) Together with this letter the pea-green footman, with a certain show of embarrassment, gave Solomin a simple note, simply stuck up without a seal, from Nezhdanov, which contained only a few words, 'Please come, you are greatly needed here and may be of great service; I need hardly say, not to Mr. Sipyagin.'

On reading Sipyagin's letter, Solomin thought: 'Quite simply! how else should I go? I never had an evening suit in my life. . . . And why the devil should I go trailing out there? . . . it's simple waste of time!' but after a glance at Nezhdanov's note, he scratched his head, and walked to the window, irresolute.

'What answer are you graciously pleased to send?' the pea-green footman questioned sedately.

Solomin stood a moment longer at the window, and at last, shaking back his hair and passing his hand over his forehead, he said, 'I will come. Let me have time to dress.'

The footman with well-bred discretion withdrew, and Solomin sent for Pavel, had some talk with him, ran over once more to the factory, and, putting on a black coat with a very long waist, made him by a provincial tailor, and a rather rusty top-hat, which at once gave a wooden expression to his face, he seated himself in the phæton, then suddenly remembered he had taken no gloves, and called the ubiquitous Pavel, who brought him a pair of white chamois-leather gloves, recently washed, every finger of which had stretched at the tip and looked like a finger-biscuit. Solomin stuffed the gloves into his pocket, and said they could drive on. Then the footman with a sudden, quite unnecessary swiftness leaped on to the box, the well-trained coachman gave a shrill whistle, and the horses went off at a trot.

While they were gradually carrying Solomin to Sipyagin's estate, that statesman was sitting in his drawing-room with a half-cut political pamphlet on his knee, talking about him to his wife. He confided to her that he had really written to him with the object of trying whether he couldn't entice him away from the merchant's factory to his own, as it was in a very bad way indeed, and radical reforms were needed! The idea that Solomin would refuse to come, or even fix another day, Sipyagin could not entertain for an instant; though he had himself offered Solomin a choice of days in his letter.

'But ours are paper-mills, not cotton-spinning, you know,' observed Valentina Mihalovna.

'It's all the same, my love; there's machinery in the one and machinery in the other . . . and he's a mechanician.'

'But perhaps he's a specialist, you know!'

'My love—in the first place, there are no specialists in Russia; and, secondly, I repeat he's a mechanician!'

Valentina Mihalovna smiled.

'Take care, my dear; you've been unlucky once already with young men; mind you don't make a second mistake!'

'You mean Nezhdanov? But I consider I attained my object anyway; he's an excellent teacher for Kolya. And besides, you know, *non bis in idem!* Pardon my pedantry please. . . . That means, facts don't repeat themselves.'

'You think not? But I think everything in the world repeats itself . . . especially what's in the nature of things . . . and especially with young people.'

'*Que voulez-vous dire?*' asked Sipyagin, flinging the pamphlet on the table with a graceful gesture.

'*Ouvrez les yeux, et vous verrez!*' Madame Sipyagin answered him; speaking French, of course, to one another, they said '*vous*'.

'H'm!' commented Sipyagin. 'Are you alluding to the student fellow?'

'To *Monsieur le student*—yes.'

'H'm! has he got . . .' (he moved his hand about his forehead . . .) 'anything afoot here? Eh?'

'Open your eyes!'

'Marianna? Eh?' (The second 'eh?' was decidedly more nasal than the first.)

'Open your eyes, I tell you!'

Sipyagin frowned.

'Well, we will go into all that later on. Just now I only wanted to say one thing. . . . This fellow will probably be rather uncomfortable . . . of course, that's natural enough, he's not used to society. So we shall have to be rather friendly with him . . . so as not to alarm him. I don't mean that for you; you're a perfect treasure, and you can captivate any- one in no time, if you choose to. *J'en sais quelque chose,*

Madame! I mention it in regard to other people; for instance, our friend there.'

He pointed to a fashionable grey hat lying on a whatnot; the hat belonged to Mr. Kallomyetsev, who happened to be at Arzhano early that morning.

'*Il est très cassant,* you know; he has such an intense contempt for the people, a thing of which I deeply disapprove! I've noticed in him, too, for some time past, a certain irritability and quarrelsomeness. . . . Is his little affair in that quarter' (Sipyagin nodded his head in some undefined direction, but his wife understood him) 'not getting on well? Eh?'

'Open your eyes! I tell you again.'

Sipyagin got up.

'Eh?' (This 'eh?' was of an utterly different character, and in a different tone . . . much lower.) 'You don't say so! I may open them too wide; they'd better be careful.'

'That's for you to say; but as to your new young man, if only he comes to-day you needn't worry yourself—every precaution shall be taken.'

And after all, it turned out that no precaution was at all needed. Solomin was not in the least uncomfortable or alarmed. When the servant announced his arrival, Sipyagin at once got up, called out loudly so that it could be heard in the hall, 'Ask him up, of course, ask him up!' went to the drawing-room door and stood right in front of it. Solomin was scarcely through the doorway when Sipyagin, whom he almost knocked up against, held out both hands to him, and, smiling affably and nodding his head, said cordially, 'This is indeed good . . . on your part! . . . how grateful I am!' and led him up to Valentina Mihalovna.

'This is my good wife,' he said, softly pressing his hand against Solomin's back, and, as it were, impelling him towards Valentina Mihalovna; 'here, my dear, is our leading mechanician and manufacturer, Vassily . . . Fedosyevitch Solomin.'

Madame Sipyagin rose and, with a beautiful upward quiver of her exquisite eyelashes, first smiled to him—simply—as to a friend; then held out her little hand, palm uppermost, her elbow pressed against her waist, and her head bent in the direction of her hand . . . in the attitude of a suppliant. Solomin let both husband and wife play off their little tricks upon him, shook hands with both, and took a seat at the first invitation to do so. Sipyagin began to fuss about him: 'Wouldn't he take something?' But Solomin replied that he did not want anything, wasn't in the least fatigued with the journey, and was completely at his disposal.

'You mean I may ask you to visit the factory?' cried Sipyagin, as though quite overcome, and not daring to believe in such condescension on the part of his guest.

'At once,' answered Solomin.

'Ah, how good you are! Shall I order the carriage? or perhaps you would prefer to walk? . . .'

'Why, it's not far from here, I suppose, your factory?'

'Half a mile, not more.'

'Then why order the carriage?'

'Ah, that's delightful, then! Boy, my hat, my stick, at once! And you, little missis, bestir yourself, and have a good dinner ready for us. My hat!'

Sipyagin was far more perturbed than his visitor. Repeating once more, 'But where's my hat?' he, the great dignitary, bustled out of the room like a frolicsome schoolboy. While he was talking to Solomin, Valentina Mihalovna was looking stealthily but intently at this 'new young man'. He was sitting calmly in his easy-chair, with his bare hands (he had not, after all, put on the gloves) lying on his knees, and calmly, though with curiosity, looking about at the furniture and the pictures. 'How is it?' she thought; 'he is a plebeian . . . an unmistakable plebeian . . . but how naturally he behaves!'

Solomin did certainly behave very naturally, and not as some do, who are simple indeed, but with a sort of intensity, as though to say, 'Look at me, understand what sort of a man I am,' but like a man whose feelings and ideas are strong without being complex. Madam Sipyagin wanted to enter into conversation with him, but, to her amazement, could not at once find anything suitable to say.

'Good heavens!' she thought, 'can I be impressed by this workman?'

'Boris Andreitch ought to be very grateful to you,' she said at last, 'for consenting to devote part of your valuable time to him. . . .'

'It's not so valuable as all that, madam,' answered Solomin; 'and I'm not come to you for very long.'

'*Voilà où l'ours a montré so patte*,' she thought in French, but at that instant her husband appeared in the open doorway, with his hat on and his stick in his hand.

Turning half round, he cried with a free and easy air: 'Vassily Fedosyevitch! Ready to start?'

Solomin got up, bowed to Valentina Mihalovna, and walked out behind Sipyagin.

'Follow me, this way, this way, Vassily Fedosyevitch!' Sipyagin called, just as though he were going through a forest and Solomin needed a guide. 'This way! there are steps here, Vassily Fedosyevitch.'

'When you are pleased to call me by my father's name,' Solomin observed deliberately, . . . 'I'm not Fedosyevitch, but Fedotitch.'

Sipyagin looked back at him over his shoulder, almost in affright.

'Ah! I beg your pardon, indeed, Vassily Fedotitch.'

'Not at all; no occasion.'

They went into the courtyard. They happened to meet Kallomyetsev.

'Where are you off to?' he inquired, looking askance at Solomin; 'to the factory? *C'est là l'individu en question?*'

Sipyagin opened his eyes wide and slightly shook his head by way of warning.

'Yes, to the factory . . . to show my sins and transgressions to this gentleman—the mechanician. Let me introduce you: Mr. Kallomyetsev, our neighbour here; Mr. Solomin. . . .

Kallomyetsev nodded his head twice, hardly perceptibly,

not at all in Solomin's direction, without looking at him. But
he looked at Kallomyetsev, and there was a gleam of something in his half-closed eyes.

'May I join you?' asked Kallomyetsev. 'You know I like
instruction.'

'Of course you may.'

They went out of the courtyard into the road, and had
not gone twenty steps when they saw the parish priest in a
cassock, hitched up into the belt, making his way home to the
so-called 'pope's quarter'. Kallomyetsev promptly left his
two companions, and with long, resolute strides approached
the priest, who was not at all expecting this and was rather
disconcerted, asked his blessing, deposited a sounding kiss on
his moist red hand, and, turning to Solomin, flung him a
challenging glance. He obviously knew 'a fact or two' about
him, and wanted to show off and to display his contempt for
this learned rascal.

'*C'est une manifestation, mon cher?*' Sipyagin muttered
through his teeth.

Kallomyetsev gave a snort.

'*Oui, mon cher, une manifestation nécessaire par le temps
qui court!*'

They went into the factory. They were met by a Little
Russian with an immense beard and false teeth, who had
succeeded the former superintendent, the German, when Sipyagin finally dismissed him. This Little Russian was a temporary substitute; he obviously knew nothing of the business,
and could do nothing but sigh and incessantly repeat 'Maybe'
. . . and 'Just so'.

The inspection of the establishment began. Some of the
factory hands knew Solomin by sight and bowed to him . . .
and to one of them he even said, 'Hullo, Grigory! you here?'
He soon saw that the business was badly managed. Money
had been laid out profusely but injudiciously. The machines
turned out to be of poor quality; many were unnecessary and
useless; many that were needed were lacking. Sipyagin kept
constantly looking at Solomin's face to guess his opinion, put

some timid questions, wished to know if he were pleased, at any rate, with the system.

'The system's all right,' answered Solomin, 'but can it give any return? I doubt it.'

Not Sipyagin only, but even Kallomyetsev, felt that Solomin was, as it were, at home in the factory, that everything in it was thoroughly familiar to him and understood to the smallest detail—that here he was master. He laid his hand on a machine as a driver lays his hand on a horse's neck; he poked his fingers into a wheel and it stopped moving or began going round; he scooped up in his hand out of the vat a little of the pulp of which the paper was made, and at once it revealed all its defects. Solomin said little, and did not even look at the Little Russian at all; in silence, too, he walked out of the factory. Sipyagin and Kallomyetsev followed him.

Sipyagin did not tell anyone to accompany him . . . he positively stamped and gnashed his teeth. He was very much disturbed.

'I see by your face,' he said, addressing Solomin, 'that you're not pleased with my factory, and I know myself that it's in an unsatisfactory state and unprofitable; however, . . . please don't scruple to speak out . . . what are really it's most important shortcomings? And what is to be done to improve it?'

'Paper-making's not in my line,' answered Solomin, 'but one thing I can tell you—industrial undertakings aren't the thing for gentlemen.'

'You regard such pursuits as degrading for gentlemen?' interposed Kallomyetsev.

Solomin smiled his broad smile.

'Oh, no! What an idea! What is there degrading about it? And even if there were, the gentry aren't squeamish as to that, you know.'

'Eh? What's that?'

'I only meant,' Solomin resumed tranquilly, 'that gentlemen aren't used to that sort of business. Commercial foresight is needed for that; everything has to be put on a different footing; you need training for it. The gentry don't understand that. We see them right and left founding cloth factories, wool factories, and all sorts, but in the long run all these factories fall into the hands of merchants. It's a pity, for the merchant's just as much of a blood-sucker; but there's no help for it.'

'To listen to you,' cried Kallomyetsev, 'one would suppose financial questions were beyond our nobility!'

'Oh, quite the contrary! the gentry are first-rate hands at that. For getting concessions for railroads, founding banks, begging some tax-exemption for themselves, or anything of that sort, none are a match for the gentry. They accumulate great capital. I hinted at that just now, when you were pleased to take offence at it. But I was thinking of regular industrial enterprises. I say *regular*, because founding private taverns and petty truck-shops and lending the peasants wheat or money at a hundred and a hundred and fifty per cent, as so many of our landowning gentry are doing now—operations like that I can't regard as genuine commercial business.'

Kallomyetsev made no reply. He belonged to just that new species of money-lending landowner whom Markelov had referred to in his last talk with Nezhdanov, and he was the more inhuman in his extortions in that he never had any personal dealing with the peasants; he did not admit them into his perfumed European study, but did business with them through an agent. As he listened to Solomin's deliberate, as it were, impartial speech, he was raging inwardly . . . but he was silent this time, and only the working of the muscles of his face betrayed what was passing within him.

'But, Vassily Fedotitch, allow me—allow me,' began Sipyagin. 'All that you are expressing was a perfectly just criticism in former days, when the nobility enjoyed . . . totally different privileges, and were altogether in another position. But nowadays, after all the beneficial reforms . . . in our industrial age, why cannot the nobility turn their energies and abilities into such enterprises? Why should they be unable to understand what is understood by the simple, often unlettered, merchant? They don't suffer from lack of education, and one may even claim with confidence that they are in some sense the representatives of enlightenment and progress.'

Boris Andreevitch spoke very well; his fluency would have had great effect in Petersburg—in his department—or even in higher quarters, but on Solomin it produced no impression whatever.

'The gentry cannot manage these things,' he repeated.

'And why not? why?' Kallomyetsev almost shouted.

'Because they will always remain mere officials.'

'Officials?' Kallomyetsev laughed malignantly. 'You don't quite realise what you are saying, I fancy, Mr. Solomin.' Solomin still smiled as before.

'What makes you fancy that, Mr. Kolomentsev?' (Kallomyetsev positively shuddered at such a 'mutilation' of his surname.) 'No, I always fully realise what I am saying.'

'Then explain what you meant by your last expression.'

'Certainly; in my idea, every official is an outsider, and has always been so, and the gentry have now *become* outsiders.'

Kallomyetsev laughed still more.

'I beg your pardon, my dear sir; that I can't make head or tail of!'

'So much the worse for you. Make a great effort . . . perhaps you will understand it.'

'Sir!'

'Gentlemen, gentlemen,' Sipyagin interposed hurriedly with an air of searching earnestly about him for someone. 'If you please, if you please . . . *Kallomyetsev, je vous prie de vous calmer.* And dinner will be ready soon, to be sure. Pray, gentlemen, follow me!'

'Valentina Mihalovna!' whined Kallomyetsev, running into her boudoir five minutes later, 'it's really beyond everything what your husband is doing! One Nihilist installed here among you already, and now he's bringing in another! And this one's the worst!'

'How so?'

'Upon my word, he's advocating the deuce knows what;

and besides—observe one thing: he has been talking to your husband for a whole hour, and *never once, not once,* did he say, Your Excellency! *Le vagabond!*'

24

BEFORE dinner Sipyagin called his wife aside into the library. He wanted to have a talk with her alone. He seemed worried. He told her that the factory was distinctly coming to grief, that this man Solomin struck him as a very capable fellow, though a trifle . . . abrupt, and that they must continue to be *aux petits soins* with him. 'Ah! if we could only persuade him to come, what a good thing it would be!' he repeated twice. Sipyagin was much irritated at Kallomyetsev's presence. . . . 'The devil brought him! He sees Nihilists on every side, and thinks of nothing but suppressing them. He's welcome to suppress them at home. He positively can't hold his tongue!'

Valentina Mihalovna observed that she would be delighted to be *aux petits soins* with this new guest, only he seemed not to care for these *petits soins* and not to notice them; not that he was rude, but very cool in a sort of way, which was extremely remarkable in a man *du commun.*

'Never mind . . . do your best!' Sipyagin besought her. Valentina Mihalovna promised to do her best, and she did do her best. She began by talking *en tête-à-tête* to Kallomyetsev. There is no knowing what she said to him, but he came to table with the air of a man who has 'undertaken' to be discreet and submissive whatever he may have to listen to. This opportune 'resignation' gave his whole bearing a shade of slight melancholy; but what dignity . . . oh! what dignity there was in every one of his movements! Valentina Mihalovna introduced Solomin to all the family circle (he

178

looked at Marianna with most attention), and made him sit beside her, on her right hand, at dinner. Kallomyetsev was seated on her left. As he unfolded his napkin, he pursed up his face with a smile that seemed to say, 'Come, now, let us go through our little farce!' Sipyagin sat facing him, and with some anxiety kept an eye on him. By Madame Sipyagin's rearrangement of the seats at table, Nezhdanov was placed not beside Marianna, but between Anna Zaharovna and Sipyagin. Marianna found her card (for the dinner was a ceremonious affair) on the dinner-napkin between Kallomyetsev and Kolya. The dinner was served in great style; there was even a *menu*— a decorated card lay beside each knife and fork. Immediately after the soup, Sipyagin turned the conversation again on his factory, and on manufacturing industry in Russia generally; Solomin, after his habit, answered very briefly. As soon as he began to speak, Marianna's eyes were fastened upon him. Kallomyetsev, as he sat beside her, had begun by addressing various compliments to her (seeing that he had been specially begged 'not to provoke an argument'), but she was not listening to him; and indeed he uttered these civilities in a half-hearted fashion to satisfy his conscience: he realised that there was some barrier between the young girl and him that he could not get over.

As for Nezhdanov, something still worse had come into existence between him and the head of the house. . . . For Sipyagin, Nezhdanov had become simply a piece of furniture, or an empty space, which he utterly—it seemed utterly—failed to remark! These new relations had taken shape so quickly and unmistakably, that when Nezhdanov during dinner uttered a few words in reply to an observation of his neighbour, Anna Zaharovna, Sipyagin looked round wonder-ingly as though asking himself, 'Where does that sound come from?'

Obviously Sipyagin possessed some of the characteristics that distinguish Russians of the very highest position.

After the fish, Valentina Mihalovna—who for her part had been lavishing all her arts and graces on her right, that is, on Solomin—remarked in English to her husband across the table that 'our guest drinks no wine, perhaps he would like beer. . . .' Sipyagin called loudly for 'ale', while Solomin turning quietly to Valentina Mihalovna said, 'You don't know, madam, I expect, that I spent over two years in England, and can understand and speak English; I tell you this in case you might want to speak of something private before me.' Valentina Mihalovna laughed and began to assure him this precaution was quite unnecessary, since he would hear nothing but good of himself; inwardly she thought Solomin's action rather queer, but delicate in its own way.

At this point Kallomyetsev broke out at last.

'So you have been in England,' he began, 'and probably you studied the manners and customs there. Allow me to inquire, did you think they were worth imitating?'

'Some, yes; some, no.'

'That's short, and not clear,' observed Kallomyetsev, trying not to notice the signs Sipyagin was making to him. 'But you were speaking this morning about the nobles. . . . You have doubtless had an opportunity of studying what's called in England the *landed gentry* on the spot?'

'No; I had no such opportunity: I moved in a totally different sphere, but I formed a notion of these gentlemen for myself.'

'Well, do you imagine that such a *landed gentry* is impossible among us, and that in any case we ought not to wish for it?'

'In the first place, I certainly do imagine it to be impossible, and, secondly, I think it's not worth while wishing for it either.'

'Why so, my dear sir?' said Kallomyetsev. The last three words were by way of soothing Sipyagin, who was very uneasy and could not sit still in his chair.

'Because in twenty or thirty years your *landed gentry* will cease to exist anyway.'

'But, really, why so, my dear sir?'

'Because by that time the land will have come into the

hands of owners, without distinction of rank.'

'Merchants?'

'Probably merchants; mostly.'

'How will that be?'

'Why, by their buying it—the land, I mean.'

'Of the nobles?'

'Yes, the nobles.'

Kallomyetsev gave a condescending smirk. 'You said the very same thing before, I remember, of mills and factories, and now you say it of the whole of the land.'

'Yes, I say the same now of the whole of the land.'

'And you will be very glad of it, I suppose?'

'Not at all, as I have explained to you already; the people will be no better off for it.'

Kallomyetsev faintly raised one hand. 'What solicitude for the people's welfare, only fancy!'

'Vassily Fedotitch!' cried Sipyagin at the top of his voice. 'They have brought you some beer! *Voyons, Siméon!*' he added in an undertone.

But Kallomyetsev would not be quiet.

'You have not, I see,' he began again, addressing Solomin, 'an over-flattering opinion of the merchants; but they belong by extraction to the people, don't they?'

'And so?'

'I supposed that everything relating to the people or derived from the people would be good in your eyes.'

'Oh, no, sir! You were mistaken in supposing that. Our people are open to reproach in many ways, though they're not always in the wrong. The merchant among us so far is a brigand; he uses his own private property for brigandage. . . . What's he to do? He's exploited and he exploits. As for the people——'

'The people?' queried Kallomyetsev in high falsetto.

'The people . . . are asleep.'

'And you would wake them?'

'That wouldn't be amiss.'

'Aha! aha! so that's what——'

'Excuse me, excuse me,' Sipyagin pronounced imperiously. He realised that the instant had come to draw the line, so to speak . . . to close the discussion. And he drew the line! He closed the discussion! With a wave of his right hand from the wrist, while his elbow remained propped on the table, he delivered a long and detailed speech. On one side he commended the conservatives, on the other approved of the liberals, awarding some preference to the latter, reckoning himself among their number; he extolled the people, but referred to some of their weak points; expressed complete confidence in the government, but asked himself whether *all* subordinate officials were fully carrying out its benevolent designs. He recognised the service and the dignity of literature, but declared that without the utmost caution it was inadmissible! He looked towards the east; first rejoiced, then was dubious: looked towards the west; first was apathetic, then suddenly waked up! Finally, he proposed a toast in honour of the trinity: 'Religion, Agriculture, and Industry!'

'Under the ægis of power!' Kallomyetsev added severely.

'Under the ægis of wise and indulgent authority,' Sipyagin amended.

The toast was drunk in silence. The empty space to the left of Sipyagin, known as Nezhdanov, did, it is true, give vent to some sound of disapprobation, but, evoking no notice, it relapsed into silence; and the dinner reached a satisfactory conclusion, undisturbed by any controversy.

Valentina Mihalovna, with the most charming smile, handed Solomin a cup of coffee; he drank it, and was already looking for his hat . . . but, softly taken by the arm by Sipyagin, was promptly drawn away into his study, and received first a most excellent cigar, and then a proposal that he should enter his, Sipyagin's, factory, on the most advantageous terms! 'You shall be absolute master, Vassily Fedotitch, absolute master!' The cigar Solomin accepted; the proposal he refused. He positively stuck to his refusal, however much Sipyagin insisted.

'Don't say "No" straight off, dear Vassily Fedotitch. Say at least that you'll think it over till to-morrow'

'But that would make no difference. I can't accept your offer.'

'Till to-morrow! Vassily Fedotitch! what harm will it do to defer your decision?'

Solomin admitted that it would certainly do him no harm . . . he left the study, however, and again went in search of his hat. But Nezhdanov, who had not till that instant succeeded in exchanging a single word with him, drew near and hurriedly whispered: 'For mercy's sake, don't go away, or it will be impossible for us to have a talk.'

Solomin left his hat alone, the more readily as Sipyagin, observing his irresolute movements up and down the drawing-room, cried, 'You'll stay the night with us, of course?'

'I am at your disposal,' answered Solomin.

The grateful glance flung at him by Marianna—she was standing at the drawing-room window—set him musing.

25

MARIANNA had pictured Solomin to herself as utterly different, before his visit. At first sight he had struck her as somehow undefined, lacking in individuality. . . . She had seen plenty of fair-haired, sinewy, thin men like that, she told herself! But the more she watched him, the more she listened to what he said, the stronger grew her feeling of confidence in him—confidence was just what it was.

This calm, heavy, not to say clumsy man was not only incapable of lying or bragging; one might rely on him, like a stone wall. . . . He would not betray one; more than that, he would understand one and support one. Marianna even fancied that this was not only her feeling—that Solomin was producing the same effect on everyone present. To what he said she attached no special significance; all this talk of merchants and factories had little interest for her; but the way he talked, the way he looked and smiled as he talked, she liked immensely. . . .

A truthful man . . . that was the great thing! that was what touched her. It is a well-known fact, though by no means easy to understand, that Russians are the greatest liars on the face of the earth, and yet there is nothing they respect like truth—nothing attracts them so much. Besides, Solomin was of a quite especial stamp, in Marianna's eyes; on him rested the halo of a man recommended by Vassily Nikolaevitch himself to his followers. During dinner Marianna had several times exchanged glances with Nezhdanov in reference to him, and in the end she suddenly caught herself in an involuntary comparison of the two men, and not to Nezhdanov's advantage. Nezhdanov's features were undoubtedly far handsomer and more pleasing than Solomin's; but his face expressed a medley of distracting emotions; vexation, embarrassment, impatience . . . even despondency; he seemed sitting on thorns, tried to speak, and broke off, laughing nervously. . . . Solomin, on the other hand, produced the impression of being, very likely, a little bored, but, anyway, quite at home; and of being, in what he did or felt, at all times utterly independent of what other people might do or feel. 'Decidedly, we must ask advice of this man,' was Marianna's thought; 'he will be sure to give us some good advice.' It was she who had sent Nezhdanov to him after dinner.

The evening passed rather drearily; luckily dinner was not over till late, and there was not much time to get through before night. Kallomyetsev was politely sulky and said nothing.

'What's the matter?' Madame Sipyagin asked him half-jeeringly. 'Have you lost something?'

'That's just it,' answered Kallomyetsev. 'They tell a story

of one of our commanders of the guards that he used to complain that his soldiers had lost their socks. "Find me that
sock!" And I say, find me the word "sir"! That word "sir"
has gone astray, and all proper respect and reverence for rank
have gone with it!'

Madame Sipyagin declared to Kallomyetsev that she was
not prepared to assist him in his quest of it.

Emboldened by the success of his 'speech' at dinner,
Sipyagin delivered a couple of other harangues, letting drop
as he did so a few statesmanlike reflections on indispensable
measures; he dropped also a few sayings—*des mots*—more
weighty than witty, he had specially prepared for Petersburg.
One of these sayings he even said over twice, prefixing the
phrase, 'if I may be permitted so to express myself'. It was
a criticism of one of the ministers of the day, of whom he said
that he had a fickle and frivolous intellect, bent on visionary
aims. On the other hand Sipyagin, not forgetting that he
had to deal with a Russian—one of the people—did not fail
to knock off a few sayings intended to prove that he was himself, not merely Russian in blood, but a real Russian bear,
every inch of him, and in close touch with the very inmost
essence of the national life! Thus, for example, upon
Kallomyetsev observing that the rain might delay getting in
the hay, he promptly rejoined, 'Let the hay be black, for then
the buckwheat'll be white'; he used proverbial terms such as,
'A store masterless is a child fatherless'; 'Try on ten times,
for once you cut out'; 'Where there is corn, you can always
find a bushel'; 'If the leaves on the birch are big as farthings
by St. Yegor's day, there'll be corn in the barn by the feast of
Our Lady of Kazan'. It must be admitted that he sometimes
got them wrong, and would say, for instance, 'Let the
carpenter stick to his last!' or 'Fine houses make full bellies!'
But the society in which these mishaps befell did not for the
most part even suspect that *'notre bon Russe'* had blundered;
and indeed, thanks to Prince Kovrizhkin, it is pretty well
inured to such Russian malapropisms. And all these saws and
sayings Sipyagin would enunciate in a peculiar hale and

185

hearty, almost thick, voice, *'d'une voix rustique'*. Such idioms, dropped in due place and season at Petersburg, set influential ladies of the highest position exclaiming, *'Comme il connaît bien les mœurs de notre peuple!'* While equally influential dignitaries of equally high position would add, *'Les mœurs et les besoins!'*

Valentina Mihalovna did her very best with Solomin; but the obvious failure of her efforts disheartened her; and as she passed Kallomyetsev she could not resist murmuring in an undertone, *'Mon Dieu, que je me sens fatiguée!'*

To which the latter responded, with an ironical bow, *'Tu l'as voulu, Georges Dandin!'*

At last, after the usual flicker-up of politeness and affability, displayed on all the faces of a bored assembly at the moment of breaking up, after abrupt handshaking, smiles and amiable simpers, the weary guests and weary hosts separated.

Solomin, who was conducted to almost the best bedchamber on the second floor, with English toilet accessories and a bathroom attached, made his way to Nezhdanov.

The latter began by thanking him warmly for consenting to stay the night.

'I know . . . it's a sacrifice for you. . . .'

'Oh, nonsense!' Solomin responded in his deliberate tones; 'much of a sacrifice! Besides, I can't say no to you.'

'Why so?'

'Oh, because I like you.'

Nezhdanov was delighted and astounded, while Solomin pressed his hand. Then he seated himself astride on a chair, lighted a cigar, and, with both elbows on the chair-back, he observed, 'Come, tell me what's the matter.'

Nezhdanov, too, seated himself astride on a chair facing Solomin, but he did not light a cigar.

'What's the matter, you ask? . . . The matter is that I want to run away from here.'

'That is, you want to leave this house? Well, what of it? Good luck to you!'

'Not to leave . . . but to run away.'

'Why? do they detain you? You . . . perhaps you've received some salary in advance? If so, you need only say the word. . . . I should be delighted.'

'You don't understand me, my dear Solomin. . . . I said, run away—not leave—because I'm not going away from here alone.'

Solomin raised his head.

'With whom?'

'With that girl you saw here to-day. . . .'

'That girl! She has a nice face. You love one another, eh? . . . Or is it simply, you have made up your minds to go away together from a house where you are both unhappy?'

'We love one another.'

'Ah!' Solomin was silent for a while. 'Is she a relation of the people here?'

'Yes. But she fully shares our convictions, and is ready to go forward.'

Solomin smiled.

'And are you ready, Nezhdanov?'

Nezhdanov frowned slightly.

'Why that question? I will prove my readiness in action.'

'I have no doubts of you, Nezhdanov. I only asked because I imagine there is no one ready besides you.'

'What of Markelov?'

'Yes, to be sure, there is Markelov; but he, I expect, was born ready.'

At that instant someone gave a light, rapid tap at the door, and, without waiting for an answer, opened it. It was Marianna. She went up at once to Solomin.

'I am sure,' she began, 'you will not be surprised at seeing me here at such an hour. . . . He' (Marianna indicated Nezhdanov) 'has told you everything, of course. Give me your hand, and, believe me, it is an honest girl standing before you.'

'Yes, I know that,' Solomin responded seriously. He had risen from his seat when Marianna appeared. 'I was looking

187

at you at dinner-time and thinking, "What honest eyes that young lady has!" Nezhdanov has been telling me, certainly, of your plan. But why do you mean to run away, exactly?'

'Why? The cause I have at heart . . . don't be surprised; Nezhdanov has kept nothing from me . . . that work is bound to begin in a few days . . . and am I to remain in this aristocratic house, where everything is deceit and lying? People I love will be exposed to danger, and am I——'

Solomin stopped her by a motion of his hand.

'Don't upset yourself. Sit down, and I'll sit down. You sit down, too, Nezhdanov. Let me tell you, if you have no other reason, then there's no need for you to run away from here as yet. That work isn't going to begin as soon as you suppose. A little more prudent consideration is needed in that matter. It's no good blundering forward at random. Believe me.'

Marianna sat down and wrapped herself up in a big plaid, which she flung over her shoulders.

'But I can't stay here any longer. I'm insulted by everyone here. Only to-day that imbecile, Anna Zaharovna, said before Kolya, alluding to my father, that the apple never falls far from the apple-tree. Kolya even was surprised, and asked what that meant. Not to speak of Valentina Mihalovna!'

Solomin stopped her again, and this time with a smile. Marianna realised that he was laughing at her a little, but his smile could never have offended anyone.

'What do you mean, dear lady? I don't know who that Anna Zaharovna may be, nor what apple-tree you are talking about . . . but come, now; some fool of a woman says something foolish to you, and can't you put up with it? How are you going to get through life? The whole world rests on fools. No, that's not a reason. Is there anything else?'

'I am convinced,' Nezhdanov interposed in a thick voice, 'that Mr. Sipyagin will turn me out of the house of himself in a day or two. He has certainly been told tales. He treats me . . . in the most contemptuous fashion.'

Solomin turned to Nezhdanov.

'Then what would you run away for, if you'll be turned away in any case?'

Nezhdanov did not at once find a reply.

'I was telling you before——' he began.

'He used that expression,' put in Marianna, 'because I am going with him.'

Solomin looked at her, and shook his head good-humouredly.

'Yes, yes, my dear young lady; but I tell you again, if you are meaning to leave this house just because you suppose the revolution is going to break out directly——'

'That's what we wrote for you to come for,' Marianna interrupted, 'to find out for certain what position things are in.'

'In that case,' pursued Solomin, 'I repeat, you can stop at home—a good bit longer. If you mean to run away because you love each other and you can't be united otherwise, then——'

'Well, what then?'

'Then it only remains for me to wish you, as the old-fashioned saying is, love and good counsel, and, if need be and can be, to give you any help in my power. Because, my dear young lady, you, and him too, I've loved from first sight as if you were my own brother and sister.'

Marianna and Nezhdanov both went up to him on the right and the left, and each clasped one of his hands.

'Only tell us what to do,' said Marianna. 'Supposing the revolution is still far off . . . there are preparatory steps to be taken, work to be done, impossible in this house, in these surroundings, to which we should go so eagerly together . . . you point them out to us, you only tell us where we are to go. . . . Send us! You will send us, won't you?'

'Where?'

'To the peasants. . . . Where should we go, if not to the people?'

'Into the forest,' thought Nezhdanov. . . . Paklin's saying recurred to his mind. Solomin looked intently at Marianna.

'You want to get to know the people?'

'Yes; that is, we don't only want to get to know the people, but to influence . . . to work for them.'

'Very good; I promise you, you shall get to know them. I will give you a chance of influencing them and working for them. And you, Nezhdanov, are ready to go . . . for her . . . and for them?'

'Of course I am ready,' he declared hurriedly. 'Juggernaut,' another saying of Paklin's, recurred to him; 'here it comes rolling along, the huge chariot . . . and I hear the crash and rumble of its wheels. . . .'

'Very good,' Solomin repeated thoughtfully. 'But when do you intend to run away?'

'Why not to-morrow?' cried Marianna.

'Very good—but where?'

'Sh . . . gently . . .' whispered Nezhdanov. 'Someone is coming along the corridor.'

They were all silent for a space.

'Where do you intend to go?' Solomin asked again, dropping his voice.

'We don't know,' answered Marianna.

Solomin turned his eyes upon Nezhdanov. The latter merely shook his head negatively.

Solomin stretched out his hand and carefully snuffed the candle.

'I tell you what, my children,' he said at last, 'come to my factory. It's nasty there . . . but very safe. I will hide you. I have a little room there. No one will find you out. You need only get there . . . and we won't give you up. You will say, "There are a lot of people at the factory." That's a very good thing. Where there are a lot of people it's easy to hide. Will that do, eh?'

'We can only thank you,' said Nezhdanov; while Marianna who had at first been taken aback by the idea of the factory, added quickly: 'Of course, of course. How good you are!

But you won't leave us there long, I suppose? You will send us on?'

'That will depend on you. . . . But in case you meant to get married, it would be very convenient for you at the factory. Close by I've a neighbour there—he's a cousin of mine—a parish priest, by name Zosim, very amenable. He would marry you with all the pleasure in life.'

Marianna smiled to herself, while Nezhdanov once more pressed Solomin's hand, and after a moment's pause inquired, 'But, I say, won't your employer, the owner of the factory, have anything to say about it? Won't he make it unpleasant for you?'

Solomin looked askance at Nezhdanov.

'Don't worry about me. . . . That's quite a waste of time. As long as the factory goes all right, it's all one to my employer. Neither you nor your dear young lady have any unpleasantness to fear from him. And the workmen will be no danger to you. Only let me know beforehand: about what time am I to expect you?'

Nezhdanov and Marianna looked at one another.

'The day after to-morrow, early in the morning, or the day after that,' Nezhdanov said at last. 'We can't put it off any longer. It's as likely as not they'll turn me out of the house to-morrow.'

'All right . . .' assented Solomin, and he got up from his chair. 'I will look out for you every morning. And, indeed, I shan't be away from home all the week. Every step shall be taken in due course.'

Marianna drew near him (she was on her way to the door). 'Good-bye, dear, kind Vassily Fedotitch . . . that is your name, isn't it?'

'Yes.'

'Good-bye . . . at least, till we meet, and thanks—thank you!'

'Good-bye. . . . Good-night, dear child.'

'And good-bye, Nezhdanov, till to-morrow . . .' she added.

Marianna went out quickly.

Both the young men remained for some time without moving, and both were silent.

'Nezhdanov . . .' Solomin began at last, and he broke off. 'Nezhdanov,' he began again, 'tell me about this girl . . . what you can tell me. What has her life been up till now? . . . Who is she? . . . and how does she come to be here?'

Nezhdanov told Solomin briefly what he knew.

'Nezhdanov,' he began again at last . . . 'you ought to take care of that girl; for . . . if anything . . . were to happen . . . you would be very much to blame. Good-bye.'

He went away, and Nezhdanov stood still for a while in the middle of the room; then muttering, 'Ah! it's better not to think,' he flung himself face downwards on the bed.

When Marianna got back to her room, she found on the table a small note, which ran as follows: 'I am sorry for you. You are going to your ruin. Think what you are doing. Into what abyss are you flinging yourself with your eyes shut? —for whom, and for what?—V.'

There was a peculiar delicate fresh scent in the room; it was clear that Valentina Mihalovna had only just gone out of it. Marianna took a pen, and, writing underneath, 'Don't pity me. God knows which of us two is most in need of pity. I only know I would not be in your place.—M.,' she left the note on the table. She had no doubt that her answer would fall into Valentina Mihalovna's hands.

The next morning Solomin, after seeing Nezhdanov, and absolutely declining to undertake the management of Sipyagin's factory, set off homewards. He mused all the way home, a thing which very seldom occurred with him; the motion of the carriage usually lulled him into a light sleep. He thought of Marianna and also of Nezhdanov. He fancied that if he had been in love, he—Solomin—he would have had quite a different face, that he would have talked and looked quite differently. 'But,' he reflected, 'since that has never happened to me, I can't tell, of course, what I should look like if it did.' He remembered an Irish girl whom he had once seen in a shop behind the counter; he remembered what won-

derful, almost black, hair she had, her blue eyes and thick
lashes, and how she had looked sadly and wistfully at him,
and how long afterwards he had walked up and down the
street before her windows, how excited he had been, and how
he had kept asking himself, should he make her acquaintance
or not? He was then staying in London. His employer had
sent him there with a sum of money to make purchases for
him. Solomin had been on the point of stopping on in London,
of sending the money back to his employer, so strong was
the impression made on him by the lovely Polly. . . . (He
had found out her name; one of the other shopgirls had
addressed her by it.) He had mastered himself, however, and
went back to his employer. Polly had been far more beautiful
than Marianna, but this girl had the same sad, wistful look
in her eyes . . . and she was a Russian. . . .

'But what am I thinking about?' said Solomin, half aloud,
'bothering my head about other men's sweethearts!' and he
gave a shake to the collar of his coat as though wishing to
shake off all unnecessary ideas; and just then he drove up
to the factory and caught a glimpse of the figure of the faithful
Pavel in the doorway of his little lodge.

26

SOLOMIN's refusal greatly offended Sipyagin—so much so that
he suddenly arrived at the opinion that this home-bred
Stevenson was not such a remarkable mechanician after all,
and that, though he might very likely not be a complete sham,
he certainly gave himself airs like a regular plebeian. 'All
these Russians, when they imagine they know a thing, are
beyond everything. *Au fond* Kallomyetsev is right.' Under
the influence of such irritated and malignant sensations, the
statesman—*en herbe*—was even more unsympathetic and

distant when he looked at Nezhdanov. He informed Kolya that he need not work with his tutor to-day—that he must form a habit of self-reliance. . . . He did not, however, give the tutor himself his dismissal, as the latter had expected; he continued to ignore him. But Valentina Mihalovna did not ignore Marianna. A terrible scene took place between them.

At about two o'clock they happened somehow to be suddenly left alone together in the drawing-room. Each of them was immediately aware that the moment of the inevitable conflict had come, and so, after a momentary hesitation, they gradually approached each other. Valentina Mihalovna was faintly smiling, Marianna's lips were compressed; they were both pale. As she moved across the room, Valentina Mihalovna looked to right and to left and picked a leaf of geranium . . . Marianna's eyes were fixed directly upon the smiling face approaching her.

Madame Sipyagin was the first to stop, and, drumming with her finger-tips on the back of the chair: 'Marianna Vikentyevna,' she said in a careless voice, 'we have, I think, entered upon a correspondence with one another. . . . Living under one roof as we do, that is rather odd, and you are aware that I am not fond of oddities of any sort.'

'It was not I began that correspondence, Valentina Mihalovna.'

'No. . . . You are right. I am to blame for the oddity this time; but I could find no other means to arouse in you a feeling of . . . how shall I say? . . . a feeling of——'

'Speak out, Valentina Mihalovna; don't mince matters—don't be afraid of offending me.'

'A feeling . . . of propriety.'

Valentina Mihalovna paused; nothing but the light tap of her fingers on the chair-back could be heard in the room.

'How do you consider I have been careless of propriety?' asked Marianna.

Valentina Mihalovna shrugged her shoulders.

'*Ma chère, vous n'êtes plus un enfant,* and you understand

me perfectly. Can you suppose your behaviour could remain
a secret to me, to Anna Zaharovna, to the whole household,
in fact? Besides, you have not taken much pains to keep it
a secret. You have simply acted in bravado. Boris Andreitch
alone has, perhaps, not observed it. . . . He is absorbed in
other matters of more interest and importance. But, except
for him, your conduct is known to all—all!'

Marianna grew steadily paler and paler.

'I would ask you, Valentina Mihalovna, to be more definite
in your expressions. With what precisely are you displeased?'

'*L'insolente!*' thought Madame Sipyagin. She still restrained herself, however.

'You wish to know what I am displeased about, Marianna?
Certainly. I am displeased at your prolonged interviews with
a young man who by birth, by education, and by social
position is far beneath you. I am displeased . . . no! that
word is not strong enough—I am revolted by your late . . .
your midnight visits to that young man's room. And that
under my roof! Do you suppose that that is quite as it should
be, and that I am to be silent, and, as it were, screen your
flightiness? As a woman of irreproachable virtue . . . *Oui,
mademoiselle, je l'ai été, je le suis, et le serai toujours*—I
cannot help feeling indignant.'

Valentina Mihalovna flung herself into an arm-chair as
though crushed by the weight of her indignation.

Marianna smiled for the first time.

'I do not doubt your virtue, past, present, and future,'
she began, 'and I say so quite sincerely; but your indignation
is needless; I have brought no disgrace on your roof. The
young man to whom you allude . . . yes, I certainly . . .
have come to love him. . . .'

'You love Monsieur Nezhdanov?'

'Yes, I love him.'

Valentina Mihalovna sat up in her chair.

'Good heavens, Marianna! why, he's a student, of no birth,
no family—why, he's younger than you are!' (There was a
certain spiteful pleasure in the utterance of these words.)

'What can come of it? and what can you, with your intellect, find in him? He's simply a shallow boy.'

'That was not always your opinion of him, Valentina Mihalovna.'

'Oh, mercy on us, my dear, let me alone. . . . *Pas tant d'esprit que ça, je vous prie.* It is you we are discussing—you and your future. Fancy! what sort of a match is it for you?'

'I must confess, Valentina Mihalovna, I had not thought of it in that light.'

'Eh? What? What am I to understand by that? You have followed the dictates of your heart, we are to suppose. . . . But all that is bound to end in marriage, isn't it?'

'I don't know. . . . I have not thought about that.'

'You have not thought about that? Why, you must be mad!'

Marianna turned slightly away.

'Let us make an end of this conversation, Valentina Mihalovna. It can lead to nothing. We shall never understand one another.'

Valentina Mihalovna got up impulsively.

'I cannot, I ought not to make an end of this conversation! It is too important. . . . I have to answer for you to . . .'. Valentina Mihalovna had meant to say 'to God', but she faltered, and said, 'to the whole world. I cannot be silent when I hear such senselessness! And why cannot I understand you? The insufferable conceit of these young people! No! . . . I understand you very well; I can see that you are infected with these new ideas which will inevitably lead you to your ruin! but then it will be too late.'

'Perhaps; but you may rest assured of one thing: even in my ruin, I shall never hold out a finger to you for aid.'

'Conceit again, this awful conceit! Come, listen to me, Marianna, listen to me,' she went on, suddenly changing her tone. . . . She was on the point of drawing Marianna to her, but Marianna stepped back a pace. *'Écoutez-moi, je vous en conjure.* After all, you know I am not so old and not so

196

stupid that it's impossible for us to understand each other. *Je ne suis pas une encroutée.* I was even regarded as a republican in my young days . . . just as you are. Listen to me; I will not affect what I don't feel. I have never felt a mother's tenderness for you, and it's not in your character to complain of that . . . but I have recognised and I do recognise that I have duties in regard to you, and I have always tried to perform them. Perhaps the match I dreamed of for you, and for which Boris Andreitch and I, both of us, would have been ready to make any sacrifices . . . that suitor did not fully answer to your ideas . . . but from the bottom of my heart——'

Marianna looked at Valentina Mihalovna—at the wonderful eyes, at the pink, faintly touched-up lips, at the white hands, with the slightly parted fingers adorned with rings, which the elegant lady was pressing so expressively to the bodice of her silk gown,—and suddenly she cut her short.

'A match, do you say, Valentina Mihalovna? Do you mean by a "match" that heartless, vulgar friend of yours, Mr. Kallomyetsev?'

Valentina Mihalovna took her fingers from her bodice.

'Yes, Marianna Vikentyevna, I mean Mr. Kallomyetsev—that cultivated, excellent young man, who will certainly make a wife happy, and whom no one but a madwoman could refuse—no one but a madwoman!'

'What's to be done, *ma tante?* It would seem I am one '

'But what fault—what serious fault—do you find with him?'

'Oh, none at all. I despise him . . . that's all.'

Valentina Mihalovna shook her head from side to side impatiently, and again sank into an arm-chair.

'Let him be. *Retournons à nos moutons.* And so you love Mr. Nezhdanov?'

'Yes.'

'And you intend to continue . . . your interviews with him?'

'Yes, I intend to.'

'Well . . . and if I forbid you to?'

'I sha'n't listen to you.'

Valentina Mihalovna bounded up in her chair.

'Oh, you won't listen to me! Oh, indeed! And that's said to me by the girl I have loaded with benefits, whom I have cared for in my own house—that is what's said to me . . . is said to me . . .'

'By the daughter of a disgraced father,' Marianna put in gloomily. 'Go on; don't mince matters.'

'*Ce n'est pas moi qui vous le fais dire, mademoiselle;* but, anyway, there's nothing to be proud of *in that.* A girl who lives at my expense——'

'Don't taunt me with that, Valentina Mihalovna! It would cost you more to keep a French governess for Kolya. . . . You know I give him French lessons.'

Valentina Mihalovna raised a hand holding a cambric hand-kerchief scented with ylang-ylang and embroidered with a huge white monogram in one corner, and tried to make some retort, but Marianna went on vehemently:

'You would have every right a thousand times over, every right to speak if, instead of all you have just been reckoning up, instead of all these pretended benefits and sacrifices, you were in a position to say, "the girl I have loved." . . . But you are too honest to tell such a lie as that.' Marianna was shaking as if she were in a fever. 'You have always hated me. At this very moment, at the bottom of your heart, as you said just now, you are glad—yes, glad—that I am justifying your constant predictions, that I am covering myself with scandal, with disgrace; all that you mind is that part of the disgrace may fall on your aristocratic, *virtuous* household.'

'You are insulting me,' faltered Valentina Mihalovna. 'Kindly leave the room.'

But Marianna could not control herself.

'Your household, you say, all your household and Anna Zaharovna and all know of my conduct! and they are all horrified and indignant. . . . But do you suppose I ask any-thing of you, or them, or any of these people? Do you suppose I prize their good opinion? Do you think the living at your expense, as you call it, has been sweet? I would prefer any poverty to this luxury. Don't you see that between your household and me there's a perfect gulf, a gulf that nothing can conceal? Can you—you're a clever woman, too—fail to realise that? And if you feel hatred for me, can't you understand the feeling I must have for you, which I don't particularise, simply because it is too obvious?'

'*Sortez, sortez, vous dis-je! . . .*' repeated Valentina Mihalovna, and she stamped with her pretty, slender little foot.

Marianna took a step in the direction of the door.

'I will rid you of my presence directly; but do you know what, Valentina Mihalovna? They say that even in Rachel's mouth in Racine's *Bajazet* that *'Sortez!'* was not effective, and you are far behind her! And something more, what was it you said? *"Je suis une honnête femme, je l'ai été, et le serai toujours."* Only fancy, I am convinced I'm a great deal honester than you! Good-bye!'

Marianna went out hurriedly, while Valentina Mihalovna leaped up from her chair; she wanted to shriek, she wanted to cry. . . . But what to shriek she did not know; and tears did not come at her bidding.

She had to be content with fanning herself with her handkerchief; but the scent with which it was saturated affected her nerves still more. She felt unhappy, insulted. She was conscious of a grain of truth in what she had just heard. But how could anyone judge her so unjustly? 'Can I be such a spiteful creature?' she thought, and she looked at herself in the looking-glass, which happened to be straight before her between two windows. The looking-glass reflected a charming face, somewhat discomposed, with patches of red coming out upon it, but still a fascinating face, exquisite, soft, velvety eyes. . . . 'I? I spiteful?' she thought again. . . . 'With eyes like those?'

But at that instant her husband came in, and she hid her face in her handkerchief again.

'What is wrong with you?' he inquired anxiously. 'What is it, Valya?' (He had invented that pet name, though he never allowed himself to use it except in absolute *tête-à-tête*, by preference in the country.)

At first she was reticent, declared there was nothing wrong, but ended by turning round in her chair, in a very graceful and touching way, and flinging her arms round his shoulders (he was standing bending over her), hiding her face in the open front of his waistcoat, and telling him everything; without any hypocrisy or hidden motive, she tried, if not to excuse, at least to some extent to justify Marianna; she threw all the blame on her youth, her passionate temperament, and the defects of her early education; she also, to some extent, and also with no double motive, blamed herself. 'With my daughter, this would never have happened! I should have looked after her very differently!' Sipyagin heard her out with indulgence, sympathy, and severity; he kept his stooping posture since she did not take her arms from his shoulders, and did not remove her head; he called her an angel, kissed her on the forehead, announced that he saw now the course of action dictated to him by his position, the position of the head of the house, and withdrew with the gait of a man of humane but energetic character, who has to make up his mind to perform an unpleasant but inevitable duty.

About eight o'clock, after dinner, Nezhdanov was sitting in his room writing to his friend Silin: 'Dear Vladimir, I am writing to you at the moment of a vital change in my existence. I have been dismissed from this house. I am going away. But that would be nothing. I am going from here not alone. The girl I have written to you about accompanies me. We are bound together by the similarity of our fate in life, the identity of our views and efforts, by our mutual feeling too. We love each other; at least, I believe I am not capable of feeling the passion of love in any other form than that in which it presents itself to me now. But I should be lying to you if I said I had no secret feeling of terror, even a sort of strange sinking at heart. The future is all dark, and we are pushing forward together into this darkness. I need not explain to you what it is we are going into, and what work we have chosen. Marianna and I are not in search of happiness; we don't want to enjoy ourselves, but to struggle on together, side by side, supporting each other. Our aim is clear to us; but what ways will lead up to it, we do not know. Shall we find, if not sympathy and help, at least freedom to work? Marianna is a splendid, honest girl; if it is decreed that we perish, I shall not reproach myself for having led her to ruin, for there is no other life possible to her now. But Vladimir, Vladimir! my heart is heavy. I am tortured by doubt, not of my feeling for her, of course, but . . . I don't know. Anyhow, it's too late to turn back. Stretch out a hand to us both from afar, and wish us patience, power of self-sacrifice, and love . . . more love. And ye, unknown of us, but loved by us with all our being, every drop of our heart's blood, Russian people, receive us not too coldly, and teach us what we are to expect from you! Farewell, Vladimir, farewell!'

After writing these few lines, Nezhdanov set off to the village. The next night, the dawn was hardly breaking in the sky when he stood on the outskirts of the birch wood at no great distance from Sipyagin's garden. A little behind him, a little peasant's cart, harnessed to a pair of unbridled horses, could be seen behind the tangled green of a broad hazel-bush; in the cart, under the seat of plaited cord, a little grey-headed old peasant lay asleep on a bundle of hay, with a patched overcoat over his head. Nezhdanov kept incessantly looking towards the road, towards the clump of willows at the garden's edge; the grey stillness of night still hung over everything, the tiny stars strove feebly to outshine each other, lost in the waste depths of the sky. Along the rounded lower edges of the stretching clouds ran a pale flush from the east; thence too came the first chill breath of early morning. Suddenly Nezhdanov started and was all alert; somewhere near at hand there was first the shrill creak, then the thump of a gate; a little feminine figure wrapped in a shawl, with a bundle in its bare hand, stepped with a deliberate movement out of the still shadows of the willows on to the soft dust of the road, and crossing it in a slanting direction, apparently on tiptoe, turned towards the copse. Nezhdanov rushed up to it.

'Marianna?' he whispered.

'It's I!' came the soft reply from under the overhanging shawl.

'This way, follow me,' responded Nezhdanov, clutching her awkwardly by the bare hand that held the bundle.

She shrank up as if she felt chilled by the frost. He led her to the cart, and waked up the peasant. The latter jumped up quickly, clambered promptly on to the driver's seat, slipped his arms into the greatcoat, and caught up the cords that served for reins. The horses shook themselves; he cautiously encouraged them in a voice still hoarse from his heavy sleep. Nezhdanov made Marianna sit down on the cord seat of the cart, first spreading his cloak on it; he wrapped her feet in a rug—the hay at the bottom of the cart was damp —placed himself beside her, and, bending over to the peasant, said softly, 'Drive on you know where.' The peasant gave a tug to the reins, the horses came out of the thicket, snorting and shaking themselves; and rattling and jolting on its narrow old wheels, the cart rolled along the road. Nezhdanov put one arm round Marianna's waist to support her; she lifted the shawl a little with her cold fingers, and turning and facing him with a smile, she said, 'How deliciously fresh it is, Alyosha!'

'Yes,' answered the peasant, 'there'll be a heavy dew!'

There was already such a heavy dew that the axles of the cart-wheels, as they caught in the tops of the tall weeds along the roadside, shook off whole showers of delicate drops of water, and the green of the grass looked bluish-grey.

Again Marianna shivered from the cold.

'How fresh, how fresh!' she repeated in a light-hearted voice. 'And freedom, Alyosha, freedom!'

27

SOLOMIN ran out to the gates of the factory as soon as they
flew to tell him that a gentleman and a lady had arrived in
a little cart and were asking for him. Without saying good-
morning to his visitors, simply nodding his head several times
to them, he at once told the peasant to drive into the yard,
and, directing him straight up to his little lodge, he helped
Marianna out of the cart. Nezhdanov leaped out after her.
Solomin led them both along a little, long, dark passage,
and up a narrow winding little staircase, in the back part of
the lodge, to the second storey. There he opened a low door,
and they all three went into a small, fairly clean room with
two windows.

'Welcome!' said Solomin, with his never-failing smile,
which seemed broader and brighter than ever to-day.

'Here are your quarters, this room, and see here, another
next to it. Not much to look at, but that's no matter; one
can live in them, and there'll be no one here to spy on you.
Here under the window you have what the landlord calls a
flower-garden, but I should call it a kitchen-garden; it lies
right up against the wall, and hedges to right and left. A
quiet little nook it is! Well, welcome a second time, dear
young lady, and you too, Nezhdanov, welcome!'

He shook hands with them both. They stood motionless,
not taking off their wraps, and with silent, half-bewildered,
half-delighted emotion they looked straight before them.

'Well, what now?' Solomin began again. 'Take off your
things! What baggage have you got?'

Marianna showed the bundle which she was still holding in
her hand.

'This is all I have.'

'And my trunk and bag are still in the cart. But I'll go
and get them directly.'

'Stand still, stand still.' Solomin opened the door. Pavel!'
he shouted into the darkness of the staircase, 'run out,
mate. There are some things in the cart . . . bring them
up.'

'Directly,' they heard the voice of the ubiquitous Pavel.

Solomin turned to Marianna, who had flung off her shawl
and was beginning to unbutton her cloak.

'And did everything go off successfully?' he inquired.

'Everything . . . no one saw us. I left a letter for Mr.
Sipyagin. I didn't take any dresses or clothes with me,
Vassily Fedotitch, because as you are going to send us . . .'
(Marianna for some reason could not make up her mind to
add 'to the people'), 'well, anyway, they'd have been of no
use. But I have money to buy what is necessary.'

'We'll arrange all that later . . . and here,' said Solomin,
pointing to Pavel, who came in with Nezhdanov's things, 'I
commend to you my best friend here; you can rely on him
fully . . . as you would on me. Did you speak to Tatyana
about the samovar?' he added in an undertone.

'It'll be here directly,' answered Pavel; 'and the cream and
everything.'

'Tatyana is his wife,' Solomin went on, 'and she is just
as trustworthy as he is. Until you . . . well . . . are a bit
used to it, she will wait on you, my dear young lady.'

Marianna flung her cloak on a little leather sofa that stood
in the corner. 'Call me Marianna, Vassily Fedotitch—I don't
want to be a young lady. And I don't want anyone to wait
on me. . . . I didn't come here to have servants. Don't look
at my dress; I had—over there—nothing else. All that must
be changed.'

The dress, of fine cinnamon-coloured cloth, was very
simple; but cut by a Petersburg dressmaker, it fell in elegant
folds about Marianna's waist and shoulders, and had
altogether a fashionable air.

'Well, not a servant, but a help, perhaps, in the American
fashion. And you must have tea, anyway. It's early days
yet, and you must both be tired. I am going off now to see

after things in the factory; we shall meet again later. Tell Pavel or Tatyana whatever you want.'

Marianna held out both hands quickly to him.

'How can we thank you, Vassily Fedotitch?' She looked at him quite moved.

Solomin softly stroked one of her hands. 'I should say, it's not worth thanking for . . . but that wouldn't be true. I'd better say that your thanks give me immense pleasure. So we're quits. Good-bye for the present! Pavel, come along.'

Marianna and Nezhdanov were left alone.

She rushed up to him, and, looking at him with just the same expression as she had looked at Solomin, only with even more delight, more emotion and gladness, 'Oh, my dear!' she said . . . 'We are beginning a new life. . . . At last! at last! You wouldn't believe how charming and delghtful this poor little lodging where we are only to spend a few days seems to me compared with that loathsome mansion! Tell me, are you glad, dear?'

Nezhdanov took her hands and pressed them to his heart.

'I am happy, Marianna, that I am beginning this new life with you! You will be my guiding star, dear, my support, my strength. . . .'

'Dearest Alyosha! But stay. I want to wash a little and make myself tidy. I'll go to my own room . . . and you, stay here. One minute. . . .'

Marianna went off into the other room, shut herself in, and a minute later half-opened the door, put her head in, and said, 'And oh! isn't Solomin nice!' Then she shut the door again, and the key clicked in the lock.

Nezhdanov went up to the window, and looked out into the little garden . . . one old, very old apple-tree for some reason riveted his attention especially. He shook himself, stretched, began opening his trunk, and took nothing out of it; he fell to musing. . . .

In a quarter of an hour Marianna returned with a beaming, freshly washed face, all gaiety and alertness; and a few instants later Pavel's wife, Tatyana, appeared with the samovar, the tea-tray, rolls and cream.

In striking contrast to her gypsy-like husband, she was a typical Russian woman, stout, with a flaxen head, with a big knob of hair tightly twisted round a horn comb, and no cap, with thick but pleasant features, and very good-natured grey eyes. She was dressed in a tidy though faded chintz gown; her hands were clean and well-shaped, though large; she bowed tranquilly, and with a firm, precise intonation, without any sort of affectation, she articulated, 'A very good health to you,' and set to work to lay the samovar and the tea things.

Marianna went up to her.

'Let me help you, Tatyana. Only give me a napkin.'

'No need, miss, we're used to it. Vassily Fedotitch has talked to me. If anything's wanted, kindly ask for it; we will do what we can with all the pleasure in life.'

'Tatyana, please don't call me miss. . . . I'm dressed like a lady, but still I'm . . . I'm quite . . .'

The steady gaze of Tatyana's keen eyes disconcerted Marianna; she broke off.

'And what then is it you will be?' Tatyana asked in her composed voice.

'I am certainly, if you like . . . I am a lady by birth; only I want to get rid of all that, and to become like all . . . like all simple women.'

'Ah, so that's it! Well, now I understand. You're one of them, I suppose, that want to be simplified. There are a good few of them about nowadays.'

'What did you say, Tatyana? To be simplified?'

'Yes . . . that's the word that's come up among us now. To be on a level with simple folks, it means—simplification. To be sure, it is a good work—to teach the peasants good sense. Only it's a difficult job! Oy, oy, di-ifficult! God give you good speed!'

'Simplification!' repeated Marianna. 'Do you hear, Alyosha? you and I are simplified creatures now!'

Nezhdanov laughed, and even repeated:

'Simplified creatures!'

'And what will he be to you—your good man or your brother?' asked Tatyana, carefully washing the cups with her large deft hands, as she looked with a kindly smile from Nezhdanov to Marianna.

'No,' answered Marianna, 'he's not my husband and not my brother.'

Tatyana raised her head.

'Then I suppose you are living in free grace. Nowadays that too is pretty often to be met with. It used to be more the way among the dissenters, but nowadays it's found among other folks too. Where there's God's blessing, one may live in peace! And there's no need of the priest for that. In our factory there are some live like that too. Not the worst chaps either.'

'What nice things you say, Tatyana! . . . "In free grace." . . . I like that very much. I'll tell you what I want to ask of you, Tatyana. I want to make myself, or to buy, a dress like yours, or rather commoner perhaps. And shoes and stockings and a kerchief, everything just as you have. I have money enough to get them.'

'To be sure, miss, we can manage all that. . . . There, I won't, don't be cross. I won't call you miss. Only what am I to call you?'

'Marianna.'

'And what are you named from your father?'

'But why do you want my father's name? Call me simply Marianna. The same as I call you Tatyana.'

'That's the same, and not the same. You'd better tell me.'

'Very well, then. My father's name was Vikent; and what was your father's?'

'Mine was Osip.'

'Well, then, I shall call you Tatyana Osipovna.'

'And I'll call you Marianna Vikentyevna. That will be capital.'

'Won't you drink a cup of tea with us, Tatyana Osipovna?'

'At this first acquaintance I might, Marianna Vikentyevna. I'll treat myself to a small cup, though Yegoritch will scold.'

'Who's Yegoritch?'

'Pavel, my husband.'

'Sit down, Tatyana Osipovna.'

'Indeed and I will, Marianna Vikentyevna.'

Tatyana seated herself on a chair and began to sip her tea through a piece of sugar. She continually turned the lump of sugar round in her fingers, screwing up her eye on the side on which she was nibbling the sugar. Marianna got into conversation with her. Tatyana answered without obsequiousness, and asked her questions and told her various things of her own accord. Solomin she almost worshipped, but her husband she put only second to Vassily Fedotitch. She was sick of factory life, though.

'You've neither the town here nor the country . . . if it weren't for Vassily Fedotitch I wouldn't stay another hour.'

Marianna listened attentively to her talk. Nezhdanov, sitting a little on one side, watched his girl friend, and was not surprised at her interest; for Marianna it was all a novelty, but it seemed to him that he had seen hundreds of similar Tatyanas, and had talked to them hundreds of times.

'Do you know, Tatyana Osipovna,' said Marianna at last, 'you think we want to teach the people; no, we want to serve them.'

'How serve them? Teach them; that's the best service you can do them. Take me, for example. When I was married to Yegoritch, neither read nor write could I; but now I've learned, thanks to Vassily Fedotitch. He didn't teach me himself, but he paid an old man to. And he taught me. You see I'm young still, for all I'm a woman grown.'

Marianna was silent for a little.

'I should like, Tatyana Osipovna,' she began again, 'to learn some trade . . . we must have a talk about that. I sew very badly; if I were to learn to cook, I might become a cook.'

Tatyana pondered.

'Why be a cook? Cooks are in rich men's houses, or merchants'; poor people do their own cooking. And to cook for a union, for workmen—well, that's quite the last thing!'

'But I might live in a rich man's house, though, and make friends with poor people. Or how am I to get to know them? I sha'n't always have such luck as with you.'

Tatyana turned her empty cup upside down in the saucer.

'It's a difficult business,' she observed at last with a sigh, 'it can't be settled off-hand. I'll show you all I know, but I'm not clever at much. We must talk it over with Yegoritch. He's such a man! He reads books of all sorts, and he can see through anything in the twinkling of an eye.' Here she glanced at Marianna, who was rolling up a cigarette. . . .

'And there's something I would say to you, Marianna Vikentyevna, if you'll excuse me; but if you really want to be simplified, you'll have to give that up.' She pointed to the cigarette. 'For in such callings as a cook's, for instance, that would never pass; and everyone would see at once that you're a young lady. Yes.'

Marianna flung the cigarette out of the window.

'I won't smoke . . . it's easy to get out of the way of it. Women of the people don't smoke, so I ought not to smoke.'

'That's a true word you've said, Marianna Vikentyevna. The male sex treat themselves to it even among us; but the female—no. . . . Ah, and here's Vassily Fedotitch himself coming up. That's his step. You ask him; he'll settle everything for you in the best way!'

She was right; Solomin's voice was heard at the door.

'May I come in?'

'Come in, come in,' called Marianna.

'That's an English habit of mine,' said Solomin as he came in. 'Well, how do you feel? You aren't dull yet? I see you're having tea here with Tatyana. You listen to her; she's a sensible person. . . . But my employer has turned up to see me to-day . . . when he's not wanted at all! And he'll stay to dinner. There's no help for it! He's the master.'

209

'What sort of man is he?' asked Nezhdanov, coming out of his corner.

'Oh, he's all right. . . . He has his eyes about him. One of the newer generation. Very affable, and wears cuffs, but pries into everything not a bit less than the old sort. He'd skin a flint with his own hands and say, "Turn a bit to this side, if you'll be so good; there's still a living spot here . . . I must give it a scouring!" Well, with me he's as soft as silk; I'm necessary to him! Only I've come to tell you that I'm not likely to manage to see you to-day. They will bring you your dinner. And don't show yourselves in the yard. What do you think, Marianna—will the Sipyagins search for you? will they make a hunt?'

'I think they won't,' answered Marianna.

'But I am sure they will,' said Nezhdanov.

'Well, anyway,' pursued Solomin, 'you must be careful at first. Later on you can do as you like.'

'Yes; only there's one thing,' observed Nezhdanov; 'Markelov must know of my whereabouts; he must be told.'

'Why?'

'It can't be helped; for the cause. He has always to know where I am. It's a promise. But he won't blab!'

'Very well. We'll send Pavel.'

'And will there be a dress ready for me?' asked Nezhdanov.

'Your get-up, you mean? to be sure . . . to be sure. It's quite a masquerade. Not an expensive one, thank goodness. Good-bye; you must have a rest. Tatyana, come along.'

Marianna and Nezhdanov were again left alone.

28

FIRST they clasped each other's hands again; then Marianna cried, 'Come, I'll help you arrange your room,' and she began unpacking his things from the trunk and the bag. Nezhdanov would have helped her, but she declared she was going to do it all alone.

'Because I must get used to making myself useful.' And she did in fact hang up his coat on nails which she found in the table drawer, and knocked into the wall, unaided, with the back of a brush for want of a hammer; the linen she laid in a little old chest which stood between the windows.

'What's this?' she asked suddenly; 'a revolver? Is it loaded? What do you want with it?'

'It's not loaded . . . but give it here, though. You ask what I want with it? How is one to get on without a revolver in our calling?'

She laughed and went on with her task, shaking out each thing separately and beating it with her hand; she even set two pairs of boots under the sofa; while the few books, a bundle of papers, and the little manuscript book of verses she arranged in triumph on a three-legged corner-table, saying it was to be the writing- and work-table, while the other round table she called the dinner- and tea-table. Then taking the book of verses in both hands, she raised it to a level with her face, and looking over its edge at Nezhdanov, she said with a smile, 'We'll read all this through together some time when we're not busy, won't we?—eh?'

'Give me that book! I'll burn it!' cried Nezhdanov. 'It's worth nothing better.'

'Why did you bring it with you, if so? No, no, I'm not going to give it you to be burnt. Though they say authors always make that threat, but never do burn their things. But anyway, I'd better carry it off!'

Nezhdanov tried to protest, but Marianna ran into the next room with the manuscript book and returned without it.

She sat down close to Nezhdanov, and instantly got up again. 'You haven't been . . . in my room yet. Would you like to see it? It's as nice as yours. Come, I'll show you.'

Nezhdanov got up too and followed Marianna. *Her* room, as she called it, was a little smaller than *his* room; but the furniture in it seemed rather newer and cleaner; in the window stood a glass vase of flowers, and in the corner a little iron bedstead.

'See how sweet of Solomin!' cried Marianna; 'only one mustn't let oneself be too much spoilt; we shan't often meet with such quarters. And what I think is, what would be nice would be to arrange things so that whatever place we have to go to we could go both together, without parting. It will be difficult,' she added after a short pause; 'well, we'll think of it. Anyway, I suppose you won't go back to Petersburg?'

'What should I do in Petersburg? Go to the university and give lessons? That would be of no use now.'

'We'll see what Solomin says,' observed Marianna; 'he'll best decide how and what to do.'

They went back to the first room and again sat down beside each other. They spoke with praise of Solomin, Tatyana, and Pavel; they mentioned Sipyagin, and said how their old life seemed suddenly so far away from them, it seemed lost in a cloud; then they pressed each other's hands again, and exchanged glances of delight; then they talked of what sort of people they ought to try to do propaganda among, and how they must behave not to be suspected.

Nezhdanov maintained that the less they thought about that, the more simply they behaved, the better.

'Of course!' cried Marianna. 'Why, we want to be simplified, as Tatyana says.'

'I didn't mean in that sense,' Nezhdanov was beginning. 'I meant to say that we ought not to be constrained——'

Suddenly Marianna laughed.

'I remembered, Alyosha, how I called us both "simplified creatures"!'

Nezhdanov smiled too, repeated 'simplified', and then sank into thought.

Marianna, too, was thoughtful.

'Alyosha!' she said.

'What?'

'I think we both feel a little awkward. Young people, *des*

nouveaux mariés,' she explained, 'the first day of their honeymoon must feel something of the sort. They are happy . . . they are very content, and a little awkward.'

Nezhdanov smiled—a forced smile.

'You know very well, Marianna, that we are not a young couple in that sense.'

Marianna got up and stood directly facing Nezhdanov.

'That depends on you.'

'How?'

'Alyosha, you know that when you tell me as an honest man—and I shall believe you, for you really are an honest man—when you tell me that you love me with that love . . . well, that love that gives one a right to another person's life—when you tell me that, I am yours.'

Nezhdanov blushed and turned a little away.

'When I tell you that . . .'

'Yes, then! But you see yourself you do not tell me so now. . . . Oh, yes, Alyosha, you certainly are an honest man. There, let us talk of matters of more importance.'

'But you know I love you, Marianna!'

'I don't doubt that . . . and I shall wait. There, I've not quite put your writing-table to rights yet. Here's something still wrapped up, something stiff.'

Nezhdanov jumped up from his chair.

'Let that be, Marianna. . . . Please . . . leave that alone.'

Marianna turned her head over her shoulder to look at him, and raised her eyebrows in amazement.

'Is it a mystery? A secret? You have a secret?'

'Yes . . . yes,' said Nezhdanov, and greatly disconcerted he added, by way of explanation, 'It's . . . a portrait.'

This word fell from him unconsciously. In the paper Marianna held in her hands there was wrapped up, in reality, her portrait, given to Nezhdanov by Markelov.

'A portrait?' she articulated, dwelling on each syllable. . . . 'A woman's?'

She gave him the little parcel, but he took it awkwardly;

213

it almost slipped out of his hands, and fell open.

'Why, it's . . . my portrait!' cried Marianna quickly. 'Well, I've a right to take my own portrait.' She took it from Nezhdanov.

'Did you sketch this?'

'No . . . not I.'

'Who, then? Markelov?'

'You've guessed. . . . It was he.'

'How did you come by it?'

'He gave it to me.'

'When?'

Nezhdanov told her how and when it had been given. Whilst he was speaking, Marianna glanced first at him and then at the portrait . . . and the same thought flashed through the heads of both: 'If *he* were in this room, he would have the right to ask.' . . . But neither Marianna nor Nezhdanov uttered this thought aloud . . . possibly because each of them was conscious of the thought in the other.

Marianna softly wrapped the portrait in the paper again, and laid it on the table.

'He's a good man!' she murmured. . . . 'Where is he now?'

'Where? . . . At home. I am going to see him to-morrow or next day to get books and pamphlets. He meant to give them to me, but I suppose he forgot it when I was leaving.'

'And do you think, Alyosha, that in giving you the portrait he renounced everything . . . absolutely everything?'

'I thought so.'

'And you hope to find him at home?'

'Of course.'

'Ah!'—Marianna lowered her eyes and dropped her hands. 'And here's Tatyana bringing us our dinner,' she cried suddenly. 'What a splendid woman she is!'

Tatyana appeared with knives and forks, table-napkins, and plates and dishes. While she was laying the table she told them what had been passing in the factory.

'The master came from Moscow by rail, and he set to

running from floor to floor like one possessed; to be sure, he knows nothing about things, he only does like that for show, to keep up appearances. But Vassily Fedotitch treats him like a babe in arms. The master thought he'd say something nasty to him, so Vassily Fedotitch suppressed him at once: "I'll throw it all up directly," says he, so our gentleman pretty soon changed his tune. Now they're dining together; and the master brought a companion with him. . . . And he does nought else but admire everything. And a moneyed man he must be, this companion, to judge from the way he holds his tongue and shakes his head. And he's stout too, very stout! A regular Moscow swell! Ah, it's a true saying: "It's downhill to Moscow from all parts of Russia; everything rolls down to her." '

'How you do notice everything!' cried Marianna.

'Yes, I'm pretty observant,' replied Tatyana. 'Come, your dinner's ready. And may it do you good. I'll sit here a little bit, and watch you.'

Marianna and Nezhdanov sat down to dinner; Tatyana leaned against the window-sill and rested her cheek in her hand.

'I watch you,' she repeated . . . 'and what poor young tender things you both are! . . . It's so pleasant to see you that it quite makes my heart ache! Ah, my dears! you're taking up a burden beyond your strength! It's such as you that the inspectors of the Tsar are ever eager to clap in custody!'

'Nonsense, my good soul, don't frighten us,' observed Nezhdanov. 'You know the saying: "If you choose to be a mushroom, you must go in the basket with the rest." '

'I know . . . I know; but the baskets nowadays are so narrow and hard to creep out of!'

'Have you any children?' Marianna asked, to change the conversation.

'Yes; a son. He begins to go to school. I had a little girl too; but she's no more, poor darling! She met with an accident; fell under a wheel. And if only it had killed her

at once! But no, she lingered in suffering a long while. Since
then I've grown tender-hearted; before then I was as hard as
a tree!'

'Why, what of your man Pavel Yegoritch? didn't you love
him?'

'Eh! that was a different matter; the feeling of a girl. And
how about you, now—do you love your man?'

'Yes.'

'Very much?'

'Yes.'

'Yes? . . .' Tatyana looked at Nezhdanov, then at
Marianna, and said no more.

It was again Marianna's lot to change the conversation.
She told Tatyana she had given up smoking; the latter
approved of her resolution. Then Marianna asked her again
about clothes; and reminded her she had promised to show
her how to cook. . . .

'Oh, and one thing more: could you get me some stout,
coarse yarn? I'm going to knit myself some stockings . . .
plain ones.'

Tatyana answered that everything should be done in due
course, and, clearing the table, she went out of the room with
her calm, resolute gait.

'Well, what shall we do now?' Marianna said, turning to
Nezhdanov; and without letting him answer, 'What do you
say? since our real work only begins to-morrow, shall we
devote this evening to literature? Let's read your poems! I
shall be a severe critic.'

For a long while Nezhdanov would not consent. . . . He
ended, however, by giving in, and began to read out of his
manuscript book. Marianna sat close beside him, and
watched his face while he was reading. She had spoken truly;
she turned out to be a severe critic. Few of the verses pleased
her; she preferred the purely lyrical, short ones, that were,
as she expressed it, non-didactic. Nezhdanov did not read
quite well; he had not the courage to attempt elocution, and
at the same time was unwilling to fall into quite a colourless

tone; the result was neither one thing nor the other. Marianna suddenly interrupted him with the question, Did he know a wonderful poem of Dobrolyubov's beginning, 'Let me die—small cause for grief'?[1] and thereupon read it to him—also not very well—in a rather childish manner.

Nezhdanov observed that it was bitter and painful to the last degree, and then added that he, Nezhdanov, could never have written such a poem, because he had no reason to be afraid of tears over his grave . . . there would be none.

'There will be, if I outlive you,' Marianna articulated slowly; and raising her eyes to the ceiling, after a brief silence, in an undertone as though speaking to herself, she queried, 'How ever did he draw a portrait of me? From memory?'

Nezhdanov turned quickly to her. . . .

'Yes, from memory.'

Marianna was amazed at his answering. It seemed to her that she had merely thought the question.

'It is astonishing . . .' she went on in the same subdued voice; 'why, he has no talent for drawing. What was I going to say?' she resumed aloud; 'oh, about Dobrolyubov's poem. One ought to write poems like Pushkin's, or such as that

> [1] And let me die—small cause for grief;
>   One thought alone frets my sick mind;
>   That death may chance to play
>   An unkind jest with me.
>
>   I dread lest over my cold corpse
>   The scalding tears should flow;
>   And lest someone with stupid zeal
>   Lay flowers upon my bier;
>
>   Lest flocking round in unfeigned grief,
>   My friends walk after it to the grave;
>   Lest as I lie under the earth,
>   I may become one loved and prized;
>
>   Lest all so eagerly desired,
>   And so in vain by me—in life,
>   May smile on me consolingly
>   Above the stone that marks my grave.
>
>   DOBR., *Works*, vol. iv. p. 615.

one of Dobrolyubov's: this is not poetry . . . though it's something as good.'

'And poems like mine,' said Nezhdanov, 'ought not to be written at all? Eh?'

'Poems like yours please your friends not because they are very fine, but because you are a fine person, and they are like you.'

Nezhdanov smiled.

'You have buried them, and me with them!'

Marianna gave him a slap on his hand and told him he was too bad. . . . Soon after she announced that she was tired and was going to bed.

'By the way, do you know,' she added, shaking her short, thick curls, 'I've got one hundred and thirty-seven roubles; what have you?'

'Ninety-eight.'

'Oh! but we're rich . . . for simplified creatures. Well, good-bye till to-morrow!'

She went out; but a few instants later her door was slightly opened, and through the narrow crack he heard first, 'Good-bye!' then more softly, 'Good-bye!' and the key clicked in the lock.

Nezhdanov sank on to the sofa and covered his eyes with his hand. . . . Then he got up quickly, went up to the door, and knocked.

'What is it?' came from within.

'Not till to-morrow, Marianna . . . but to-morrow!'

'To-morrow,' responded a gentle voice.

29

THE next day early in the morning Nezhdanov again knocked at Marianna's door.

'It's I,' he said in answer to her 'Who's there?' 'Can you come out to me?'

'Wait a minute . . . directly.'

She came out, and uttered a cry of astonishment. For the first minute she did not recognise him. He had on a long full-skirted coat of threadbare, yellowish nankin, with tiny buttons and a high waist; he had combed his hair in the Russian style, with a straight parting in the middle; his neck was wrapped in a blue kerchief; in his hand he held a cap with a broken peak; on his feet were unpolished high boots of calf leather.

'Good gracious!' cried Marianna; 'how . . . horrid you look!' and thereupon she gave him a rapid embrace, and a still more rapid kiss. 'But why are you dressed like that? You look like a poor sort of shopkeeper . . . or a pedlar, or a discharged house-serf. Why that coat with skirts, and not simply a peasant's smock?'

'That's just it,' began Nezhdanov, who in his get-up did really resemble a pedlar, and he was conscious of this himself, and was full of vexation and embarrassment at heart; he was so much embarrassed that he kept striking himself on the breast with the outspread fingers of both hands, as though he were brushing himself.

'In a smock I should have been recognised at once, so Pavel declared; and this costume . . . in his words . . . looked as though I'd never had any other dress cut for me in my life! Not very flattering to my vanity, I may remark in parenthesis.'

'Do you really mean to go out at once . . . to begin?' Marianna inquired with keen interest.

'Yes; I shall try, though . . . in reality . . .'

'Happy fellow!' interrupted Marianna.

'This Pavel is really a wonderful man,' Nezhdanov went on; 'he knows everything, directly he sets eyes on you; and then all of a sudden he purses up his face, as though he were outside it all—and wouldn't meddle in anything! He serves the cause himself—and makes fun of it all the while.

219

He brought me the pamphlets from Markelov; he knows him and speaks of him as Sergei Mihalovitch. But for Solomin he'd go through fire and water.'

'And so would Tatyana,' observed Marianna. 'Why is it people are so devoted to him?'

Nezhdanov did not answer.

'What sort of pamphlets did Pavel bring you?' asked Marianna.

'Oh! the usual things. "The Tale of Four Brothers" . . . and others too . . . the ordinary well-known things. However, those are best.'

Marianna looked round anxiously.

'But what of Tatyana? She promised to come so early.'

'Here she is,' said Tatyana, coming into the room with a small bundle in her hand. She was standing at the door, and had heard Marianna's exclamation.

'You need not be in a hurry; it's not such a treat as all that.'

Marianna fairly flew to meet her.

'You have brought it!'

Tatyana patted the bundle.

'Everything's here . . . fully prepared. . . . You've only got to put the things on . . . and go out in your finery for folks to admire you.'

'Ah, come along, come along, Tatyana Osipovna, dear. . . .'

Marianna drew her into her room.

Left alone, Nezhdanov paced twice up and down with a peculiar stealthy gait . . . (he imagined for some reason that that was just how small shopkeepers walked); he sniffed cautiously at his own sleeve, and the lining of his cap—and frowned; he looked at himself in a little looking-glass hanging on the wall near the window, and shook his head; he certainly looked very unattractive. 'All the better, though,' he thought. Then he took up a few pamphlets, stuffed them in his skirt pocket, and murmured a few words to himself in the accent of a small shopkeeper. 'I fancy that's like it,' he thought again; 'but after all, what need of acting? my get-up will answer for me.' And at that point Nezhdanov recollected a German convict, who had to run away right across Russia, and he spoke Russian badly, too; but thanks to a merchant's cap edged with cat's-skin, which he had bought in a provincial town, he was taken everywhere for a merchant, and had successfully made his way over the frontier.

At that instant Solomin came in.

'Aha! brother Alexey,' he cried; 'you're studying your part! Excuse me, brother; in that disguise one can't address you respectfully.'

'Oh, please do. . . . I'd meant to ask you to call me so.'

'Only it's awfully early yet; but, there, I suppose you want to get used to it. Well, then, all right. But you'll have to wait a bit; the master's not gone yet. He's asleep.'

'I'll go out later on,' answered Nezhdanov. 'I'm going to walk about the neighbourhood till I get instructions of some sort.'

'That's right! Only I tell you what, brother Alexey . . . I may call you Alexey, then?'

' 'Lexey, if you like,' said Nezhdanov, smiling.

'No; we mustn't overdo it. Listen! good counsel is better than money, as they say. I see you have pamphlets there; you can give them to whom you please—only not in the factory!'

'Why not?'

"Because, in the first place, it would be risky for you; secondly, I have pledged myself to the owner that there shall be nothing of the sort going on—after all, the factory's his, you know; and thirdly, we have something started there—schools and so on. . . . And—well—you might ruin all that. Act as you please, as best you may—I will not hinder you; but don't touch my factory-hands.'

'Caution never comes amiss . . . hey?' Nezhdanov remarked with a malignant half-smile.

Solomin smiled his own broad smile.

'Just so, brother Alexey; it never comes amiss. But who is this I see? Where are we?'

These last exclamations referred to Marianna, who appeared in the doorway of her room in a sprigged chintz gown, that had seen many washings, with a yellow kerchief on her shoulders and a red one on her head. Tatyana was peeping out from behind her back, in simple and kindly admiration of her. Marianna looked both fresher and younger in her simple costume; it suited her far better than the long full-skirted coat suited Nezhdanov.

'Vassily Fedotitch, please don't laugh,' Marianna entreated, and she flushed the colour of a poppy.

'What a pretty pair!' Tatyana was exclaiming, meanwhile clapping her hands. 'Only you, my dear laddie, don't be angry, you're nice, very nice—but beside my little lass here you cut no figure at all.'

'And, really, she's exquisite,' thought Nezhdanov; 'oh! how I love her!'

'And look-ee,' went on Tatyana, 'she's changed rings with me. She's given me her gold one and taken my silver one.'

'Girls of the people don't wear gold rings,' said Marianna. Tatyana sighed.

'I'll take care of it for you, dearie, never fear.'

'Well, sit down; sit down, both of you,' began Solomin, who had been all the time watching Marianna, with his head a little bent; 'in old days you remember folks always used to sit down together for a bit when they were setting off on their road. And you've both a long, hard road before you.'

Marianna, still rosy red, sat down; Nezhdanov too sat down; Solomin sat down; and last of all Tatyana too sat down on a thick log of wood standing on end.

Solomin looked at all of them in turn:

> 'Step back a bit
> And look at it,
> How nicely here we all do sit . . .'

he said, slightly screwing up his eyes; and all of a sudden he burst out laughing, but so nicely that, far from feeling offended, they were all delighted.

But Nezhdanov suddenly got up.

'I'm off,' he said, 'this minute; though this is all very delightful—only a trifle like a farce with dressing-up in it. Don't be uneasy,' he turned to Solomin; 'I won't touch your factory-hands. I will do a little talking about the suburbs, and come back, and I'll tell you all my adventures, Marianna, if only there's anything to tell. Give me your hand for good luck!'

'A cup of tea'd be as well first,' observed Tatyana.

'No! tea-drinking indeed! If I want anything I'll go to a tavern or simply a gin-shop.'

Tatyana shook her head.

'Those taverns swarm along our highroads nowadays like fleas in a sheepskin. The villages are all so big—why, Balmasovo . . .'

'Good-bye, till we meet . . . may I leave good luck with you!' Nezhdanov added, correcting himself and entering into his part as a small shopkeeper. But before he had reached the door, Pavel poked his head in from the corridor under his very nose, and handing him a long thin staff, peeled, with a strip of bark running round it like a screw, he said: 'Please take it, Alexey Dmitritch; lean on it as you walk; and the further you hold the stick away from you the better effect it will have.'

Nezhdanov took the staff without speaking and went off; Pavel followed him. Tatyana was about to go away too; Marianna got up and stopped her.

'Wait a little, Tatyana Osipovna; I want you.'

'But I'll be back in a minute with the samovar. Your comrade went off without any tea—he was in such a desperate hurry. . . . But why should you deny yourself? Later on things'll be clearer.'

Tatyana went out; Solomin too rose. Marianna was standing with her back to him, and when she did at last turn round to him—seeing that for a very long time he had not uttered a single word—she caught in his face, in his eyes which were fastened upon her, an expression she had never seen in him

223

before, an expression of inquiry, of anxiety, almost of curiosity. She was disconcerted and blushed again. And Solomin seemed ashamed of what she had caught sight of in his face, and he began talking louder than usual:

'Well, well, Marianna . . . here you've made a beginning.'

'A fine beginning, Vassily Fedotitch! How can one call it a beginning? I feel somehow very stupid all of a sudden. Alexey was right; we are really acting a sort of farce.'

Solomin sat down again on his chair.

'But, Marianna, let me say . . . How did you picture it to yourself—the beginning? It's not a matter of building barricades with a flag over them, and shouting "hurrah! for the republic!" And that's not a woman's work either. But you now to-day will start training some Lukerya in something good, and it'll be a hard task for you, as Lukerya won't be over-quick of understanding, and she'll be shy of you, and will fancy too that what you're trying to teach her won't be of the least use to her; and in a fortnight or three weeks you'll be struggling with some other Lukerya, and meanwhile you'll be washing a child or teaching him his A B C, or giving medicine to a sick man . . . that will be your beginning.'

'But the sisters of mercy do all that, you know, Vassily Fedotitch! What need, then . . . of all this?' Marianna pointed to herself and round about her with a vague gesture. 'I dreamt of something else.'

'You wanted to sacrifice yourself?'

Marianna's eyes glistened.

'Yes . . . yes . . . yes!'

'And Nezhdanov?'

Marianna shrugged her shoulders.

'What of Nezhdanov! We will go forward together . . . or I will go alone.'

Solomin looked intently at Marianna.

'Do you know what, Marianna . . . you will excuse the unpleasantness of the expression . . . but to my idea, combing the mangy head of a dirty urchin is a sacrifice, and a great sacrifice, of which not many people are capable.'

'But I would not refuse to do that, Vassily Fedotitch.'

'I know you wouldn't! Yes, you are capable of that. And that's what you will be doing for a time; and afterwards, maybe—something else too.'

'But to do that I must learn from Tatyana!'

'By all means . . . get her to show you. You will scour pots, and pluck chickens. . . . And so, who knows, maybe you will save your country!'

'You are laughing at me, Vassily Fedotitch.'

Solomin shook his head slowly.

'O my sweet Marianna! believe me, I am not laughing at you; and my words are the simple truth. You now, all of you, Russian women, are more capable, and loftier too, than we men.'

Marianna raised her downcast eyes.

'I should like to justify your expectations, Solomin . . . and then—I'm ready to die!'

Solomin got up.

'No, live . . . live! That's the great thing. By the way, don't you want to find out what is taking place in your home now, as regards your flight? Won't they take steps of some sort? We need only drop a word to Pavel—he'll reconnoitre in no time.'

Marianna was surprised.

'What an extraordinary man he is!'

'Yes . . . he's rather a wonderful fellow. For instance, when you want to celebrate your marriage with Alexey—he'll arrange that too with Zosim. . . . You remember I told you there was a priest. . . . But I suppose there's no need of him for a while? No?'

'No.'

'No, then.' Solomin went up to the door that separated the two rooms—Nezhdanov's and Marianna's—and bent down over the lock.

'What are you looking at there?' asked Marianna.

'Does it lock?'

'Yes,' whispered Marianna.

Solomin turned to her. She did not raise her eyes.

'Then, there's no need to find out what are Sipyagin's intentions?' he observed cheerfully; 'no need, eh?'

Solomin was about to go away.

'Vassily Fedotitch . . .'

'What is it?'

'Tell me, please, why is it you, who are always so silent, are so talkative with me? You don't know how much it pleases me.'

'Why is it?'—Solomin took both her little soft hands in his big rough ones—'Why?—Well, it must be because I like you so much. Good-bye.'

He went out. . . . Marianna stood a little, looked after him, thought a little, and went off to Tatyana, who had not yet brought in the samovar, and with whom she did—it is true—drink tea, but she also scoured pots, and plucked chickens, and even combed out the tangled mane of a small boy.

About dinner-time she returned to her little apartments. . . . She had not long to wait for Nezhdanov.

He returned, weary and covered with dust, and almost fell on to the sofa. She at once sat down beside him. 'Well? well? Tell me!'

'You remember those two lines,' he answered in a weak voice:

> ' "It would all have been so comic
> If it had not been so sad"

Do you remember?'

'Of course I do.'

'Well, those lines apply precisely to my first expedition. But no! There was positively more of the comic in it. In the first place, I'm convinced that nothing's easier than to play a part; no one dreamt of suspecting me. But there was one thing I had not thought of—one wants to make up some sort of story beforehand . . . they keep asking one—where you're from, and what you're doing—and you have nothing ready. However, even that's hardly necessary. One's only to propose a dram of vodka at the gin-shop, and lie away as one pleases.'

'And you . . . did tell lies?' asked Marianna.

'I lied . . . the best I could. The second point is: all, absolutely all the people I talked to are discontented; and no one even cares to know how to remedy this discontent! But at propaganda I seem to be a very poor hand; two pamphlets I simply left secretly in a room—one I thrust into a cart. . . . What'll come of them the Lord only knows! I offered pamphlets to four men. One asked was it a religious book, and did not take it; another said he could not read, and took it for his children as there was a woodcut on the cover: a third began by agreeing with me. "To be sure, to be sure . . ." then all of a sudden fell to swearing at me in the most unexpected way, and he too did not take one; the fourth at last took one, and thanked me very much for it, but I fancy he couldn't make head or tail of what I said to him. Besides that, a dog bit my leg; a peasant woman brandished a fire-shovel at me from the door of her hut, shouting, "Ugh! you beast! You Moscow loafers! Will nothing drown you?" And a soldier on furlough, too, kept shouting after me, "Wait a minute, we'll put a bullet through you, my friend"; and he'd got drunk on my money!'

'Anything more?'

'Anything more? I've rubbed a blister on my heel; one of my boots is awfully big. And now I'm hungry, and my head's splitting from the vodka.'

'Have you drunk much, then?'

'No, not much—only to set the example; but I've been in five gin-shops. But I can't stand that filth—vodka—a bit. And how our peasant can drink it passes my understanding! If one must drink vodka to be simplified, I'd rather be excused.'

'And so no one suspected you?'

'No one. An innkeeper, a stout, pale man with whitish

eyes, was the only person who looked at me suspiciously. I heard him tell his wife to "keep an eye on that red-haired chap . . . with the squint". (I never knew till then that I squinted.) "He's a sharper. Do you see how ponderously he drinks?" What ponderously means in that context I didn't understand; but it could hardly be a compliment. Something after the style of Gogol's "movy-ton" in the *Revising Inspector;* do you remember? Perhaps because I tried to pour my vodka under the table on the sly. Ugh! it's hard, it's hard for an æsthetic creature to be brought into contact with real life.

'Better luck next time,' Marianna consoled Nezhdanov. 'But I'm glad that you look at your first attempt from a humorous point of view. . . . You weren't bored really?'

'No, I wasn't bored; in fact, I was amused. But I know for a certainty I shall begin to think over it now, and I shall feel so sick and so sad.'

'No, no! I won't let you think. I'm going to tell you what I've been doing. Dinner'll be brought us in directly; by the way, I must tell you I've scoured out most thoroughly the pot Tatyana's cooked the soup in. . . . And I shall tell you . . . everything over every spoonful.'

And so she did. Nezhdanov listened to her chat, and looked and looked at her . . . so that several times she stopped to let him tell her why he was looking at her like that. . . . But he was silent.

After dinner she offered to read aloud to him some of Spielhagen. But before she had finished the first page, he got up impulsively, and, going up to her, fell at her feet. She stood up, he flung both his arms round her knees, and began to utter passionate words—disconnected and despairing words! 'He would like to die, he knew he would soon die. . . .' She did not stir, did not resist; she calmly submitted to his abrupt embrace, calmly, even caressingly, looked down at him. She laid both hands on his head, that was shaking convulsively in the folds of her dress. But her very calmness had a more powerful effect on him than if she had repulsed him. He got up, murmured: 'Forgive me, Marianna, for what has passed to-day and yesterday; tell me again that you are ready to wait till I am worthy of your love, and forgive me.'

'I have given you my word . . . and I can't change.'

'Thank you; good-bye.'

Nezhdanov went out; Marianna locked herself in her room.

30

A FORTNIGHT later, in the same place, this was what Nezhdanov was writing to his friend Silin, as he bent over his little three-legged table, on which a tallow candle gave a dim and niggardly light. (It was long after midnight. On the sofa and on the floor lay mud-stained garments, hurriedly flung off; a fine, incessant rain was pattering on the window-panes, and a strong, warm wind breathed in great sighs about the roof.)

'DEAR VLADIMIR,—I am writing to you without putting an address, and this letter will even be sent by a messenger to a distant posting-station, because my presence here is a secret; and to tell it you might mean the ruin not of myself alone. It will be enough for you to know that I have been living at a large factory, together with Marianna, for the last fortnight. We ran away from the Sipyagins' the very day I wrote to you last. We were given a home here by a friend. I will call him Vassily. He is the chief person here—a splendid fellow. Our stay in this factory is only temporary. We are here till the time comes for action—though, to judge by what has happened so far, this time is hardly likely ever to come! Vladimir, my heart is heavy, heavy. First of all, I must tell you that though Marianna and I have run away

229

together, we are so far as brother and sister. She loves me . . .
and has told me she will be mine if . . . I feel I have the right
to ask it of her.

'Vladimir, I don't feel I have the right! She believes in
me, in my honesty—I'm not going to deceive her. I know I
have never loved anyone and never shall love (that's pretty
certain!) anyone more than her. But, for all that, how can
I unite her fate for ever to mine? A living being—to a
corpse? Well, not a corpse—to a half-dead creature! Where
would one's conscience be? You will say, if there were a
strong passion—conscience would have nothing to say. That's
the very point that I am a corpse; an honest, well-meaning
corpse, if you like. Please don't cry out that I always
exaggerate. . . . All I am telling you is the truth! the truth!
Marianna is a very concentrated nature, and now she is all
absorbed in her activity, in which she believes. . . . While
I?

'Well, enough of love and personal happiness, and everything of that sort. For the last fortnight now I have been
"going to the people", and alack and alack! anything more
absurd you cannot imagine. Of course, there the fault lies
in me, and not in the work itself. Granted, I'm not a
Slavophil; I'm not one of those who find their panacea in the
people, in contact with them; I don't lay the people on my
aching stomach like a flannel bandage. . . . I want to have
an influence on them myself; but how? How accomplish that?
It appears when I am with the people that I am always only
stooping to them, and listening; and when it does happen
that I say anything, it's beneath contempt! I feel myself I'm
no good. It's like a bad actor in the wrong part.
Conscientiousness is quite out of place in this, and so is
scepticism, and even a sort of pitiful humour directed against
myself. . . . It's all not worth a brass farthing! It's
positively sickening to remember; sickening to look at the rags
I drag about on me, at this masquerade, as Vassily expresses
it! They maintain one ought first to study the people's talk,
learn their character and habits. . . . Rubbish! rubbish!

230

rubbish! One must *believe* in what one says, and then one
may say what one likes. I once chanced to hear something
like a sermon from a sectarian prophet. There's no saying
what rot he talked; it was a sort of hotch-potch of ecclesiastical
and bookish language, with simple peasant idioms, and that
not Russian, but White Russian of some sort. . . . And you
know he kept pounding away at the same thing, like a plover
calling! "The spirit has dee-scended, the spirit has dee-
scended!" But then his eyes were ablaze, his voice firm and
hoarse, his fists clenched—he was like iron all over! The
listeners did not understand, but they revered him! And they
followed him! While I start speaking like a criminal—I'm
begging pardon all the while. I ought to go to the sectarians,
really; their art is not great . . . but there's the place to get
faith, faith! Marianna there has faith. She's at work from
early morning, busy with Tatyana, a peasant woman here,
good-natured and not a fool; by the way, she says of us that
we want simplification, and calls us simplified folks;—well,
Marianna busies herself with this woman, and never sits down
a minute; she's a regular ant! She's delighted that her hands
are getting red and rough; and looks forward to some day, if
necessary, the scaffold! While awaiting the scaffold, she has
even tried giving up shoes; she went somewhere barefoot, and
came back barefoot. I heard her afterwards washing her feet
a long while; I see she walks cautiously on them—they're sore
from not being used to it; but she looks as joyful, as radiant,
as though she had found a treasure, as though the sun were
shining on her. Yes, Marianna's first-rate! And when I try
to talk to her of my feelings, to begin with, I feel somehow
ashamed, as though I were laying hands on what's not mine;
and then that look . . . oh, that awful, devoted, unresist-
ing look. . . . "Take me," it seems to say . . . *"but
remember!* And what need of all this? Isn't there something
better, higher upon earth?" That is, in other words, "Put on
your stinking overcoat, and go out to the people." . . . And
so, you see, I go out to the people. . . .

'Oh, how I curse at such times my nervousness, delicacy,

sensitiveness, squeamishness, all I have inherited from my aristocratic father! What right had he to shove me into life, supplying me with organs utterly unfit for the surroundings in which I must move? To hatch a chicken and shove it into the water! An artist in the mud! a democrat, a lover of the people, whom the mere smell of that loathsome vodka, "the green wine", turns ill and nearly sick?

'See what I've worked myself up to—abusing my father! And, indeed, I became a democrat of myself; he'd no hand in that.

'Yes, Vladimir, I'm in a bad way. I have begun to be haunted by some grey, ugly thoughts! Can it be, you will ask me, that I have not even during this fortnight come across anything consolatory, any good, live person, however ignorant? What shall I say? I have met something of the sort . . . I've even come across one very fine, splendid, plucky chap. But turn it which way I will, I'm no use to him with my pamphlets, and that's all about it! Pavel— a man in the factory here—(he's Vassily's right hand, a very clever, very sharp fellow, a future "head" . . . I fancy I wrote to you about him)—he has a friend, a peasant, Elizar is his name . . . a clear brain, too, and a free spirit, untrammelled in every way; but directly we meet, it's as though there's a wall between us! his face is nothing but a "No!" And again another fellow I met with . . . he was one of the hot-tempered sort, though. "Now then, sir," says he, "no soft soap, please, but say straight out, are you giving up all your land, as it is, or not?" "What do you mean?" I answered; "I'm not a gentleman!" (and I even added, I remember, "Lord bless you!"). "But if you're a common man," says he, "what sort of sense is there in you? Do me the favour to let me alone!"

'And another thing. I've noticed if anyone listens to you very readily, takes pamphlets at once, you may be sure he's one of the wrong sort, a featherhead; or you'll come on a fine talker, an educated fellow, who can do nothing but keep repeating some favourite expression. One, for instance, simply drove me distracted; everything with him was "product". Whatever you say to him, he keeps on, "To be sure, a product!" Ugh, to the devil with him! One remark more. . . . Do you remember at one time, a long while ago, there used to be a great deal of talk about "superfluous" people—Hamlets? Fancy, such "superfluous" people are to be found now among the peasants! with a special tone of their own, of course. . . . Moreover, they're for the most part of consumptive build. Interesting types, and they come to us readily; but for the cause they're no good—just like the Hamlets of former days. Come, what is one to do, then? Found a secret printing-press? Why, there are books enough as it is, both of the sort, "Cross yourself and take up the hatchet," and the sort that say, "Take up the hatchet" simply. Write novels of peasant life, filled out with padding? They wouldn't get printed, most likely. Or first take up the hatchet? . . . But against whom, with whom, what for? So that the national soldier may shoot you down with the national rifle! Well, that's a sort of complex suicide! It would be better to make an end of myself. At least I shall know when and how, and shall choose myself what part to aim at. . . . Really, I fancy if there were a war of independence going on now anywhere, I would set off there, not to liberate anybody whatever (the idea of liberating others when one's own people are not free!), but to make an end of myself.

'Our friend Vassily, the man who has taken us in here, is a happy man; he is of our camp, and a quiet fellow in a way. He's not in a hurry. Another man I should abuse for that . . . but him I can't. And it seems as though the whole basis of it doesn't lie in convictions, but in character. Vassily has a character you can't pick holes in. Well, to be sure, he's right. He sits a great deal with us, with Marianna. And here's a curious fact. I love her and she loves me (I can see you smiling at that phrase, but, by God, it's so!); and we have hardly anything to say to one another. But she argues and discusses with him, and listens to him. I'm not jealous of him; he's taking steps for getting her into some place, at least she asks him about it; only my heart aches when I look at them. And yet imagine: if I were to falter out a word about marriage, she'd agree at once, and the priest, Zosim, would put in an appearance: "Esaias, be exalted," and all the rest in due order. Only, it would make it no better for me, and *nothing would be changed*. . . . There's no way out of it! Life's cut me on the cross, dear Vladimir, as you remember our friend the drunken tailor used to complain of his wife.

'I feel, though, that it won't last long, I feel that something is preparing. . . .

'Haven't I demanded and proved that we ought to "act"? Well, now we are going to act.

'I don't remember whether I wrote to you of another friend of mine, a dark fellow, a relation of the Sipyagins. He may, very likely, cook a kettle of fish that won't be swallowed too easily.

'I quite meant to finish this letter before, but there! Though I do nothing, nothing at all, I scribble verses. I don't read them to Marianna, she doesn't much care for them, but you . . . sometimes even praise them; and what's of most importance, you won't talk about them to anyone. I have been struck by one universal phenomenon in Russia. Anyway, here they are—the verses:

SLEEP

A long while I had not been in my own land. . . .
But I found in it no change to notice——
Everywhere the same deathlike, senseless stagnation,
Houses without roofs, walls tumbling down,
And the same filth and stench and poverty and boredom!
And the same slavish glance, now insolent, now abject!
Our people were made free; and the free arm
Hangs as before like a whip unused.
All, all is as before. . . . And in one thing alone
Europe, Asia, the whole world we have outstripped!
No! never yet have my dear countrymen
Sunk into a sleep so terrible!

Everything is asleep; everywhere, in village and in town,
In cart, in sledge, by day, by night, sitting and standing . . .
The merchant, the official sleeps; the sentinel at his post
Stands asleep in the cold of the snow and in the burning heat!
And the prisoner sleeps; and the judge snores;
Dead asleep are the peasants; asleep, they reap and plough;
They thresh asleep; the father sleeps, the mother and children
All are asleep! He that flogs is asleep, and he too that is flogged!
Only the Tsar's gin-shop never closes an eye;
And grasping tight her pot of gin,
Her brow on the Pole and her heels on the Caucasus,
Lies in interminable sleep our country, holy Russia!

'Please forgive me: I didn't want to send you such a melancholy letter without giving you a little amusement at the end (you'll certainly notice some halting lines . . . but what of it!). When shall I write to you again? Shall I write again? Whatever becomes of me, I am sure you will not forget your faithful friend,

'A.N.

'*P.S.*—Yes, our people is asleep. . . . But I fancy if anything ever does wake it, it won't be what *we* are thinking of. . . .'

After writing the last line Nezhdanov flung down the pen, and saying to himself, 'Well, now try to sleep and forget all this rot, rhymester', he lay down on the bed . . . but it was long before sleep visited his eyes.

Next morning Marianna waked him, passing through his room to Tatyana; but he had only just had time to dress when she came back again. Her face expressed delight and agitation; she seemed excited.

'Do you know, Alyosha, they say that in the T—— district, not far from here, it has begun already!'

'Eh? what has begun? who says so?'

'Pavel. They say the peasants are rising, refusing to pay taxes, collecting in mobs.'

'You heard that yourself?'

'Tatyana told me. But here's Pavel himself. Ask him.'

Pavel came in and confirmed Marianna's tale.

'There's disturbance in T—— district, that's true!' he said, shaking his beard and screwing up his flashing black eyes. 'It's Sergei Mihalovitch's work, one must suppose. It's five days now he's not been at home.'

Nezhdanov snatched up his cap.

'Where are you going?' asked Marianna.

'Where? . . . there,' he answered, scowling, and not raising his eyes; 'to T—— district.'

'Then I'll go with you. You'll take me, won't you? Only let me put a big kerchief over my head.'

'It's not a woman's work,' said Nezhdanov sullenly, as before looking down as though irritated.

'No! . . . no! . . . You do right to go; or Markelov would think you a coward. . . . And I will go with you.'

'I'm not a coward,' said Nezhdanov in the same sullen voice.

'I meant to say he would take us both for cowards. I'm coming with you.'

Marianna went into her room for the kerchief, while Pavel uttered in a sort of stealthy inward whistle, 'Ah-ha, aha!' and promptly vanished. He ran to warn Solomin.

Marianna had not reappeared when Solomin came into Nezhdanov's room. He was standing with his face to the window, his forehead resting on his arm, and his arm on the window-pane. Solomin touched him on the shoulder. He turned quickly round. Dishevelled and unwashed, Nezhdanov had a wild and strange look. Though indeed Solomin too had changed of late. He had grown yellow, his face looked drawn, his upper teeth were slightly visible. . . . He too seemed unhinged, so far as his 'well-balanced' nature could be.

'So Markelov could not control himself,' he began; 'this may turn out badly, for him chiefly . . . and for others too.'

'I want to go and see what's going on . . .' observed Nezhdanov.

236

'And I too,' added Marianna, making her appearance in the doorway.

Solomin turned slowly to her.

'I would not advise you to, Marianna. You might betray yourself and us; without meaning to and utterly needlessly. Let Nezhdanov go and see what's in the air a little, if he likes . . . and the less of that the better!—but why should you?'

'I don't like to stay behind when he goes.'

'You will hamper him.'

Marianna glanced at Nezhdanov. He stood immovable, with an immovable, sullen face.

'But if there's danger?' she said.

Solomin smiled.

'Don't be afraid . . . when there's danger, I'll let you go.'

Marianna silently took the kerchief off her head and sat down.

Then Solomin turned to Nezhdanov.

'And do you, brother, really look about a little. Perhaps it's all exaggerated. Only, please, be careful. Someone shall go with you, though. And come back as quick as possible. You promise? Nezhdanov, do you promise?'

'Yes.'

'Yes, for certain?'

'Since everyone obeys you here, Marianna and all.'

Nezhdanov went out into the passage without saying good-bye. Pavel popped up out of the darkness and ran down the staircase before him, his iron-shod boots ringing as he went. Was *he* then to accompany Nezhdanov?

Solomin sat down by Marianna.

'You heard Nezhdanov's last words?'

'Yes; he's vexed that I listen to you more than to him. And indeed it's the truth. I love *him,* but I obey *you.* He's dearer to me . . . but you're nearer.'

Solomin cautiously stroked her hand with his.

'This . . . is a most unpleasant affair,' he observed at last. 'If Markelov's mixed up in it—he's lost.'

Marianna shuddered.

'Lost?'

'Yes. . . . He does nothing by halves, and he won't hide behind others.'

'Lost!' murmured Marianna again, and the tears ran down her face. 'O Vassily Fedotitch! I am very sorry for him. But why can't he be victorious? Why must he inevitably be lost?'

'Because in such undertakings, Marianna, the first always perish, even if they succeed. . . . And in the work *he's* plotting for, not only the first and the second, but even the tenth . . . and the twentieth.'

'Then we shall never live to see it?'

'What you are dreaming of? Never. With our eyes we shall never look upon it; with these living eyes. In the spirit . . . to be sure, that's a different matter. We may gratify ourselves by the sight of it that way now, at once. There's no restriction there.'

'Then how is it you, Solomin——'

'What?'

'How is it you are going along the same way?'

'Because there's no other; that is, speaking more correctly, my aim is the same as Markelov's; but our paths are different.'

'Poor Sergei Mihalovitch!' said Marianna mournfully. Solomin again gave her a discreet caress.

'Come, come; there's nothing certain yet. We shall see what news Pavel brings. In our . . . work one must be of good courage. The English say, "Never say die." A good proverb. Better than the Russian, "When trouble comes, open the gates wide." It's useless lamenting beforehand.'

Solomin got up from his seat.

'And the place you meant to get me?' asked Marianna suddenly. The tears were still glistening on her cheeks, but there was no sadness in her eyes.

Solomin sat down again.

'Do you want so much to get away from here as soon as possible?'

'Oh, no! but I should like to be of use.'

'Marianna, you are of great use even here. Don't forsake us, wait a little. What is it?' Solomin asked of Tatyana, who came in.

'Well, there's some sort of a female article asking for Alexey Dmitritch,' answered Tatyana, laughing and gesticulating. 'I was for saying that he wasn't here, not here at all. We don't know any such person, says I. But then it——'

'Who's—it?'

'Why, this same female article took and wrote her name on this slip of paper here, and says I'm to show it, and that'll admit her; and that if Alexey Dmitritch really isn't at home, then she can wait.'

On the paper stood in large letters, 'Mashurina.'

'Show her in,' said Solomin. 'You won't mind, Marianna, if she comes in here? She, too, is one of ours.'

'Oh, no! indeed!'

A few seconds later Mashurina appeared in the doorway, in the same dress in which we saw her at the beginning of the first chapter.

31

'Is Nezhdanov not at home?' she asked; then, seeing Solomin, she went up to him and gave him her hand. 'How are you, Solomin?' At Marianna she simply cast a sidelong glance.

'He will soon be back,' answered Solomin. 'But let me ask, from whom did you find out . . . ?'

'From Markelov. Though indeed it's known in the town . . . to two or three people already.'

'Really?'

'Yes. Someone has blabbed. Besides, they say Nezhdanov himself has been recognised.'

'So much for this dressing-up business!' muttered Solomin. 'Let me introduce you,' he added aloud. 'Miss Sinetsky, Miss Mashurin! Pray sit down!'

Mashurina gave a slight nod and sat down.

'I have a letter for Nezhdanov; and for you, Solomin, a verbal message.'

'What sort of message? From whom?'

'From a person you know. . . . How are things with you? . . . is everything ready?'

'Nothing is ready.'

Mashurina opened her tiny little eyes as wide as she could.

'Nothing?'

'Nothing.'

'You mean absolutely nothing?'

'Absolutely nothing.'

'Is that what I'm to say?'

'That's what you must say.'

Mashurina pondered a minute, then she took a cigarette out of her pocket.

'A light—can you give me?'

'Here's a match.'

Mashurina lighted her cigarette.

'They expected something quite different,' she began. 'And all around—it's not as it is with you. However, that's your affair. I'm not here for long. Only to see Nezhdanov and to give him the letter.'

'Where are you going?'

'Oh, a long way from here.' (She was in fact going to Geneva, but she did not care to tell Solomin so. She did not regard him as altogether trustworthy; besides, there was an 'outsider' sitting there. Mashurina, who hardly knew a word of German, was being sent to Geneva, in order to hand to a person there utterly unknown to her a torn scrap of cardboard with a vine-branch sketched on it, and two hundred and seventy-nine roubles.)

240

'Where's Ostrodumov? Is he with you?'

'No. He's near here . . . he got stuck on the way. But he'll come when he's wanted. Pimen's all right. No need to worry about him.'

'How did you come here?'

'In a cart . . . how else should I? Give me another match. . . .'

Solomin gave her a lighted match.

'Vassily Fedotitch!' a voice whispered all at once at the door. 'Please, sir!'

'Who's there? What do you want?'

'Please come,' the voice repeated with persuasive insistency. 'There's some strange workmen come here; they keep jawing away, and Pavel Yegoritch isn't here.'

Solomin excused himself, got up and went out.

Mashurina fell to staring at Marianna, and stared at her so long that the latter was quite out of countenance.

'Forgive me,' she said suddenly in her gruff, abrupt voice; 'I'm a rough sort, I don't know how to put things. Don't be angry; you needn't answer if you don't want to. Are you the girl that ran away from the Sipyagins'?'

Marianna was somewhat disconcerted; however, she said, 'Yes.'

'With Nezhdanov?'

'Well, yes.'

'If you please . . . give me your hand. Forgive me, please. You must be good, since he loves you.'

Marianna pressed her hand.

'Do you know Nezhdanov well?'

'Yes, I know him. I used to see him in Petersburg. That's what makes me say so. Sergei Mihalitch, too, told me. . . .'

'Ah, Markelov! You have seen him lately?'

'Yes. Now he's gone away.'

'Where?'

'Where he was ordered.'

Marianna sighed.

'Ah, Miss Mashurin, I fear for him.'

241

'To begin with, I'm not "Miss". You ought to cast off all such manners. And, secondly . . . you say, "I fear." That won't do either. You will come not to fear for yourself, and to give up fearing for others. Though indeed I'll tell you what strikes me: it's easy for me, Fekla Mashurina, to talk like that. I'm ugly. But of course . . . you're a beauty. That must make it all the harder for you.' (Marianna looked down and turned away.) 'Sergei Mihalovitch told me. . . . He knew I had a letter for Nezhdanov. . . . "Don't go to the factory," he said to me, "don't take the letter; it will be the breaking-up of everything there. Stay away! They're both happy there. . . . So let them be! Don't meddle!" I should be glad not to meddle . . . but what was I to do about the letter?'

'You must give it without fail,' Marianna assented. 'But oh, how kind he is, Sergei Mihalitch! Can it be that he will be killed, Mashurina . . . or be sent to Siberia?'

'Well, what then? Don't people come back from Siberia? And as for losing one's life! Life's sweet to some, and to some it's bitter. His life is not made of refined sugar either.'

Mashurina again turned an intent and inquisitive gaze on Marianna.

'Yes, you are certainly beautiful,' she cried at last, 'a perfect little bird! I'm beginning to think Alexey's not coming. . . . Shouldn't I give you the letter? Why wait?'

'I will give it him, you may rest assured.'

Mashurina rested her cheek in her hand, and for a long, long time she did not speak.

'Tell me,' she began . . . 'excuse me . . . do you love him very much?'

'Yes.'

Mashurina shook her heavy head.

'Well, there's no need to inquire whether he loves you. I'm going, though, or perhaps I shall be too late. You tell him that I have been here . . . sent my greetings to him. Tell him Mashurina has been. You won't forget my name? No?

Mashurina. And the letter. . . . Wait a bit, where have I put it to? . . .'

Mashurina stood up, turned away, making a pretence of rummaging in her pockets, but meanwhile she rapidly put into her mouth a little folded scrap of paper and swallowed it. 'Ah, my goodness! What a piece of idiocy! Can I have lost it? Lost it really is. What a misfortune! If anyone were to find it! . . . No; it's nowhere. So it has turned out as Sergei Mihalitch wished, after all!'

'Look again,' whispered Marianna.

Mashurina waved her hand.

'No! What's the use? It's lost!'

Marianna went up to her.

'Well, kiss me, then!'

Mashurina suddenly took Marianna in her arms and pressed her to her bosom with more than a woman's force.

'I wouldn't have done that for anybody,' she said thickly, 'it's against my conscience . . . it's the first time! Tell him to be more careful. . . . And you too. Mind! It'll soon be a bad place for you here, very bad. Get away, both of you, while . . . Good-bye!' she added in a loud sharp voice. 'But there's something else . . . tell him. . . . No, there's no need. It's no use.'

Mashurina went out, slamming the door, and Marianna was left pondering in the middle of the room.

'What does it all mean?' she said at last; 'why, that woman loves him more than I love him! And what was the meaning of her hints? And why did Solomin go out so suddenly and not come back?'

She began walking up and down. A strange sensation—a mixture of dismay and annoyance and bewilderment—took possession of her. Why had she not gone with Nezhdanov? Solomin had dissuaded her . . . and where was he himself? And what was going on all around her? Mashurina of course had not given her that fatal letter, out of sympathy for Nezhdanov. . . . But how could she bring herself to such an act of insubordination? Did she want to show her magnanimity? What right had she? And why had *she*, Marianna, been so much touched by that action? And was she really touched by it? An ugly woman was attracted by a young man. . . . After all, what was there out of the way in that? And why did Mashurina assume that Marianna's devotion to Nezhdanov was stronger than her sense of duty? Perhaps Marianna had not at all desired such a sacrifice! And what could have been contained in the letter? A call to immediate action? What then?

'And Markelov? He is in danger . . . and are we doing anything?' she asked herself. 'Markelov spares us both, gives us the chance of being happy, won't separate us . . . what is that? Magnanimity too . . . or contempt?

'And did we run away from that detestable house only to be together, billing and cooing like doves?'

Such were Marianna's meditations. . . . And stronger and stronger was the part played in her feelings by the same exasperated annoyance. Moreover, her vanity had been wounded. Why had everyone left her alone—*everyone?*

This 'fat' woman had called her a beauty, a little bird . . . why not a doll at once? And why was it Nezhdanov had gone not alone but with Pavel? As though he needed someone to look after him! And after all, what were Solomin's convictions really? He wasn't a revolutionist at all! And was it possible anyone imagined that her attitude to it all was not a serious one?

Such were the thoughts that whirled chasing one another in confusion through Marianna's heated brain. Compressing her lips and folding her arms like a man, she sat down at last by the window, and again stayed immovable, not leaning back in her chair, all alertness and intensity, ready to spring up any minute. Go to Tatyana, work, she would not; she wanted to do one thing only; to wait! And she waited, obstinately, almost spitefully. From time to time her own mood struck her as strange and incomprehensible. . . . But it made no difference! Once it even occurred to her to wonder whether jealousy was not at the root of all her feeling. But recalling the figure of poor Mashurina, she merely shrugged her shoulders and dismissed the idea with a mental wave of her hand.

Marianna had long to wait; at last she caught the sound of two persons' steps mounting the stairs. She turned her eyes on the door . . . the steps drew nearer. The door opened and Nezhdanov, supported under Pavel's arm, appeared in the doorway. He was deadly pale, and without his cap; his dishevelled hair fell in moist tufts over his brow; his eyes were staring straight before him, seeing nothing. Pavel led him across the room (Nezhdanov's legs moved with an uncertain, feeble totter) and seated him on the sofa.

Marianna jumped up.

'What is it? What's wrong with him? Is he ill?'

But as he settled Nezhdanov, Pavel answered her with a smile, looking round over his shoulder.

'Don't worry yourself, miss, it'll soon pass off. . . . It's just from not being used to it.'

'But what is it?' Marianna queried insistently.

'He's a little tipsy. Been drinking on an empty stomach; that's all!'

Marianna bent over Nezhdanov. He was half-lying across the sofa; his head had sunk on to his breast, his eyes were glassy. . . . He smelt of spirits; he was drunk.

'Alexey!' broke from her lips.

He raised his heavy eyelids with an effort and tried to smile.

'Ah! Marianna!' he stammered, 'you always talked of sim-sim-plification; see now, I'm really simplified. For the people's always drunk, so——'

He broke off; then muttered something indistinct, closed his eyes and fell asleep. Pavel laid him carefully on the sofa.

'Don't be worried, Marianna Vikentyevna,' he repeated, 'he'll sleep a couple of hours and wake up as good as new.'

Marianna was on the point of asking how it had happened; but her questions would have detained Pavel; and she wanted to be alone . . . that is, she did not want Pavel to see him in such a disgraceful state before her longer than could be avoided. She turned away to the window, while Pavel, who had taken in the situation at a glance, carefully covered Nezhdanov's legs with the skirts of his long coat, put a pillow under his head, once more murmured, 'It's nothing!' and went out on tiptoe.

Marianna looked round. Nezhdanov's head sank heavily into the pillow: on his white face could be seen a tense immobility, as on the face of a man mortally sick.

'How did it happen?' she thought.

32

THIS was how it had happened.

On taking his seat in the cart with Pavel, Nezhdanov suddenly fell into a state of intense excitement; and directly they drove out of the factory yard and began rolling along the highroad towards T—— district, he began shouting, stopping the peasants that passed, and addressing them in brief, disconnected sentences. 'Eh, are you asleep?' he would say. 'Rise! the time has come! Down with the taxes! Down with the landowners!' Some peasants stared at him in amazement; others went on, paying no attention to his shouts—they took him for a drunken man; one even said when he had got home that he had met a Frenchman shouting some stammering, incomprehensible stuff. Nezhdanov had enough sense to know how unutterably stupid and even meaningless what he was doing was; but he gradually worked himself up to such a point that he did not realise what was sense and what was nonsense. Pavel tried to quiet him, told him he couldn't really go on like that; that soon they would reach a large village, the first on the borders of T—— district, 'Lasses' Springs,'— that there they could reconnoitre. . . . But Nezhdanov did not listen . . . and at the same time his face was strangely sad, almost despairing. Their horse was a very plucky round little beast with a clipped mane on his scraggy neck; he plied his sturdy little legs very actively, and kept pulling at the reins, as though he were hastening to the scene of action and taking persons of importance there. Before they reached 'Lasses' Springs', Nezhdanov noticed, just off the road, before an open corn barn, eight peasants; he sprang at once out of the cart, ran up to them with sudden shouts and back-handed gestures. The words, 'Freedom! forward! Shoulder to shoulder!' could be distinguished, hoarse and noisy, above a multitude of other words less comprehensible. The peasants, who had met before the granary to deliberate how it could be filled, if only in appearance (it was the commune granary, and consequently empty), stared at Nezhdanov and seemed to be listening to his address with great attention; but can hardly have understood much, as when at last he rushed away from them, shouting for the last time, 'Freedom!', one of them, the most acute, shook his head with an air of deep reflection, and commented, 'Wasn't he severe?' while another observed, 'Some captain, seemingly!', to which the acute peasant rejoined, 'To be sure—he wouldn't strain his throat for nothing. That's what they give us nowadays for our money'. Nezhdanov himself, as he clambered into the cart and sat beside Pavel, thought to himself, 'Lord! what idiocy! But there, not one of us knows just how one ought to stir up the people—isn't that it, perhaps? There's no time to analyse now. Tear along! Does your heart ache? Let it!'

They drove into the village street. In the very middle of it a good many peasants were crowding round a tavern. Pavel tried to restrain Nezhdanov; but he flew head over heels out of the cart, and with a wailing shout of 'Brothers!' he was in the crowd. . . . It parted a little; and Nezhdanov again fell to preaching, looking at no one, in a violent passion as it seemed, and almost weeping.

But here the result that followed was quite different. A

gigantic fellow with a beardless but ferocious face, in a short greasy coat, high boots, and a sheepskin cap, went up to Nezhdanov, and clapping him on the shoulder with all his might, 'Bravo! you're a fine chap!' he bellowed in a voice of thunder; 'but stop a bit! don't you know, dry words scorch the mouth? Come this way! It's much handier talking here.' He dragged Nezhdanov into the tavern; the rest of the crowd trooped in after them. 'Miheitch!' bawled the young giant, 'look sharp! two penn'orth! My favourite tap! I'm treating a friend! Who he is, what's his family, and where he's from, old Nick knows, but he's laying into the gentry pretty hot. Drink!' he said, turning to Nezhdanov, and handing him a full heavy glass, moist all over the outside as though perspiring, 'drink—if you've really any feeling for the likes of us!' 'Drink!' rose a noisy chorus around. Nezhdanov grasped the pot (he was in a sort of nightmare), shouted, 'To your health, lads!' and emptied it at a gulp. Ugh! He drank it off with the same desperate heroism with which he would have flung himself on a storm of battery or a row of bayonets. . . . But what was happening in him? Something seemed to dart along his spine and down his legs, to set his throat, his chest, and his stomach on fire, to drive the tears into his eyes. . . . A shudder of nausea passed all over him, and with difficulty he kept it down. . . . He shouted at the top of his voice, if only to drown the throbbing in his head. The dark tavern room seemed suddenly hot, sticky, stifling, full of crowds of people! Nezhdanov began talking, talking endlessly, shouting wrathfully, malignantly, shaking broad, horny hands, kissing slobbery beards. . . . The young giant in the coat kissed him too, he almost crushed his ribs in. And he showed himself a perfect demon. 'I'll split his gullet for him!' he roared, 'I'll split his gullet for him! if anyone's rude to our brother! or else I'll pound his skull into a jelly. . . . I'll make him squeak! I'm up to it, I am; I've been a butcher; I'm a good hand at that sort of job!' And he shook his huge freckled fist. . . . And then, good God! someone bellowed again, 'Drink!' and again Nezhdanov gulped down that loathsome poison. But this second time it was terrible! He seemed to be full of blunt hooks tearing him to pieces inside. His head was on fire, green circles were going round before his eyes. There was a loud roar, a ringing in his ears. . . . Oh, horror! A third pot. . . . Was it possible he had emptied it? Purple noses seemed to creep up close and hem him in, and dusty heads of hair, and tanned necks and throats ploughed over with networks of wrinkles. Rough hands caught hold of him. 'Hold on!' raging voices were bawling. 'Talk away! The day before yesterday another, a stranger, talked like that. Go on! . . .' The earth seemed reeling under Nezhdanov's feet. His own voice sounded strange to him, as if it came from a long way off. . . . Was it death, or what?

And all of a sudden . . . a sense of the fresh air on his face, and no more hubbub, no red faces, no stench of spirits, sheepskins, pitch and leather. . . . And again he was sitting in the cart with Pavel, at first struggling and shouting, 'Stop! Where are you off to? I'd not time to tell them anything, I must explain . . .' then adding, 'And you yourself, you sly devil, what are your views?' To which Pavel replied, 'It would be nice if there were no gentry, and the land was all ours—what could be better? but there's been no order to that effect so far', while he stealthily turned his horse's head, and suddenly lashing him on the back with the reins, set off at full trot away from the din and clamour . . . to the factory. . . .

Nezhdanov dozed and was jolted about, but the wind blew sweetly in his face, and kept back gloomy thoughts.

Only he was vexed that he had not been allowed to explain himself fully. . . . And again the wind soothed his heated face.

And then the momentary vision of Marianna, a momentary burning sense of disgrace, and sleep, heavy, death-like sleep. . . .

All this Pavel told afterwards to Solomin. He made no secret of the fact that he had not hindered Nezhdanov's getting drunk . . . he could not have got him away else. The others wouldn't have let him go.

'But there, when he was getting quite feeble I begged them with many bows: "Honest gentlemen," says I, "let the poor boy go; see, he's quite young. . . ." And so they let him go. "Only give us half a rouble for ransom," says they. And so I gave it them.'

'Quite right,' said Solomin approvingly.

Nezhdanov slept; and Marianna sat at the window and looked into the little enclosure. And, strange to say, the angry, almost wicked thoughts and feelings that had been astir within her before Nezhdanov's arrival with Pavel left her all at once; Nezhdanov himself was far from being repulsive or disgusting to her; she pitied him. She knew very well that he was neither a rake nor a drunkard, and was already pondering what to say to him when he should wake up: something affectionate, that he might not be too much distressed and ashamed. 'I must manage so that he should tell of his own accord how this mishap befell him.'

She was not excited; but she felt sad . . . desperately sad. It was as if a breath had blown upon her from that real world which she had been struggling to reach . . . and she shuddered at its coarseness and darkness. What Moloch was this to which she was going to sacrifice herself?

But no! It could not be! This was nothing; it was a chance event, and would be over directly.

It was the impression of an instant, which had impressed her only because it was unexpected. She got up, went to the sofa, on which Nezhdanov was lying, passed a handkerchief over his pale brow, which was contracted with suffering even in his sleep, and pushed back his hair. . . .

Again she felt sorry for him, as a mother pities her sick child. But it made her heart ache a little to look at him, and she softly went away into her room, leaving the door ajar.

She did not take up any work, and sat down again, and again a mood of musing came upon her. She felt the time melting away, minute after minute flying past, and it was positively sweet to her to feel it, and her heart beat, and again she fell to waiting for something.

Where had Solomin got to?

The door creaked softly, and Tatyana came into the room.

'What do you want?' asked Marianna almost with annoyance.

'Marianna Vikentyevna,' began Tatyana in an undertone, 'look here. Don't you upset yourself, for it's a thing that will happen in life, and thank God too——'

'I'm not the least upset, Tatyana Osipovna,' Marianna cut her short. 'Alexey Dmitritch isn't quite well; it's of no great consequence! . . .'

'Well, now, that's first-rate! But here have I been thinking, my Marianna Vikentyevna doesn't come, what's wrong with her, thinks I? But for all that I wouldn't have come in to you, for in such cases the first rule is, "Mind your own business!" Only here's someone—I don't know who—come to the factory. A little man like this, and a bit lame; and nothing'll content him but to get at Alexey Dmitritch! It seems so queer; this morning that female came asking for him . . . and now here's this lame man. "And if," says he, "Alexey Dmitritch's not here," we're to let him see Vassily Fedotitch! "I won't go without," says he, "for," says he, "it's very important business." We try to pack him off like that female; tell him Vassily Fedotitch isn't here . . . has gone away, but this lame man keeps on, "I'm not going," says he, "if I've to wait till midnight. . . ." So he's walking in the yard. Here, come this way into the passage; you can see him from the window. . . . Can you tell me what sort of a fine gentleman he is?'

Marianna followed Tatyana—she had to pass close by Nezhdanov—and again she noticed his brow contracted painfully, and again she passed her handkerchief over it. Through the dusty window-pane she caught sight of the visitor, of whom Tatyana had been speaking. He was a stranger to her, But at that very instant Solomin came into sight round the corner of the house.

The little lame man went rapidly to him, and held out
his hand. Solomin took it. He obviously knew the man.
Both of them vanished. . . .

But now their steps could be heard on the stairs. . . . They
were coming up. . . .

Marianna went back hurriedly into her room and stood still
in the middle, hardly able to breathe. She felt dread . . .
of what? She did not know.

Solomin's head appeared in the doorway.

'Marianna Vikentyevna, allow us to come in to you. I have
brought a person whom it's absolutely necessary for you to
see.'

Marianna merely nodded in reply, and behind Solomin in
walked—Paklin.

33

'I'M a friend of your husband's,' he said, bowing low to
Marianna and trying, as it seemed, to conceal his scared and
excited face; 'I'm a friend, too, of Vassily Fedotitch's. Alexey
Dmitritch is asleep; he is, I hear, unwell; and I have unfortunately brought bad news, which I have already communicated in part to Vassily Fedotitch, and in consequence
of which decisive measures must be taken.'

Paklin's voice broke continually, like that of a man who is
parched and tortured by thirst. The news he brought was
really very bad! Markelov had been seized by the peasants
and carried off to the town. The stupid clerk had betrayed
Golushkin; he had been arrested. He, in his turn, was betray-
ing everything and everyone, was eager to go over to ortho-
doxy, was offering to present the high school with the portrait
of the bishop Filaret, and had already forwarded five
thousand roubles for distribution among 'crippled soldiers'.
There was not a shadow of doubt that he had betrayed

Nezhdanov; the police might make a raid upon the factory any minute. Vassily Fedotitch, too, was in some danger. 'As far as I'm concerned,' added Paklin, 'I'm surprised really that I'm still walking about at liberty; though to be sure I have never taken any part precisely in politics and had no hand in any plans. I have taken advantage of this forgetfulness or oversight on the part of the police to warn you and consult you as to what means may be employed . . . to avert all unpleasantness.'

Marianna heard Paklin to the end. She was not frightened —she even remained perfectly serene. . . . But, to be sure, some steps would have to be taken! Her first action was to look to Solomin.

He, too, seemed composed; only the muscles were faintly twitching about his lips, with something unlike his habitual smile.

He understood what her look meant; she was waiting for him to say what steps were to be taken.

'It's rather a ticklish business, certainly,' he began; 'it would be as well, I imagine, for Nezhdanov to keep in hiding for a time. By the way, how did you learn that he was here, Mr. Paklin?'

Paklin waved his hand.

'An individual told me. He'd seen him wandering about the neighbourhood making propaganda. Well, he kept an eye on him, though with no evil intent. He is a sympathiser. Pardon me,' he added, turning to Marianna, 'but really, our friend Nezhdanov has been very . . . very indiscreet.'

'It's no use blaming him now,' Solomin began again. 'It's a pity we can't talk things over with him; but his indisposition will be over by to-morrow, and the police are not so rapid in their movements as you imagine. You, too, Marianna Vikentyevna, ought to go away with him, I suppose.'

'Undoubtedly,' Marianna replied, thickly but resolutely.

'Yes,' said Solomin. 'We shall have to think things over; we shall have to find ways and means.'

'Allow me to lay one idea before you,' began Paklin; 'the

253

idea entered my head as I came in here. I hasten to observe that I dismissed the cabman from the town, a mile away.'

'What is your idea?' asked Solomin.

'I'll tell you. Let me have horses at once . . . and I will gallop off to the Sipyagins.'

'To the Sipyagins!' repeated Marianna. . . . 'What for?'

'You shall hear.'

'But do you know them?'

'Not in the least! But listen. Consider my proposition thoroughly. It seems to me simply a stroke of genius. You see, Markelov's Sipyagin's brother-in-law, his wife's brother. Isn't that so? Is it possible that gentleman will do nothing to save him? And moreover, Nezhdanov himself! Granting that Mr. Sipyagin is angry with him. . . . Still, you see, for all that, Nezhdanov has become a relation of his by marrying you. And the danger hanging over our friend's head——'

'I'm not married,' observed Marianna.

Paklin positively started.

'What? Not managed that all this time! Well, never mind,' he went on; 'one can fib a little. It's just the same thing; you're going to be married directly. Indeed, one can't devise any other plan! Take into consideration the fact that Sipyagin up till now has not gone so far as to persecute you. Consequently, he has a certain . . . magnanimity. I see that expression's not to your taste; let's say, a certain affectation of generosity. Why shouldn't we utilise it in the present case? Think of it!'

Marianna raised her head and passed her hand over her hair.

'You may utilise what you please for Markelov's benefit, Mr. Paklin . . . or for your own; but Alexey and I desire neither the protection nor the patronage of Mr. Sipyagin. We did not leave his house to go knocking at his door as beggars. We will owe nothing either to the magnanimity nor the affectation of generosity of Mr. Sipyagin or his wife!'

'Those are most praiseworthy sentiments,' responded Paklin (but, 'My! that's a nice wet blanket!' was his inward comment), 'though, on the other hand, if you come to reflect . . . However, I am ready to obey you. I will exert myself on Markelov's account, our dear, good Markelov only! I venture only to observe that he is not his blood relation, but only related to him through his wife, while you——'

'Mr. Paklin, I beg you!'

'Oh, yes . . . yes! But I can't refrain from expressing my regret, for Sipyagin is a man of great influence.'

'So you've no fears for yourself?' queried Solomin.

Paklin straightened his chest.

'At such moments one must not think of oneself,' he said proudly. And all the while, it was just of himself he was thinking. He wanted (poor, feeble little creature!) to be the first in the field, as the saying is. On the strength of the service rendered him, Sipyagin might, if need arose, speak a word for him. For as a fact, he too—say what he would—was implicated; he had listened . . . and even gone chattering about himself.

'I think your idea's not a bad one,' observed Solomin at last, 'though I put little confidence in its success. Anyway, you can try. You will do no harm.'

'Of course not. Come, supposing the very worst; suppose they kick me out. . . . What harm will that do?'

'There'll certainly be no harm in that. . . .' ('*Merci!*' thought Paklin.) While Solomin went on: 'What o'clock is it? Five o'clock. No time to waste. You shall have the horses directly. Pavel!'

But instead of Pavel, on the threshold they saw Nezhdanov. He staggered, steadying himself on the doorpost, and opening his mouth feebly, stared with bewildered eyes, comprehending nothing.

Paklin was the first to approach him.

'Alyosha!' he cried, 'you know me, don't you?'

Nezhdanov gazed at him, blinking slowly.

'Paklin?' he said at last.

'Yes, yes; it's I. You are not well?'

'Yes . . . I'm not well. But . . . why are you here?'

255

'I'm here . . .' But at that instant Marianna stealthily touched Paklin on the elbow. He looked round, and saw she was making signs to him. . . . 'Ah, yes!' he muttered. 'Yes . . . to be sure! Well, do you see, Alyosha,' he added aloud, 'I've come on important business, and must go on further at once. . . . Solomin will tell you all about it—and Marianna . . . Marianna Vikentyevna. They both fully approve of my plan—it's a matter that concerns us all: that is, no, no,' he interpolated hurriedly in response to a gesture and a glance from Marianna. . . . 'It's a matter concerning Markelov, our common friend Markelov; him alone. But now, good-bye! Every minute's precious—good-bye, friend. . . . We shall meet again. Vassily Fedotitch, will you come with me to give orders about the horses?'

'Certainly. Marianna, I'd meant to say to you, keep up your spirits! But there's no need. You're the real thing!'

'Oh, yes! oh, yes!' chimed in Paklin: 'you're a Roman woman of the time of Cato! Cato of Utica! But come along, Vassily Fedotitch, let us go!'

'You've plenty of time,' observed Solomin with a lazy smile. Nezhdanov moved a little aside to let them both pass. . . . But there was still the same uncomprehending look in his eyes. Then he took two steps, and slowly sat down on a chair facing Marianna.

'Alexey,' she said to him, 'everything is discovered; Markelov has been seized by the peasants he was trying to incite; he's under arrest in the town, and so is that merchant you dined with; most likely the police will soon be here after us. Paklin has gone to Sipyagin.'

'What for?' muttered Nezhdanov, hardly audibly. But his eyes grew clearer, his face regained its ordinary expression. The stupor had left him instantly.

'To try whether he will intercede.'

Nezhdanov drew himself up. . . . 'For us?'

'No; for Markelov. He wanted to beg for us too . . . but I would not let him. Did I do right, Alexey?'

'Right?' said Nezhdanov, and without getting up from his

chair, he held out his hands to her. 'Right?' he repeated, and, drawing her close to him and hiding his face against her, he suddenly burst into tears.

'What is it, dear? what is it?' cried Marianna. Now, too, as on that day when he had fallen on his knees before her, faint and breathless with a sudden torrent of passion, she laid her two hands on his trembling head.

But what she felt now was not at all what she had felt then. Then she had given herself up to him. She had submitted, and simply waited for what he would say to her. Now she pitied him, and thought of nothing but how to comfort him.

'What is it, dear?' she said. 'What are you crying for? Surely not because you came home in rather . . . a strange state! That can't be! Or are you sorry for Markelov, and afraid for me and you? Or are you grieving for our shattered hopes? You didn't expect everything to run smoothly, you know!'

Nezhdanov suddenly raised his head.

'No, Marianna,' he said, gulping down his sobs, 'I'm not afraid for you nor for myself. . . . But yes . . . I am sorry——'

'For whom?'

'For you, Marianna! I'm sorry you have bound up your life with a man unworthy of it.'

'Why so?'

'Well, if only because he can be shedding tears at such a moment!'

'It's not you weeping; it's your nerves!'

'My nerves and I are all one! Come, Marianna, look me in the face: can you really say now that you don't regret . . .'

'What?'

'That you ran away with me?'

'No.'

'And will you go further with me? Everywhere?'

'Yes!'

'Yes? Marianna . . . Yes?'

'Yes. I have given you my word, and so long as you are the man I loved, I will not take it back.'

Nezhdanov went on sitting in his chair; Marianna stood before him. His arms lay about her waist; her hands rested on his shoulders. 'Yes, no,' thought Nezhdanov . . . 'but yet—before, when it was my lot to hold her in my arms, just as at this moment, her body was at least motionless; but now, I feel it gently and perhaps against her will shrink away from me!' He loosened his arms . . . Marianna did, in fact, scarcely perceptibly draw back.

'I tell you what!' he said aloud, 'if we must run away . . . before the police discover us . . . I suppose it would be as well for us to be married first. Most likely we shouldn't meet with such an accommodating priest as Zosim anywhere else!'

'I'm ready,' said Marianna.

Nezhdanov looked intently at her.

'Roman maiden!' he said with an evil half-smile. 'What a sense of duty!'

Marianna shrugged her shoulders.

'We must speak to Solomin.'

'Yes . . . Solomin . . .' Nezhdanov drawled. 'But he too, I suppose, is in some danger. The police will seize him too. It strikes me he has done more and known more about it than I.'

'I know nothing about that,' said Marianna. 'He never talks about himself.'

'Unlike me in that!' thought Nezhdanov. 'That was what she meant! Solomin . . . Solomin,' he repeated after a long silence. 'Do you know, Marianna, I should not pity you, if the man with whom you had linked your life for ever had been like Solomin . . . or had been Solomin himself.'

Marianna, in her turn, looked intently at Nezhdanov.

'You had no right to say that,' she said finally.

'I'd no right! How am I to understand those words? Do they mean that you love me? or that I ought not anyway to touch on that question?'

'You had no right to say it,' repeated Marianna.

Nezhdanov's head drooped.

'Marianna!' he articulated in a somewhat changed voice.

'Well?'

'If I were now . . . if I put you that question—you know?
. . . No, I ask nothing of you . . . good-bye.'

He got up and went out; Marianna did not try to keep
him. Nezhdanov sat down on the sofa and hid his face in
his hands. He was frightened by his own thoughts, and tried
not to think. He had one feeling only, that a sort of dark,
underground hand seemed to have clutched at the very root
of his being, and would not let him go. He knew that that
sweet, precious woman he had left in the next room would
not come out to him; and he dared not go in to her. And
what would be the use? What could he say?

Rapid, resolute footsteps made him open his eyes.

Solomin walked across his room, and, knocking at
Marianna's door, went in.

'Make way for your betters!' muttered Nezhdanov in a
bitter whisper.

34

IT was ten o'clock in the evening in the drawing-room of
the mansion of Arzhano. Sipyagin, his wife, and Kallomyetsev were playing cards, when a footman came in and
announced the arrival of a stranger, Mr. Paklin, who wanted
to see Boris Andreitch on the most urgent and important
business.

'So late!' wondered Valentina Mihalovna.

'Eh?' queried Boris Andreitch, wrinkling up his handsome
nose. 'What did you say was the gentleman's name?'

'He said Paklin, sir.'

'Paklin!' cried Kallomyetsev. 'A truly rural name.

Paklin' (*i.e.* stuffing) '. . . Solomin' (*i.e.* strawing) '. . . *De vrais noms ruraux, hein?*'

'And you say,' pursued Boris Andreitch, turning to the footman with the same expression of displeasure, 'that his business is important, urgent?'

'So the gentleman says, sir.'

'H'm . . . some beggar or swindler' ('Or both together,' put in Kallomyetsev). 'Quite likely. Ask him into my study.' Boris Andreitch got up. *'Pardon, ma bonne.* Have a game of écarté while I'm gone, or wait for me. I'll be back directly.'

'Nous causerons . . . allez!' said Kallomyetsev. When Sipyagin came into his study and saw Paklin's pitiful, feeble little figure meekly huddled against the wall between the fireplace and the door, he was seized with that truly ministerial sensation of lofty compassion and fastidious condescension so characteristic of the Petersburg higher official.

'Mercy on us! What a poor little plucked bird!' he thought, 'and I do believe he's lame too!'

'Be seated,' he said aloud, giving vent to the benevolent baritone notes of his voice, and affably throwing back his little head; and he took a seat before his visitor.

'You are tired from your journey, I presume; take a seat, and let me hear what is the important business that has brought you to me so late.'

'Your Excellency,' began Paklin, dropping discreetly into a chair, 'I have made bold to come to you——'

'Wait a bit, wait a bit,' Sipyagin interrupted him; 'I've seen you before. I never forget a face I have once met; I always recollect it. Eh . . . eh . . . eh . . . precisely . . . where have I met you?'

'You are right, your Excellency. . . . I had the honour of meeting you in Petersburg at a person's who . . . who . . . since then . . . has unfortunately . . . incurred your displeasure.'

Sipyagin got up quickly from his chair.

'At Mr. Nezhdanov's! I remember now. Surely you haven't come from him?'

'Oh, no, your Excellency; quite the contrary . . . I . . .'
Sipyagin sat down again.

'That's as well. For in that case I would promptly have
asked you to leave the house. I can give no admittance to
any mediator between me and Mr. Nezhdanov. Mr.
Nezhdanov has shown me one of those affronts which are not
forgotten. . . . I am above revenge, but I wish to know
nothing of him, nor of the girl—more depraved in mind than
in heart' (this phrase Sipyagin must have repeated thirty
times since Marianna's flight)—'who could bring herself to
leave the home where she had been cared for to become the
mistress of a base-born adventurer! It's enough for them
that I consent to forget them!'

At this last word Sipyagin made a downward motion of
his wrist away from him.

'I forget them, sir!'

'Your Excellency, I have already submitted to you that
I have not come here from them, though I may nevertheless
inform your Excellency, among other things, that they are
already joined in the bonds of lawful matrimony.' . . .
('There, it's all one!' thought Paklin; 'I said I'd lie a bit
here, and I'm lying. Here goes!')

Sipyagin moved his head restlessly to right and left against
the back of his easy-chair.

'That is a matter of no interest to me, sir. One foolish
marriage the more in the world, that's all. But what is this
most urgent business to which I am indebted for the pleasure
of your visit?'.

'Ugh! the damned director of a department!' Paklin
thought again. 'That's enough of your airs and graces, you
ugly English monkey-face.'

'Your wife's brother,' he said aloud—'Mr. Markelov—has
been seized by the peasants he had meant to incite to in-
surrection, and is now in custody in the governor's house.'

Sipyagin jumped up a second time.

'What . . . what did you say?' he stammered, not at all
in his ministerial baritone, but in a sort of piteous guttural.

'I said your brother-in-law had been seized and is in chains. Directly I learned this fact, I took horses and came to warn you. I imagined that I might be rendering a service both to you and to that unfortunate man whom you may be able to save!'

'I am much obliged to you,' said Sipyagin in the same feeble voice; and with a violent blow on a bell shaped like a mushroom, he filled the whole house with its clear, metallic ring. 'I am much obliged to you,' he repeated more sharply; 'though let me tell you, a man who has trampled underfoot every law, human and divine, were he a hundred times my kinsman, is in my eyes not to be pitied; he is a criminal!'

A footman darted into the room.

'Your orders, sir?'

'The coach! This minute the coach and four! I am driving to the town. Filip and Stepan to come with me!' The footman darted out. 'Yes, sir, my brother-in-law is a criminal; and I am driving to the town, not to save him! Oh, no!'

'But, your Excellency . . .'

'Such are my principles, sir; and I beg you not to trouble me with objections!'

Sipyagin fell to walking up and down the room, while Paklin's eyes grew round as saucers. 'Ugh, you devil!' he was thinking; 'and you call yourself a liberal! Why, you're a roaring lion!' The door opened, and with quick steps there entered first Valentina Mihalovna, and behind her Kallomyetsev.

'What is the meaning of this, Boris? you have ordered the coach out? you are going to the town? what has happened?'

Sipyagin went up to his wife, and took her by her arm, between the wrist and the elbow. *'Il faut vous armer de courage, ma chère.* Your brother is arrested.'

'My brother? Sergei? What for?'

'He has been preaching Socialistic theories to the peasants!' (Kallomyetsev gave vent to a faint whistle.) 'Yes! He has been preaching revolution! he has been making propaganda!

They seized him, and gave him up. Now he's—in the town.'

'The madman! But who has told you this?'

'Mr. . . . Mr. . . . what's his name? Mr. Konopatin brought this news.'

Valentina Mihalovna glanced at Paklin. He gave a forlorn bow. 'My! what an elegant female!' was his thought. Even at such painful moments . . . alas, how susceptible was poor Paklin to feminine charms!

'And you mean to go to the town—so late?'

'I shall find the governor still up.'

'I always predicted that it must end so,' put in Kallom-yetsev. 'It could not be otherwise! But what splendid chaps our Russian peasants are! Delightful! *Pardon, madame, c'est votre frère! Mais la vérité avant tout!'*

'Can you really mean to go, Boris?' asked Valentina Mihalovna.

'I'm convinced too,' continued Kallomyetsev, 'that that fellow too, that *tutor*, Mr. Nezhdanov, has had a hand in it. *J'en mettrais ma main au feu.* They're all in one boat! Has he been caught? You don't know?'

Again Sipyagin made a downward gesture from his wrist. 'I don't know, and I don't want to know! By the way,' he added, turning to his wife, *'il paraît qu'ils sont mariés.'*

'Who said so? The same gentleman?' Valentina Mihalovna again looked at Paklin, but this time she screwed up her eyes as she did so.

'Yes.'

'In that case,' put in Kallomyetsev, 'he knows where they are for a certainty. Do you know where they are? Do you know where they are? Eh? eh? eh? Do you know?' Kallomyetsev began pacing up and down before Paklin, as though to bar the way to him, though the latter showed not the faintest inclination to escape. 'Speak! Answer! Eh? Eh? Do you know? Do you know?'

'If I did know,' Paklin said with annoyance—his wrath was stirred at last and his little eyes flashed—'if I did know, I should not tell you.'

'Oh . . . oh . . . oh!' muttered Kallomyetsev. 'You hear . . . you hear! Why, this fellow, too . . . this fellow, too, must be one of their gang!'

'The coach is ready!' a footman announced. Sipyagin seized his hat with a graceful, resolute gesture; but Valentina Mihalovna begged him with such insistence to put off going till next morning—she laid before him such cogent reasons, the darkness on the road, and everyone would be asleep in the town, and he would merely be upsetting his nerves and might catch cold—that Sipyagin at last was persuaded by her, and exclaiming, 'I obey!' with a gesture as graceful, but no longer resolute, he laid his hat on the table.

'Take out the horses!' he commanded the footman; 'but to-morrow at six in the morning precisely let them be ready! Do you hear? You can go! Stop! The visitor . . . the gentleman's conveyance can be dismissed! Pay the man! Eh? I fancy you spoke, Mr. Konopatin? I'll take you with me to-morrow, Mr. Konopatin! What do you say? I don't hear. . . . You will take some vodka, I dare say? Some vodka for Mr. Konopatin! No! You don't drink it? In that case, Fyodor, show the gentleman to the green room! Good-night, Mr. Kono——'

Paklin lost all patience at last.

'Paklin!' he roared, 'my name is Paklin!'

'Yes, yes; well, that's much the same. It's not unlike, you know. But what a powerful voice you have for one of your build! Good-night, Mr. Paklin. . . . I've got it right now, eh? *Siméon, vous viendrez avec nous?*'

'*Je crois bien!*'

And Paklin was led off to the green room. And he was even locked in there. As he got into bed, he heard the key turn in the ringing English lock. Violently he swore at himself for his 'stroke of genius', and he slept very badly.

Early next morning, at half-past five, he was called. Coffee was handed him; while he drank it, a footman with embroidered shoulder-knots waited with the tray in his hands, and shifted from one leg to the other, as though he would say,

'Hurry up, you're keeping the gentlemen waiting!' Then he was conducted downstairs. The coach was already standing before the house. There, too, was Kallomyetsev's open carriage. Sipyagin made his appearance on the steps in a camel's-hair cloak with a round collar. Such cloaks had not been worn for many years except by a certain very important dignitary whom Sipyagin was trying to please and to imitate. On important official occasions, therefore, he wore such a cloak.

Sipyagin greeted Paklin fairly affably, and with an energetic gesture motioned him to the coach and asked him to take his seat. 'Mr. Paklin, you will come with me, Mr. Paklin! Put Mr. Paklin's bag on the box! I am taking Mr. Paklin!' he said, with an emphasis on the word Paklin, and an accent on the letter *a*, as though he would say, 'You've a name like that and presume to feel insulted when people change it for you! There you are, then! Take plenty of it! I'll give you as much as you want! Mr. Paklin! Paklin!' The unlucky name kept resounding in the keen morning air. It was so keen as to set Kallomyetsev, who came out after Sipyagin, muttering several times in French, 'B-r-r-r! B-r-r-r! B-r-r-r!' and wrapping himself more closely in his cloak he seated himself in his elegant open carriage. (His poor friend the Servian prince, Mihal Obrenovitch, on seeing it had bought one exactly like it at Binder's . . . *vous savez Binder, le grand carrossier des Champs-Élysées?*) From the half-open shutters of a bedroom Valentina Mihalovna peeped out 'in the trailing garments of the night', as the poet has it.

Sipyagin took his seat and kissed his hand to her.

'Are you comfortable, Mr. Paklin? Drive on!'

'*Je vous recommande mon frère; épargnez-le!*' Valentina Mihalovna was heard to say.

'*Soyez tranquille!*' cried Kallomyetsev, glancing smartly up at her from under the edge of a travelling-cap that he had designed himself, with a cockade in it. . . . '*C'est surtout l'autre qu'il faut pincer!*'

'Drive on!' repeated Sipyagin. 'Mr. Paklin, you're not cold? Drive on!'

The two carriages rolled away.

For the first ten minutes both Sipyagin and Paklin were silent. The luckless Sila in his shabby little suit and greasy cap seemed a still more pitiful figure against the dark-blue background of the rich silky material with which the inside of the coach was upholstered. In silence he looked round at the delicate, pale-blue blinds that ran up rapidly at a mere finger's touch on a button, and at the rug of soft white sheep-skin at their feet, and the box of red wood fitted in in front, with a movable tray desk for letters, and even a shelf for books. (Boris Andreitch did not much care to work in his coach, but he wished to make people believe he liked to work on his journeys like Thiers.) Paklin felt intimidated. Sipyagin glanced at him twice over his glossily shaven cheek, and with majestic deliberation pulled out of his side-pocket a silver cigar-case with a curly monogram on it in old Slavonic type, and offered him . . . positively offered him a cigar, balancing it between the second and third fingers of a hand in an English glove of yellow dogskin.

'I don't smoke,' muttered Paklin.

'Ah!' responded Sipyagin, and he himself lighted the cigar, which appeared to be a most choice regalia.

'I ought to tell you . . . dear Mr. Paklin,' he began, puffing affably at his cigar, and emitting delicate rings of fragrant smoke . . . 'that I . . . am in reality . . . very grateful . . . to you. . . . I may have seemed . . . somewhat short . . . to you yesterday . . . though that is not a . . . characteristic . . . of mine at all' (Sipyagin intentionally cut his sentence up meaningly), 'I venture to assure you of that. But, Mr. Paklin, put yourself in my . . . place' (Sipyagin rolled the cigar from one corner of his mouth to the other). 'The position I occupy makes me . . . so to say . . . conspicuous; and all of a sudden . . . my wife's brother . . . compromises himself . . . and me in this incredible manner! Eh! Mr. Paklin? You perhaps think that's of no great matter?'

266

'I don't think that, your Excellency.'

'You don't know for what precisely . . . and where exactly, he was arrested?'

'I heard it was in T—— district.'

'From whom did you hear that?'

'From . . . from a man.'

'Well, it would hardly be from a bird. But what man?'

'From . . . from an assistant of the director of the business of the governor's office.'

'What's his name?'

'The director?'

'No, the assistant.'

'His . . . his name is Ulyashevitch. He's a very good public servant, your Excellency. When I heard of that occurrence, I hurried at once to you.'

'To be sure, to be sure! And I repeat that I am very grateful to you. But what madness! Isn't it madness? eh? Mr. Paklin? eh?'

'Perfect madness!' cried Paklin, and the perspiration zigzagged in a hot rivulet down his back. 'It comes,' he went on, 'of not in the least understanding the Russian peasant. Mr. Markelov, so far as I know him, has a very kind and generous heart; but he has never understood the Russian peasant' (Paklin glanced at Sipyagin, who, turning slightly towards him, was scanning him with a chilly but not hostile expression). 'The Russian peasant cannot ever be induced to revolt except by taking advantage of his devotion to a higher authority, some sort of Tsar. Some sort of legend must be invented—you remember the false Demetrius— some sort of regal insignia, branded in burnt patches on the breast.'

'Yes, yes, like Pugatchev,' interrupted Sipyagin in a tone that seemed to say, 'I've not forgotten my history . . . you needn't enlarge!' and adding, 'It's madness! madness!' he turned to the contemplation of the swift coil of smoke rising from the end of his cigar.

'Your Excellency!' observed Paklin, gathering courage, 'I

267

told you just now I didn't smoke . . . but that's not quite accurate. I do smoke at times; and your cigar smells so delicious. . . .'

'Eh? what? what's that?' said Sipyagin, as though waking up; and without letting Paklin repeat what he had said, he proved in the most unmistakable manner that he had heard him, and had uttered his reiterated questions solely for the sake of his dignity, by offering him his open cigar-case.

Paklin discreetly and gratefully lighted a cigar.

'Now, I fancy, is a good moment,' he thought; but Sipyagin anticipated him.

'You spoke to me, too, do you remember?' he said carelessly, interrupting himself to look at his cigar, and to jog his hat forwards on to his forehead, 'you spoke . . . eh? you spoke of . . . that friend of yours who has married my . . . relation. Do you see them? They are settled not far from here?'

'Aha!' thought Paklin, 'Sila, look out!'

'I have seen them only once, your Excellency! they are living, as a fact . . . at no great distance from here.'

'You understand, of course,' Sipyagin went on in the same manner, 'that I have no further serious interest, as I explained to you, either in that frivolous girl or in your friend. Good heavens! I've no prejudices, but you will agree with me, this is beyond everything. It's folly, you know. Though I imagine they have been more drawn together by political sympathies' ('Politics!' he repeated with a shrug of his shoulders) 'than by any other feeling.'

'Indeed I imagine so, your Excellency!'

'Yes, Mr. Nezhdanov was a red-hot republican. I must do him the justice to admit that he made no secret of his opinions.'

'Nezhdanov,' Paklin hazarded, 'has been led away, perhaps, but his heart——'

'Is good,' put in Sipyagin: 'to be sure . . . to be sure, like Markelov's. They all have good hearts. Probably he too has taken part—and will be too . . . We shall have to protect him too.'

Paklin clasped his hands before his breast.

'Ah, yes, yes, your Excellency! Extend your protection to him! Indeed . . . he deserves . . . deserves your sympathy.'

'H'm,' said Sipyagin; 'you think so?'

'If not for his own sake, at least . . . for your niece's; for his wife's!' ('O Lord! O Lord!' Paklin was thinking, 'what lies I'm telling!')

Sipyagin puckered up his eyes.

'You are, I see, a very devoted friend. That's excellent; that's very praiseworthy, young man. And so, you say, they're living near here?'

'Yes, your Excellency; at a large establishment . . .' Paklin bit his tongue.

'Tut . . . tut-tut . . . at Solomin's! so they're there! I was aware of that—indeed, I'd been told so, I'd been informed. . . . Yes.' (Mr. Sipyagin was not in the least aware of it, and no one had told him so; but recollecting Solomin's visit, and their midnight interview, he dropped this bait. . . . And Paklin rose to it at once.)

'Since you know that,' he began, and a second time he bit his tongue. . . . But it was too late. . . . From the mere glance flung at him by Sipyagin he realised that he had been playing with him all the while, as a cat plays with a mouse.

'I must tell your Excellency, though,' the luckless wretch faltered, 'that I really know nothing. . . .'

'And I ask you no questions, upon my word! What do you mean? What do you take me, and yourself, for?' said Sipyagin haughtily, and he promptly withdrew into his ministerial heights.

And again Paklin felt himself a wretched little, entrapped creature. . . . Till that instant he had kept his cigar in the corner of his mouth, remote from Sipyagin, and had stealthily puffed the smoke on one side; now he took it out of his mouth altogether, and ceased smoking.

'Good Lord!' he groaned inwardly—and the sweat

269

trickled over his shoulders more plentifully than before. 'What have I done! I have betrayed everything and every-one! . . . I've been fooled, bought with a good cigar! . . . I'm an informer . . . and what can be done to undo the harm now? Lord!'

There was nothing to be done. Sipyagin began to doze with the same dignified, solemn ministerial air, wrapped up in his camel's-hair cloak. . . . And before another quarter of an hour had passed, both the carriages stopped in front of the governor's house.

35

THE governor of the town of S—— was one of those good-natured, careless, worldly generals, those generals endowed with an exquisitely well-washed white body, and an almost equally pure soul, those well-born, well-bred generals, kneaded, so to speak, of the most finely sifted flour, who, though they never lay themselves out to be 'shepherds of the people', do nevertheless give proof of very tolerable administrative abilities; and doing very little work, for ever sighing for Petersburg and dangling after pretty provincial ladies, are of the most unmistakable service to their province and leave pleasant memories behind them. He had only just got out of bed, and, sitting in a silk dressing-gown and a loose night-shirt before his looking-glass, he was dabbing his face and neck with eau-de-Cologne, after taking off a perfect collection of little amulets and relics as a preliminary—when he was informed of the arrival of Sipyagin and Kallomyetsev on important and urgent business. With Sipyagin he was very intimate, called him by his Christian name, had known him from his youth up, was continually meeting him in Peters-burg drawing-rooms, and of late he had begun, every time his name occurred to him, to ejaculate mentally a respectful 'Ah!' as on hearing the name of a future statesman. Kallomyetsev he knew rather less and respected much less, seeing that for some time past 'unpleasant' complaints had begun to be made against him; he regarded him, however, as a man —*qui fera chemin*—one way or another.

He gave orders that the visitors should be asked into his study, and promptly came into it in the same silk dressing-gown, and without even an apology for receiving them in such an unofficial attire; and he shook hands cordially with them. Only Sipyagin and Kallomyetsev had, however, been conducted to the governor's study; Paklin had been left in the drawing-room. As he crawled out of the coach, he had tried to sneak off, muttering that he had business at home; but Sipyagin with courteous firmness had detained him (Kallomyetsev had skipped up and whispered in Sipyagin's ear: *'Ne le lâchez pas! Tonnerre de tonnerre!'*) and taken him in along with him. To the study, however, he had not led him, but had requested him, still with the same courteous firmness, to wait in the drawing-room till he should be sent for. Paklin even here hoped to slink off . . . but, at a hint from Kallomyetsev, a stalwart gendarme showed himself at the door. . . . Paklin remained.

'You guess, no doubt, what has brought me to you, *Voldemar?*' began Sipyagin.

'No, dear boy, I can't guess,' answered the amiable epicurean, while a smile of welcome curved his rosy cheeks and showed a glimpse of his shining teeth, half hidden by silky moustaches. . . .

'What? . . . Don't you know about Markelov?'

'What do you mean?—Markelov?' the governor repeated with the same expression. He had, to begin with, no clear recollection that the man arrested the day before was called Markelov; and he had besides utterly forgotten that Sipyagin's wife had a brother of that surname. 'But why are you standing, Boris? sit down; won't you have some tea?'

But Sipyagin was in no mood for tea.

271

When he explained at last what was the matter and for what reason he and Kallomyetsev had made their appearance, the governor uttered a pained exclamation, and slapped himself on the forehead, while his face assumed an expression of grief.

'Yes . . . yes . . . yes!' he repeated; 'what a misfortune! And he's here now—to-day—for a while; you know we never keep *that sort* with us longer than one night; but the commander of police is out of the town, so your brother-in-law's been detained. . . . But to-morrow they will forward him. Dear me! how very unfortunate! How distressed your wife must be! What is it you wish?'

'I should have liked to have an interview with him, here—if it's not contrary to law.'

'My dear fellow! laws are not made for men like you. I *do* feel for you! . . . *C'est affreux, tu sais!*'

He gave a peculiar ring. An adjutant appeared.

'My dear baron, if you please—some arrangements here.' He told him what he wanted. The baron vanished. 'Only fancy, *mon cher ami*, you know they all but murdered him. They tied his hands behind him, clapped him in a cart, and off they went with him! And he—fancy! isn't in the least angry with them—not a bit indignant—dear, dear! He's so composed altogether. . . . I was astonished! but there, you will see for yourself. *C'est un fanatique tranquille.*'

'*Ce cont les pires,*' Kallomyetsev pronounced sententiously. The governor gave him a dubious look.

'By the way, I must have a word with you, Semyon Petrovitch.'

'Why, what is it?'

'Oh, something's amiss.'

'And what?'

'Well, I must tell you; your debtor, that peasant who came to me with a complaint——'

'Well?'

'He's hanged himself, you know.'

'When?'

'It's of no consequence when: but it's a bad business.'

Kallomyetsev shrugged his shoulders, and with a dandified swing of his elegant person moved away to the window. At that instant the adjutant brought in Markelov.

The governor had spoken truly about him; he was unnaturally calm. Even his habitual moroseness had vanished from his face and was replaced by an expression of a sort of indifferent weariness. It did not change when he saw his brother-in-law, and only in the glance he flung at the German adjutant escorting him was there a momentary flash of his old hatred for that class of persons. His coat had been torn in two places and hurriedly sewn up with coarse thread; on his forehead, over one eyebrow, and on the bridge of his nose could be seen small scars covered with clotted blood. He had not washed, but had combed his hair. Stuffing both hands up to the wrists into his sleeves, he stood not far from the door. His breathing was quite even.

'Sergei Mihalovitch!' Sipyagin began in an agitated voice, going two steps towards him, and stretching out his right hand so that it might touch him or stop him if he were to make a forward movement. 'Sergei Mihalovitch! I am not here to express to you our amazement, our deep distress— that you cannot doubt! You have yourself *willed* your own ruin! And you have ruined yourself! But I desired to see you so as to say to you . . . er . . . er . . . to render . . . to give you the chance of hearing the voice of common sense, honour, and friendship! You may still mitigate your lot; and, believe me, I will, for my part, do all that lies in my power, and the honoured head of this province will support me in this.' Here Sipyagin raised his voice: 'Unfeigned penitence for your errors, and a full confession without reserve, which shall be duly represented in the proper quarters . . .'

'Your Excellency,' Markelov began all at once, addressing the governor, and the very sound of his voice was quiet, though a little hoarse, 'I imagined it was your pleasure to see me to make a further examination of me or something. . . . But if you have summoned me only at the desire of Mr.

273

Sipyagin, give orders, please, for me to be taken back; we can't understand one another. All he says . . . is so much Greek to me.'

'Greek . . . indeed!' Kallomyetsev intervened in a haughty treble; 'but it's not Greek to you to set peasants rioting! That's not Greek, is it? Eh?'

'What have you here, your Excellency? some sub in the secret police, eh? So zealous in his work?' queried Markelov, and a faint smile of pleasure quivered on his pale lips.

Kallomyetsev, with a hiss of anger, was stamping. . . . But the governor stopped him.

'It's your own fault, Semyon Petrovitch. Why do you interfere in what's not your business?'

'Not my business! . . . I should say it's the public business . . . of all us noblemen! . . .'

Markelov scanned Kallomyetsev with a cold, prolonged gaze, as though it were for the last time, and turned a little towards Sipyagin. 'And since you, brother-in-law, want me to explain my views to you, here you are. I recognise that the peasants had the right to arrest me and give me up if they didn't like what I said to them. They were free to do that. *I* had come to them; not they to me. And the government, if it sends me to Siberia . . . I'm not going to grumble— though I don't regard myself as guilty. It's doing its own work, for it's guarding itself. Is that enough for you?'

Sipyagin flung up his hands.

'Enough! What a thing to say! That's not the question, and it's not for us to criticise the action of the government; what I want to know is, do you feel . . . do you, dear Sergei, feel'—(Sipyagin resolved to try an appeal to the feelings)—'the senselessness, the madness of your attempt? are you prepared to prove your *repentance* in act? and can I answer, to a certain extent answer, for you, Sergei?'

Markelov knitted his bushy brows.

'I have said my say . . . and I don't want to repeat it.'

'But repentance! What of your repentance?'

Suddenly Markelov grew restive.

'Ah, let me alone with your "repentance"! Do you want to crawl inside my soul? Leave that at least to me.'

Sipyagin shrugged his shoulders.

'There, you are always like that; you will never listen to the voice of reason! You have still a possibility of extricating yourself without scandal or dishonour.'

'Without scandal or dishonour . . .' Markelov repeated grimly. 'We know those phrases! They are always used to suggest a man's doing something scoundrelly. That's what they mean!'

'We sympathise with you,' Sipyagin continued to exhort Markelov, 'and you hate us.'

'A nice sort of sympathy! You pack us off to Siberia to hard labour; that's how you show your sympathy for us! Ah, let me alone . . . let me alone, for mercy's sake!'

And Markelov's head sank on his breast. There was great confusion in his soul, quiet as he was outwardly. More than all he was fretted and tortured by the thought that he had been betrayed by none other than Eremey of Goloplyok! Eremey in whom he had believed so blindly! That Mendely, the Sulker, had not followed him had not really surprised him. . . . Mendely had been drunk and was frightened. But Eremey! To Markelov, Eremey was a sort of personification of the Russian peasantry. . . . And he had deceived him. Then, was all Markelov had been toiling for, was it all wrong, a mistake? And was Kislyakov a liar, and were Vassily Nikolaevitch's orders folly, and were all the articles and books, works of socialists and thinkers, every letter of which had seemed to him something beyond doubt, beyond attack—was all that too rubbish? Could it be? And that splendid simile of the swollen abscess, ready for the stroke of the lancet, was that too a mere phrase? 'No! no!' he murmured to himself, and over his bronzed cheeks flitted a faint tinge of brick-dust colour; 'no; it's all true; all . . . it is *I* am to blame, I didn't understand, I didn't say the right thing, I didn't go the right way to work! I ought simply to have given orders, and if anyone had tried to hinder or resist, put a bullet through his head! What's the use of explanations here? Anyone not with us has no right to live . . . spies are killed like dogs, worse than dogs!'

And all the details of his capture passed before Markelov's mind. . . . First the silence, the leers, the shouts at the back of the crowd. Then one fellow comes up sideways as if to salute him. Then that sudden rush! And how they had flung him down! . . . 'Lads . . . lads! . . . what are you about?' And they, 'Give us a belt here! Tie him!' . . . The shaking of his bones . . . and helpless wrath . . . and the stinking dust in his mouth, in his nostrils. . . . 'Toss him . . . toss him into the cart.' Someone guffawing thickly . . . ugh!

'I didn't go the right way—the right way to work!' That was just what fretted and tormented him; that he himself had fallen under the wheel was his personal misfortune: it had no bearing on the cause in general; that he could bear . . . but Eremey! Eremey!

While Markelov stood, his head sunk on his breast, Sipyagin drew the governor aside and began talking to him in undertones, with slight gesticulations and a shake of two fingers on his forehead, as though he would suggest that the poor fellow was not quite right in that region, and would try altogether to arouse, if not sympathy, at least indulgence for the crazy creature. And the governor shrugged his shoulders, turned up and then half-closed his eyes, regretted his own helplessness in the matter, but gave some vague promises. . . . *'Tous les égards . . . certainement, tous les égards,'* . . . the delicately lisped words were heard softly uttered through his scented moustaches. . . . 'But you know, dear boy, the law!' 'Of course—the law!' Sipyagin assented with a sort of stoical submissiveness.

While they were conversing in this way in the corner, Kallomyetsev simply could not stand still; he moved up and down, cleared his throat, hummed and hawed, exhibiting every sign of impatience. At last he went up to Sipyagin, and hurriedly remarked: *'Vous oubliez l'autre!'*

'Ah, yes!' said Sipyagin aloud. *'Merci de me l'avoir rappelé.* I must lay the following fact before your Excellency,' he said, turning to the governor. . . . (He used this formal address to his dear Voldemar intentionally, not to compromise the prestige of authority before a revolutionist.) 'I have good grounds for supposing that my *beau-frère's* mad attempt has certain ramifications; and that one of those branches, that is, one of the suspected persons is at no great distance from this town. Send, he added, in an undertone, 'for the man . . . there, in your drawing-room . . . I brought him with me.'

The governor glanced at Sipyagin, thought with reverence, 'What a fellow!' and gave the necessary order. A minute later, the 'servant of God', Sila Paklin, stood before him.

Sila Paklin was beginning to make a low bow to the governor; but catching sight of Markelov he did not complete his salutation—he remained as he was, bent in half, twisting his cap about in his hands. Markelov cast a heedless glance in his direction, but can hardly have recognised him; for he sank again into thought.

'Is this—the branch?' queried the governor, pointing at Paklin with a large white finger adorned with a turquoise.

'Oh, no!' responded Sipyagin with a half-smile. 'However,' he added, after a moment's thought, 'here, your Excellency,' he began again aloud, 'before you is one Mr. Paklin. He is, to the best of my belief, a resident in Petersburg, and an intimate friend of a certain person who filled the position of tutor in my family, and left my house, taking with him—I blush to add—a young girl, a relative of my own.'

'Ah! oui, oui,' muttered the governor, and he flung up his head; 'I had heard something . . . the Countess was telling me . . .'

Sipyagin raised his voice.

'That person is a certain Mr. Nezhdanov, strongly suspected by me of perverted ideas and theories . . .'

'Un rouge à tous crins,' put in Kallomyetsev.

'Of perverted ideas and theories,' repeated Sipyagin still more distinctly, 'and is certainly not without a share in all this propaganda; he is . . . in hiding, as I have been informed by Mr Paklin, in the factory of the merchant Faleyev . . .'

At the words 'I have been informed', Markelov glanced a second time at Paklin, but only smiled, slowly and indifferently.

'Excuse me, excuse me, your Excellency,' cried Paklin, 'and you, Mr. Sipyagin; I never . . . never . . .'

'You say the merchant Faleyev?' said the governor, addressing Sipyagin, and merely twirling his fingers in Paklin's direction, as much as to say, 'Silence there, my good man.' 'What's coming to them, our respectable bearded shop-keepers? Yesterday they caught another one about the same business. You may have heard his name—Golushkin, a rich man. But there, he'll never make a revolution. He's grovelling on his knees now.'

'The merchant Faleyev does not come into the affair,' Sipyagin struck off; 'I know nothing of his views; I am speaking only of his factory, in which, according to Mr. Paklin's story, Mr. Nezhdanov may be found at this moment.'

'I didn't say so!' Paklin wailed again. 'It was *you* said so!'

'Excuse me, Mr. Paklin,' Sipyagin went on, uttering every word with the same relentless distinctness. 'I respect the sentiment of friendship which inspires your denial.' ('Why—he's a regular Guizot!' the governor was thinking to himself.) 'But I will venture to put myself before you as an example. Do you suppose the sentiment of kinship is less strong in me than your feeling of friendship? But there is another feeling, sir, which is stronger still, and which ought to be our guide in all our deeds and actions—the feeling of duty!'

'*Le sentiment du devoir,*' Kallomyetsev explained.

Markelov scanned both the speakers.

'Mr. Governor,' he observed, 'I repeat my request: order me, if you please, to be removed from these chatterers.'

But here the governor lost patience a little.

'Mr. Markelov!' he exclaimed, 'I should advise you, in your position, to show more restraint in your language, and more respect for your superiors . . . especially when they are expressing patriotic sentiments such as you have just heard from the lips of your *beau-frère*. I shall be very happy, my dear Boris,' added the governor, turning to Sipyagin, 'to bring your noble action before the notice of the minister. But where precisely is this Mr. Nezhdanov to be found—in this factory?'

Sipyagin knit his brows.

'He is with a certain Mr. Solomin, the overseer of the machinery there—so this Mr. Paklin has informed me.'

It seemed to afford Sipyagin a peculiar satisfaction to torment poor Sila; he was making him pay now for the cigar he had given him in the carriage, and the familiarity of his behaviour, and even some little flattery wasted on him.

'And this Solomin,' put in Kallomyetsev, 'is an unmistakable radical and republican, and it would be quite as well for your Excellency to turn your attention to him too.'

'Do you know these people . . . Solomin . . . and what's his name—Nezhdanov?' the governor questioned Markelov in a rather authoritative nasal.

Markelov's nostrils dilated vindictively.

'And do you, your Excellency, know Confucius and Livy?'

The governor turned away.

'*Il n'y a pas moyen de causer avec cet homme,*' he observed, shrugging his shoulders. 'Baron, here, please!'

The adjutant darted up to him; and Paklin, seizing the opportunity, limped hobbling up to Sipyagin.

'What are you doing?' he whispered; 'do you want to ruin your own niece? Why, she's with him, with Nezhdanov! . . .'

'I am ruining no one, sir,' Sipyagin responded aloud; 'I am obeying the dictates of my conscience, and——'

'And your wife, my sister, who keeps you under her thumb?' Markelov put in quite as loudly.

Sipyagin, at the phrase, did not turn a hair. . . . It was too much beneath him!

'Listen,' Paklin continued, whispering—his whole body was shaking with excitement and possibly with fear—and his eyes glittered with hate and the tears made a lump in his throat; tears of pity for *the others,* and anger with himself; 'listen, I told you she was married—that's not true—I told you a lie!—but this marriage must take place now—and if you prevent this, if the police make a raid on them, there will be a stain on your conscience which nothing can wipe off, and you——'

'The fact you have communicated,' Sipyagin interrupted still louder, 'if only it is true, which I have good reason to doubt, can only hasten the measure I should think it necessary to take; and as to the purity of my conscience, sir, I will ask you not to concern yourself about it.'

'It's polished, brother,' Markelov put in again; 'there's a coat of Petersburg varnish laid on it; nothing will touch it! Ah, Mr. Paklin, you may whisper as you will, you'll never whisper your way out of this business, no fear!'

The governor thought it needful to cut short these recriminations.

'I presume,' he began, 'that you have said all you need to, gentlemen; and so, my dear baron, you may remove Mr. Markelov. *N'est-ce pas,* Boris, you have no further need . . . ?'

Sipyagin made a deprecating gesture.

'I have said all I could!'

'Very well. . . . My dear baron . . .'

The adjutant approached Markelov, clinked his spurs, made a horizontal motion with his arm. . . . 'If you please!' Markelov turned and went out. Paklin—only in imagination, it must be owned, but with bitter sympathy and pity—shook his hand.

'And we'll send our fellows to the factory,' pursued the governor. 'Only there's one thing, Boris; I fancy—this gentleman'—(he indicated Paklin with a turn of his chin)—

'gave you some information about your young relation. . . .
Possibly she is there, in the factory. . . . If so . . .'

'She could not be arrested in any case,' observed Sipyagin
profoundly; 'possibly she will come to her senses and return.
If you will permit it, I will write her a little note.'

'I shall be obliged if you will. And, of course, you may
rest assured. . . . *Nous coffrerons le quidam . . . mais
nous sommes galants avec les dames . . . et avec celle-là
donc!*'

'But you are taking no measures with regard to that
Solomin!' Kallomyetsev exclaimed, plaintively. He had been
all the while on the alert trying to catch the governor's
remarks a little aside to Sipyagin. 'I assure you, he's the
ringleader! I've an instinct in these things . . . a perfect
instinct!'

'*Pas trop de zèle*, dear Semyon Petrovitch,' observed the
governor with a smirk. 'Remember Talleyrand! If there's
anything amiss, he won't escape us either. You'd much better
devote your thoughts to your . . .' The governor made a
gesture suggesting a noose round the neck. . . . 'And by the
way,' he turned again to Sipyagin—'*et ce gaillard-là*' (he again
indicated Paklin by a turn of his chin), '*qu-en ferons-nous?*
He doesn't look formidable.'

'Let him go,' said Sipyagin softly, and he added in
German: '*Lass den Lumpen laufen!*'

He imagined, for some unknown reason, that he was
making a quotation from Goethe, from *Götz von Berlichingen*.

'You can go, sir!' observed the governor aloud. 'We have
no further need of you! Good-bye, till we meet again.'

Paklin made a general bow and went out into the street,
utterly crushed and humiliated. Good God! this contempt
annihilated him!

'What am I?' he thought in unutterable despair; 'both
coward and informer? Oh, no . . . no; I'm an honest man,
gentlemen, and I'm not quite devoid of all manliness!'

But what was this familiar figure standing on the steps of
the governor's house, gazing at him with dejected eyes, full of

reproach? Why, it was Markelov's old servant. He had, seemingly, come to the town after his master, and would not move away from his prison. . . . But why did he look like that at Paklin? It was not he who had betrayed Markelov!

'And what induced me to go poking my nose where I was no manner of use?' he thought again in desperation. 'Why couldn't I have kept quiet and minded my own business? And now they'll talk, and most likely write: "A certain Mr. Paklin has told of everything, he has betrayed them . . . his friends, betrayed them to the enemy!"' He recalled at this point the glance Markelov had flung at him, he recalled his last words: 'You'll never whisper your way out, no fear!'—and then those aged, dejected, despairing eyes! And as it is written in the scriptures, 'he wept bitterly,' and made his way to the oasis, to Fomushka and Fimushka, to Snanduliya. . . .

36

WHEN Marianna, the same morning, came out of her room, she saw Nezhdanov dressed and sitting on the sofa. In one hand he held his head, the other lay weak and motionless on his knees. She went up to him.

'Good morning, Alexey. . . . You've not undressed? you've not slept? How pale you are!'

His heavy eyelids rose slowly.

'No, I didn't undress, I've not been asleep.'

'Are you ill, or is it the result of yesterday?'

Nezhdanov shook his head.

'I couldn't sleep after Solomin went into your room.'

'When?'

'Yesterday evening.'

'Alexey, are you jealous? Well, that's something new! And what a time you've chosen to be jealous! He only stayed with me a quarter of an hour. . . . And we were talking about his cousin, the priest, and how to arrange our marriage.'

'I know he only stayed a quarter of an hour; I saw when he came out. And I'm not jealous, oh, no! But still, I couldn't get to sleep, after that.'

'Why?'

Nezhdanov did not speak.

'I kept thinking . . . thinking . . . thinking!'

'What about?'

'You . . . and him . . . and myself.'

'And what conclusion did you come to?'

'Must I tell you, Marianna?'

'Yes, tell me.'

'I thought that I'm in your way . . . and his . . . and my own.'

'Mine? his? I can fancy what you mean by that, though you do declare you're not jealous. But your own?'

'Marianna, there are two men in me, and one won't let the other live. So that I suppose in fact it would be better for both to cease to live.'

'Come, hush, Alexey, please! What makes you want to torture yourself and me? We ought to be considering now what steps we must take. . . . They won't leave us in peace, you know.'

Nezhdanov took her hand affectionately.

'Sit beside me, Marianna, and let us talk a little, like friends. While there is still time. Give me your hand. I think it would be as well for us to explain ourselves, though, they do say, explanations of all sorts only lead to greater confusion. But you are kind and wise; you will understand it all, and what I don't say out, you will think for yourself. Sit down.'

Nezhdanov's voice was very soft, and a peculiar affectionate tenderness was apparent in his eyes, which were fixed intently on Marianna.

She sat down readily at once beside him and took his hand.

'Thank you, dear one. Now listen. I won't keep you long. I've gone over all I want to say, in my head, during the night. Well, don't think that what happened yesterday has upset me unduly; I was certainly very ridiculous and even a little disgusting; but you thought nothing base or low of me, I know . . . you know me. I said that what happened hasn't upset me; that's not true, it's nonsense . . . it has upset me, not because I was brought home drunk, but because it has been the final proof to me of my failure! And not only because I can't drink as Russians drink, but in everything! everything! Marianna, I'm bound to tell you that I have no faith now in the cause which brought us together; for which we left that house together; to tell the truth, I had grown lukewarm when your enthusiasm warmed me and and set me on fire again. I don't believe in it! I don't believe in it!'

He laid the hand that was free over his eyes and was silent for an instant. Marianna too uttered not a word and looked down. . . . She felt that he had told her nothing new.

'I used to think,' Nezhdanov went on, taking his hand away from his eyes, but not looking again at Marianna, 'that I did believe in the cause itself, and only doubted of myself, my own power, my own fitness; my abilities, I thought, do not correspond with my convictions. . . . But it seems these two things can't be separated, and what's the object of deceiving oneself? No, I don't believe in the *cause itself*. And you do believe in it, Marianna?'

Marianna sat up and raised her head.

'Yes, Alexey, I do believe in it. I believe in it with all the strength of my soul, and I will devote all my life to this cause! To my last breath!'

Nezhdanov turned towards her and scanned her from head to foot in a touched and envious glance.

'Yes, yes; I expected that answer. So you see that there

is nothing for us to do in common; you have severed our tie yourself at one blow.'

Marianna did not speak.

'Now Solomin,' began Nezhdanov again, 'though he does not believe . . .'

'What?'

'No! He does not believe . . . but he does not need to; he moves calmly forward. A man going along a road to a town doesn't ask himself whether the town has a real existence. He goes on and on. That's like Solomin. And nothing more's needed. But I . . . can't go forward; I don't want to go back; standing still I'm sick of. Whom could I presume to ask to be my companion? You know the proverb, "One at each end of the pole and the burden is borne easily"; but if one cannot hold up his end, what becomes of the other?'

'Alexey,' Marianna ventured uncertainly, 'I think you are exaggerating. We love one another, don't we?'

Nezhdanov gave a heavy sigh.

'Marianna . . . I revere you . . . and you pity me, and each of us trusts implicitly in the other's honesty; that's the real truth! But there's no love between us.'

'Stop, Alexey, what are you saying? Why, this very day, directly, there will be a search for us. . . . We must set off together, you know, and not part. . . .'

'Yes; and go to the priest Zosim to get him to marry us, as Solomin proposes. I know very well that in your eyes this marriage is nothing but a passport; a means of avoiding annoyance from the police . . . but, nevertheless, it does in a way pledge us . . . to life in common, side by side . . . or if it does not *pledge* us, at least it presupposes a desire to live together.'

'What do you mean, Alexey? Are you going to stay here?'

'Yes,' all but broke from Nezhdanov's lips, but he recollected himself and said:

'N . . . n . . . no.'

'Then you are going away from here, but not where I go?'

Nezhdanov warmly pressed the hand which still lay in his.

'To leave you without a protector, without a champion, would be a crime, and I won't do that, mean as I may be. You shall have a champion. . . . Do not doubt it!'

Marianna bent down towards Nezhdanov, and, putting her face close to his, tried anxiously to look into his eyes, into his soul—into his very soul.

'What is the matter with you, Alexey? What is in your heart? Tell me! . . . You frighten me. Your words are so enigmatical, so strange. . . . And your face! I have never seen you with such a face!'

Nezhdanov gently turned her away, and gently kissed her hand. This time she did not resist, and did not laugh, and still looked at him with anxiety and alarm.

'Don't alarm yourself, please! There's nothing strange in it. The whole trouble is this: Markelov, they say, was beaten by the peasants; he felt their fists, they bruised his ribs. . . . I've not been beaten by the peasants—they even drank with me, drank my health . . . but they have bruised my soul worse than Markelov's ribs. I was born all out of joint. . . . I tried to set myself right, but only put myself more out of joint than ever. That's just what you see in my face.'

'Alexey,' said Marianna slowly, 'it would be very wrong of you not to be open with me.' He clasped her hands.

'Marianna, my whole being is before you, as it were in your hand; and whatever I do, I tell you beforehand, you will be surprised at nothing, nothing in reality!'

Marianna wanted to ask for an explanation of those words, but she did not ask for it . . . besides, at that instant Solomin came into the room.

His movements were sharper and more rapid than usual. His eyes were screwed up, his wide lips were drawn tight, his whole face looked as it were sharper, and wore a dry, hard, almost surly expression.

'My friends,' he began, 'I've come to tell you that delay's out of the question. Get ready. . . . It's time for you to go.

286

You must be ready within an hour. You must go to your wedding. There's no news whatever from Paklin; his horses were first kept at Arzhano and then sent back. . . . He remained there. Probably they took him to the town. He wouldn't tell tales, of course, but there's no knowing, he might let something out, perhaps. Besides, they might find out from the horses. My cousin has been told to expect you. Pavel will go with you. He will be the witness.'

'And you, Solomin . . . Vassily?' asked Nezhdanov. 'Aren't you coming? I see you're dressed for a journey,' he added, glancing at the high boots Solomin was wearing.

'Oh, I put them on . . . it's muddy out of doors.'

'But aren't you going to answer for us, Vassily?'

'I don't suppose . . . anyway, that's my affair. So in an hour's time. Marianna, Tatyana wants to see you. She has been preparing something out there.'

'Oh, yes! And I was meaning to go to her. . . .'

Marianna was moving to the door. . . .

Something strange, something akin to terror, misery, came out on Nezhdanov's face. . . .

'Marianna, are you going away, dear?' he said suddenly in a failing voice.

She stopped.

'I'll be back in half an hour. It won't take me long to pack.'

'Yes; but come to me. . . .'

'Certainly, what for?'

'I wanted to have one more look at you.' He took a long, slow look at her. 'Good-bye, good-bye, Marianna!' She was bewildered.

'Why . . . what on earth am I talking about? I'm talking rubbish. Why, you'll be back in half an hour, won't you? Eh?'

'Of course.'

'To be sure. . . . Forgive me. My head's reeling from want of sleep. I too will . . . pack up directly.'

Marianna went out of the room. Solomin was about to follow her.

Nezhdanov stopped him.

'Vassily!'

'Well?'

'Give me your hand. I have to thank you, dear friend, for your hospitality.'

Solomin laughed.

'What an idea!' However, he gave him his hand.

'And something more,' Nezhdanov went on: 'if anything happens to me, may I rely on you, Vassily, not to leave Marianna?'

'Your wife that is to be?'

'Yes, Marianna!'

'To begin with, I'm sure nothing will happen to you; but you can set your mind at rest: Marianna is as precious to me as she is to you.'

'Oh! I know that . . . I know that! That's right, then. Thanks. In an hour, then?'

'Yes.'

'I will be ready. Good-bye!'

Solomin went out and overtook Marianna on the stairs. He had it in his mind to say something to her about Nezhdanov, but he was silent. And Marianna on her side was aware that Solomin had it in his mind to speak to her, and about Nezhdanov, too, and that he was silent. And she was silent too.

37

DIRECTLY Solomin went out, Nezhdanov jumped up from the sofa, walked twice from one corner to the other, then stood still for a minute in a sort of petrified stupefaction in the middle of the room; suddenly he shook himself, hurriedly flung off his 'masquerading' get-up, kicked it into a corner, took out and put on his own former attire. Then he went up to the three-legged table, took out of the drawer two sealed envelopes and another small article, which he thrust into his pocket; the envelopes he left on the table. Then he crouched down before the stove, and opened the little door. . . . In the stove lay a whole heap of ashes. This was all that was left of Nezhdanov's manuscripts, of his book of verse. . . . He had burned it all during the night. But there in the stove, on one side, sticking close against one wall, was Marianna's portrait, given him by Markelov. It seemed he had not had the heart to burn the portrait too! Nezhdanov took it carefully out and laid it on the table beside the sealed envelopes. Then with a resolute gesture he clutched his cap and was making for the door . . . but he stopped short, turned back, and went into Marianna's room. There he stood a minute, looked around him, and, approaching her little narrow bed, bent down, and with one stifled sob pressed his lips, not to the pillow, but to the foot of the bed. . . . Then he got up at once, and, pulling his cap over his eyes, rushed out.

Meeting no one, either in the corridor, on the stairs, or below, Nezhdanov slipped out into the little enclosure. It was a grey day with a low-hanging sky, and a damp breeze that stirred the tops of the grasses and set the leaves on the trees shaking; the factory made less rattle and roar than at the same time on other days; from its yard came a smell of coal, tar, and tallow. Nezhdanov took a sharp, searching look round, and went straight up to the old apple-tree which had attracted his attention on the very day of his arrival, when he had first looked out of the window of his little room. The stem of this apple-tree was overgrown with dry moss; its rugged, bare branches, with reddish-green leaves hanging here and there upon them, rose crooked into the air, like old bent arms raised in supplication. Nezhdanov stood with firm tread on the dark earth about its roots, and took out of his pocket the small object that he had found in the table drawer. Then he looked attentively at the windows of the little lodge. . . .

'If anyone catches sight of me this minute,' he thought, 'then, perhaps, I will put it off.' . . . But nowhere was there a sign of one human face . . . everything seemed dead, everything had turned away from him, gone for ever, left him to the mercy of fate. Only the factory thickly roared and hummed, and overhead fine keen drops of chilly rain began falling.

Then Nezhdanov, glancing through the crooked branches of the tree under which he was standing, at the low, grey, callously blind, damp sky, yawned, shrugged, thought, 'There's nothing else left—I'm not going back to Petersburg, to prison,' flung away his cap, and feeling already all over a sort of mawkish, heavy, overpowering languor, he put the revolver to his breast, pulled the trigger. . . .

Something seemed to strike him at once, not very violently even . . . but he was lying on his back, trying to understand what had happened to him, and how he had just seen Tatyana. . . . He even tried to call her, to say, 'Ah, I don't want . . .' but now he was numb all over, and there was a whirl of muddy green turning round and round over his face, in his eyes, on his head, in the marrow of his bones—and a sort of terrible flat weight seemed crushing him for ever to the earth.

Nezhdanov had really caught a glimpse of Tatyana at the very minute when he pulled the trigger of the revolver. She had gone up to one of the windows, and had caught sight of him under the apple-tree. She had hardly time to think, 'Whatever is he doing in this rain under the apple-tree without a hat on?' when he rolled over on his back like a sheaf of corn. She did not hear the shot—the report was very faint—but she at once saw something was wrong, and rushed in hot haste down into the garden. . . . She ran up to Nezhdanov. . . . 'Alexey Dmitritch, what's the matter?' But already darkness had overtaken him. Tatyana bent over him, saw blood.

'Pavel!' she cried in a voice not her own—'Pavel!'

In a few instants, Marianna, Solomin, Pavel, and two of

the factory-hands were in the enclosure. They lifted Nezhdanov up at once, carried him into the lodge, and laid him on the very sofa on which he had spent his last night.

He lay on his back with half-closed, fixed eyes, and face fast turning grey. He gave slow, heavy gasps, sometimes with a sob, as though he were choking. Life had not yet left him. Marianna and Solomin were standing one on each side of the sofa, both almost as pale as Nezhdanov himself. Shaken, agitated, stunned, they were both—especially Marianna—but not astounded. 'How was it we did not foresee this?' they were thinking, and at the same time it seemed to them that they had . . . yes, they had foreseen it. When he had said to Marianna, 'Whatever I do, I tell you beforehand, nothing will come as a surprise to you,' and again when he had talked of the two men within him who could not live together, had not something stirred within her akin to a vague presentiment? Why had she not stopped at once and pondered on those words, on that presentiment? Why was it she did not dare now to look at Solomin, as though he were her accomplice . . . as though he too were feeling a sting of conscience? Why was it she was feeling, not only boundless, despairing pity for Nezhdanov, but a sort of horror and dread and shame? Could it be, it had rested with her to save him? Why was it they had neither dared utter a word? Scarcely dared breathe—and waited . . . for what? Merciful God!

Solomin sent for a doctor, though of course there was no hope. On the small wound, now black and bloodless, Tatyana laid a large sponge of cold water; she moistened his hair too with cold water and vinegar. All at once Nezhdanov ceased gasping and stirred a little.

'He is coming to himself,' whispered Solomin.

Marianna was on her knees near the sofa. . . .

Nezhdanov glanced at her . . . up till then his eyes had had the fixed look of the dying.

'Oh, I'm . . . still alive,' he articulated, scarcely audibly.

'Failed again . . . I'm keeping you.'

'Alyosha!' moaned Marianna.

'Oh, yes . . . directly. . . . You remember, Marianna, in my . . . poem . . . "With flowers then deck me . . ." where are the flowers? But you're here instead. . . . There, in my letter. . . .'

He suddenly shivered all over.

'Ah, here she is. . . . Give each other . . . both . . . your hands—before me. . . . Quick . . . take . . .'

Solomin grasped Marianna's hand. Her head lay on the sofa, face downwards, close to the wound.

Solomin stood stern and upright, looking dark as night.

'Yes . . . good . . . yes . . .'

Nezhdanov began to sob again, but in a strange, unusual way. . . . His breast rose, his sides heaved. . . .

He obviously was trying to lay his hand on their clasped hands, but his hands were dead already.

'He is passing,' murmured Tatyana, who stood in the doorway, and she began crossing herself.

The sobbing gasps grew briefer, fewer. . . . He still sought Marianna with his eyes . . . but a sort of menacing, glassy whiteness was overspreading them. . . .

'Good . . .' was his last word.

He was no more . . . and the linked hands of Solomin and Marianna still lay on his breast.

This was what he had written in the two short letters he left. One was addressed to Silin, and consisted of only a few lines :

'Good-bye, brother, friend, good-bye! By the time you get this scrap of paper, I shall be dead. Don't ask how and why, and don't grieve; believe that I'm better off now. Take our immortal Pushkin and read the description of the death of Lensky in *Yevgeny Onyegin*. Do you remember?—"The windows are whitewashed; the mistress has gone. . . ." That's all. It's no good my talking to you . . . because I should have too much to say, and there's no time to say it. But I could not go away without telling you; or you would have thought of me as living still, and I should be wronging our friendship. Good-bye; live. Your friend.—A.N.'

The other letter was somewhat longer. It was addressed to Solomin and Marianna. This was what it contained: 'My children!' (Immediately after these words there was a break; something had been erased, or rather smudged over as though tears had fallen on it.) 'You will think it strange, perhaps, that I address you in this way. I am almost a child myself, and you, Solomin, are older of course than I am. But I am dying, and standing at the end of life I regard myself as an old man. I am much to blame to both of you, especially you, Marianna, for causing you such grief (I know, Marianna, you will grieve) and having given you so much anxiety. But what could I do? I could find no other way out of it. I could not *simplify myself;* the only thing left was to blot myself out altogether. Marianna, I should have been a burden to myself and to you. You are great-hearted, you would have rejoiced in the burden, as another sacrifice . . . but I had no right to take such a sacrifice from you; you have better and greater work to do. My children, let me unite you, as it were, from the grave. . . . You will be happy together. Marianna, you will infallibly come to love Solomin; as for him . . . he has loved you ever since he first set eyes on you at the Sipyagins. That was no secret to me though we did run away together a few days after. Ah, that morning! How glorious it was, how sweet and young! It comes to me now as a token, as a symbol of your life together—yours and his—and I was merely by accident in his place that day. But it's time to make an end; I don't want to work on your feelings. . . . I only want to justify myself. To-morrow you will have some very sorrowful moments. . . . But there's no help for it! There's no other way, is there? Good-bye, Marianna, my good, true girl! Good-bye, Solomin! I leave her in your care. Live happily—live to the good of others; and you, Marianna, think of me only when you are happy. Think of me as a man who was true and good too, but one for whom it was somehow more fitting to die than to live. Whether I really loved you, I don't know, my dear; but I know that I have never felt a feeling stronger, and that it would have been more terrible to me to die without that feeling to carry with me to the grave.

'Marianna! if you ever meet a girl called Mashurina—Solomin knows her, I fancy—by the way, you have seen her too—tell her I thought of her with gratitude not long before my death. . . . She will understand.

'But I must tear myself away. I looked out of the window just now; among the rapidly moving clouds there was one lovely star. However rapidly they moved, they had not been able to hide it. That star made me think of you, Marianna. At this instant you are sleeping in the next room, and suspecting nothing. . . . I went to your door, listened, and I fancied I caught your pure, calm breathing. . . . Good-bye, good-bye, my dear! good-bye, my children, my friends!—Your A.

'Fie! fie! How came I, in a last letter before death, to say nothing of our great cause? I suppose because one can't tell lies on the point of death. . . . Marianna, forgive me this postscript. . . . The falsehood's in me, not in what you have faith in!

'Oh! something more: you will think, perhaps, Marianna, "He was afraid of the prison where they would certainly have put him, and he thought of *this* expedient to escape it." No; imprisonment's nothing of any consequence; but to be in prison for a cause you don't believe in—that's really senseless. And I am putting an end to myself, not from dread of being in prison. Good-bye, Marianna! Good-bye, my pure, spotless girl!'

Marianna and Solomin read this letter in turn. After that she put her portrait and the two letters in her pocket, and stood motionless.

Then Solomin said to her:

'Everything is ready, Marianna; let us go. We must carry out his wishes.'

Marianna approached Nezhdanov, touched his chill brow

with her lips, and turning to Solomin said, 'Let us go.'

He took her by the hand, and together they went out of the room.

When a few hours later the police made a descent on the factory, they found of course Nezhdanov—but a corpse. Tatyana had laid the body out decorously, put a white pillow under his head, crossed his arms, and even put a nosegay of flowers on the little table beside him. Pavel, who was primed with all needful instructions, received the police officers with the profoundest obsequiousness and a sort of derision, so that the latter hardly knew whether to thank him or to arrest him too. He described circumstantially how the suicide had taken place, and regaled them with Gruyère cheese and Madeira; but professed perfect ignorance of the whereabouts at the moment of Vassily Fedotitch and the lady who had been staying there, and confined himself to assuring them that Vassily Fedotitch was never away long, on account of his work; that he'd be back to-day, or else to-morrow, and he would then, without losing a minute, give notice of the fact. He was the man for that—accurate!

So the worthy police officers went away with nothing, leaving a guard in charge of the body and promising to send the coroner.

38

Two days after all these events, there drove into the court-yard of the 'accommodating' priest Zosim a little cart in which sat a man and a woman, already well known to the reader, and the day after their arrival they were legally married. Soon afterwards they disappeared, and the worthy Zosim never regretted what he had done. At the factory Solomin had left a letter addressed to the owner and delivered to him by Pavel; in it was given a full and exact account of the state of the business (it was doing splendidly), and a request was made for three months' leave of absence. This letter had been written two days before Nezhdanov's death, from which it may be concluded that Solomin even then thought it necessary to go away with him and Marianna and keep out of sight for a time. Nothing was revealed by the inquiry held over the suicide. The body was buried; Sipyagin cut short all further search for his niece.

Nine months later Markelov was tried. At the trial he behaved himself just as he had done before the governor, with composure, a certain dignity, and some weariness. His habitual sharpness was softened, but not by cowardice; there was another, nobler feeling at work. He made no defence, expressed no regret, blamed no one and mentioned no names; his emaciated face with its lustreless eyes preserved one expression—submission to his fate, and firmness; his mild but direct and truthful answers awakened in his very judges a sentiment akin to sympathy. Even the peasants who had seized him and gave witness against him—even they shared this feeling, and spoke of him as a 'simple', good-hearted gentleman. But his guilt was too apparent; he could not possibly escape punishment, and it seemed as though he himself accepted this punishment as his due. Of his fellow-conspirators, few enough, Mashurina kept out of sight; Ostrodumov was killed by a shopkeeper whom he was inciting to revolt, and who gave him an 'awkward' blow; Golushkin, in consideration of his 'heartfelt penitence' (he almost went out of his senses with alarm and agitation), received a light sentence; Kislyakov was kept a month under arrest and then set free, and even allowed to 'gallop' about the provinces unchecked; Nezhdanov was set free by death; Solomin, through lack of evidence, was left undisturbed though under suspicion. (He did not, however, avoid trial, and made his appearance when wanted.) Of Marianna nothing ever was said; and Paklin completely evaded all difficulties—indeed, no notice was taken of him at all.

A year and a half had gone by, the winter of 1870 had

come. In Petersburg—Petersburg where the privy councillor and chamberlain Sipyagin was beginning to take an important position, where his wife patronised the arts, gave musical evenings, and founded soup-kitchens, and where Mr. Kallomyetsev was regarded as one of the most promising secretaries of his department—along one of the streets of Vassily Ostrov walked, hobbling and limping, a little man in a shabby overcoat with a catskin collar. It was Paklin. He had changed a good deal of late; a few silver threads could be seen among the long tufts of hair that stuck out below his fur cap. There chanced to be coming towards him along the pavement a rather stout, tall lady, closely muffled in a thick cloth cloak. Paklin cast an indifferent glance in her direction, passed her by . . . then suddenly stood still, thought a minute, flung up his arms, and quickly turning and overtaking her, he looked up under her hat at her face.

'Mashurina?' he said in a low voice.

The lady scanned him majestically, and without uttering a word walked on.

'Dear Mashurina, I recognise you,' Paklin went on, hobbling along beside her, 'only don't you, please, be afraid. I wouldn't betray you, I am too delighted to have met you! I'm Paklin, Sila Paklin, you know, Nezhdanov's friend. . . . Come and see me; I live only a step or two away. Please do!'

'*Io sono contessa Rocca di Santo Fiume!*' the lady answered in a low voice, but in a wonderfully pure Russian accent.

'Come, nonsense! . . . a fine contessa! . . . Come and see me. Let us have a chat. . . .'

'But where do you live?' the Italian countess asked suddenly in Russian. 'I've no time to lose.'

'I live here, in this street—that's my house, the grey one there, with three storeys. How kind it is of you not to persist in trying to mystify me! Give me your hand, come along. Have you been here long? And how are you a countess? Have you married some Italian count?'

Mashurina had not married an Italian count. She had been provided with a passport made out in the name of a certain

297

Countess Rocca di Santo Fiume, who had died not long before, and with this she had with the utmost composure returned to Russia, though she did not know a word of Italian and had the most Russian of faces.

Paklin conducted her to his humble lodgings. The hunch-backed sister with whom he was living came to meet the visitor from behind the screen that separated the tiny kitchen from the equally tiny passage.

'Here, Snapotchka,' he said, 'I commend to you a great friend of mine; give us some tea as quick as you can.'

Mashurina, who would not have gone to Paklin's if he had not mentioned Nezhdanov's name, took off her hat, and, passing her masculine hand over her still cropped hair, bowed and sat down in silence. She was altogether unchanged, she was even wearing the very same dress that she had worn two years before; but in her eyes there was a sort of immovable grief, which added something touching to the habitually stern expression of her face.

Snanduliya went for the samovar, while Paklin placed himself opposite Mashurina, lightly patted her on the knee, and hung down his head; but when he tried to speak, he was obliged to clear his throat; his voice broke and tears glistened in his eyes. Mashurina sat stiff and motionless, without leaning back, in her chair, and looked morosely away.

'Yes, yes,' began Paklin, 'those were times! Looking at you, I remember . . . many things, and many people, dead and living; my poll parrots too are dead . . . but you didn't know them, I fancy; and both on the same day, as I foretold. Nezhdanov . . . poor Nezhdanov! . . . you know, of course . . . ?'

'Yes, I know,' said Mashurina, still looking away.

'And do you know about Ostrodumov, too?' Mashurina merely nodded. She wanted him to go on talking of Nezhdanov, but she could not bring herself to ask him about him. He understood her without that.

'I was told that in the letter he left he mentioned you—was that true?'

Mashurina could not answer at once.

'It is true,' she brought out at last.

'He was a marvellous fellow! Only, he got out of his right track! He was about as good a revolutionist as I was. Do you know what he really was? The idealist of realism! Do you understand me?'

Mashurina flung a rapid glance at Paklin. She did not understand, and indeed she did not care to take the trouble to understand him. It struck her as strange and unsuitable that he should dare to compare himself with Nezhdanov; but she thought, 'Let him brag now.' (Though he was not bragging at all, but rather, to his own ideas, humbling himself.)

'A fellow called Silin found me out here,' Paklin continued. 'Nezhdanov had written to him too just before his death. And he, this Silin, was inquiring whether one couldn't get hold of any of his papers. But Alyosha's things had been put under seal . . . and besides, there were no papers among them; he burned everything, he burned his poems too. You didn't know perhaps that he wrote poetry? I am so sorry about them; I am sure some of them must have been very good. All that has vanished with him, all lost in the common vortex, and dead for ever! Nothing's left but the memories of his friends till they pass away in their turn!'

Paklin paused.

'The Sipyagins,' he went on again: 'do you remember those condescending, dignified, loathsome swells? They're at the tip-top of power and glory by now!'

Mashurina did not 'remember' the Sipyagins in the least; but Paklin hated them both, especially Mr. Sipyagin, to such a degree that he could not deny himself the pleasure of 'pulling them to pieces'. 'They say there's such a high tone in their house! they're always talking about virtue! But I've observed, whenever there's too much talk about virtue, it's for all the world like too much smell of scent in a sickroom; you may be sure there's some hidden nastiness to conceal! It's a suspicious sign! Poor Alexey! they were the ruin of him, those Sipyagins!'

'How's Solomin doing?' asked Mashurina. She had suddenly ceased to feel any inclination to hear anything about *him* from this man.

'Solomin!' cried Paklin. 'That's a first-rate fellow. He has got on splendidly. He threw up his old factory and carried off the best workmen with him. There was one chap there . . . a regular firebrand, they say! Pavel was his name . . . he took him along with him. Now they say he has a factory of his own, a small one, somewhere out Perm way, on co-operative principles. He's a man that'll stick to what he's about! He'll carry anything through! He's a sharp fellow, ay, and a strong one too. He's first-rate! And the great thing is: he's not trying to cure all the social diseases all in a minute. For we Russians are a queer lot, you know, we expect everything; someone or something is to come along one day and cure us all at once, heal all our wounds, extract all our diseases like an aching tooth. Who or what this panacea is to be—why, Darwinism, the village commune, Arhip Perepentyev, a foreign war, anything you please! Only, we must have our teeth pulled out for us! It's all sluggishness, apathy, shallow thinking! But Solomin's not like that—no, he's not a quack doctor, he's first-rate!'

Mashurina waved her hand as though she would say, 'He may be dismissed, then.'

'Well, and that girl,' she inquired—'I've forgotten her name—who ran away with him, with Nezhdanov?'

'Marianna? Oh, she's that same Solomin's wife now. It's more than a year since she was married to him. At first it was only formal, but now they say she really is his wife. Yes, yes.'

Mashurina waved her hand again. Once she had been jealous of Marianna for Nezhdanov's sake; now she felt indignant with her for being capable of infidelity to his memory. 'I dare say there's a baby by now,' she commented contemptuously.

'Very likely, I don't know. But where are you off to?' Paklin added, seeing that she was taking up her hat. 'Stay a little, Snapotchka will give us some tea directly.' It was not so much that he wanted to keep Mashurina particularly, as that he could not let slip an opportunity of giving utterance to all that had accumulated and was seething in his breast. Since Paklin had returned to Petersburg, he had seen very few people, especially of the younger generation. The Nezhdanov affair had scared him; he had grown very cautious and avoided society, and the younger men on their side looked very suspiciously upon him. One young man had even abused him to his face as an informer. With the elder generation he did not much care himself to consort; so that it had sometimes been his lot to be silent for weeks together. He did not speak out freely before his sister—not that he supposed her to be incapable of understanding him, oh no! He had the highest opinion of her intellect. . . . But with her he would have had to talk seriously and perfectly truthfully; directly he fell into 'playing trumps', as they say, she would begin gazing at him with a peculiar intent and compassionate look; and he was ashamed. And how is a man to get on without a little 'trumping', just a low 'trump' occasionally! And so life in Petersburg had begun to be a weariness of the flesh to Paklin, and he even thought about moving elsewhere, to Moscow perhaps. Reflections of all sorts, speculations, fancies, epigrams, and sarcasms, were stored up within him, like water in a closed mill. . . . The floodgates could not be raised; the water had grown stagnant and stale. Mashurina had turned up . . . so he lifted the floodgates and talked and talked. . . . He fell upon Petersburg, Petersburg life, and all Russia. No one and nothing was spared. Mashurina took a very limited interest in all this, but she did not contradict or interrupt him . . . and that was all he wanted.

'Yes, indeed,' he said, 'these are nice little times, I can assure you! In society the stagnation's absolute; everyone bored to perdition! In literature a vacuum clean swept! In criticism . . . if an advanced young reviewer has to say that "it's characteristic of the hen to lay eggs", it takes him twenty whole pages to expound this mighty truth, and even then he doesn't quite manage it! They're as soft, these fellows, let me tell you, as feather-beds, as greasy as cold stew, and foaming at the mouth they utter commonplaces! In science . . . ha! ha! ha! we've a renowned *Kant* of our own indeed, if it's only the *Kant'* (*i.e.* braiding) 'on our engineers' collars! In art it's just the same! If you care to go to the concert to-day, you will hear the national singer Agremantsky. . . . He is having an immense success. . . . And if a stuffed bream, a *stuffed bream,* I tell you, were possessed of a voice, it would sing precisely like that worthy! And Skoropihin even —you know our time-honoured Aristarchus—praises him! It's something, he declares, quite unlike Western art! He praises our miserable painters too! He used once to rave, he says, over Europe, over the Italians; but he has heard Rossini and thought: "Pooh, pooh!"; he has seen Raphael—"Pooh, pooh!" And that "pooh" is quite enough for our young men; they repeat "pooh" after Skoropihin, and they're contented if you please! And meanwhile the people's poverty is fearful, they are utterly crushed by taxes, and the only reform that's been accomplished is that all peasants have taken to caps while their wives have given up coifs. . . . And the famine! The drunkenness! The usurers!'

But at this point Mashurina yawned, and Paklin saw he must change the subject.

'You have not yet told me,' he said to her, 'where you have been these two years, and whether you have been here long, and what you have been doing and how you came to be transformed into an Italian, and why——'

'There's no need for you to know all that,' Mashurina interrupted; 'what's the use? That's not in your line now.'

Paklin felt a pang, and to hide his confusion he laughed a short, forced little laugh.

'Well, that's as you please,' he rejoined. 'I know I'm regarded as out-of-date by the present generation; and to be sure, I can't reckon myself . . . among the ranks of those who . . .' He did not complete his sentence. 'Here is Snapotchka bringing us some tea. You must take a cup, and

302

listen to me. . . . Perhaps in my words you may find something of interest to you.'

Mashurina took a cup and a small lump of sugar, and began to sip the tea and nibble at the sugar.

Paklin's laugh was genuine this time.

'It's as well there are no police here, or the Italian Countess . . . what is it?'

'Rocca di Santo Fiume,' said Mashurina, with imperturbable gravity, as she imbibed the scalding liquid.

'Rocca di Santo Fiume!' repeated Paklin, 'and she sips her tea through the sugar! That's too unlikely! The police would be on the alert in a minute.'

'Yes,' observed Mashurina, 'a fellow in uniform bothered me abroad; he kept asking me questions; I couldn't stand it at last. "Let me alone, do, for mercy's sake!" I said.'

'Did you say that in Italian?'

'No, in Russian.'

'And what did he do?'

'He? Why, walked off, to be sure.'

'Bravo!' cried Paklin. 'Hurrah for the Contessa! Another cup, do! Well, what I wanted to say to you was, you spoke rather coolly of Solomin. But do you know what I can assure you? Fellows like him—they are the real men. One doesn't understand them at first, but they're the real men, take my word for it; and the future's in their hands. They're not heroes; not even the "heroes of labour", about whom some queer fish—an American or an Englishman—wrote a book for the edification of us poor wretches; they're sturdy, rough, dull men of the people. But they're what s wanted now! Just look at Solomin; his brain's clear as daylight, and he's as healthy as a fish. . . . Isn't that a wonder! Why, hitherto with us in Russia it's always been the way that if you're a live man with feelings and a conscience, you're bound to be an invalid! But Solomin's heart, I dare say, aches at what makes ours ache, and he hates what we hate—but his nerves are calm, and his whole body responds as it ought . . . so that he's a splendid fellow! Yes, indeed, a man with an ideal, and no nonsense about him; educated—and from the people; simple—and a little shrewd. . . . What more do you want . . . ?

'And never you mind,' pursued Paklin, working himself up more and more, and not noticing that Mashurina had long ceased to attend, and was once more gazing away into the distance; 'never mind if there are swarms of all sorts in Russia: Slavophils and officials and generals, plain and decorated, and epicureans and imitators and queer fish of all sorts. (I used to know a lady called Havronya Prishtehov, who suddenly without rhyme or reason turned legitimist, and assured everyone that when she died they need only open her body and they would find the name of Henri V engraved in her heart . . . on the heart of Havronya Prishtehov!) Never mind all that, my dear madam, but let me tell you our only true way lies with the Solomins, coarse, plain, shrewd Solomins! Recollect *when* I am saying this to you, in the winter in 1870, when Germany is making ready to crush France—when——'

'Silushka,' Snanduliya's soft little voice was heard saying behind Paklin's back, 'I think in your speculations on the future you forget our religion and its influence. . . . And besides,' she added hurriedly, 'Madame Mashurina is not listening to you. . . . You had better offer her another cup of tea.'

Paklin pulled himself together.

'Ah, yes, dear lady—won't you really?'

But Mashurina slowly turned her gloomy eyes upon him, and said absently, 'I wanted to ask you, Paklin, haven't you any notes of Nezhdanov's or his photograph?'

'I have a photograph . . . yes; and I fancy rather a good one, in the table. I'll find it for you directly.'

He began rummaging in the drawer, while Snanduliya went up to Mashurina, and with a long, intent look of sympathy she clasped her hand like a comrade.

'Here it is! I have found it!' cried Paklin, and he gave her the photograph. Mashurina, with hardly a glance at it,

304

and without a word of thanks, crimsoning all over, thrust it quickly into her pocket, put on her hat, and was making for the door.

'Are you going?' said Paklin. 'Tell us, at least, where you live?'

'As it happens.'

'I understand, you don't wish me to know, then! Well, tell me, please, one thing anyway: are you still working under the orders of Vassily Nikolaevitch?'

'What is that to you?'

'Or perhaps of some other—Sidor Sidoritch?'

Mashurina made no answer.

'Or does someone anonymous direct you?'

Mashurina was already across the threshold.

'Perhaps it is someone anonymous!'

She slammed the door behind her.

A long while Paklin remained standing before this closed door.

'Anonymous Russia!' he said at last.

Selected List of Grove Press
Drama and Theater Paperbacks

E312   ARDEN, JOHN / Serjeant Musgrave's Dance / $2.45 [See also Modern British Drama, Henry Popkin, ed. GT614 / $5.95]

E471   BECKETT, SAMUEL / Cascando and Other Short Dramatic Pieces (Words and Music, Film, Play, Come and Go, Eh Joe, Endgame) / $1.95

E96   BECKETT, SAMUEL / Endgame / $1.95

E318   BECKETT, SAMUEL / Happy Days / $2.45

E226   BECKETT, SAMUEL / Krapp's Last Tape, plus All That Fall, Embers, Act Without Words I and II / $2.45

E33   BECKETT, SAMUEL / Waiting For Godot / $1.95 [See also Seven Plays of the Modern Theater, Harold Clurman, ed. GT422 / $4.95]

B79   BEHAN, BRENDAN / The Quare Fellow* and The Hostage**: Two Plays / $2.45 *[See also Seven Plays of the Modern Theater, Harold Clurman, ed. GT422 / $4.95] **[See also Modern British Drama, Henry Popkin, ed. GT614 / $5.95]

B117   BRECHT, BERTOLT / The Good Woman of Setzuan / $1.95

B80   BRECHT, BERTOLT / The Jewish Wife and Other Short Plays (In Search of Justice, The Informer, The Elephant Calf, The Measures Taken, The Exception and the Rule, Salzburg Dance of Death) / $1.65

B90   BRECHT, BERTOLT / The Mother / $1.45

B108   BRECHT, BERTOLT / Mother Courage and Her Children / $1.50

B333   BRECHT, BERTOLT / The Threepenny Opera / $1.45

B88   BRECHT, BERTOLT / The Visions of Simone Machard / $1.25

E344   DURRENMATT, FRIEDRICH / The Visit / $2.75

E130   GENET, JEAN / The Balcony / $2.95 [See also Seven Plays of the Modern Theater, Harold Clurman, ed. GT422 / $4.95]

E208   GENET, JEAN / The Blacks: A Clown Show / $2.95

E577   GENET, JEAN / The Maids and Deathwatch: Two Plays / $2.95

E374   GENET, JEAN / The Screens / $1.95

E456   IONESCO, EUGENE / Exit the King / $2.95

E101   IONESCO, EUGENE / Four Plays (The Bald Soprano, The Lesson, The Chairs,* Jack, or The Submission) / $1.95 *[See also Eleven Short Plays of the Modern Theater, Samuel Moon, ed. B107 / $2.45]

E646   IONESCO, EUGENE / A Hell of a Mess / $3.95

E506   IONESCO, EUGENE / Hunger and Thirst and Other Plays / $1.95

E189   IONESCO, EUGENE / The Killer and Other Plays (Improvisation, or The Shepherd's Chameleon, Maid to Marry) / $2.45

E613   IONESCO, EUGENE / Killing Game / $1.95

E259   IONESCO, EUGENE / Rhinoceros* and Other Plays (The Leader, The Future is in Eggs, or It Takes All Sorts to Make a World) / $1.95 *[See also Seven Plays of the Modern Theater, Harold Clurman, ed. GT422 / $4.95]

E485   IONESCO, EUGENE / A Stroll in the Air and Frenzy for Two: Two Plays / $2.45

E119   IONESCO, EUGENE / Three Plays (Amédée, The New Tenant, Victims of Duty) / $2.95

E387   IONESCO, EUGENE / Notes and Counter Notes / $3.95

B354   PINTER, HAROLD / Old Times / $1.95

E315   PINTER, HAROLD / The Birthday Party* and The Room: Two Plays / $1.95 *[See also Seven Plays of the Modern Theater, Harold Clurman, ed. GT422 / $4.95]

E299   PINTER, HAROLD / The Caretaker* and The Dumb Waiter: Two Plays / $1.95 *[See also Modern British Drama, Henry Popkin, ed. GT422 / $5.95]

E411   PINTER, HAROLD / The Homecoming / $1.95

E432   PINTER, HAROLD / The Lover, Tea Party, The Basement: Three Plays / $1.95

E480   PINTER, HAROLD / A Night Out, Night School, Revue Sketches: Early Plays / $1.95

E626   STOPPARD, TOM / Jumpers / $1.95

B319   STOPPARD, TOM / Rosencrantz and Guilderstern Are Dead / $1.95

GROVE PRESS, INC., 196 West Houston St., New York, N.Y. 10014